Esther

Esther

C.M. Huddleston

Interpreting Time's Past Press
2023

Esther

Published by:
Interpreting Time's Past Press
Text copyright © 2023 by C. M. Huddleston
First Edition

All rights reserved. No part of this book may be used or reproduced in any manner whatsoever without written permission except in the case of brief quotations embodied in critical articles and reviews. For information, please address Connie Huddleston at Interpreting Time's Past Press
connie@interpretingtimespast.com

Cover design by Samantha Fury
Photograph by Pamela Sale

ISBN-13: 979-8-9852672-2-8
Library of Congress Control Number: 2023916517

Publisher's Cataloging-in-Publication data

Names: Huddleston, Connie Marie, author.
Title: Esther / C. M. Huddleston.
Description: Crab Orchard, KY: Interpreting Time's Past Press, 2023.
Identifiers: LCCN: 2023916517 | ISBN: 979-8-9852672-2-8 (paperback) | 979-8-9852672-4-2 (paperback) | 979-8-9852672-3-5 (ebook)
Subjects: LCSH United States--History--Revolution, 1775-1783--Fiction. | Brothers and sisters--Fiction. | Family--Fiction. | North Carolina--History--Fiction. | Watauga Settlement (North Carolina)--Fiction. | Virginia--History--Revolution, 1775-1783--Fiction. | BISAC FICTION / Historical / Colonial America & Revolution
Classification: LCC PS3608 .U32 E78 2020 | DDC 813.6--dc23

For all my ancestors
who believed in,
fought for
and achieved
our Independence

May our Flag Forever Wave!

For Aunt Esther

Many, many thanks to
Pamela Sale
and
Sherron Lawson
for my beautiful cover illustration
and their friendship

A Bit About the American Revolution
– our nation's first civil war

American colonists loyal to the King – called Tories, Loyalists, King's men

American colonists seeking freedom – called Whigs, American Whigs, Patriots, Revolutionaries, Continentals (troops serving the Continental Congress)

Militia – a body of *citizen* soldiers as distinguished from professional soldiers. Each colony had their own militia, militia terms of enlistment, and appointed their own officers. Both Loyalists and Patriots militias existed in each colony.

Timeline:

Lead-in To War: 1763 to 1774 (Events before the beginning of the novel)

February 10, 1763
The Treaty of Paris ended the Seven Years War (called the French and Indian War in America). France surrendered all its North American possessions east of the Mississippi River to Britain. This ended a source of insecurity for the British colonists along the Atlantic coast. The costs of the French and Indian War and maintaining an army in the colonies led the British government to impose new taxes on its American colonists.

March 22, 1765
Britain passed the Stamp Act, imposing a tax on legal documents, newspapers, even playing cards. This was the first direct tax on the American colonists and was forcibly resisted. "Taxation without representation" became a rallying cry.

October 1768
British troops landed in Boston to enforce the Townshend duties (taxes on paint, paper, tea, etc., passed in June 1767) and to clamp down on local radicals. The troops' presence led to outrage and street fights. One clash between soldiers and a mob in March 1770 left five dead. This incident became known as the Boston Massacre.

Spring 1772
Patriots established the Committees of Correspondence throughout the colonies to coordinate American response to British colonial policy. Many Patriot men secretly joined the Sons of Liberty. This was the first important move toward cooperation, mutual action among the colonies, and the development of a national identity among Americans.

March to June, 1774
The British Parliament passed the Coercive Acts, often called the Intolerable Acts in America. Britain closed the port of Boston and required British troops to be housed in taverns and vacant buildings. The acts generated considerable sympathy for Massachusetts among other colonies.

Independence Declared: 1775 to 1777 (while Ballinger siblings lived in Virginia)

April 19, 1775
The first shots of the Revolutionary War were fired at Lexington and Concord in Massachusetts. News of the bloodshed spread along the eastern seaboard. Thousands of volunteers converged—*called Minute Men*—on Cambridge, Mass. These men became the beginnings of the Continental Army.

November 1775
The British governor of Virginia, Lord Dunmore, issued a proclamation offering freedom to any slaves of rebellious Americans who surrendered to British forces. Throughout the course of the war, tens of thousands of African Americans sought their freedom by supporting the British. They were

forced to labor in return for their food and protection. Men were often separated from their families. A smaller number of slaves and free Blacks fought for the Patriots, despite policies that discouraged their enlistment.

June 17, 1775
In the first major action of the war, inexperienced colonial soldiers held off hardened British veterans for over two hours at Breed's Hill. Although eventually forced to abandon their position, including the high ground of Bunker Hill overlooking Boston, the patriots showed they were not intimidated by the King's long lines of red-coated infantrymen. Of the 2,200 British who saw action on this date, over 1,000 ended up dead or wounded.

February 27, 1776
A force of Loyalists, most of them of Scots descent, was defeated by a Patriot army at the Battle of Moore's Creek Bridge in North Carolina. This setback quieted Loyalist activity in the Carolinas for three years.

June 28, 1776
A British invasion force mounted an all-day attack on a Patriot force on Sullivan's Island, off Charleston, South Carolina. The invaders were unable to land their troops on the island. Additionally, the tricky waters of Charleston Harbor frustrated the British navy. The British fleet retired in defeat, and South Carolina remained untouched by the enemy for three more years.

July 1776
The Second Continental Congress adopted the Declaration of Independence. Following a decade of agitation over taxes and a year of war, representatives made the break with Britain. King George III stood unwilling to let his subjects go without a fight. Loyalist sentiment remained strong in many areas. Americans' primary allegiance was to their states. Nationalism grew slowly over the coming years.

December 1776 to January 1777
In a bold move, General George Washington moved his troops

across the Delaware River into New Jersey on Christmas night. The Patriots then surprised a force of German troops, called Hessians, fighting for Britain, at Trenton on December 26. They achieved a similar victory over British troops at Princeton on January 3, reviving hopes that the war just might be winnable. Washington's army then encamped for the winter at Morristown, New Jersey.

War in the North: 1777 to 1778 (occurred while Ballinger siblings lived at Watauga)

August 1777
American Fort Schuyler (also called Fort Stanwix, located in central New York) survived a three weeklong siege forcing allied British forces under Barry St. Leger to retreat. St. Leger's goal of securing New York's Mohawk Valley for General Burgoyne failed. American Colonel Peter Gansevoort and the fort's garrison were commended by the Continental Congress for their efforts.

October 17, 1777
General John Burgoyne's attempt to separate the rebellious New England colonies from those farther south ended in a spectacular failure, with the surrender of 6,000 British regulars at Saratoga, NY. This event shocked London and helped induce France to enter the war on the American side.

December 1777 (Benjamin served at Valley Forge)
With the British occupying Philadelphia just 20 miles away, the Continental Army entered winter quarters at Valley Forge, Pennsylvania. Supply failures continued to cause severe problems for Washington's troops. During the winter, various supply arrangements improved, and the Continental troops drilled and emerged as a more disciplined, unified fighting force.

February 1778
As a result of the Patriot victory at Saratoga and American diplomatic efforts, France allied itself with the new American

government. French financial and military aid would prove critical in winning the war. The Continental Army learned of the French Alliance in May.

May to December, 1778
With barely 150 men, Virginian George Rogers Clark captured several British posts in the Ohio Territory (present-day Illinois and Indiana) and convinced French-speaking inhabitants of Kaskaskia and Cahokia to support the Patriot side. Although Native American tribes continued to oppose white settlement for three decades, Clark's exploits paved the way to expand the U.S. north of the Ohio River.

Southern Campaigns: 1779 to 1781 (Ballinger siblings lived at Watauga)

April 14, 1780
A British victory at the Battle of Monck's Corner, South Carolina, successfully cut off Patriot communication to Charleston, South Carolina, and dispersed Patriot reinforcements. The victory allowed the British to lay siege to Charleston with limited Patriot interference.

May 12, 1780
The British captured Charleston, S.C., including a large portion of the Patriot army, and dealt the Patriots one of their worst defeats of the war. The British move on Charleston was part of a broader British strategy to hold the southern colonies, as the war remained stalemated in Pennsylvania and New York.

May 29, 1780
The Battle of Waxhaw's Creek, sometimes called Waxhaw's Massacre or Buford's Massacre, was a military engagement between Colonel Abraham Buford's mostly Continental forces against a British militia force led by Lieutenant Colonel Banastre Tarleton, near Lancaster, South Carolina.

June 20, 1780
In early June, Lieutenant Colonel John Moore and Major Nicholas Welch, both Loyalists, returned to Lincoln County,

North Carolina, where they issued a call for local Loyalists to assemble and support the British. By the evening of June 19, over 1,000 men and boys, many of them unarmed were camped on the west bank of Clark's Creek, opposite a gristmill operated by Jacob Ramsour. Nearby a Patriot militia force of some 400 men gathered to disperse the Loyalists. On 20 June, as a heavy fog blanketed the area around the mill, the Patriots marched into battle, coming close before being discovered. Two hours later, all fighting had ceased. Scores of dead and wounded lay scattered across the battlefield. Some 70 men lay dead beside 200 wounded, many so severely that they died within days. Casualties were about equally divided between the two sides, although the Patriot's loss in officers was quite high.

August 16, 1780
The Battle of Camden was a major victory for the British in the Southern theater. On August 16, 1780, British forces under Lieutenant General Charles, Lord Cornwallis routed the numerically superior American forces led by Major General Horatio Gates about four miles north of Camden, South Carolina. This victory strengthened the British hold on the Carolinas following the capture of Charleston.

October 7, 1780
Patriot militia from the Carolinas, Virginia, and present-day Tennessee surrounded and defeated a force of Loyalists under Major Patrick Ferguson at King's Mountain, South Carolina. Ferguson was the only British soldier on the field of battle. King's Mountain was truly a battle between Americans to determine their future.

January 17, 1781
Continental soldiers and Patriot militiamen under General Daniel Morgan defeated a British force under Banastre Tarleton at Cowpens, South Carolina. Coming on the heels of the victory at King's Mountain, Cowpens helped convince worried Patriots that the British southern strategy could be defeated and the war turned to their advantage.

March 15, 1781

British troops won a costly victory over Continentals and militia at Guilford Courthouse, North Carolina. The battle was part of Patriot General Nathanael Greene's strategy of engaging the British on ground of his choosing. Without winning a single clear-cut victory, he wore down the British army through hit-and-run tactics and set-piece battles.

May to June, 1781

General Nathanael Greene laid siege to the isolated British garrison at Ninety Six, South Carolina. The approach of a British relief column led Greene to make a final, unsuccessful assault on the fort on June 18. The events at Ninety Six underlined the fact that Britain had too few troops to hold the southern hinterlands.

September to October, 1781

Joint French and American Patriot forces trapped a large British army on Virginia's Yorktown peninsula. Unable to evacuate or receive reinforcements because a French fleet had driven off the British fleet, British General Cornwallis was forced to surrender. Although New York City and Charleston, South Carolina remained in British hands until a peace treaty was signed two years later, the war for American independence was essentially over.

> "...who knows but that you have come to your royal position for such a time as this?" Esther 4:14, *The Bible*

Beginning - 1805

The Corn Planting moon, spring's second full moon, hung high above the hillside's hardwood as she settled herself on the rough-hewn bench, now worn so smooth it felt like the silk she'd donned on special occasions. Esther slowly inhaled a long, cleansing breath, taking in the May evening. It being sometime long after dusk, the day's chores mostly completed, she let the quiet stillness surround and hold her softly in its arms. Even as she felt her age-old body go limp as it eased into much-needed rest, she knew the moon, sliding softly into morn, would most likely find her still alight the bench despite many hours passing. As was her habit, rifle across her knees, Esther sat silently in the moon's glow, sinking tired bones into the evening's stillness, and found peace from the day's labors. She whispered her prayers, few though they were.

As the moon rose, sounds deepened in the surrounding hills and hollows. Unseen tree frogs squeaked and chirped. In the distance, a fox issued its screaming bark, calling its mate hither; the answer rose from near the stream just southeast of the cabin. Glow flies glimmered across the meadow, which ran gently down the hillside to the southwest. As the moon's luminous glow crossed a small patch near the stream, ox-eye daisies shimmered gently in the almost still air. Earlier that day, farther down that same hillside, in a shaded area, she'd discovered a cluster of *self-heal* blooming, the tiny blue-lavender flowers coloring a patch of ground near several cedars. Perhaps tomorrow, she'd decide to gather some to dry, both leaves and flowers, to prepare tinctures and teas as might be needed during the coming season. As a soft breeze ruffled her homespun shift, she caught a whiff of honeysuckle, sweet to the nose and the tongue. Underlying the sweetness, the rancid smell of skunk lingered on the air. She laid aside her book and blew out her lantern.

Jeb, her old red dog, stretched across the cabin's hewn limestone rock step nearby her feet. It's smoothness still held the heat of the day. He growled softly, perhaps warning of a nearby wolf. Jeb only growled at two beings—Indians being the second. For years now, Esther had doubted Indians were ever nearby, figuring a wolf's scent was more likely to have disturbed Jeb's sleep and caused his grumbling. Or maybe he only dreamed. A solitary whippoorwill still called from nearby. Knowing birds most often fell silent when man crept about the surrounding forest, she left the rifle where it lay. Resting her head back against the cabin wall, she followed the moon's progression across the sky before it sank below the distant hills to the southwest. As so often was her way, her thoughts tumbled about, keeping sleep far, remembering, reminiscing, dreaming, wishing. . ..

Thoughts of long, long years ago. Almost of another world, another lifetime. She recalled how her mother'd named all her first eight children from the Bible. She, herself, became *Esther*, the first daughter after three sons—Benjamin (allowed to be named for their father only because Benjamin was a Biblical name), followed by Samuel, and then Joshua. She learned years later how her mother had decided her first baby girl needed a royal name, the name of a queen. Some thought she'd chosen the name since it is the Greek version of her Latin *Hester*. In Persian, *Esther* means star, while in Hebrew, *Hadassah* is myrtle. Upon learning she could have been called Myrtle, a still-young Esther had rejoiced in her mother's classical education and religious training. Like her mother in only this one small way, she considered *Myrtle* to be a somewhat common name. One not fit for a first daughter.

Born and raised in England, Hester Hollowell Ballinger— always *Mother* to her children—claimed to descend from noble blood. And perhaps she did. All her daughter ever knew was Hester's own father, a strict religious man, had raised his daughter alongside her two brothers, providing all three children with a liberal education in the Bible, Latin, Hebrew, Greek, the classics, mathematics, music, and art. What he failed to teach Hester was any acceptance of the failings of others, the joy of life, freedom of choice, and the benefits of love. How he'd failed his daughter thus, Hester's own children could never understand. But, then again, they'd never met their grandfather.

In the 1740s, upon their father's death, Hester's brothers had sold their vast English holdings and come to America to establish their place in the new world. Why each would give up such riches and chance their livelihood upon the rough, unrefined land, Hester's children also never learned. Hester, herself, resented their foolishness in bringing her to this solitary life where there was no *society*. As for the brothers, Esther had met them for the first time at her mother's funeral, though they resided not more than a day's ride from her own home in rural Virginia.

Like her father, Benjamin Ballinger, Michael, and Gabriel Hollowell each owned large estates. Still, those men and her family lived in ways so different from each other. While their uncles owned many African slaves, Dr. Benjamin refused to own a human being and, instead, hired newly arrived immigrants, indenturing each for only five years instead of the accepted seven. He treated them well and often paid wages to those who worked hard in addition to supplying their housing and food. Most every man and woman the good doctor employed came to respect and care for their employer, serving him faithfully and well. Many stayed on, working for even higher wages once their indenture ended.

All her older children learned from Hester's frequent dinner table rants about the economic benefits of holding slaves and how enslaved labor would have increased the family's earnings and, in her mind, their prestige. Throughout her life, she believed and stated, to all of a mind to listen, how "anyone not white, not educated, and not English, is lower than the beasts of the field." She especially included Scots, Irish, Germans, Indians, and Negroes. Her children surely knew if she'd ever met anyone from Asia, she would have included them as well. They also knew not to argue with her or even state their opinions on the matter. Consequently, they learned to avoid many subjects at the dinner table. During the late months of Hester's pregnancies, she would take to her room and refuse to come to the table. During these times of her absence, Dr. Benjamin led the children in hearty debates about all the facts of life, religion, government, and family.

Esther's father, the good doctor, held with none of his wife's many prejudices. Raised in Virginia, he'd attended William and Mary College before traveling to Edinburgh, Scotland, to attend medical school. A medium-height man with dark hair and green eyes, he still possessed his own family's Scottish burr. Dr. Benjamin saw all men as his equal, despite their heritage, their skin color, their education, or their religion. A congenial man, he enjoyed meeting men and women from far-off places and learning about their ways of life. Despite Hester's almost constant protests, he employed tutors from Germany, Scotland, France, and even one from Italy, for his children. Unfortunately, the well-liked Italian tutor turned out to be a colossal failure and had to be dismissed.

Privately, the older children often wondered among themselves why their father had chosen Hester Hollowell as his wife. Their own eyes revealed their petite, blonde, blue-eyed mother to be a beauty. She spoke softly, sang beautifully, and could play the pianoforte with precision—and sometimes with lyrical sensitivity. Yes, she was educated, a rarity among women of the age. Still, their father was so different in thoughts, beliefs, and even spirit than their mother. Her children only ever learned, from overhearing conversations, that their parents had met in Williamsburg. No one ever mentioned a courtship or their wedding. The couple's own children rarely saw them together, except at mealtimes. They heard no terms of endearment, witnessed no displays of affection.

Despite all this, Mother bore nine children. Despite their mother's icy demeanor, theirs became a loving family. Despite her attitudes, or maybe because of them, Dr. Benjamin showered each child with affection every single day. The older brothers adored their new little sister, Esther, and every child who came after.

In the rolling hills of Virginia's Goochland County, Dr. Ballinger provided his wife and each of the children with more than enough. They lived in a large, palatial home filled with expensive furniture, much of it from England. The portico across the front faced a small stream, called Tuckahoe Creek, where the children often fished or played in the swimming hole on a hot summer's afternoon. Luckily, this deep stand of water lay downstream, outside their mother's hearing, as they were not to disturb her quiet times. The land surrounding the house provided an abundance of subsistence crops to feed the family and to sell at the local markets. Dr. Ballinger enjoyed breeding horses, and each child learned to ride at an early age. Life was excellent as far as the children were concerned.

Hester decorated each room of the two-story home with linen and silk, most often in blue and white. Many years afterward, her children could remember vividly the elegant, painted entrance hall with its mosaic floor of alabaster, turquoise, and black. Hester had declared it must be painted just as in the Biblical palace of King Ahasuerus, husband to Queen Esther.

Their extensive household staff included a cook, a cook's helper, maids, a butler, a driver, footmen, and their mother's personal maid. Indentured women often performed some chore within the house, the kitchen garden, or the laundry. Never could a speck of dust or dirt be found within Hester's notice. Her boys learned to shed their dirty or wet clothing outside the kitchen door and dash up the servant's stairs to their rooms. Hester never learned this led to more than one of her sons running stark naked through the kitchen and up the backstairs.

At Hester's insistence, Benjamin hired a wet nurse for each baby and later nannies for the children until they were old enough to spend the day in the classroom. Afterward, the children had tutors. His three oldest sons and his two daughters received the same education. Upon reaching the milestone of thirteen years of age, the good doctor expected each son to announce his choice of occupation. *Their own choice, without interference from either parent.* While Hester secretly, and often publicly, tried to influence each, Dr. Benjamin stood patiently behind his ideal of how to raise responsible adults. He believed in only giving advice when asked his opinion.

"Hester, my dear, our son has reached the age when a boy becomes a man. He, and he alone, must decide. Keep your opinion to yourself and let the man choose." He uttered these words in a soft, but demanding, voice each time one of the boys reached thirteen.

And choose they did. Benjamin followed in his father's footsteps and off he went to William and Mary, and then to Edinburgh, to become a doctor. Samuel, as all the younger ones suspected he would, remained on the family estate to learn the responsibilities of overseer. Samuel loved the land and wanted to be a planter. Joshua—probably only to spite their mother—worked the land alongside the hired men for two years after his thirteenth birthday, before leaving for Virginia's westernmost settlements.

The older children vividly remembered his leaving the house—out the kitchen door, as their mother would allow no one to use the front entrance unless dressed properly. Esther watched from the schoolroom window as Joshua, who now wore rough homespun and buckskins, and carried a simple pack, a bedroll, and a rifle, silently mounted his horse—a gift from his father—and rode quickly into the distance one early spring morning. Dr. Benjamin had paid him the wages, the same as the hired men earned, for his two years of labor. He'd watched his son ride out alone, with tears in his eyes, knowing the boy's own mother's harsh words had driven him to leave. She had expected him to become a lawyer. Dr. Benjamin remained proud of the young man who now followed his own dreams.

Joshua had grown up in Virginia's woods. Early on, he learned to use a musket to take game, often coming home with squirrels and rabbits for the table. His clothes would be torn and filthy, but a smile of happy accomplishment graced his face. Before his thirteenth birthday, Joshua frequently slipped out of a morning, missing all his lessons, to traipse about the surrounding forest. Their father seemed to understand Joshua's need to be out of doors and alone. He let him be, let him learn, and let him grow into the man he became. Without Mother's knowledge, Dr. Benjamin presented Joshua with a long rifle on his thirteenth birthday.

At leaving on that early spring day, determined to see places unknown and explore the western lands, Joshua'd said his goodbyes early on to his family. He'd come, in private, to his younger siblings, taking all in big hugs. He'd promised to return someday, knowing full well he most likely would never come home as long as his mother lived. He'd wished all well during tearful goodbyes, all except his mother. Hester'd refused to allow him to go; therefore, she refused to hear his farewell. She retreated to her room and locked the door.

Upon his departure, and expecting her ninth child, Hester's health wavered. The day Joshua rode away, smiling and hollering with joy, his mother took to her bed.

In mid-spring, on a day just warm enough to enjoy the outdoors, Hester Ballinger birthed a baby girl. Dr. Benjamin named her Lydia, for Hester passed from this world just as the tiny baby entered. Tiny Lydia lingered only long enough to whimper her first and only small cry. Dr. Benjamin and his remaining children buried them together.

Two days later, Micah, only four years old, was the first to come down with the fever. Micah lasted one fitful day. The twins, Peter and Isaiah, died within days of Micah. Dr. Benjamin had nursed each, refusing to sleep or eat while the twins suffered, yet typhoid fever took each one in succession. Immediately after they buried their six-year-old twin brothers, Samuel, Esther, and Lovely watched as their father slipped slowly to the ground. He never stood upright again, suffering mightily for nine days before the Lord carried him home. In a way, his children felt relieved. They had watched his growing agony of body and mind and understood he died mostly of a broken heart. Only three remained at the house, Esther, her sister, only two years younger than her own thirteen years, and Samuel, barely seventeen.

So, in the early summer of 1775, while they awaited their brother, Benjamin's return, three children lived in a bewildering world of grief—saddened, alone, and in mourning for their beloved father as the world around them turned swiftly to war.

7

"Life is a daring adventure or nothing" Helen Keller

The Year 1775

By early summer, though one considered himself grown, three children had buried their parents and four younger siblings. Their lives descended into turmoil. They no longer possessed parents, embraced no leadership, and looked to no one for advice nor comfort.

No one paid the nanny or the tutors, so each left. Many of the indentured servants disappeared as well, for no one remained to tell them to do so or even urge them to stay. Some stole their indenture papers from Dr. Ballinger's desk. Samuel, Esther, and Lovely silently wished them well. The three children would awaken, morning after morning, and find yet another person gone from their small, sheltered world.

A little over two weeks later, the three learned of their uncles' treachery, for Michael and Gabriel had named the children to the governor as revolutionaries. Even going so far as to name their dead father as such. Going before Lord Dunmore, Virginia's crown governor, the uncles demanded they be named as legal guardians in Benjamin's absence. All that legally belonged to Benjamin, already of age at twenty-one and his father's legal heir—the land, house, and its belongings—was placed totally under the uncles' control. All except Benjamin's funds, held separately for his education and living. With Benjamin still residing in Scotland and unaware of their circumstances, Samuel and Esther held little hope for his return, and for their future. Then, the Hollowell brothers sent an overseer to take control.

Around them the world fell apart. As even before their mother's and father's deaths, in those first months of 1775, news sheets, arriving at their rural home weeks after their publication, belatedly revealed how fellow Virginian, Patrick Henry had declared, "Give me liberty or give me death." From across the colonies, events they read about weeks, even months afterward, captured their attention. In Boston, Paul Revere and William Dawes had ridden through the night to warn of the Redcoats' arrival. Later, the children read of the clashes at Lexington and Concord. Yet, it felt so far away and had so little effect on their daily lives. Still, after their parents' deaths, Samuel, Esther, and Lovely grasped at each and every story, reading them over and over. For within these stories from afar, there seemed to be a minuscule speck of hope. They found within these newspapers a feeling of escape from their own troubles, their grief.

A lover of stories, of the written word, Esther wondered if this war for independence was only a fable, a good story, told in sequels. Samuel and Esther often spoke of the rebellion as if it were only a tall tale, until news arrived of the Second Continental Congress meeting in Philadelphia. Their pride swelled as they learned Virginia's own George Washington, a family acquaintance, had been named as commander-in-chief just two days before the battle at Breed's Hill. Suddenly, hopefully, they believed in the tale and held hopes of being free of England's tyranny. Dinner table discussions from times when Hester did not attend had led the children to an understanding of their place in the world and under the Crown. They also knew their uncles remained loyal to the king.

Their own father, a believer in freedom of expression and freedom from tyranny, had taught them to think for themselves, to find their own way in the world. Those events, carried out in places only known from maps and news sheets, diverted their thoughts from the grief surrounding them. Samuel and Esther grabbed onto this promised dream of liberty, for it also granted a bit of hope of resuming the life they had known before their personal springtime crisis. Lovely listened to their dreams, their stories of the far-distant war, and said little. Lovely seemed to exist in a world of her own making, a quiet world without turmoil.

Day by day, Samuel tried to keep the house and farm running smoothly. In those first few weeks, Cook directed the household staff. That is, in the days before the staff began to disappear. Hester's personal maid disappeared one evening, taking with her much of their mother's jewelry. There was no one to send after her, to have her arrested for theft.

Esther spent those early days of grief, gathering flowers for the family graves, and caring for *Lovely*, her younger sister. Eleven years earlier, not long after the girl's birth, their father had declared the small baby to be such, and his description became her sobriquet. Overnight, at only thirteen years of age, Esther became both mother and nursemaid to a child only two years younger than herself.

Lovely, a quiet, shy child, experienced a grief that outwardly seemed much deeper than that of either Esther's or Samuel's — perhaps because the two older children each felt the need to take on the responsibilities of one parent or the other. They each expressed little grief throughout the day, whereas Lovely withdrew into herself. She often refused to eat. Though she seldom cried, Lovely sometimes sat inside the cemetery gate for hours at a time, not speaking, just staring into some distant thought or time. At night, terrors invaded her sleep, causing her to scream out. Always for her father. Never once for her mother.

Esther stolidly accepted her role as mother to Lovely and all the responsibility as the female head of house. These duties, she carried out with some effort, as she had little training in daily household chores. Hester had always insisted her girls didn't need to learn how to cook or clean or such. Instead, each was to focus on their looks, their deportment, their charm, and their feminine wiles. Neither daughter had any idea what feminine wiles consisted of.

Only a few months earlier, Esther had timidly approached her father, asking, "Daddy, Mother instructed me to practice my feminine wiles on the menfolk around here, so next year when we go into Richmond, I'll be able to attract a suitor. I don't know what feminine wiles are, and Mother won't tell me. She says I should know by now."

"Esther, your mother is, despite her best intentions and education, a woman full of nonsense and foolish ideas. Best you just pretend to listen to her gibberish and carry on with being a child. No need to be thinking of suitors, beaus, or husbands," he snapped back. "No! No! No daughter of mine requires feminine wiles. Instead, she needs an education. Now off you go. Read a book."

Defiantly, she answered, "Perhaps I've read them all."

"I have no doubt, not one, that you have already read every book in my library, that is except my medical journals. Perhaps you might find a new book on my nightstand. Or go outside and ride Athena," he replied, smiling.

In a whisper, as she practically ran toward his bedroom to grab up the new book, Esther allowed these words to escape, "I've read many of the journals, Papa." A chuckle behind her told her he had heard.

Despite her father's wishes to keep her a child, as she grew into a woman, most who saw her considered Esther a beauty. They commented on her looks at social events and gatherings among their community of friends. Her long dark hair, with hints of mahogany, fell to past her waist in waves and curls. Its contrast to her green eyes—an inheritance from her father—her rosy skin often attracted attention. Esther's smile, a genuine one, and her laughing manner, revealed her loving, happy nature. Like the Biblical Esther, men noticed her. At thirteen, she had grown to five feet, six inches with a willowy, but showy figure. She carried herself with dignity and poise.

That summer, Esther's looks became a problem and caused her deep regret, given their current circumstances. Mr. Watson, the overseer the children's uncles had hired, seemed to consider Esther his property from the very first day of his arrival. In those first few days, he treated her with the deference due her, but his eyes often fell upon the girl with malicious gazes, noticed first by Samuel, then by Cook. Within a week, he took to touching Esther whenever he found her alone. Scared and wary of his manner, unable to avoid his hands and resenting his constant attention, Esther, who understood his lascivious intentions, hesitantly approached Cook and Samuel to address her unease about the man and to seek a solution.

After some discussion, the three, Samuel, Esther, and Cook, hatched a simple plan. Each day, Esther was to remain either with Samuel or Cook from the time she arose from her bed until she entered her room at night. Although this caused many awkward situations, the girl resolutely stayed within sight of one or the other. They even escorted her to the privy. Using Lovely's nightmares as an excuse, Esther took her sister to her bed each night. The girls blocked the bedroom door with a heavy trunk.

After sending letters to each absent brother by passing travelers, Samuel and Esther decided to await either Joshua's or Benjamin's return before making a decision as to their future. The two older siblings, after a long discussion outside of Lovely's hearing, had declared their eleven-year-old sister "too young and heartbroken to have a say in any but the most inconsequential decisions." Samuel, Esther, and Cook babied the girl and protected her from the harshness of their new existence. Esther sometimes carried out Lovely's chores along with her own, for the last of their household staff abandoned them soon after the overseer's unexpected arrival. Only Cook remained.

Whenever given the chance of reading or learning from travelers the most recent war news, the older siblings quietly took in each tidbit about battles and Continental Congress debates. These times of departure from their new existence allowed each to escape to a world apart. They analyzed each new military engagement based on their knowledge of history and the classics. To their dismay, and despite General Washington's taking command, the war effort faltered. Everything looked dismal. Their own situation somehow became intertwined with their country's desire for freedom.

With their Hollowell uncles' unexpected arrival in late summer, Samuel, only seventeen, struggled to find his place in their world. Never a particularly outgoing boy, he had grown into a competent, quiet man who understood his duties and the farm's management. As the older brother, Samuel tried to shelter his sisters from their uncles' wrath and debauchery, for each had brought along a slave woman who served their carnal needs. Samuel recognized soon after their arrival that these women, barely older than Esther, lived in fear. Soon he discovered each had old stripes, and sometimes open sores, from Gabriel's whip across their back and legs.

Immediately upon arrival, Michael Hollowell, the oldest brother, took over their father's room as his own and installed his concubine there. Gabriel occupied their mother's, which lay diagonally across the hallway from Esther's. Each night, cries of pain and lust disturbed the sisters' sleep.

Soon, the siblings lived in constant fear and often hunger. Any suspicious behavior or suspected insolence from the Ballinger youngsters brought about swift and unjust punishment from their uncles. Gabriel used his crop to enforce his will. A slash across Samuel's face, precipitated by what began as a discussion of how the crops could be harvested with the now severe lack of labor on the farm, cut deeply and damaged the sight in his left eye.

Not only had all their indentured servants departed, but all around their community, farmers struggled as the younger men joined the various militias or the Continental Army. Across their district, this left only the remaining few older men and young boys to carry out the continuing labor of planting and harvesting crops and caring for livestock.

With the loss of the Ballinger indentured servants, for which Michael blamed Samuel, they had no laborers besides themselves. Unable to gain access to all the doctor's accounts, Gabriel and Michael used their own funds to purchase several male slaves. This outraged Esther and Samuel. While Esther held her tongue, Samuel argued vehemently against the use of slaves on their land. Such arguments often led Michael to send the siblings to bed without supper.

Toward the end of August, Gabriel struck Lovely with his whip after she refused to sleep in her own bed. Lovely, still so much a child in mind and action, feared both her uncles. That evening, her screams and cries continued until Michael intervened, allowing her one more night in Esther's room.

The next night, Lovely slipped quietly into her own bed, hungry and sobbing with every step. Samuel slept wrapped in a quilt at the end of the hallway, keeping watch. Lovely, at eleven, with the corn-silk blonde hair and pale skin of her mother, defined her name. Samuel had seen desire in Gabriel's gray eyes as he gazed upon his nieces. Esther, secretly, took to carrying a large kitchen knife in her apron pocket.

Two days later, Esther, returning from bringing in the last of the summer vegetables, found Lovely, hiding under Esther's bed, shaking with silent sobs. Despite the late summer heat, she had bundled herself into several quilts and blankets. Strangely, Lovely said no words, and made no sounds beyond her quiet sobs. She stared straight ahead when Esther forced her to open her eyes. She refused to speak. In Esther's arms, she began to shake.

Although Cook and Esther at last calmed her, hushing her sobs, and convinced her to drink a cup of chamomile tea, Lovely refused to keep her eyes open. Her personal darkness and that of the late evening brought about terrors. Even after sleep overtook Lovely, she awoke screaming throughout the night. Yet, she issued forth no words. Esther, Samuel, and Cook feared the worst. Cook declared Lovely's mind had broken. Esther gathered Lovely's fear into herself and decided the child would never fear again, or be left alone to face the uncles, for she knew in her heart one or the other of their uncles was to blame for Lovely's sorrow. Samuel schemed, plotted, and paced.

So, with little planning and only a slight diversion to mislead their uncles, on the second of September, Samuel and Esther sneaked from the house, under a waxing quarter moon, just before midnight, taking only their own three horses, long-ago gifts from their father. Their packs held what food they could carry, clothing and blankets. They stuffed what little jewelry and coin they had hidden away after their uncles' arrival in their pockets. With a still silent Lovely in tow, they struck out to find Joshua.

Samuel, who had hidden away Joshua's old musket soon after their uncles' arrival, brought it along for protection. He wasn't a very good shot and had found only a little powder and ball shot about the house. After scrounging through their brothers' old rooms, Esther and Lovely, now dressed as boys, hair plaited and hidden in boy's caps, rode astride into the night, away from the only home they knew. Samuel served as their guide and protector.

Earlier, Cook had slipped a strong sedative, found in their father's pharmacy, into the uncles' evening meal to give the children extra time for their escape. A middle-aged Negro woman who had spent her adult life at the Ballinger home, Cook departed later that same evening. She planned simply to walk into the darkness, carrying her few belongings. She insisted her staying would put her in even greater danger than just leaving. She'd declined the children's offer of taking her with them, and simply melted into the dusk. After that night, the Ballinger children never heard what became of her. Esther prayed for Cook's health and safety for years afterward.

Avoiding the obvious paths from their home to neighbors who might have been sympathetic to their plight, instead, Samuel led them first due south far into the dark, until they reached the James River. Only then did they turn west, for there was no way to cross except for the ferry. Samuel knew the ferryman had retired for the evening and that he would have reported their crossing. Samuel and Esther both assumed the uncles would believe the siblings had sought refuge with local family friends. They hoped this roundabout diversion would give them more time for their escape.

Totally unprepared for such a journey, the three youngsters somehow survived that first week. They roughly followed the James River west, often straying off the river and riding along wooded paths. The weather stayed mild and dry, and they had food. Minor problems, like riding for hours at a stretch, relieving themselves in the forest, and sleeping on the ground, were new experiences for the girls. Neither Lovely nor Esther had ever been in the saddle for hours at a time. Though they were accomplished riders, it had previously been only for an hour, or maybe two. None of the three had realized they would have to do without the use of a privy, or the chamber pot in their room. Nor had the two girls ever slept rough. While Esther quickly adapted, Lovely often cried and rebelled when evening came.

As the days passed, the three rode from sunup to dusk. They stopped only to water and rest the horses at midday. They rode farther and farther into the wilderness, avoided the few cabins they chanced to see, and remained more afraid of what lay behind than what lay ahead. Samuel, knowing little about the wilderness, feared he'd led them far from their desired destination. They crossed forested hills, using deer paths, and sometimes followed dirt trails marked by wagon ruts. Soon, they could see the Blue Ridge mountains rising on the western horizon.

After riding late into the night under a full moon, weeks into their journey, Lovely, asleep in her saddle, slid from her horse, and landed with a light thud and a splash. Had she not awoken screaming, Esther and Samuel would have continued laughing.

"Please take me home," Lovely sobbed, while wiping mud from her clothing and then thrashing about, trying to strip her muddy clothes from her body. Taking her in hand, and holding her tight to his chest, Samuel first spoke quietly and finally sang, in his sweet tenor, an old Scottish lullaby their nanny had sung.

Blow the wind, blow;
Swift and low;
Blow the wind o'er the ocean.
Breakers rolling to the coastline;
Bringing ships to harbor;
Gulls against the morning sunlight;
Flying off to freedom!

Samuel sang the lyrics over and over again, rocking Lovely back to sleep while sitting beside the small stream. At last, she lay quietly in his arms. Esther placed their blankets in a nearby clearing, just off the path they'd trod earlier. Placing Lovely there, Samuel and Esther wept in each other's arms. Fear, relief, and exhaustion took over. After settling and hobbling their horses, each lay to one side of Lovely and all slept until late into the following day.

They awoke, ate bread and cheese Samuel had purchased from a farm the previous day, and resumed their journey. That day it rained, continuing well into the night. The rain brought the cold. The next morning proved even more chilly as the siblings donned their remaining clothing, now damp from the seeping rain. For three more days, they traveled. The rain came again and again. Despite their waterproof cloaks, all three shivered with the chill of the wind, the rain, and fear.

For three nights, they hid, and on each, rationed their food. They took to sleeping bundled together, covered in all the now damp blankets. On the fourth morning, only a small slice of cheese and a hunk of dry bread remained. Samuel handed it to Lovely.

Samuel insisted they hide deeper into the forest and give the horses rest and time to graze. So, they spent a peaceful day except for their ever-present worries about starving. The skies cleared, and the sun shone down, drying their belongings. That night they slept warm. The following morning found them mounted and ready to travel. Three grubby children, each now several pounds thinner, rode farther from home into the unknown, thinking only of food. Several hours passed before they rode through a small village where five small cabins stood beside a small river ford. Samuel and Esther bargained for food, paying with several of their few remaining coins.

An elderly woman approached as they made to cross a stream at the edge of the village and handed Esther a small bundle. Placing it in her pack, Esther insisted upon paying her with another coin. She held out the colonial farthing with its image of George III.

"No, child, no. God keep ye," she whispered, turning away. "We never seen ye. Run far."

Somehow, she knew.

18

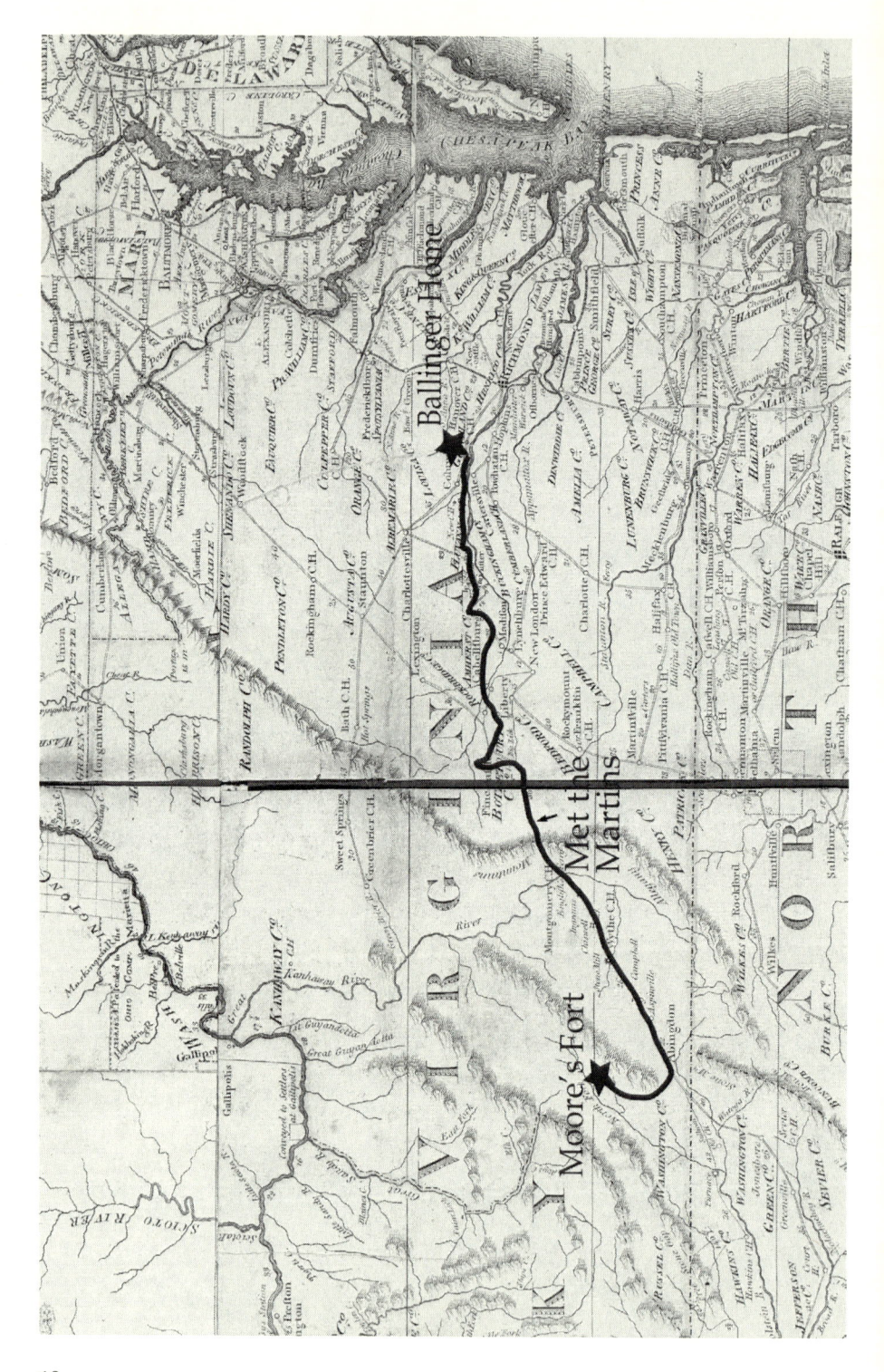

"For I know the plans I have for you," declares the LORD, "plans to prosper you and not to harm you, plans to give you hope and a future."
Jeremiah 29:11 *The Bible*

Late 1775 - 1776

Days passed into weeks. They learned their way, somewhat. The older two quickly realized how much Lovely hated insects of all kinds. Each morning, as they checked each other for ticks and insect bites, Lovely whimpered and cried. Mosquitoes and horse flies pestered them constantly during the day, often causing more tears from Lovely. While Samuel mostly maintained his composure, Esther's temper finally reached its peak. One morning while saddling the horses, a large, greenish-black horsefly bit Lovely on the cheek. Her scream rang out through the trees, disturbing the birds and her siblings.

"Lovely, shut up," Esther cried, tears now forming in her own eyes. "It will only hurt for a few minutes. Would you rather it was Uncle Gabriel's whip? Hush! Grow up! Stop being such a baby."

Immediately, upon seeing the expression on Lovely's countenance, Esther despaired over her words of anger. Her own tears calmed her anger as they streaked down her dirty face.

Samuel stepped between the two girls and gathered them both into his arms. Soon, all three wept together. Lovely wept over the harsh words of her sister and her stinging cheek. Samuel wept as he felt responsible for their suffering. Esther's tears flowed from loss, from hunger, and from fear for her sister and her brother.

Once calmed, Esther pulled peppermint oil from a small satchel where she had secreted several small bottles from her father's pharmacy. Using a clean cloth, she soothed the sting and then applied a drop of the oil as her father had done so many times to his own children.

"I didn't know you raided Father's pharmacy."

"I did, not long after the uncles arrived. I hid away things for which I understood their use. Bandages, ointments, oils, and the small surgical kit. Not that I know how to use it, but I thought it might be needed," Esther replied sheepishly.

Shaking his head over his sister's thoughtfulness, Samuel walked away and finished saddling Lovely's horse, then helped her up into the saddle.

Despite having a rough map that showed a few main roads and small villages, the three had no inkling so many rivers and streams flowed through the Virginia landscape. Each day, it seemed, they were forced to cross bodies of water, often swimming their horses. The hills and valleys of the Blue Ridge foothills slowed their rate of progress.

The weather created more unexpected hardships. They learned to ride on during thunderstorms. Being wet, damp, cold, or hot, and always hungry, left each with a frayed, short temper. Some days Lovely cried almost constantly, yet she never again begged to go home. Seems fear of the known was much worse than that of the unknown.

At times they became lost, or at least convinced themselves they were lost. Samuel had a bearing compass, and the rough, hand-drawn map he'd found in their father's desk. On day fifteen, Samuel heard a large group of riders approaching. Terrified of being returned home, they hid Lovely and their horses well off the traveled path, deep within the surrounding forest.

"Samuel, who are those men?" Esther asked, staring through a small gap in the trees after they had crept back toward the road.

"Probably militia," he answered, cautiously.

"Would they help us? Could we ask for directions?" Esther whispered, her voice breaking.

"Hush, you know they might be Tories. I can't tell. We can't take the chance."

Watching until the group rode out of sight, Samuel realized how close they'd come to discovery. He led his sisters farther into the forest, where they remained until almost dusk. In a small clearing, they dismounted and let their horses graze while either Samuel or Esther kept watch. They slept away the rest of the day, each in turns.

They lost count of the days as they wandered alone, avoiding all other travelers. What felt like months after leaving home, the chill of late autumn took its toll. Just east of the Blue Ridge Mountains, practically starving, shaking with fear and exhaustion, near dusk on a late October day, Samuel, Esther, and Lovely stumbled upon a kindly young couple, who they soon learned planned to move on to the new settlements in Kentucky come spring. But first, they would winter at the Clinch River settlements, at Castle's Woods.

Wrapping Lovely in a dry blanket, Evie Martin bundled her close and handed her a clean rag for her nose and eyes. Meanwhile, Samuel and Esther spoke quietly with Mr. Martin, who insisted they call him Mark, as he and Evie, who had married in the spring, were only two years older than Samuel. Upon hearing their story, Mark insisted the children travel with them. Being somewhat naïve and exhausted, they'd told Mark and Evie their tale of woe and their real names.

Later, sharing a much-needed hot meal of roasted rabbit and sweet potatoes, Mark suggested, "Samuel, Esther, perhaps ye might adopt a different surname? Instead of Ballinger, how about Ball? Evie and I ken a large family named Ball near abouts our old place." Upon seeing their hesitation, he continued with a smile, "We could rightly tell people ye be cousins on my mama's side and that ye'd lived nearby us."

"We be good at secrets," Evie chimed in. "Be proud to have ye as cousins. 'Sides, once we reach the Clinch settlements, no one give a mind to ye. Still, be best to be family. No sense givin' people reason to be speculatin' about ye."

So, they became the Martins' cousins, with the surname Ball. Their new *cousins* shared their food and supplies. Evie, a short, plump young woman, apparently starved for female company, talked constantly with Esther. Evie could neither read nor write and loved hearing from Esther of books she had read. Mark, a strong, muscular young man, stood only a few inches taller than this wife. His ability with an ax and a rifle provided all five with plenty of meat and warm fires each evening.

Mark explained they were in Bedford County and needed to pass over the Blue Ridge mountains through Buford's Gap. On the other side, they would be in the Shenandoah River Valley where the trails and roads would provide for easier and faster traveling.

The children contributed what they could when they rode through settlements where supplies might be purchased, as Mark and Evie held very limited funds. Daily, Mark taught the Ballinger children new skills, such as how to build a simple lean-to shelter and how to start a fire more quickly with flint and steel. He even improved Samuel's marksmanship.

Evie taught Lovely and Esther how to clean game and fish, cook over an open flame, and even to catch fish. Soon Lovely could make and cook corncakes and corn porridge. Their journey became more pleasant, not only because of the skills they learned but also because they had companions. Changes in Lovely's demeanor and behavior came slowly, but she soon began contributing her labor to all the chores except cleaning fish and game. She smiled again, easing herself from her cocoon of grief and fear. Still, she spoke little.

By the time the party reached the Clinch River settlements, Samuel and Esther considered themselves almost capable in the ways of the frontier. They soon realized how much more they had to learn.

Naively, Samuel and Esther had believed life might be easier once they reached Moore's Fort, one of several fortified stations nearby the Clinch River in southwestern Virginia. Hidden behind a new name, the trio felt safe from discovery, as only two people knew their history. Instead, what the teenagers quickly discovered was the drudgery of frontier life. Theirs became a scramble to survive; each day, every moment, life presented them with a new challenge.

Lovely struggled even more.

First came the supreme disappointment of Moore's Fort. The fort itself sat on a lonely rise about three miles east of the Clinch River. Roughly and quickly constructed, only a year earlier, of upright logs of differing lengths sunk several feet into the ground, the small stockade housed a few tiny cabins placed along the interior walls. Locals and the militia had built the fort simply to furnish the residents of Castle's Woods with a place of refuge in times of Indian trouble. These frontier forts offered not much more than shelter from attack. The fort was rustic, dirty, foul-smelling, and barely adequate. The dozen or so cabins and four corner blockhouses housed only a few full-time residents, but also provided shelter to travelers and the local militia of about twenty men, though all twenty rarely gathered at the fort.

With little regard to British authority, Castle's Woods, first settled around 1769, sat among southeastern Virginia's mountains. Settlers and hunters had unlawfully moved over the mountain passes into the lands west of the commonly called Donelson Line, established by the Proclamation of 1763. According to the story told thereabout, the first of these frontiersmen was one Jacob Castle, an albino man who had once lived among the Indians and was accused of raiding with them. A posse, organized to capture Castle, fell under fire and had to flee back across the river. In this skirmish, one man fell into the river, was captured, killed, and scalped. His name being Clinch, the river was forevermore named for him. More settlers had arrived after Castle, and they soon established several small, almost completely self-reliant communities. With more and more people settling the area of the Clinch, the Virginia legislature took notice, and created a new county, Botetourt.

The valley, full of tillable land surrounded by forested hills filled with game, and streams brimming with fish, fresh-water mussels, and such, drew men looking for freedom and free land. By the time of Lord Dunmore's War, Botetourt County's population had grown to a considerable number of residents. Forts sprang up for defense, and men such as William Russell had established large land holdings. Men, women, and families came and went. Some planned on traveling even farther west, while others headed south into the Watauga settlement. In 1775, Castle's Woods offered the Ballinger children what they deemed to be the only realm of safety where they might linger for the winter.

As they neared the settlements along the Clinch, Lovely whispered, "Esther, what day will we arrive at the castle?"

"Castle? What castle?"

"The one in castle's woods."

"Oh, Lovely, there is no castle. Castle was a person, not a building like in fairy tales. The area is called Castle's Woods, for a man, not a castle."

Esther watched as Lovely's face showed her disappointment at the news there would be no castle to house them. Sometimes she wondered at Lovely's understanding of their plight, and then remembered her sister was only eleven and had been sheltered and pampered as the youngest girl in their family.

Upon arrival, Mark and Samuel went off immediately to find one of the militia officers to arrange for two cabins—or one, if only one was available. Esther and Lovely dismounted and led their horses to a nearby stream for water.

"My, goodness, mercy be, ye two girls look plum tuckered out. Surely, ye not be traveling alone?"

Esther turned to find an older woman, probably in her early sixties, addressing them. She carried a bucket in one hand and a covered basket in the other. Her brown linsey-woolsy skirt, though patched and darned in many places, hung clean and free of mud, unlike their own pilfered wool trousers. A bonnet of once brightly printed calico, worn thin and faded from use, covered her gray braids. Deep brown eyes belied a kind nature and trustworthiness.

"No, mistress, we traveled with our brother and some cousins. I am Esther Ball," she answered, after having suddenly remembered to use her adopted name, "and this is my sister Lovely. We are seeking to find our brother believed to be in this area."

"My, my child, perhaps I might be of help. Girls, turn your horses out to graze and come to my cabin. Ye'll find me in the back west corner. My door will be open to ye. I be Sarah Porter."

Lovely and Esther, too tired to refuse her invitation, unsaddled all three horses, and placed their belongings near where Evie sat awaiting Mark's return.

"Evie, one of the residents, an older woman, invited us to her cabin. Would you like to join us? I'm sure she wouldn't mind. I am eager to ask about our brother, or I would not leave you alone."

"No, just be sittin' here and enjoy'n the sunshine. Mark soon be 'long with news, then me and him be settin' up camp here under the trees or move'n our goods into a cabin. Be glad to tell Samuel where ye be." Evie smiled and leaned back against the packs that contained all their household belongings.

Lovely and Esther easily found the small cabin and Mistress Porter. After helping them wash up with real soap and a clean towel, Sarah sat them down and pushed bread, butter, and honey toward each girl. Lovely began to cry and soon found herself wrapped in Sarah Porter's powerful arms and comforted as only a mother can do. After Lovely quieted, Esther asked after Joshua.

"Mistress Porter, we came west to find our brother Joshua. He left home in the spring, headed west. Since then, our parents died, and we three are all alone. Joshua is tall, several inches over six feet, has sandy blond hair, and is only just now sixteen, though he looks older. Have you, by chance, seen him?

"Perhaps, child, for there be several militia boys with those looks. I remember one very tall boy. Can't say as I ever knew his name. Have ye girls no other family?"

"Yes, ma'am. Our brother, Samuel, came west with us. He's somewhere about, looking for us a cabin. We have an older brother studying medicine in Scotland. We sent him word of our whereabouts." Esther knew that last statement held a partial lie. They had been afraid to send a letter or leave word with anyone about their plans.

When Samuel located his sisters, Lovely lay sleeping on Sarah Porter's bed. He and Esther left her undisturbed while they created what comfort they could in a tiny cabin along the west wall of Moore's Fort. Mark and Evie took over a cabin on the east wall. Seeing how little they possessed, Mistress Porter lent the siblings several items to make their cabin more comfortable.

Only days after their arrival, Joshua rode into the fort with two older men, all of them militia. Samuel spotted him immediately and called out, "Joshua, Joshua!" As the brothers embraced, those nearby guessed rightly of their relationship. Samuel, barely two years older, stood only an inch shorter than Joshua and had the same long, lanky torso, sandy hair, and crooked smile.

Sadly, Joshua had never received their letter, or any news, detailing the events of the previous spring and summer. Grief ignited, along with Joshua's anger. Over a small rough table, within a minuscule log cabin at Moore's, Samuel and Esther told Joshua all that had occurred and why they had fled. Joshua's tears mixed with their own as he learned how little family he had left after losing all their younger siblings, the pain and grief the uncles had inflicted, and his remaining siblings' struggle to survive. Upon hearing their tale, Joshua seemed unable to forgive himself, believing his departure had brought about all their grief and trouble.

Joshua took the death of their mother upon himself. In his grief he ranted about how, perhaps if he had not left, she might still live and the tiny baby sister as well. Samuel tried to dispel such thoughts, but Esther knew they would remain with Joshua for many years, guilt being a hard sentiment to be shed of. All cried tears of renewed grief.

After a serious family discussion, four of the five remaining Ballinger siblings abandoned their surname and called themselves *Ball*. Joshua had enlisted in the militia with the name Ballinger, but went to his captain and asked his name to be changed on the official documents. Never did the siblings imagine it would be many years before they felt safe to resume using the name Ballinger. On bartered paper, Esther wrote to Benjamin, making him aware of their circumstances. They had little hope the letter would reach him, as now a war stood sentinel between four siblings and their oldest brother.

Winter came in hard that year, only a few weeks after their arrival. With Joshua's help, they found safety within the fort, living in that small one-room cabin that shared a wall on each side with the cabin next door. Cabins within the fort were often exchanged, used with or without permission, and rented as travelers came and went. Like many of the others, their cabin's dirt floor seemed always damp and cold. A rough-hewn table, one leg shorter than the other three, and two even rougher benches became their only furniture, if one could call it that. At nighttime, they rested upon bedding made up of corn husk stuffed, duck-cloth mattresses, a small luxury as the cloth had cost Esther a small gold brooch, a gift on her twelfth birthday from her mother. A stone fireplace provided heat against the snow and wind, and a place to prepare meals. With Mistress Porter's help, the four children stood together and began life in the wilderness of far western Virginia.

Others within the fort supplied them with some necessary household goods in exchange for labor. Yet, they mostly did without. To earn bits of coin or to trade for foodstuffs, Esther and Lovely cleaned, did laundry, cooked, and cared for small children. Poor as church mice and often exhausted, the girls relied on each other. Joshua and Samuel both served in the militia, receiving irregularly paid minute wages. With the militia, they patrolled the nearby settlements, stations, isolated cabins, and forts.

Although Lord Dunmore's War had ended in 1774 with the Battle of Point Pleasant, the western settlements, especially those at Castle's Woods, still existed under a tenuous peace. Indians,

Cherokee and Shawnee in particular, often passed through the region and sometimes caused minor skirmishes.

Mark and Evie Martin helped the girls to settle in too, and they frequently shared the chore of preparing meals with Evie. Mark brought in game, sometimes deer, once a bear, and most often squirrel or possum. Lovely refused to eat possum, as the greasy meat tasted extremely gamy. Otherwise, Lovely regained some of her lost weight and carried out her chores without complaint, though she rarely talked. Her nightmares continued to haunt their sleep.

Esther quickly regained her confidence, spoke with all the women of the fort, and developed the necessary skills to make their small cabin a home. She also became a favorite of the militia, all of whom treated her with respect.

The brothers' militia service occasionally left Lovely and Esther alone for weeks at a time. Unable to afford another rifle, Esther took to carrying their large carving knife in a belt at her waist. At night, she placed it under the edge of her corn-husk pallet, for Moore's population consisted mainly of unmarried men, who often drank the easily available corn liquor to excess. Esther only slept well when either Samuel or Joshua was about, even if the two boys slept in the adjoining blockhouse.

As winter deepened, Joshua and Samuel helped keep the family in game, so they rarely went truly hungry. When a trader came through, they sometimes purchased cornmeal. Lovely's one true talent, developed under their mother's tutelage, lay in sewing. Her stitches, always tight and true, made for beautiful workmanship. So, Lovely often traded her sewing skills for herbs and the occasional small weight of beans.

Things improved slightly in mid-winter as Esther found additional employment teaching some of the young girls to read and write. The fort had a schoolmaster; however, he refused to allow the young girls to attend. Evie attended these classes when possible. By late winter, she had learned her letters and could write her name.

Sarah Porter taught Esther and Lovely to make and bake bread in the fort's small communal beehive oven. By late December, Lovely could make a passable loaf of sourdough bread when wheat flour became available from traders. At other times, corn cakes filled their need for bread.

Winter kept all the womenfolk and children close to the fort, creating a sense of confinement among the residents. Still, they stayed constantly busy. Firewood needed to be gathered and chopped, game to be cleaned and prepared, and washing to be done. Esther insisted they have clean clothing, unlike many of the fort who had no change of clothing or even the desire to shed their bodily dirt. The girls had given up their brothers' garb when they arrived and donned simple wool skirts and bodices. Each had two, one to wear and one for spare. Samuel, like Joshua, had taken to wearing buckskins, as the militia did not have uniforms. Esther packed away Samuel's good clothing, hoping one day it might, once again, be of use.

Late that winter, a fever laid low many of the fort's younger children. Esther sometimes volunteered to sit with a child, especially at night, to give the mother a bit of rest. In so doing, she began learning about remedies to bring down fevers, treat sore throats, headaches, and minor injuries, for most everyone at the fort turned to Mistress Porter in times of sickness or injury.

Sarah Porter had come to Castle's Woods four years earlier with her husband, William. They'd built a small cabin, planted crops, fought off Indians four times, and lived what they considered to be a passable life. Still, life had more to give Sarah, or take, as it was. William had just stepped out to chop wood for the fire in February 1774 when Sarah heard his sharp cry of pain.

Instantly, he cried out, "Sarah, bar the door!"

First, Sarah had opened the door farther, hoping to pull William inside. Instead, she saw a large Indian jerk William's head back and begin the cut to take his scalp. The arrow, still embedded in a stomach wound, drained his blood out upon the woodpile. Remembering William's words, she slammed the door shut, dropped the iron bar, and grabbed her musket. Firing from one of the slots cut into the cabin's logs for just that purpose, Sarah took down one warrior. She had, over the many years of necessity that came with frontier living, become an excellent shot. Next, she grabbed William's rifle and took down another. By the time she'd reloaded each weapon, all was quiet outside. Peeking out through the slot, Sarah saw William's mutilated body lying in a puddle of his own blood. She knew he was dead. She knew what he expected of her — to save herself.

For that entire day and the following night, Sarah sat in a chair facing the door, musket and rifle loaded and primed. Although she might have dozed a bit, she never slept. At dawn, Sarah heard voices. *English!* she thought immediately.

Captain David Gass of the militia knocked quietly. "Sarah Porter, ye there? It be Captain Gass."

They'd buried William near the cabin. Someone, she couldn't remember who, came from the fort with a small cart and helped her pack up their belongings. After Sarah moved to the fort, only once did she venture back to their cabin. On a lovely spring day, she'd visited William's grave and planted a small dogwood tree at its head.

Mistress Sarah, as she insisted the siblings call her, constantly carried a leather pack filled with little cloth sacks containing such things as dried chamomile flowers to help calm patients. Seeing Esther's interest, she began teaching the young woman about the uses of various plants and herbs. Esther first learned how to use purple cone flower in teas to reduce fevers and inflammation, and black raspberry roots to brew a tea for coughs. As she learned more, she began a small notebook soon filled with sketches of the plants, notes on where they could be found, how each must be used, and which ones could be dangerous. Mistress Sarah, one of the few women at the fort who could read and write, would go over the notes with her, and help illustrate her sketches with distinguishing markings on plants to make recognition easier. Soon, Esther developed a kind, helping manner, and often found herself sought out during times of illness or injury.

Sarah and Lovely became friends as well. Lovely would tend Sarah's cabin during the woman's absences to tend the sick. Lovely always made sure Mistress Sarah had clean water and kept her fire burning. As the winter progressed, Lovely and Esther often spent nights with Sarah, especially when their brothers were on patrol together. If Mark Martin had gone out hunting, and planned to stay out for several days, Evie would join them. The women and girls ate, giggled, told stories, and shared their secrets. Even Lovely contributed to the fun. Evie told them first, even before Mark, that she was carrying a child. Sarah's grief lessened, and she knew she once again possessed a family.

"Choose the great adventure of being brave and afraid at the exact same time." Brené Brown

1776

News filtered sporadically in from the east, mostly as new settlers came into the fort. Of course, few traveled west during the dead of winter. In late March, a new militia officer arrived, bringing the latest war news. Soon the Battle of Moore's Creek Bridge, fought in eastern North Carolina, sat foremost on everyone's mind. A month earlier, on the twenty-seventh of February, far from Moore's Fort—though they shared a name—almost one thousand Patriots had quietly waited for Loyalist forces to cross a partially dismantled bridge. During the previous days, the Patriots had removed the bridge flooring and smeared, with grease, tallow, and soap, the remaining portions, in particular the standing piers and support rails. With cannons and muskets ready to rain fire upon their enemy, the ragtag Patriots stood firm behind an embankment until the Loyalist forces charged. Loyalist General MacDonald—shouting in Gaelic, "King George and broadswords!"—led the charge. MacDonald had recruited heavily among the colony's former Scottish Highlanders.

After the cannons and muskets fired, the Patriots—many of whom were also Scottish Highlanders, who each held a deep hatred for England—charged with broadswords, each man calling out his own Highland battle cry! At long last, listening as the newcomer related the tale, the residents and the Ballinger siblings heard of the Patriots winning a battle. At Castle's Woods, spirits rose. Young boys fought the battle across a nearby creek each day, arguing each time who would be a Patriot and who would be forced to play a Loyalist. There were always more Patriots. Some days, they fought against an invisible enemy, for among the children none agreed to be a Loyalist.

Moore's residents spoke often of their own Lieutenant Colonel William Russell and his Fincastle Rangers who worked to build a fort on the north side of the South Fork of the Holston River near the upper end of Long Island. This stockade wall with bastions at the corners would enclose three acres on the bluff above the Holston. Russell's force and the fort were to provide additional protection against the Cherokee, led by Dragging Canoe, who had been defeated on the twentieth of July at that same location. Russell named the fort for Virginia's first governor Patrick Henry.

Using their minimal savings, the siblings sent a notice to Purdie's Virginia Gazette to be run weekly for one month. It read: *If an oldest brother, returning from his training, should seek his siblings, he should ask along the Clinch.* Being as the *Virginia Gazette* supported the revolution, they had little worried the uncles would be frequent readers of such a news sheet. Despite the danger of discovery, they posited posting the advertisement might be their only chance to contact Benjamin.

Regularly, as the warmer days of spring arrived, it seemed more and more travelers came into the settlement from the east and brought with them the latest war news. Although Loyalists' activities had quieted in the Carolinas after the Battle of Moore's Creek Bridge, Virginia's westernmost settlements remained vulnerable to such Loyalist activities and spies. Hatred grew against those who still supported the king. Most Loyalists in Castle's Woods packed up and moved back east.

Throughout that winter, the Ballinger children kept to themselves when outsiders appeared. However, with spring's arrival, and now desperate for any type of news, they flocked to the fort's common when newcomers arrived.

Benjamin found them in the summer. Lovely saw him first as he rode in with a group of rough-looking men. She had been sitting in the sunlight, mending a torn apron when she let out a little gasp and then ran toward the horses, screaming his name. Benjamin, seeing her approach, leaped down to grab her out of harm's way. Attracted by all the noise, particularly Lovely's scream, Esther watched from their cabin doorway as sister and brother, having not seen each other for over five years, hugged, heads together, hands clasped. Both weeping and laughing together. Esther's tears flowed with joy, for perhaps now their time of turmoil would end.

Soon, all five siblings gathered within the now severely crowded cabin. They listened as Benjamin told all the news of their former home, still held by the uncles who had each returned to their own plantation, leaving the overseer in charge. To their dismay and shame, slaves now toiled their land, under the whip of a man much despised by the three who knew him.

Having confronted the overseer and learning nothing more than that the children had fled. Benjamin had then asked about at nearby plantations. At one, he had learned from one of their cooks a tale of his siblings fleeing west to join up with Joshua.

Benjamin told of going from village to village, cabin to cabin on his way west, asking after his siblings. After listening to only negative replies, he had been overjoyed to meet one older woman who declared she had seen the three headed west. She also handed him a news sheet, one which just happened to have their notice printed neatly in the third column of the second page.

They listened to tales of Benjamin's studies, his friends in Scotland, and his journey home across a sea filled with warships and privateers. Benjamin relayed all the latest on the revolution. He'd brought gifts, books for Lovely and Esther, cloth for new clothing, a warm cape for each sister, and a new long rifle each for Joshua and Samuel.

Benjamin had stopped long enough in their old community of friends to learn, that despite his being their father's heir, the current courts held always with Loyalists. Their uncles' statements about their father's political views would sway the magistrates to side with the Hollowell brothers. He didn't dare challenge them at this time. Besides, Benjamin was desperate to find his remaining family. He envisioned there would be time to reclaim his inheritance.

That evening, emotions flowed like a soft river with their ever-ebbing grief, brutishly with their anger, and tenderly with the overwhelming joy of being together again. They spoke together well into darkness, Benjamin holding a sleeping Lovely in his lap. Dawn broke not long after the older four had retired to their shared pallets.

As always, morning brought activity. That day, it flowed in a different direction. Samuel and Joshua went off to find the fort's leaders to discuss their need for a larger, or an additional, cabin. Lovely fetched water with Benjamin at her side. Esther tidied the cabin and prepared the morning's cornmeal cakes and butter. Sarah Porter had moved to the fort, leading a dairy cow and calf. Being a kind and generous woman, Sarah shared the luxury of milk, cream, and butter with all.

After they broke their fast, Benjamin asked, "Esther, dearest sister, might ye take a walk with me." Minutes later, they left the fort and walked west toward a small rocky-bed stream, good for fishing and quiet contemplation. Benjamin appeared to be enjoying the view, but Esther recognized something troubled him. At the stream's bank, the two stopped, and he pulled out a small pistol and placed it in Esther's hand.

"Esther, I carried this in Scotland when I went wandering. Unlike the Scots, British law allowed me to have a firearm. I want you to keep this on your person, always. I'll teach you how to use it over the coming weeks."

"Benjamin, you'll need this more than I."

"No, sister. I own another now. Besides, I've seen the lust and violence on the faces of drunk men in Scotland and here. You've become a beautiful lassie, sister."

Esther shook her head, scoffing at Benjamin's words.

"No sister, believe me. I've seen the looks. Men do and will continue to notice you. Keep the pistol. It will ease my thoughts as to your safety." As she accepted the gift and placed it in her apron pocket, Benjamin softly continued, "Esther, tell me about Lovely. She seems so much a child, despite her twelve years."

As Esther talked about Lovely's response to their parents' death, events after their uncles' arrival, her behavior on their journey west, and her current mental condition, Benjamin listened quietly.

"I suspected as much after observing her last night. I don't know a lot about mental instability, but I suspect Lovely may never recover from all that has happened. If she does, it may take years. You and Samuel were right to protect her from the harshness of this world. I believe Lovely's spirit is damaged. I worried most about her upon hearing from our neighbors of your treatment at our uncles' hands, for father always babied her even after all the younger ones came along. One of our neighbors said Cook had come their way and informed them of your treatment. She also told them of your fleeing. In my heart, I knew you would be the strong one, despite all that happened.

"Did you know Samuel sent a letter with Cook? While the letter stated that the three of you would seek refuge in a town, it also told in great detail of Joshua's wish to go west over the mountains. Somehow, upon reading it, I knew this was Samuel's way of telling me you would attempt to follow Joshua."

"I didn't know of the letter. I spoke against leaving any written communication as to our intended plans. I'm glad Samuel wrote, for now we can be together again."

Benjamin pulled Esther against him as he spoke, and she recognized how much of a man he'd become—taller than their father, respectful of others. Truly, his time in Scotland had made him a gentleman. He sported a head full of sandy hair, held neatly in a queue, and a short, neat beard that matched exactly, in color, that of his head. During his years of absence from them, Benjamin had matured into an attractive man. Like her, his face held their father's green eyes—eyes that reflected his quiet demeanor and his intelligence.

"Samuel and I tried to protect Lovely. But there was no pleasing Uncle Gabriel. After Father died, she became withdrawn and quiet. Then Gabriel struck her across her backside with his whip. Cook treated her wound. Later, whispering a warning to Samuel and me about how Gabriel most likely wanted to . . . .

"No need to say those abhorrent words, sister. I know what he desired. You and Samuel did the correct thing in leaving, for Gabriel would have defiled her had you not departed. He or Michael would have raped you as well. From what Samuel has said, the Negro girl Gabriel was abusing was not much older than you."

"Perhaps he did, for something happened the day before we departed that left Lovely speechless for days into our journey. Her nightmares increased, and she withdrew more so within herself."

"Oh Esther . . . Ye have each endured too much," Benjamin replied, wondering to himself what all Esther might not be sharing.

Suddenly shaking, scared, tired, and despondent with thoughts of those days, Esther quietly admitted to herself how much more horrendous their treatment might have been had they stayed. In her heart, she knew Samuel would have tried to defend his sisters and would have most likely died in his attempt. As Benjamin held Esther, they talked for a long, long while. Tears flowed from both, tears of grief each had held in for much too long. As their talk moved on to other topics, both felt a release—a calm.

Benjamin saw in Esther a woman grown. A woman who had adopted the role of mother long before her time should have come. A caring and loving woman, who, at all costs, would protect Lovely, Samuel, and Joshua. He saw in this beautiful creature his father's strength, his father's love, and his father's wisdom. So unlike was she to their own mother, except for her beauty. It seemed Esther's heart had little room for hatred or prejudice.

Later in the day, Samuel and Joshua returned with good news, lifting the spirits of all as they once again crowded into that tiny cabin. The brothers had located a new home for the family and had already ridden out to check its condition. As Benjamin had coin from an account their father'd set up for him many years ago, he paid a small sum to Captain Thomas Gass, renting the cabin for a year. It lay roughly one-half mile outside the fort's walls. Gass, whose brother David had once been the militia captain before he moved out to Boonesborough that spring, had told the brothers the Boone family had lived there until they left for Kentucky the previous September.

Beside the cabin, which stood close enough to the fort that they could easily and quickly flee inside during times of distress, lay a small pasture where their horses could graze. The cabin's garden plot was located nearby, and a lean-to attached to the cabin's back wall would shelter their horses in bad weather.

A tiny grave marked only with stones lay nearby. After they settled, Lovely took to tending it. She dug wildflowers and placed them among the stones. Lovely seemed happier now that they had privacy and didn't have to live within the crowded, and constantly odoriferous, fort.

Since their arrival at Moore's, she'd slept beside Esther, always a hand upon her, except on the nights she stayed with Sarah. All night she touched Esther, reaching out for her in sleep if her sister moved or turned. She still cried out some nights and woke sobbing. Once they settled in the cabin outside the walls, Lovely came back to herself in bits and pieces. Her fears seem to disappear. She became happy once again but remained very much a child.

Almost immediately after his arrival, people within the fort started calling on Doctor Benjamin for all sorts of ailments and injuries. Soon the family acquired, as payment for his services, two hens, a young dairy cow — payment for delivering twins — and three piglets. Few people paid in coin. Still, their larder never lay empty.

Esther often went along as his assistant, and thereby learned more about treatments and medicines. Her notebook grew with each visit as she diligently added tidbits about the treatment of wounds and illnesses. Benjamin, seeing her interest, spent time explaining procedures and theories about how the organs in the body worked. Mistress Sarah welcomed Benjamin and his medical training. They began working together when someone became injured or ill.

Their nightly discussions now included another option for the future. Being of maturity at two and twenty, and their father's heir, Benjamin could now challenge the uncles' control and force the return of their lands and home. Yet, with the war's stalemate, his chances were not good. After many such talks, the Ballinger children tabled that discussion.

Of an evening, in the coming weeks and months, laughter often rang from the small cabin. Sometimes voices rang out in song as Benjamin taught his siblings tunes learned in Edinburgh's public houses. In the following days, Esther could often be heard singing or humming bits and pieces of her favorite *The Bonnie Lass o' Fyvie*.

It's braw, aye it's braw, a captain's lady for to be
And it's braw to be a captain's lady-o
It's braw to ride around and to follow the camp
And to ride when your captain he is ready-o

O I'll give you ribbons, love, and I'll give you rings
I'll give you a necklace of amber-o
I'll give you a silken petticoat with flounces to the knee
If you'll convey me

The five Ballinger children—now called Ball by all at the fort—found happiness in each other, in relative safety, in family, and in brotherly love.

On other evenings, the five discussed heading farther west into Kentucky. Mark and Evie Martin had already joined a party headed into the wilderness. Evie, her pregnancy now showing, had ridden away to start her family in the wilds beyond the mountains.

The siblings knew the small settlements at Boonesborough or Fort Harrod might provide them with a more distant hiding place. Joshua pushed the most for moving west, while Benjamin and Samuel always resisted any such move. The older brothers wanted the younger siblings to remain in Virginia, for each planned to join the militia or Continental Army to fight for their country's freedom. Benjamin's skills as a trained surgeon were much in demand by both groups, whereas Samuel simply wanted revenge upon their uncles and believed they could regain their heritage if the colonies proved successful. Neither wanted the additional worry of Joshua, Lovely, and Esther being so far away in Kentucky.

Still, the five made no decision, although Joshua most often brought up the subject of moving farther west, or even southwest to the Watauga settlement. Then, in early August, a lone traveler brought news from the east. Since their own arrival, among the visitors to the fort had come all sorts of people. Scots, Irish, English, and Germans all ventured west, looking for land. Many who had been in the colonies for several generations came for the new opportunities available. For free land, to escape their poor existence. To hide.

This particular traveler fell into neither group. Instead, he was just a wanderer. Not a tall man—no, what might even be called dumpy—he was heavy of body and limbs. His head, covered by a nest of unkept black hair, appeared to have never seen the likes of a comb. His hair fell only to his shoulders, and some joked it was as if he had cut it with his own hunting knife. He wore buckskin pants topped with a white shirt—once stylish, now worn and filthy—under a brocade waistcoat with a variety of bright buttons. Some gold, some silver, and some bone! Over his shirt and waistcoat, he proudly bore an old black wool frock coat, mended and patched in various places with different colors of wool cloth. It had no buttons. None at all, even on the frayed too-long sleeves. He wore moccasins on his feet. Strangely, he spoke with an educated air and had manners to match.

As he conversed with all those gathered around following his booming request, they learned the most important bits of his information came from newspapers, sheets, he'd carried west to share with settlers along the way. This being his way of making coin. Soon, quiet overtook the group so all could listen. They stood that night in early August and heard him read aloud the *Declaration of Independence*. By his reading's end, some had tears, some shouted with joy, and others—the few among the gathering loyal to the king—scoffed and turned away. Benjamin, Joshua, Samuel, Lovely, and Esther stood, listening as the man read, once again, those powerful words—a declaration of freedom—for many in the crowd had begged to hear him read the words once more—powerful words of tyranny wrought by men, men who shared their desire for freedom from an unseen king across distant waters.

Proving quite the storyteller, the haphazardly dressed man then relayed sad news from the Watauga settlement. Tales of its fort having been attacked by Cherokee warriors, first in June, and then again in mid-July. Of how many of that place now feared, even more so, for their lives. He described the carnage, the brutal deaths, and even cried out the Cherokee war cries while dancing around with a tomahawk and pretending to be an Indian. He delivered even more details of the second attack, perpetrated on the twenty-first of July, which began in the early morning as the women of the fort remained outside the walls milking their cows. He acted out the women running for the fort's gates while trying to carry pails full of milk. Those in his audience could almost hear their terrified screams, the cries of their pursuers, and the pleas of encouragement shouted from within the walls.

Their troubadour's words revealed the thrilling story of how bonnie Kate Sherrill had been pulled by her arms up and over the wall by John Sevier. He told of Kate's great beauty, her athletic prowess, her amazing shooting skills, and how the men of the fort each desired her devotion. Next, he described the actions of the fort's militia officers to organize a defense. He relayed how the initial attack had been short-lived, only three or so hours, although at one point the fighting became extremely fierce, causing the fort's women to act on their own. According to his tale, a woman named Ann Robertson Johnson, the fort commander's sister, had poured scalding water over the heads of the Cherokee men attempting to set the walls on fire. Ann had continued her efforts, although slightly wounded, with the help of other women, until the Cherokee men gave up their attempt at setting fire to the fort's walls.

Keeping up the deadly drama, he explained how, for over two weeks, the fort's occupants remained under siege. Sleepless nights and days of terror held the fort's occupants hostage, over one hundred of them in that small fort.

Just when the listeners thought the story could get no worse, the bearer of news began to describe additional events of the initial attack of that July day, for the Cherokee had captured a young man, Samuel Moore—near to Esther's own age—outside the walls and taken him to the nearby village of Tuskegee, where he was to be burned at the stake. Another captive, Mistress Lydia Bean, was mother to a large family who lived nearby the fort on Boone's Creek. The Cherokee had captured Lydia as she attempted to rush home to their nearby cabin after hearing the initial attack. They said her husband, a Scotsman named William Bean, the original settler in the area and a leader of the settlement, watched as Cherokee warriors captured his wife, beating her when she resisted. Like the youth, Lydia had been taken to their village and sentenced to death in the same horrendous manner.

By now, the gathering had seated themselves in a circle around the chronicler. Others leaned against cabin walls. Fascinated and horrified, they silently listened to a tale that could be their own at any time, wanting to hear the ending, needing to know all was now well at Watauga. They listened, dreading to hear news of friends, and even family, at that settlement. Each one needed to hear there was hope for themselves should they be attacked.

The Ballinger siblings sat quietly, listening, Esther beside Benjamin, who held Lovely upon his knee. Esther noticed her sister's silently falling tears and wished they had left her at the cabin.

"Now those murdering Cherokee pulled Mistress Bean screaming and crying to their village, where the Cherokee women threw rocks and such at her. They tied her to a stake and left her beaten and miserable, without water or food, as they first tortured and then burned alive the youth. Mistress Bean, forced to watch and listen to his horrible screams, begged them for mercy on the boy's behalf, crying out that he was only a boy, a child. They say Samuel cried out first for his own mother, and then for the end to come. Mistress Bean later told how she'd prayed for a quick end to his anguish, and for hers when her time came.

"Now, burning the poor boy to death didn't end their frenzy, and they stripped Mistress Bean stark naked and tied her to yet another stake at the center of the village. At some point, her arm had been broken and her shoulder dislocated. She had other injuries as well. In excruciating pain, tied there, surrounded by kindling, with a torch being lit, she prayed to her God for deliverance. Seems our good Lord listened because a Cherokee Beloved Woman rushed in and saved that dear mother's life. This Cherokee woman stopped the burning and had Mistress Bean carried to her own cabin. There, she nursed her, clothed her, and kept her safe.

"Now you might ask why this Cherokee woman had such power. Well, those who know her story say Nanyehi—that be her Cherokee name—was named a Ghigau, a Beloved Woman of the Cherokees years earlier. Those Cherokee believe she speaks with the spirit world, and so, she is greatly honored by her people, all because as a young woman she joined her husband in a battle against the Creek Indians and even led them to victory after her husband's death. Nowadays, Nanyehi occupies a seat next to the war chief and peace chiefs at the ceremonial fire in Chota. That's their main village. She leads the women's council and has a vote in all tribal decisions—in all matters of war and peace. Seems Nanyehi also has absolute power over the fate of all prisoners taken in raids and battles.

"Mistress Bean and Nanyehi, who is married to a white trader and now called Nancy Ward by the settlers, became fast friends and traded skills during the time Mistress Bean recovered at Nancy's cabin. Lydia Bean, it is said, taught Nancy to make butter and to weave cloth. You see, Mistress Bean and her daughters are all excellent weavers.

When Nancy arranged for Lydia's return to her family, Lydia presented her with two dairy cows."

As the evening grew dark, more stories followed, but none as exciting as the tale of Lydia Bean and Nancy Ward. The Ballinger siblings listened on for over an hour before returning to their cabin. As Lovely fell asleep, the older four discussed the news, and Benjamin read aloud from one of the news sheets he had purchased.

> "Let me not pray to be sheltered from dangers,
> but to be fearless in facing them.
> Let me not beg for the stilling of my pain,
> But for the heart to conquer it."
> Rabindranath Tagore

Late 1776 - 1777

As their second winter at Moore's Fort began, the Ballinger siblings established a daily routine that kept them safe, warm, fed, and spiritless with the routines of life. Their boredom changed in February when the news of General Washington's Christmas Day move from New Jersey, across the Delaware River in the dead of night, to take on the Hessians at Trenton, finally reached the Clinch River settlements. Even those living in the most isolated frontier lands had heard of the Hessian troops, hired by King George III to supplement his forces. They feared these well-trained, brutal men. Yet, a fellow Virginian had taken on those elite troops in a surprise attack and persevered. Now, they had something new, something uplifting, to fuel their evening discussions.

While the events of the war buoyed spirits at the fort, they also led to major changes in the little family. As the weather broke in early spring, Benjamin and Samuel packed up, saddled their horses, and rode off to join the rebellion. Before Benjamin departed, he gave the remaining three most all his coin. They held enough to survive for a while longer, even without the income from Benjamin's doctoring. Broken-hearted, yet proud, three siblings watched their older brothers ride away. Esther and Joshua worried most about Samuel. He had no experience in fighting. While he had become a steady shot, no one would name him as a sharpshooter, for the damage to his eye from Gabriel's whip had left him with trouble seeing things at a distance clearly.

They believed Benjamin would remain out of danger being he was a surgeon.

Once again, Lovely withdrew into herself. She spoke little and spent hours of her time with the two books Benjamin had gifted the girls the previous summer. Few at the fort owned a book, besides the Bible, probably because even fewer of the settlement could read or write. Esther's book was Dr. Samuel Johnson's *A Journey to the Western Islands of Scotland*. Benjamin had purchased the newly published volume in Glasgow just before his departure. Lovely's book, *Poems by Mrs. Robinson*, contained verses and sonnets concerning the values desirable in women.

In the evening, the three siblings often read aloud. Lovely's favorite poem was "Cupid's Sleeping." She chose this one to read so frequently that Samuel and Esther grew to despise even its name. However, Lovely believed the poem foretold of a sweetheart for herself, as she held strong to her childish romantic beliefs, learned from fairy tales read to the siblings by their nannies and tutors. Esther could often be heard to declare she had seen and heard too much of "love" to believe it could be that soft, that pure. Yet, for many years, she could recite that poem word for word.

> CLOSE in a woodbine's tangled shade,
> The BLOOMING GOD asleep was laid;
> His brows with mossy roses crown's;
> His golden darts lay scatter'd round;
> To shade his auburn, curled head,
> A purple canopy was spread,
> Which gently with the breezes play'd,
> And shed around a soften'd shade.
> Upon his downy smiling cheek,
> Adorned with many a "dimple sleek,"
> Beam'd glowing health and tender blisses,
> His coral lip which teem'd with kisses
> Ripe, glisten'd with ambrosial dew,
> That mock'd the rose's deepest hue.-
> His quiver on a bough was hung,
> His bow lay carelessly unstrung:

His breath mild odour scatter'd round,
His eyes an azure fillet bound:
On every side did zephyrs play,
To fan the sultry beams of day;
While the soft tenants of the grove,
Attun'd their notes to plaintive Love.
Thus lay the Boy- when DEVONS feet
Unknowing reach'd the lone retreat;
Surpriz'd, to see the beauteous child
Of every dang'rous pow'r beguil'd!
Approaching near his mossy bed,
Soft whisp'ring to herself she said:-
" Thou little imp, whose potent art
" Bows low with grief the FEELING HEART;
" Whose thirst insatiate, loves to sip
" The nectar from the ruby lip;
" Whose barb'rous joy is prone to seek
" The soft carnation of the cheek;
" Now, bid thy tyrant sway farewell,
" As thus I break each magic spell: "
Snatch'd from the bough, where high it hung,
O'er her white shoulder straight she flung
The burnish'd quiver, golden dart,
And each vain emblem of his art;
Borne from his pow'r they now are seen,
The attributes of BEAUTY'S QUEEN!
While LOVE in secret hides his tears;
DIAN the form of VENUS wears!

When Esther or Joshua's time came to read, they explored, through words, the next Scottish isle or locale Dr. Johnson had visited and described. Before Benjamin departed, he would often offer his own views of the place or describe to his siblings his recollections of the natural elements, castles, and animals mentioned by Dr. Johnson. After the trio finished the first entire reading of each book, they simply turned to the beginning and read it again. On Sundays, one or the other read from the Bible unless they attended one of the infrequent services held at the fort.

Joshua continued to serve in the local Virginia militia, which meant the two girls were often alone except for a half-grown puppy they had adopted the previous autumn. Samuel had named him *Woody* for his coloring. With his short, shaggy, bark-like hair of multi colors, he looked like a scrambled mixture of pine, oak, and cherry. Woody grew to be an exceptionally large, tall dog, covered in wiry hair with ears that perked at any sound. His bark rang out magnificently, booming and echoing around the cabin, often an early warning of anyone approaching their home. His very protective manner of Lovely and Esther kept most visitors at a great distance, especially when he growled. Though rarely heard, Woody's growl could shake rafters and scare away bears.

In the spring, Esther and Lovely took on the tasks required for a substantial garden. They purchased seeds from a peddler, and Lovely drew out a plan. She and Esther had spent the warmer days of winter building a wicker rabbit fence around the small plot. Lovely also placed one around the small grave. Over the last year, they'd learned the grave held the body of a newborn child, borne of Mistress Boone just days before that family left for Kentucky.

Twice during March, Esther and Lovely heard the warnings of Indians nearby and fled to the fort. Events during their third stay inside the walls ultimately led to their decision to leave Moore's Fort.

On a mid-morning in April, after hearing once again the shouted warnings from the fort's militia, Lovely and Esther fled on horseback to the safety of the fort's walls, carrying only their old musket. The weather was unseasonably warm and humid, yet a sharp wind blew. Woody howled and barked the entire way from the cabin to the fort and could not be hushed. Once safely within the fort's walls, Lovely took Woody into Sarah's cabin with her to distract him. Still, Woody would not be silenced.

Directly after their arrival, men pushed the gates closed, barring them with strong timbers. The girls watched as the local men and the militiamen stood ready along the ramparts.

Inside the fort, confusion reigned as women gathered children and livestock, pulled down washing hung earlier that morning, and headed for their cabins or the empty blockhouses. All about, militiamen loaded rifles and prepared the fort for attack.

Esther placed their horses within the small paddock and went to find Lovely and Sarah. Inside her small cabin, the girls helped by tearing and rolling linen strips to make bandages, while Sarah prepared a poultice, knowing one might be needed.

As the day grew warmer still, the wind blew fiercely, whipping items about the fort. At times, the wind made it difficult to walk. Still, from outside the fort, they could occasionally hear war cries and the sharp reports of both rifles and muskets booming out. In the early afternoon, Sarah and the two girls gathered with the fort's other wives and daughters to find solace in prayer. Each prayed for those who had not made it into the fort and for the militiamen who were somewhere out on patrol. Joshua being among them, Lovely prayed and pleaded for his safe return through her tears.

By mid-afternoon, dark storm clouds whirled on the southwestern horizon. The wind blew in sharper, heavier gusts. Anything loose about the fort had to be weighed down or brought inside. Those standing guard on the parapets clung to the upright posts to keep their balance, yet none could stand down, as they could occasionally see and hear Cherokee in the surrounding forest.

About five o'clock in the afternoon, in the paddock, horses began running about. Agitated, their whinnying cries filled the air. Dairy cows, some tied outside cabins, mooed, and pulled at their tethers, while the fort's few dogs, now including Woody, took to barking and howling. The noise terrified all, but especially the babies and children. While Lovely tried to soothe Woody, Esther ran to the paddock to help the older boys who strove unsuccessfully to calm the horses. It wasn't long before each realized their presence accomplished little more than to put themselves in danger of being trampled.

Suddenly, all grew quiet as the wind died. Everything seemed to stand in stilled silence. Just as quickly as the wind had gone, a roaring noise filled their ears. Louder and louder, as if a monstrous creature approached, coming closer and yet even closer, howling with each step a cry so thunderous as to overcome all their senses. The air pushed down upon them, heavier and then thinner, filled with an odor of lightning.

Drawn outside their cabins by the commotion fueled by the animals and the wind, a few women watched as their menfolk tried to climb down from the walls, some leaping the six feet to the ground. Those that could, then scrambled toward the walls and cabins, calling for all to find shelter. Knocked to the ground by the wind, Esther raised her head and watched as the fort's main gate shattered and fell into broken bits of log and timber. She expected Indians to rush in. Instead, she watched as trees, massive trees, branches, limbs, roots, and a man flew past, propelled by some thunderous monster, outside the opening where their gate, their protection, had stood moments before. Objects of all sizes moved horizontally across the opening.

Those who witnessed this phenomenon screamed, though unless they were within arm's reach of others, their cries of terror were not heard over the roaring storm. Cedar shakes flew from roofs with such force as to be more dangerous than an Indian's arrow. The wind flung a wagon up against the fort's wall, splintering it into a thousand pieces, leaving the men who had earlier sheltered below the wagon exposed to the rock-hard hail that now pounded the earth. With one concerted move, all the horses ran from the paddock. Jumping or breaking down the fence, they ran for the forest. Two still wore saddles and packs.

Exposed, Esther lay on the ground. Hailstones the size of ripe persimmons, but nowhere as soft, pelted her. Abruptly aware of a softness beside her, she gathered Woody close, sensing, feeling, his anxious growl. Beaten and stunned, she could not regain her feet to find shelter. She shook with the cold as wetness enveloped her. Then darkness.

Esther slowly awoke, hours later, as Lovely placed a buffalo hide over the numerous quilts that she had already piled upon her sister. Now dressed only in her thin cotton shift, Esther still shivered with cold and remembered her fear. Her back, her limbs, and her head ached from the bruises inflicted by the hailstones. Slowly, she recognized soft rain now falling on what remained of the cabin's roof and water dripping about the room, turning the dirt floor to mud.

"Lovely! Sister! Stop fussing and fretting. Are you safe? How did I get here? Is anyone hurt? Where is Woody?"

"She's awake, Mistress Sarah, she woke up!" Lovely cried out, and then, sobbing, she fell across Esther.

"Oh, Esther, girl, ye gave us a fright. Lovely here believed ye to be at death's door, though I kept telling her ye would wake. How do ye get on, child? Are ye still cold?" Sarah rambled. Her eyes glowed with unshed tears as her voice shook with emotion. "Lovely, rise and fetch her a cup of tea and quiet ye tears. Ye sister will live. She be one of the lucky ones."

Esther had no broken bones, but the back of her body remained covered with deep purple bruises for weeks. Sitting proved difficult and painful. Woody stayed at her side, quiet now. For days she suffered a fever, and it was only after she had regained some strength that she moved about the fort and discovered the destruction wrought by the tornado. Three men had suffered serious injuries, including one with a broken back. He died on the fourth morning after the storm. They did not find the body of another man. Esther knew he was likely the one she saw fly by. A few others had minor injuries, such as broken bones, and yet, amid it all, a baby girl had been born.

Men and women alike worked to repair roofs and the fort's two gates, both of which had blown down, shattered and useless. Lovely described to her the path of destruction found outside the fort. A great swath of downed trees now lay in a straight line all the way past their small cabin, which stood roofless. She relayed how their winter's toil, the rabbit fence, was nowhere to be found and told how the lean-to across the back of their cabin had collapsed into a pile now only useful as firewood.

When the militiamen returned later in the week, Joshua and Lovely rounded up their horses, but couldn't locate their cow or chickens. Their cow wandered up near the fort, with two others, over a week later. With Joshua's help, the girls gathered their few belongings from the cabin and brought everything inside the fort. While Lovely and Esther stayed with Mistress Porter, Joshua slept in one of the remaining blockhouses. Again, three Ballinger children were homeless.

While the siblings remained in the fort, Lovely's silence deepened. She spoke only when answering a direct question. Sarah and Esther worried over her lack of appetite and her continuing night terrors. After Joshua's term of enlistment with the militia ended, increasingly of an evening, they discussed moving on. By now, Sarah Porter knew their entire story. With no one to keep her at Moore's Fort, she expressed her desire to travel with the Ballinger children if they decided to leave. They agreed that only Captain Gass be told of their destination, in case either Benjamin or Samuel came looking for them or sent a letter.

Still, they did not leave. They stalled, hoping one of their brothers might return, or for the war's end, or for every feasible solution to their untenable situation. With every new day, they expected a traveler to bring news of the war or a letter from a brother. They fretted, they often despaired, and and they existed in a realm of uncertainty and hope.

"Have I not commanded you? Be strong and courageous. Do not be afraid; do not be discouraged, for the Lord your God will be with you wherever you go." Joshua 1:9 *The Bible*

Summer 1777

In the two months after the tornado, Moore's citizenry changed. Some families moved on, as there was little to keep them near the fort. Many had lost their cabin and all their belongings. Others, determined to remain on their holdings, began rebuilding, for theirs was not the only cabin damaged by the tornado. The fort's protection was now gone, as the walls urgently needed repairs. Families turned back east. Others traveled over the mountains into the west, where land could be had in exchange for hard work.

Meanwhile, drifters took over the few cabins left standing. Thefts, fights, and drunkenness reigned, especially during the evenings' darkness. Slovenly, lazy residents allowed the fort to slip further into disrepair. The smell of refuse and human waste filled the air with odors often unbearable to decent folks.

Danger from men now lay within as well as outside Moore's walls. Lovely and Esther learned never to leave Mistress Porter's cabin after dark. Without prompting, Woody slept against the door and gave warning when any tried to enter, a not uncommon occurrence.

Even sunlight did not deter the more belligerent men, especially when liquor had been imbibed. The women of the fort took to traveling in pairs to the nearby spring and to carry out their daily chores. Even Mistress Sarah took care after being pushed down by a drunkard, leaving her bruised and sore. Twice, Esther defended herself with the knife she still carried. Neither time was she injured, nor did she injure her assailant. She had no more ammunition for Benjamin's pistol, and none was available for purchase or barter. At fifteen, she'd grown another inch or so, and due to strenuous labor, had grown stronger and more agile. Despite Joshua's and Sarah's warning about leaving the fort alone, Esther's abilities and confidence led her to believe she could defend herself.

On a late afternoon in early June, carrying two wooden buckets, Esther left the fort for the walk to a nearby spring where the water ran cleaner than that in the fort's well. No one stood available to walk with her. Desperation for cool, clean water overrode her fears, for only a day earlier, one woman had pulled her bucket from the well to find a dead rat floating atop. Esther's walk out past the fort's walls and into the forest was peaceful. After leisurely filling her buckets, Esther sat for some minutes, enjoying the fresh untainted air before she started for the fort's gate.

Carrying the now-laden buckets, she kept her eyes downcast upon the path, carefully watching her step. Just as she reached the edge of the forest, where she would be within sight of the fort, a large hand roughly grabbed her shoulder and spun her around. Unaware of her assailant's identity and without thinking, Esther screamed and flung one bucket onto her foe's back, drenching him in cold water. Infuriated, he slapped her hard across the face, then pulled her once more against his chest.

"Quiet girl, or ye and Lovely both will feel my cock this night," he whispered against Esther's ear, pinning her arms against her sides.

His breath smelled horrid—sour and rancid—and his rough beard even worse. This close, Esther could see fragments from recent meals and such in his hair and beard. It crawled with lice. His body's odor overwhelmed her. She gagged. She struggled to free herself. Responding, he pulled at her now well-worn bodice, ripping it down the front, leaving her mostly exposed from the waist up. She screamed again.

Using his free hand, he grabbed her breast and squeezed.

Esther struggled harder to be free. She stomped firmly upon his moccasin-clad foot. He released her right hand and, pulling back, punched her full in the pit of her stomach. Breath rushed from her body, leaving her limp, suffering. She shook with pain.

Dazed, barely able to stand, she felt him push her roughly backward along the earthen path, into the forest and completely out of view and hearing of the fort's watchmen.

Once sheltered from any who might intervene, he forced Esther to the ground while attempting with one hand to pull her skirt up above her knees.

Dazed and hurting, Esther focused her every effort to bring her breathing under control and to find the breath to scream. Despite his words of warning, Esther understood her dilemma and its consequences. Her life depended entirely upon her own actions.

A full minute, or perhaps more, passed before she pulled air into her lungs.

Sitting astride her legs, her assailant pinned her left arm above her head and, using his other hand, fumbled with his crotch. Esther gasped sharply and grabbed the knife from her waist with her right hand. She inhaled deeply, finding strength and air.

Screaming out, Esther stabbed at him twice. Being left-handed and still short of air, her awkward movements inflicted little damage other than to increase his anger.

Cursing, he backhanded her twice before grabbing for the knife. With her increasing will to persevere and her waning strength, she moved to end her struggle.

Esther sliced deeply into his hand and wrist, severing tendons and muscles, forcing him to draw back in pain.

Screaming in agony, he grabbed at his wounded hand and, in so doing, released her left hand. Blood shot from his palm and wrist, showering both with its warmth.

Esther's hand flew up. Striking during his moment of weakness. Strengthened by a fierce, growing anger, she placed her left hand over her right and pushed the knife into his throat.

As he fell backward across her lower legs, gasping for breath and bleeding heavily, Esther pulled her body from under his weight and began kicking him. She screamed over and over, not for help, instead with anger and a hatred she had never realized could exist within herself.

As she shook, crying and screaming, two soft, powerful hands reached out and pulled her upright. "Esther, Esther, it be me, Joshua. Ye be safe. I be here. Quiet, sister, quiet," he murmured against her ear, holding her in his peaceful, brotherly, loving arms.

"Joshua, oh, Joshua." Esther collapsed against him.

As blood gushed from his wrist and his throat to puddle on the hard dirt of the path, Esther's attacker died at her feet. Though she told few in the coming years, she always believed she died a bit that day as well. Sarah said it wasn't the death of her soul she felt, but the death of her innocence.

"Esther," Joshua now whispered, continuing to soothe her fears. "I be here. He cannot hurt ye ever again."

They stood for a long while, holding each other upright, sharing tears. And in those minutes, Joshua's strength became hers. He took her fear into himself and gave her safety in return.

"Is he dead?"

"Yes, sister. Dead. He'll never hurt ye again. Let's get ye back to Mistress Sarah. Can ye walk?"

"No, Joshua, I came for water. Sarah needs fresh water," Esther answered forcefully, looking around for the wooden pails as shock continued to cloud her mind and befuddle her senses.

Seeing one bucket lying in scattered pieces at the bottom of a large oak, Joshua found the other. Hand in hand, they returned to the spring. As the minutes passed, Esther realized what had occurred and what was to come.

"Joshua, how did you find me?"

"Lovely told me where you'd gone. I'd seen Matt headed in the same direction. Something worried me about him leaving so soon after you. Esther, did he, did he . . . "

"No, brother, but some shall see my clothing and believe he did. Will they call it murder? Will they hang me for his death?"

Not answering, Joshua carried the remaining bucket of water, placing his other arm around his sister's shoulders to hold the neck of her bodice in place. As dusk rapidly moved toward darkness, they approached the gate. A sentry called out.

"Joshua, that ye? Did ye hear those screams?"

"Yes, David, 'twas my sister, Esther. She's injured. Matt Bowen lies dead, down at the forest edge, on the path to the spring. Hurry, open the small gate for us."

"Indians? Should I sound the alarm?"

"No need. There be no Indians."

As Joshua and Esther moved toward Sarah's door, men rushed about, gathering a stretcher and rifle, each man calling out questions about what had happened. Neither Ballinger sibling answered. Each knew answers were needed, but Joshua remained determined Esther would not be answering to a crowd of rough men while standing exposed in her torn, disheveled, ruined clothing.

As Lovely and Mistress Sarah stepped out to investigate all the ruckus, brother turned to sister and whispered, "Go with Mistress Sarah. I'll return soon. All will be well, I promise ye."

"Come, child, come. I'll see to ye." Firmly, Mistress Sarah took Esther from Joshua's arms and used her own strength to move the young woman into her cabin. As she reached to pull the door closed, Sarah whispered to Joshua, "Delay them for as long as possible. I be seeing to yer sister."

Lovely grabbed the bucket of water as they retreated inside the small cabin. Sarah barred the door while quietly instructing Esther to sit on the bed. Within a minute, she bathed Esther's face and arms with cool water, wiping away all traces of blood, and then helped remove her ruined clothing, throwing each piece into the hearth fire. All without a word. Without a question.

Woody now sat at Esther's side, whimpering. Throughout Esther's earlier absence, the mutt had growled and pawed at the door until Sarah had bribed him with a deer bone. Even then, he had refused to move away from the door.

Tears running silently down her face, Lovely brought her sister a fresh nightgown and a shawl. Esther could hear men shouting. She heard women's questions and shouted terse words. Yet, throughout it all, Sarah's face remained soft and loving. She shed no tears, knowing her strength would be necessary in the coming hours and days. All this she did, though her heart silently broke for a young woman she now considered her own child.

The evening's darkness enveloped the fort before the knock came to the door.

"Mistress Sarah, it be Captain Gass. I must speak with Esther."

"Ye'll be softer and kinder than yer knock if ye want to speak with this child tonight, Thomas Gass, ye hear me?" Sarah demanded, her voice full of stern authority.

"Yes, Mistress Sarah, but I need to hear her answers."

"Ye may come in then and ask. You be remembering my words. Be kind and be gentle, for this child has seen the worst roughness of men today and needs no more to be dealing with. I'm not afraid of throwing ye back out my door should ye be rough in words or deeds. Don't care if you do be a captain."

"Yes, Mistress Sarah, I shall be a gentleman with the girl. Ye have my word of honor."

"I trust ye shall," and finally, she opened the door.

Silently, Esther sat wrapped in her gown, her shawl, and a blanket, for despite the warm weather, she shook with remembered fear. Chilled. Still unable to pull warmth within herself, she held a cold compress to her split lip and swollen face.

"Esther, be this yer knife?" he asked, holding out the blood-covered weapon.

"Yes, Captain Gass."

"Did ye stab Matt Bowen?"

"Yes, Captain, I did. I also cut him across his hand. I must have cut his wrist as well, though that was not my intention."

After a quiet moment, his voice now a whisper, he asked, "Did he . . . did he rape ye?"

Esther could tell, by his hesitation, the militia captain really did not want to hear or know her answer. Yet, as a man of authority and honor, Gass knew his duty. Still, he wished not to know, not to acknowledge what Matt might have done to the young woman, a woman most all in the fort respected for her caring ways for those injured or ill.

"No," Esther sobbed out, her voice breaking. "He tried . . . he tried."

As her tears flowed, Esther once again gathered her strength into herself and found a strong young woman waiting. Her words now flowed in a rush, softly at first, and then with force and determination. "Captain, Matt Bowen, if that was his name, accosted me as I carried water from the spring. First, I hit him with a bucket. You'll find it in pieces near his body. Then he threatened me with rape. I could see in his eyes he meant to do it no matter how much I screamed or struggled. He slapped me, he punched me in the stomach, and he backhanded me across the face. He tore my clothing and pushed me to the dirt, placing his putrid body over mine, he began fumbling for his cock. That's when I cut him and then stabbed him. Now, may I have my knife back?"

Thomas Gass, his face now softer, pulled up a stool and sat himself down. "Mistress Sarah, please take Lovely outside to Joshua. I be holdn' my questions until ye return."

"See ye do, Thomas," Sarah snapped as she took Lovely's hand and led the pale, trembling girl from her cabin.

Several minutes passed before the door opened again. Sarah entered alone. Without a word, she busied herself by fixing them both a cup of tea. Esther moved from the edge of the bed to the bench at Sarah's small table. All three remained quiet as Sarah filled each cup and then sat beside Esther, taking her hand in her own.

"Esther, I hate this. Still, I must answer to the Major when he returns. I need to understand exactly what happened. Did Bowen rape ye?"

"No. I stabbed him before he could get his cock out of his trousers," Esther repeated with obvious displeasure, before continuing more softly. "Captain, when he first grabbed me . . . his words . . . he let me know of his intentions toward me . . . and Lovely if I screamed. He tore my bodice and struck me numerous times. I had no choice. I'd decided his words, his threats against me, made no difference. I knew if he raped me, he would kill me and try the same with Lovely. In fear of him harming my sister, I struck him again and again. I didn't mean, not at first, mean to kill him, but . . . I struck repeatedly to stop him . . . in so doing I killed him. I have no regrets."

Sarah gasped and then sobbed as she pulled Esther against her. "Can't ye see this girl has been through enough for one day?"

The three sat for a few soft quiet minutes and sipped their tea. Esther worked silently to control her emotions. Captain Gass thought of his own young daughters. Sarah's thoughts ran only to Esther and what this would mean to her in the future.

At length, Sarah broke the silence, stating firmly, "Thomas Gass, many will not believe Esther's story, that she not be raped, unless you make it so that they do. Some saw her torn clothing. Already the tales be spreading. I be depending on ye, as Captain, to walk out that door right now and make it known how she defended herself before that vermin of a man carried out his threats."

Sarah's firm voice led Gass to understand he had no choice. In her mind, she had become Esther's mother. Her defense against all evil. Her protector of body and reputation.

Nodding to Sarah, the Captain stood to go. "Esther, ye rest. On my authority, there will be no charges against ye. I be returning your knife to Joshua so that he can clean it for ye."

"Sir, perhaps you might . . . please . . . not let it be known that he threatened Lovely. I would not have my sister know."

"I understand. Rest easy. Goodnight to ye both. I be posting a sentry nearby tonight to keep ye safe and undisturbed. I will instruct him to let no one in except Lovely and Joshua. I ken no reason for more questions."

"If your world doesn't allow you to dream, move to one where you can."
Billy Idol

Late Summer 1777

Captain Gass kept his word. Despite his efforts, people talked. Whispered rumors and accusations flew among the newer men at the fort. As Esther's wounds healed, and she took up her former activities, those women who'd lived at the fort long enough to call Esther a friend readily believed her story. They, themselves, had often feared for their lives and their virtue. More troubling to Esther and her family were the occasional whispers from women among the newcomers. Esther knew several of these women wondered if she now carried a child.

Esther worried that if more and more believed her to have killed Matt Bowen for reasons other than his attempt to rape her, they might put her on trial. Stories about her virtue, or lack thereof, were bantered about and overheard by both Joshua and Sarah. If Lovely heard them, she never spoke of it. Likewise, she never referred to the events of that evening.

Before that fateful day, Moore's militiamen had, to a man, treated Esther with respect and deference. Several would have courted her had Joshua not warned them off. They now acted as her protectors, asking about her wellbeing, quietly watching out for her. They offered to carry water or firewood. They escorted her whenever she left the fort, always keeping her in sight but giving her space to herself if she asked to be alone. Even then, they kept watch from a distance. Esther began to depend on them and kept each in her prayers.

Outwardly, Esther appeared to have moved forward after that day. She carried on most days as if nothing had occurred. Though Sarah often noticed the young woman staring into space and jumping at sudden noises, she convinced herself Esther would recover. Esther, herself, was not as sure. Often, in her dreams, Matt Bowen appeared already dead, with blood flowing from his many wounds, to threaten her again and again. Her dream would end with a sudden awakening, leaving her shaking and terrified. She would lie awake until morning. Yet, she never spoke of these dreams to anyone. If anyone dared to ask, Esther always stated she felt no guilt for Matt Bowen's death, though she regretted being the instrument of his demise. The first a lie, and the second a truth.

The incident's effect on Lovely proved more profound, as the child grew even more silent in the coming weeks. She would not read aloud, nor would she join in casual conversation. She became afraid of leaving the fort and would not do so without Joshua with her. Neither Esther nor Sarah could convince her to do so. At thirteen, with her pale corn silk-colored hair, petite figure — a figure just beginning to reveal her coming of age — and green eyes, Lovely had become what her name foretold. Esther feared for Lovely more than for herself. Matt Bowen's threat stayed foremost in her mind. The fort's population now contained many, many more rough, uncivilized men.

In the years since Joshua left for the wilderness, his skills had improved with the instruction of others more familiar with frontier living. Around Moore's, the young man's natural skills and abilities had blossomed. Always an excellent shot, Joshua had worked to improve in other skills such as how to read a trail. He could walk almost silently through the forest, and always returned from hunting trips carrying enough to fill the kettles hanging over many a fire. A likable, quiet man, his sense of humor made him a favorite around the post. Captain Gass soon recognized in Joshua all the makings of a leader and capable courier.

Of an evening, Joshua urged his sisters to consider moving on to Kentucky until a militia courier from the settlements there brought news of recent attacks upon frontier forts, including Fort Harrod in early March, Boonesborough in early April and again in mid-July, and Fort Logan in late May. The courier had come with an urgent request for men and ammunition. As the danger seemed too great, Joshua and Esther made their decision and tabled all talk of moving farther west.

Recognizing the time had come for them to move on, they decided as to where and when. After drafting letters to their brothers and leaving them with Captain Gass, on a mid-July morning, Esther, Joshua, and Sarah packed their few belongings onto horses and led Lovely out of Moore's. They turned southeast, toward the settlement of Abington. From there they would travel along the Holston River Valley to the Watauga settlement of far-western North Carolina.

As they rode quietly but with joy of leaving behind troubles and cares, Woody trotted alongside, giving warning to and of squirrels, rabbits, deer, and any other creature about the trail. His gaiety reflected not only their mood but his own relief at no longer being restricted to the fort's enclosure.

Wisely, the siblings traveled with two large families, both of whom had older boys who could readily handle a rifle. Three former Virginia militiamen joined the party of travelers. Each being particular friends of Joshua's, they were fond of his two sisters. While Captain Gass and several of Moore's militia had warned them all to wait and join an even larger group, each family felt compelled to move on, and therefore ignored all predictions of Indian attacks along the trail.

Since the first white men had moved into the western hills of Virginia and North Carolina, Indian attacks had occurred frequently along the trails between settlements and isolated cabins. Having heard the stories of attacks, murders, and kidnappings, members of the party realized they might encounter Shawnee from the north or Chickamauga Cherokee from the south.

Within the last year, the Chickamauga band had rejected the land purchases made by the Transylvania Company and the Watauga Association. Beginning in the summer of 1776, the Chickamauga Cherokee had attacked many settlements along the Watauga, Holston, Nolichucky, and Doe rivers. All these *overmountain* settlements, as many called them, were illegal under British law, as they lay well west of the Donelson Line of 1763. The Indians knew of this law and highly resented the settlers' encroachment on their lands.

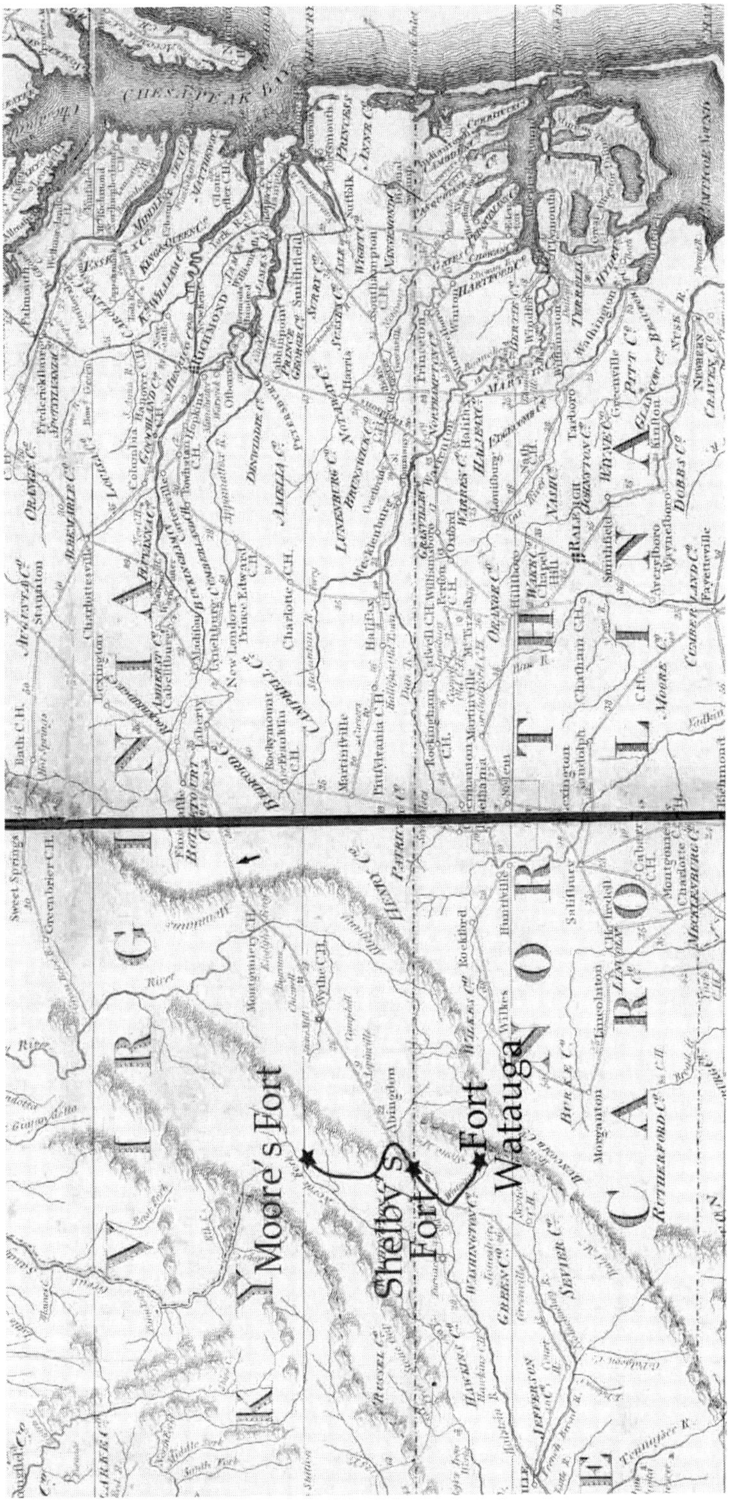
Moore's Fort
Shelby's Fort
Fort Watauga
VIRGINIA
NORTH CAROLINA
CHESAPEAK BAY
RICHMOND
Abingdon
Wythe C.H.
Sweet Springs
Greenbrier C.H.

As the war raged in the east, Indian attacks grew more frequent in the lands across the Appalachians. Despite knowing of and fearing such attacks, men, families, and the militia traveled the far western trails, for such was life in the wilderness.

Besides the threats of Indian attacks, all frontier travelers heard tales of robbers, evil men, white like themselves, attacking and killing along the backcountry roads and trails. In response to both types of threat, colonial militiamen had built several log stations along the various trails, both south and west, to provide refuge for travelers. These somewhat evenly spaced stations provided shelter during times of trouble, attack, or harsh weather. Most travelers made use of these stations when convenient.

As only seventy or so miles separated the two forts, the party that left Moore's that July day estimated a journey of five to six days. While the trip could be made much faster, their party traveled encumbered with several small children and trailed by a small herd of livestock, mainly cows and a few hogs.

Esther and Joshua felt excited to be moving on, though they had little expectation of a better life at Watauga. They did anticipate leaving behind unfortunate memories of Moore's, knowing distance might be a soothing balm. Mistress Sarah reckoned to herself how memories, rumors, and accusations would most likely follow Esther for years.

Now in her late sixties, Sarah, feeling a great motherly attachment to Esther and Lovely, also thought of Joshua as her son. At their asking her to go along to the Watauga settlements, Sarah had no qualms in saying yes. Her only tie to Castle's Woods lay outside a burned-out cabin. There stood her husband's grave, a pile of stones and a small dogwood tree she had transplanted a year or so earlier to mark its existence. While she could do no more for William, Sarah felt these siblings needed her. So, Sarah packed her meager belongings, sent a letter west to her sons at Kentucky's Fort Harrod, and moved south.

Their party traveled only some ten or so miles that first day. Mostly southeast, along a wooded path, up and down hills, they rode. They had started not long after dawn, and by noon,

Sarah could see that Lovely was already fatigued. By dusk, the child could barely stay in her saddle. When they stopped for the evening, with Esther's help, the two made up a pallet under the boughs of a large cedar and let her sleep.

That evening, lying beside Lovely and Sarah, Esther remembered the night noises, the screeches of owls and howls of wolves she'd heard on their first journey across Virginia. As others slept, she heard the plaintive cry of a panther. Only toward morning did she fall into a deep sleep. Yet she awoke rested and eager to move on.

On the second day, under a blazing late afternoon sun, they passed a log station. While they might have taken shelter there for the night, the two-story log structure currently housed a sick family who'd taken refuge several days earlier. Three of their children suffered from a pox. While Esther and Sarah's fellow travelers moved on without them, leaving only a militiaman to accompany them onward, the two women offered what help they could safely give before rejoining their group. Several miles later, their party settled in beside the trail for the night.

On the following morning, Esther woke to sounds of the men preparing the horses for the day's journey, and to find her monthly courses upon her. Knowing her moon cycle, she'd prepared herself and carried the necessary items. Esther had donned a pair of Samuel's old buckskin trousers for the journey, making her able to care for her needs for the day ahead with ease. Still, in the late afternoon, the need to relieve herself and care for her padding caused Esther to slip away into the woods along a nearby stream they had followed most of the afternoon. After voiding, she stooped by the steam to wash out her cloths. Humming softly, she hung the clean rags over a nearby branch to drip as she worked. As she finished with the last one, cleaned her hands, and turned to gather up her belongings, she came face to face with a young Cherokee man.

"Quiet," he whispered without moving towards her, "Waya mean no harm. Others nearby do."

Stunned and, despite his words, anxious to be with her family, Esther turned to go around him, when he placed his hand firmly on her arm, "Stay, wait. Others soon move on. You be safe. No harm."

Scared, Esther stared at the man, yet something of his demeanor made her believe his words. His hand rested upon her arm, yet he did not hold her in place. She stopped and waited, reasoning that if he'd meant her harm, he wouldn't have warned her. Instead, she would already lie dead or be a captive. Waiting, Esther took in his appearance and saw that Waya stood taller than her by several inches. Despite the heat of summer, he wore buckskin trousers and moccasins with a linen shirt, each of good repair. His long black hair was not plucked on the sides of his scalp like so many Cherokee warriors but pulled back in a queue and tied with a leather thong, just as Joshua wore his. Waya carried a well-maintained rifle. A knife and a tomahawk hung from his belt.

"Your English is very good," she whispered, smiling, after they had stood in silence for several minutes.

"My mother's sister mated white trader. He teach me your words. Listen, tis safe, now. Move quickly to friends. Find shelter for night."

Esther reached for her belongings as he slipped, almost silently, into the stream and hurried out of sight. Upon returning to their party, now almost one-half mile away, she motioned Joshua to one side of the trail.

"Joshua, a Cherokee man just warned me of other Indians about in this area," Esther whispered, holding tight to her brother's strong arm.

"Where?"

"By the stream, as I was . . ."

"Did he give his name?" Joshua interrupted, guessing her reluctance to explain.

"Waya. He spoke decent English."

"Wolf, Waya means Wolf in English. I know him. He often carries messages to Captain Gass from Watauga. He is Nancy Ward's nephew. You remember, the Cherokee woman who saved Mistress Bean?"

After a few more quiet words, Joshua and Esther moved back to their party. He relayed the message to the others. As dusk approached, at Joshua's urging, the travelers stopped early as they'd come upon another station. This one stood empty. Like most all stations, it was built of logs, stacked without windows and only two doors. One front and one back. Firing slits and small holes in the chinking allowed them to take defensive action if attacked. Stations rarely had chimneys, and this one followed that pattern.

Lovely, Esther, and Sarah took one of the two upper story rooms, reached by climbing a shaky ladder of sturdy branches held in place by rope and vines. The Holbrooke family claimed the other. Taking up with them only their bedrolls and nightly necessities, they settled in.

Joshua and the former militiamen slept on the first floor with the women and children of the Robertson family. They'd hobbled all the horses in a nearby clearing and left two men standing guard, knowing each could quickly reach the station if attacked.

A stash of firewood stacked behind the cabin fueled a roaring fire and provided the travelers with a hot meal. All slept well, with the men switching off to stand sentry. At dawn, they arose and began their fourth day of travel.

By now, each realized their trip would necessarily take longer than the planned six or seven days. Their livestock, consisting of cattle, milk cows, and pigs, moved slower than their horses. Piglets and hatchling chickens filled bags hung behind several riders. One such bag held a mama cat and her kittens. Not wanting to leave the young men and boys tending the livestock trailing too far behind, they often halted to allow them to catch up. All remembered the deaths of the Boone boy and Henry Russell during that party's aborted first attempt to settle in Kentucky.

Adding to their slow rate of travel, the Robertson families had two small children and a newborn, making it even more difficult to begin each day's travel quickly. As it was mid-summer, the heat of the afternoon became oppressive, despite the frequent canopy of trees, requiring them to stop frequently for water for themselves and their livestock.

Several days later, as they started their day, Lovely took one of the two-year-old girls on to her saddle with her. Esther could hear Lovely singing softly to the girl and telling her stories. Being out of the fort had changed Lovely in ways neither Sarah nor the girl's siblings expected. She smiled more often, spoke with most of the women during the day, and seemed at ease. Still at night, she withdrew into herself and slept, once again touching either Esther or Sarah.

Riding yet many miles from Fort Caswell, called Fort Watauga by most all, the party moved along in silence. In the late morning, Joshua rode ahead to scout for trouble and returned with two hunters, each leading a loaded packhorse. They were returning to their homes near Watauga.

Gathering all the men about him, Joshua spoke quietly, "This be William Bean, son of William Bean of Watauga, and his brother, Robert. They tell me there be Chickamauga Cherokee about, and we need to find shelter. Shelby's Fort lies about four miles ahead. A bit off our path but not far. They see as half the men and all the women and children should ride ahead to the fort. The rest might stay with our livestock and the boys. The Bean brothers be willing to escort the first party to safety."

"How about you, militia boy? You going ahead or staying?" Mr. Holbrooke asked. Holbrooke always seemed to speak sharply, having a rough way about him, though Esther and Sarah had discovered he was a gentle, loving man with great faith in the Lord.

"I be aimin' to stay. I suggest ye and yer younger son travel with the womenfolk and children. Yer older son can stay with us if he's a mind to. My friends can each make their own decision,"

Joshua answered, knowing his comrades would act in the best interest of the travelers.

The party split into two groups. The Bean brothers led the Robertsons and Holbrooke families, except for their oldest boys, forward toward Shelby's Fort. Two of the Robertson younger boys also stayed behind, as did their father. Joshua's militia friends, Michael and David, volunteered to stay as well. The other former militiaman, Sean, joined the first party to provide them with another rifle.

As the lead party departed, Joshua, Michael, and David helped the men and boys gather all the livestock into a tighter herd and push them swiftly toward the fort.

In the forward group, Esther rode directly beside Lovely, now holding a sleeping child nestled before her on her saddle. Sean rode on the other side of her. All the women rode in near silence, hushing their children and keeping each close. The Bean brothers split up. One rode in front of the column and the other in back. After a tense journey, with only brief stops for water and to relieve themselves, the first party arrived at Shelby's Fort mid-afternoon. They had encountered no one along the trail, neither friend nor foe.

At Shelby's, the Bean brothers escorted them into a palisaded area of about one and one-half acres. A large two-story, hewn log structure stood directly on the higher middle ground. Between it and the outer vertical log walls, the ground lay cleared. An area around the fort's outer walls had also been cleared of trees and brush. The fort's few permanent occupants welcomed the Bean brothers, whom they had known for years, before leading all their horses to a nearby paddock.

Lovely returned the sleeping child to her mother and followed the womenfolk inside the station, while Esther began unloading their pack horse and bringing their supplies and scarce belongings into the log structure. Noticing the lovely young woman, Robert Bean quickly offered to help her.

"Thank you, sir, I could use the help," Esther replied to Robert's offer to unload and feed their horses. "Do you and your brother live near here?"

"No, William's family and mine both live near Fort Watauga on Boone's Creek. Actually, most all of my family lives nearby the fort, except a few older cousins still in Virginia. There be seven of us children, with four still at home with Ma and Pa. The youngest is Russell. He be eight. There be only the two girls, Jane be thirteen and Sarah be nine. Jesse be nigh on one and twenty. He be in the militia and lives at the fort most times, but is home often enough for Ma's cooking."

As they worked, Esther kept one eye on the gate, willing Joshua and the rest of their party into safety. As she brushed down Lovely's horse, Robert asked, "So is the older woman traveling with ye yer relative? I think ye called her Sarah."

"No, we met Sarah at Moore's. She's become like a mother to us and has no more family in Virginia, so she came along. I have only Joshua and Lovely with me. Two older brothers left to serve in the war. One is a doctor." Feeling she had said enough, Esther quickly asked, "So, who owns this fort?"

"Ah, that be Evan Shelby. Ol' Evan moved to the area about 1771 and settled his family nearby. This here tis mostly only his trading post. Still, it tis a good site to take refuge in times of trouble."

"I've heard tell of Isaac Shelby. Is he related to Evan?"

"Yes, ma'am, Ol' Evan's son. There be seven of those children, all grown now. Both Evan and Isaac fought at Point Pleasant back in 1774, under Captain John Fields. When Fields got killed, Evan stepped up as commander. Isaac stayed on and served at Point Pleasant for a while after the battle. Good, brave men, both of them. Just heard Governor Patrick Henry done commissioned Isaac to secure provisions for the militia here over the mountains. He be at Fort Patrick Henry now. Just heared yesterday that the government done signed a treaty with the Cherokee to insure peace. They been holding talks for nigh on weeks now led by some man called Waithstill Avery. Now ain't that a name!

"But I talk too much, Miss Esther. 'Cuse me, and I'll be gettin' these things in the station for ye. I 'spect yer brother and them be along any time now."

Several hours later, the rest of the travelers rode into Shelby's Fort just after dusk. Tired, dirty, and hungry, they unloaded the horses after heading all the livestock into a paddock. With them rode Waya, whom Esther thought had been traveling on foot during their earlier meeting.

As they settled in, a quiet darkness surrounded the fort and talk consumed the interior. She learned Waya had carried his message to Moore's and been sent back on horseback to Shelby's and Watauga. Seems several Chickamauga Cherokee warriors had been seen with Shawnee warriors on the Ohio River. All settlements, forts, and as many isolated cabins, as possible, were to be warned to take precautions.

"Happiness doesn't have just one address." Unknown

Autumn 1777

As the Ballinger siblings soon discovered, their mother would have despised the Watauga settlement for oh so many reasons. Foremost would have been its mixture of uneducated English, Highland Scots, and Irish, with a few German pioneers thrown in. To make matters even more abhorrent to their late mother's sensibilities, there always seemed to be peaceable Cherokee men and women about.

Few among Watauga's residents had more than a basic education, and only occasionally would they discover someone who could read and write. Instead, these frontier folks knew how to survive on their own by living off the land, hunting, and fishing, and raising crops and livestock. Almost all lived in one- or two-room, hewn-log cabins, few had windows and none with glass. Most cabins possessed a loft, and all had a chimney of sorts, be it of mud and sticks or stacked stone. The community worked together, providing for each other as needed, helping to build new cabins and small barns. They cleared land for gardens and crops. Each family knew the importance of their shared security. Warnings quickly passed from homestead to homestead when necessary.

Yet, unlike Moore's Fort, Watauga had a trader who somehow brought in goods needed by the community. Several residents practiced trades, including two blacksmiths, a potter, a gunsmith, and a couple of millers. At a nearby creek, an older man had built a powder mill, where he made gunpowder from guano found in local caves. His competition was a woman miller who make gunpowder at her home. Another had harnessed a flowing stream to grind corn.

Having established this settlement beyond the Appalachian Mountains in 1772, in what was considered part of the North

Carolina colony, the settlers had declared their independence and created for themselves the entirely separate Watauga Association with its own laws and court system with elected commissioners and several justices of the peace, including William Bean and his brother-in-law, George Russell. Although only related by marriage, both men typified the frontier standard. Each stood not over six feet tall and carried no extra weight. Each had strong, muscular frames developed from hard labor and long journeys on foot or horseback. Both had dark brown hair, streaked with gray at the temple, yet neither looked the least elderly.

In the fall of 1775, the Watauga residents met, deciding to hold with the American cause. At that same meeting, they formed a committee and declared themselves the Washington District. Soon afterward, now recognized by North Carolina, William Bean and twenty others were appointed justices of the peace for Washington County.

In that same year, to make their existence west of the mountains more legal, the Association followed the example set by Richard Henderson, of the Transylvania Company. Henderson had purchased from the Cherokee a large tract of land in an area known as Kentucky, or Caintuck, in far western Virginia. The first settlement soon became known as Boonesborough. Likewise, the Watauga settlers obtained legal ownership of their settlement for the sum of two thousand pounds paid directly to the Cherokee.

Still, frequent attacks kept the community on edge as some Cherokee and Shawnee violently disputed the Association's ownership and occupation of the land. Occupants of outlying cabins remained ever vigilant. Men and women alike carried rifles when venturing far from home to carry out chores.

Heeding frequent warnings and after spending several weeks at Shelby's Fort, the travelers from Moore's had joined with several other families and moved south to the Watauga settlement. Once again, needing a home, Joshua arranged for them to live in a small, deserted log cabin on Boone's Creek, named for an earlier rough cabin constructed in part by Daniel Boone. The cabin they occupied had once housed, briefly, the Boone family. Seems they were destined to live in cabins left empty by the well-known frontiersman.

Their cabin lay back in a hollow along the creek, somewhat isolated. Nearby cabins on Boone's Creek included that of William and Lydia Bean and those of their married children, in particular Will and Rob. Brother George Bean's family lived farther away. The large Russell family, Lydia's family, also lived nearby.

Esther, Lovely, and Sarah settled in quietly. The small cabin was a bit larger than theirs outside Moore's. This one had two beds built into corners and a loft across one third of the interior space. Its well hewn and stacked logs needed little chinking. Two small, shuttered window openings allowed fresh air to flow through the cabin even on warm summer days. Esther and Sarah were happy to find that the chinking needed only small repairs, the chimney drew well, and a puncheon floor, a later addition to the cabin, meant no more sweeping dirt. All rejoiced upon seeing this improvement to their living situation.

Boone's Creek contained fresh water and many fish. Nearby, a spring sprung from limestone provided them with fresh cool water all summer. The women created a home with their few possessions and settled in.

Woody, in particular, loved their new home. He often spent his days lying in the sunshine near their door with brief respites in the creek where he tried, always without success, to catch fish.

Once again, Joshua joined the North Carolina militia along with Michael and David, as each needed income and felt the need to serve. During their journey and their weeks at Shelby's, Joshua's three friends had become like brothers, and therefore, protectors of Esther, and even more so, of Lovely and Sarah. Sometimes one or two, and occasionally all three young men, would sit with them for meals, help with chores, and make sure they had all their needs attended to. Esther purchased powder and shot for her small pistol, their musket, and Joshua's old rifle, and David taught her how to be a more accurate shot. Sean taught Lovely how to load a rifle and musket, but she refused to learn to shoot.

Esther and Sarah came to depend on the three young men much as they did Joshua. Lovely would chat with dark-haired Michael, a quiet young man in his early twenties, and pale blond David, only nineteen but experienced in backwoods living. However, she seemed to like Sean best. His Scottish burr made her giggle with glee. Sean's father had emigrated with his entire family not long after the Scottish defeat at Culloden in 1746. Sean's family remained in eastern North Carolina, and Esther had written several letters for him, as he could neither read nor write. Sean loved to hear Lovely read from Dr. Johnson's book, and often her blonde head and his dark auburn one could be seen bent over the pages as she tried to teach him to read while reading to him about his father and mother's homeland.

Several months after their arrival at Watauga, Sean joined a party of long hunters and moved off into the mountains to the south. Lovely seemed to miss him most of all, and always asked about him when any visitors arrived at their small cabin. Many, many months later, Joshua came to the cabin to tell his sisters of Sean's death at the hands of Chickamauga Cherokee. Esther wrote to his parents, as she remembered their whereabouts.

Despite the calm, civilized life of the area, Indian troubles continued to plague the community regularly. While the local Cherokee remained somewhat friendly, the Chickamauga band seemed determined to drive the settlers east, back across the Alleghenies, or to kill them outright.

As summer waned, they each helped bring in harvests at various nearby cabins, for they had arrived too late for planting a summer garden. In exchange for their labor, they put aside stores of corn, squash, and pumpkins for use during the winter. Esther bartered cream and milk from their cows for several small chicks. Sarah returned to healing and often came back to the cabin carrying cuts of deer or small game for the stew pot. Leaning on each other for their subsistence, they shared laughter, told talesand often invited both Michael and David for meals. It became a happy cabin.

Once again, Lovely took in sewing. Her skills quickly became known throughout the settlement and were especially noted by

Lydia Bean. The Bean's oldest daughter, Jane, also thirteen, was learning to weave cloth on the family's large loom. Jane, a gangly girl with soft brown hair and a ready smile, looked much like her mother. A giggling, happy friendship blossomed between the two girls. Lovely broke from her shell. She spoke with others and laughed often. Sarah, Joshua, and Esther marveled at the change their move and a new friendship had brought about.

Lydia, a weaver of great skill, taught Lovely to spin and weave linsey-woolsy. This plain woven, coarse twill fabric used linen or flax as the warp with wool as the weft. The Bean families each grew flax, but the womenfolk also collected wild flax and hemp for weaving. Soon Lovely began spending more and more time at the Bean cabin, often staying overnight with the large family. She and Jane became particular friends, though they often included Jane's younger sister, Sarah, in their number.

The first letter from Benjamin and Samuel arrived in late October. Its long journey across the war-torn colonies included being forwarded by Captain Gass after its arrival at Moore's. To Esther's great surprise, Waya delivered it. As mail service was almost non-existent in the colonies, Benjamin had sent the letter by military courier.

"Morning, Miss Ball. Captain Gass say bring letter to Joshua or you. No one else," he stated, quietly, holding the small, folded letter out to Esther, after she had discovered him standing outside their cabin scratching Woody's ears.

"Thank you kindly, Waya. Would you like to come in and join us for our evening meal?" Sarah asked from behind Esther. Having frequently seen the Cherokee man about the area and with Joshua, Waya had become a familiar of the family.

"Thank you. Must go to fort. Have letters for Captain Carter. All is quiet."

Esther and Sarah watched the young man walk silently away, though Sarah turned back long before Esther.

"Lovely, come, we have a letter from Benjamin. I would wait for Joshua but . . . no, he will understand. Come, let us read it together."

Dearest, Esther, Lovely, and Joshua,

With my best regards, I hope you are all well and safe. Mistress Sarah as well. Samuel is here with me. I cannot at this time reveal to you of our association with the military as this letter might well be intercepted by our enemies.

My work continues, and I rarely sleep as illnesses and injuries are the constant companion of the military. We have lost men to dysentery, cholera, measles, and various poxes since my arrival. There are also the ever-occurring injuries, most often from daily life instead of battle. Yet, those also occur. After one recent battle, I treated a young Frenchman, an officer, who continued to lead his men and cover the retreat of others of our forces even after his being severely wounded. This remarkable young man arrived from France and volunteers in our time of need. He is greatly admired by his men and has become a favorite of his superiors.

As you know from my earlier letters, Samuel serves as an aide to the medical staff. In times of need, he often carries wounded men from the battlefield. His position does not keep him always from harm but places him near to me. His eyesight is much worse than I expected and prevents him from serving on the battle's front lines.

Esther, your skills at healing would be much appreciated here. As would Mistress Sarah's. We often have no one skilled at nursing the sick and wounded. We lose many due to a lack of care. Yet, I would never want my sister to be exposed to military life, though there are those women who follow the army from place to place. They take in washing, mend clothes, and cook when rations allow. Some are tolerable as nurses, but have no knowledge of healing. What a horrible life it is for them! Our commanders often express their desire to send them away, back to their homes and safety. Perhaps, soon, they will do so.

Samuel and I recently met a young man from near our old home. His news of our place proved very disturbing. It seems our uncles have now "turned Patriot" after being threatened and abused by the local *militia. They abandoned Father's property after their overseer was hung for murdering two young local boys he had hired to help with the spring planting. There is more to the story, but not one I'd be willing to place in writing. We now know our home is burned and our fields lie abandoned. Samuel plans to ride south in late November after his term of enlistment is met, to survey and secure our holdings. It is not safe for you to return at this time.*

I cannot tell you where to write to us. It is not safe. Take care and know that we will do the same. Perhaps write in care of old neighbors, and Samuel can collect any letters upon his return to our home.

Please give Mistress Sarah our best wishes. With all our love, your brothers,

Benjamin and Samuel

In the weeks to come, each of the Ballinger children read the letter over and over, memorizing each line. Joshua and Esther reveled in the part their brothers now played in the war for independence. They speculated about where their brothers served, in whose command they'd enlisted, and even Benjamin's rank.

"Is he an officer?" Lovely asked.

"Surely, he be. I mean to say," Joshua insisted, "Benjamin be an educated man from a prestigious Virginia family. Why, our own father once treated Patrick Henry!" Joshua's pride in his brothers serving with the Continental Army was widely known.

Waya heard all this discussion and listened intently as Benjamin's letter was once again read aloud when he accompanied Joshua back to their cabin one evening later that week. The young men had become fast friends, often traveling together from station to station, carrying news and warning residents of raids.

Soon it became their routine at the little cabin to set an extra place for Waya on those evenings when Joshua was expected to return. Occasionally, like Joshua, the Cherokee man slept on the floor before the fire instead of returning to the fort. The little cabin never seemed empty. If Joshua and Waya were out on patrol, David or Michael might appear at dusk and stay the night before the fire. The women felt protected, as they rarely spent a night without at least one of the four young friends nestled before their fire.

On a cold, blustery evening, in early November, Sarah and Esther had just sat down to a dish of stew and griddle cakes when a loud knock, accompanied by Woody's barking, disturbed their quiet repast.

"My turn," whispered Sarah, as Esther rose and grabbed their musket.

"Mistress Sarah," a male voice called, "Mistress Sarah, you be needed at the fort."

Esther relaxed her grip and returned the musket to its place as Sarah opened the door to Michael, having recognized the young man's voice.

"Michael, what be the trouble?" Sarah asked patiently, while donning her cloak and reaching for her bag.

"A family just comed at the fort. In my mind, the woman should nay be travelin' for she be giving birth as we speak. I heared from others in the party, how the woman's husband be a worryin' sort. He done shouted for more help than just the local women at the fort. So, I came for ye. Good evening, Esther, do ye wish to come as well?" he replied, all in a rush. Then asked, "Where be Lovely, be she with the Beans again?"

"Yes, Michael, do step in," Esther answered.

"No need, no need," busied Sarah. "I believe I can birth a baby all on my own without too much trouble. Will ye help with my horse, Michael?"

"Oh, yes, ma'am. I mean no. I be ordered to be escortin' you by Captain Carter. I brung two horses. Can't have ye out alone on a night raw and dark as this. Here, let me tote yer bag. Esther, bar the door. David and me both be on duty so we cannot stop by this evening. Ye be good alone?"

"Yes, Michael, go on, go on," she said with a smile to stop his rambling, and pushed them on their way. "Take care, Sarah. My prayers be with you and the new mother. Oh, and you too Michael."

So, leaving Esther alone, for Lovely was with the Beans, Sarah and Michael left for the fort. Relieved at not having to go out on a night so brisk, Esther finished her stew, washed up, and made herself a cup of tea. As she added another log to the fire, once more a knock came at the door. This one was so quiet she believed for a moment she had misheard it. Yet, Woody stood near the door whining.

"Miss Esther? Mistress Sarah?" a wavering voice called.

"Waya, is that you?"

"Please, help."

Swiftly grabbing and raising the bar, Esther pulled open the door. There she found Waya, blood streaming from a head wound, leaning against the rough wood frame. Glancing about, Esther pulled him inside, where he collapsed at her feet. Taking care first to secure the door, Esther reached and placed their musket nearby before moving to care for their injured friend.

Knowing head wounds bleed profusely, Esther covered the now-unconscious Waya in a warm quilt and cushioned his head. With cloths dipped in cold water, she bathed away the blood before applying yarrow leaves to staunch the bleeding. As the bleeding eased, Esther bandaged Waya's wound—a deep cut surrounded by a now purple lump just over his left ear—before checking him for other injuries. Strangely, she found none.

Pulling hides and quilts from their beds, Esther created a pallet on the floor near the fire and, as gently as possible, moved Waya onto it. She covered him with her own wool blanket and cradled his head on another.

Still, Waya did not wake. Knowing she dared not go for help, as she was completely unaware of by whom and where he had been injured, and what dangers might lie outside their cabin,

Esther sat beside him all night and well into the next morning. Alone, for Sarah did not return. Neither did Joshua. Esther kept the cabin warm. She slept little. She worried. She watched. She prayed.

Watching Waya sleep, she took in everything about him. His smooth face, unburdened by whiskers, his soft lips, and his long black, shining hair. Waya, like most of the young men at the fort, was muscular from constant labor and long, arduous journeys. In many ways, he resembled Joshua, especially in the clothing he wore—buckskin leggings, moccasins, a linen shirt covered almost entirely by a heavy, fringed hunting jacket. Esther noticed Waya's knife still hung at his belt, although he'd arrived with neither his rifle nor a powder horn.

Finally, the sun broke through the gray clouds, and the wind died. Still, Esther did not leave the cabin. Waya slept, never moving.

Sitting at the table, sometime after noon, stress and lack of sleep overcame her. Esther settled her weary head against her folded arms resting on the table and fell deeply asleep. Hours passed, and the sun sat on a full day before Sarah knocked at the door.

"Esther, Esther," Waya whispered. "Wake, Mistress Sarah calls."

Startled, Esther awoke and, seeing Waya awake, she smiled before going to unbar the door and grant Sarah entrance.

Sarah checked Waya's wound and found it already beginning to heal. She and Esther carried out the morning chores, fetched fresh water and firewood—one working while the other carried the musket.

Waya stayed with the women for three more days. At first, he was too weak and lightheaded to do much more than sit up. On the second day, he walked with Esther's help twice about the cabin. By the third evening he could keep down food and walk without help, though he still suffered from occasional head pain.

More serious was his lack of memory as to how and where the injury had occurred.

As Waya recovered, he, Sarah, and Esther spoke of many things. Sarah told of the latest birth at the fort. "Never seen nor heard a man so anxious about the birth of a baby. It be his and her first, but that young man 'twas convinced she would die. Captain Carter and Michael finally took him aside and forced upon him a few swallows of ol' Gilbert's spirits. Don't believe he had e'er tasted such strong drink. Before long, he snored quietly in the opposite blockhouse, leaving his young wife to her work. New mother declared herself t*o be relieved to be rid of my worryin' nuisance of a husband* and seemed to enjoy the quiet just before that wee baby boy arrived with nary a problem."

"Cherokee women send men far away when time for babe to come. Make someone take him for hunt or fish. Cherokee women never shout like white women. Much quieter," Waya informed them.

Later in the day, Waya asked, "Esther, ye can read the marks in those books?"

"Yes, my father insisted all his children have an education. We learned to read and write at an early age. Surely you know Joshua can read.

"Waya cannot read. Joshua or Captain reads messages to him to learn and recite. Waya have good memory. Joshua tell me stories from your book called the Bible. My aunt's man, the trader, tells me stories when I visit. I learn story from the Bible about how Earth was made. My people have story about Earth's creation. It much the same."

"Oh, I would love to hear it. Can you tell us your story?"

Esther and Sarah settled in to listen after coaxing Waya to tell his people's tale.

"As young children, elders tell us stories every ceremonial fire. We learn the words. Waya knows this story well. . .

"Earth floats upon the water like a big island hanging from four rawhide ropes tied to the top of the sky at all four sacred directions. Ropes tied to top of world to sky made of rock crystal. If the ropes break, the world will come down and all things will fall, and the world will die. It will be as before the beginning and water will cover it."

Waya paused, and then added, "Many of my people believe the white man will make this happen," before continuing his tale.

"In the beginning, home was up there, above the rainbow, and all lived crowded together on the water. Man, woman, child, animals, plants. Every living thing lived in that place. Man decided he needed more room. Women agreed. Animals and plants said world was too crowded. So, wanting to know what was below the water, the animals sent Water Beetle. He skimmed the water but could see nothing. So bravely he dived down and came up with a bit of mud. Before our eyes, the mud spread out in all four directions and created the island all creatures live on. The Earth.

"Someone Powerful then fastened it to the sky ceiling with cords. The new Earth was flat and only mud. It held no weight. The animals sent birds down to land and see if the Earth would support their weight. They all returned, one after another.

"Then the animals send Grandfather Buzzard. He flew close to the Earth where the Cherokee now live and found the Earth, the mud getting harder. He flew and flew. Now tired and weary, he flew close to the Earth. As his wings went down, they created valleys and when they went up, they created mountains. The animals watching from above the rainbow made him come back as he created too many mountains. That is why the Cherokee land stands tall with mountains.

"At last, the Earth became hard enough, and the animals came down, but all was dark as they had no sun or moon. They pulled the sun from above the rainbow and showed him a path to go from east to west.

"Now earth too hot, so one man pushed the sun back up from the earth. It was not far enough. So, a man stood on his shoulders and pushed the sun higher. Too hot. So, four men stood on his shoulders and pushed. Everyone satisfied."

Sarah and Esther listened in awe to the ages-old story, passed down from generation to generation. As Waya paused to take a drink, Sarah asked, "Is there more to the story, Waya?"

"Yea, Waya can tell ending."

"Please," Esther begged.

"Now before humans came to be, Someone Powerful created plants and animals and told them to stay awake for seven days and seven nights. They were to watch. Now that is what men do to prepare for some ceremonies. Some animals could not do this. Some slept after one day, others after two days, and some after three. Only the owl and the mountain lion stayed awake after seven days and seven nights. To honor them, Someone Powerful gave them eyes that see so they can hunt at night.

"Some plants also could not stay awake, only the cedar, pine, holly, and laurel were still awake on the eighth morning. Someone Powerful rewarded them, allowing them to keep their green all winter.

"After creating the plants and animals, Someone Powerful had made a man and his sister. The man poked her with a fish and told her to give birth. After seven days she had a child, in seven more days she had another, and then another. The humans increased too quickly! Someone Powerful changed this so the woman could have only one child each year.

"Someone Powerful also taught us about the world below ours. The world through the center of the Earth.

This world be reached by going down a spring hole, through the water. One must be guided by underworld people or would be forever lost. This world be opposite to ours. In our summer, it be winter and in our winter it be summer. The Cherokee know this to be true, for water springing from the earth is warmer than the air in winter and cooler than the air in summer."

Several moments of quiet passed after Waya finished his tale with this proclamation of proof of another world. Sarah and Esther recognized the similarities with the creation story told in their own Bible. Finally, Esther spoke. "That is a beautiful story, Waya. I can see how it is like our creation story, the one in the Bible. Thank you for sharing. Do your people tell more such tales about the fire?"

"Yea, many more. My people have storytellers who remember the stories of our people and repeat them to us over fires so we can learn and pass them on to our children and then their children and then their children. Someday, Waya will tell this story to his children. My wife will also tell the story, and my children will learn of our beginnings and pass the story on to their children. Every Cherokee learns these stories. The ones who tell them best, with actions and different voices, become our storytellers."

Only after Joshua returned on the fourth evening did they begin to understand some of what had happened the night Waya was attacked. After much searching, Joshua discovered Waya's bedroll beside the trail leading to their cabin. There, he also found many moccasin prints and blood. He did not find Waya's rifle or powder horn.

On the following morning, both young men returned to the fort and spoke with their commander, Captain Carter.

"Wolf, do you know of anyone who might wish to harm you?" asked Carter.

"Yea, a few of my people dislike my work for the militia. They say Waya be no longer Cherokee. He be traitor. My aunt, Nancy, you call her, has warned me of the talk."

After a bit more discussion, Waya left for his aunt and uncle's trading post, while Joshua and Michael searched the area surrounding where Joshua had found Waya's bedroll. They discovered nothing more. After a few days of quiet, the incident was mostly forgotten.

"Perseverance is also key to success in any endeavor, but without perseverance in combat, there can be no victory." Jocko Willink

November 1777

In mid-November, their old acquaintance from Moore's, the purveyor of news and stories, arrived at Watauga. He immediately announced his intention to share "news, fables, and tall tales" at dusk. Quickly the word spread, and from all around the settlement, residents came to listen. Each brought a small token for their storyteller, a coin, a bit of cornmeal, cuts of meat, or such in payment. David came by the Ballinger cabin to share the invitation. He agreed to come back, mid-afternoon, to walk with the ladies to the fort, as Joshua was absent on a trip to Evan Shelby's home.

So, on a cool but pleasant evening at sunset, some of those few who could read purchased news sheets from their visitor. Others settled in to listen as the chronicler shared his tales of the world. Still dressed in rags and looking down-at-the-heel and careworn, as though he had nothing, no wisdom, no knowledge, and no voice with which to share his tales, the traveling storyteller jumped, straight up in one quick motion, upon a hickory stump and relayed, in his strong and steady baritone, stories from far and wide. His listeners lent him their ears—their unwavering attention.

He began with bits and pieces, insignificant events from around the colonies. He spoke of rising prices for commodities and shortages of essentials across the region. He relayed small skirmishes by the various colonial militia units, and then more important news, such as how on the fourteenth of June, the Second Continental Congress had adopted an official flag for their new republic. He told how a Boston woman, a seamstress named Betsy Ross, had sewn the first flag from strips and bits of cloth she had about her house. He showed off a small example, only two by three feet, adorned with a circle of white stars on a blue field bordered by red and white stripes, by waving it about while his audience clapped and cheered.

Then, after settling the crowd and making shushing noises to a crying baby, he began divulging more serious reports. This was the news each wished so desperately to hear.

"'Twas almost mid-September, when General Washington, our glorious commander, a planter from Virginia whom many of you remember served during the French and Indian War, well, he determined, 'twas his duty and 'twas expected of him, to prevent those evil, red-coated bastards, sent by the Satan we once called our king, from capturing our glorious Congress, who even then tended to their business in our capital of Philadelphia.

"Taking up positions at all the fords across Brandywine Creek, in southeastern Pennsylvania, which lay between our enemy and our capital, our forces prepared to meet their adversary. Across that body of water, marched, nearer and nearer, some over fifteen thousand men under the command of Sir William Howe. Howe's army consisted of British soldiers and those most hated of all — Hessians!"

Booing and shouting broke out amongst the crowd. He let them express their ire before continuing several minutes later.

"Hush now and listen. On the eleventh of September, General Knyphausen led his Hessian troops opposite our men, where they fired upon our brave soldiers across Brandywine Creek at Chadds Ford. Our men fought bravely, not knowing this was nothing more than a ruse. A bewilderment to keep our men occupied as the enemy moved forward. For unbeknownst to all in our command, some miles farther upstream, Howe's forces even then crossed the Brandywine at another ford!

"Yet, our brave men fought on as the hours passed, for they remained unaware of the danger approaching on their right flank. The Hessians kept up a steady stream of fire with cannons and muskets. Our stalwart and steady men suffered losses! Some wounded and some dead. Still, without pause, they fought and held their ground against superior numbers. In the late afternoon, a heavy fog floated onto the battlefield and obscured the instability and vulnerability of our men's position. The battle raged on and on!

"Suddenly, out of the fog, Redcoats appeared to the right. Always prepared, General Washington quickly sent forces under generals Sullivan and Alexander to shore up this flank. Those soldiers, our own valiant men, fought like wildcats, firing and reloading, firing and reloading, again and again, until overrun by Howe's devils. Even then, they fought hand to hand.

"It happened exactly as that scheming Howe had planned, for those Hessian devils rushed across Brandywine Creek at Chadds Ford just as Howe's men attacked on the right flank. Suddenly, the battle turned, and our Continentals could hold no more. Our line collapsed under overwhelming numbers from those damned Redcoats and those even more devilish Hessians!

"Calling upon his audacious and inspired leaders, one more time, to save our army from total defeat, Washington asked General Nathanael Greene's division to cover their retreat. That Fighting Quaker, as he is called, for General Greene was raised a Quaker, took up the gauntlet and led his men in a counterattack. They fought hand to hand, toe to toe, along the crest of Birmingham Hill while our remaining troops fell back in an orderly retreat led by a Frenchman! A Frenchman, I say! One who came over to fight alongside our brave soldiers. He's a Marquis, a young, brave, and exceedingly handsome nobleman, named Gilbert du Motier, Marquis de Lafayette! Despite his wounds, received in the earlier battle, de Lafayette kept our men moving and led them to safety.

"Oh! the sorrow of defeat, the losses of this battle! In the end, that villain Howe captured Philadelphia. Still, I beg you! Despair not, listeners! Despair not! Fast riders, warning of the coming danger, and our men's bravery gave our representatives time to escape. Escape they did, by horseback, by carriage, by wagon, and on foot! Likewise, led by our brave generals, Washington and Greene, our Continentals gathered to fight once more.

"Ladies, lest I forget to tell you, the hero of the day, de Lafayette, survived his wounds due to the excellent care of our own doctors. I hear tell, to this day, the Marquis remains steadfast in his desire to ensure our victory in the coming campaigns."

Again, he paused his story and yelled out over the shouts and cries of many among the crowd, for they had begun to comment and grew anxious over the events of his story.

"Despair not my friends, I shout despair not!

"Give me your attention, listen! Hear! For our brave men, while they retreated, they also fought. As all this initial battle occurred at Brandywine Creek and Philadelphia, there came south from Canada into the colony of New York, British General John Burgoyne and his army with the goal, all our important and educated men believe, of subduing the northernmost colonies. With Burgoyne marched over seven thousand red-coated hellions, prepared to kill, rape, and pillage! Marching toward him came some nine thousand Continentals under General Horatio Gates, who all desired to stop this indecency.

"The two armies met first on the nineteenth of September at a place called Freeman's Farm, near Saratoga, where Gates had entrenched his men and lay in wait. Although the British overran our men in the end, our own men killed or wounded over 600. Let it be known our own American losses counted much lower.

"As Gates moved south to join forces with General Washington, Burgoyne awaited reinforcements. By the seventh of October, this British general decided he could wait no longer. He attacked! This time our Continentals held firm, and as the battle progressed, they moved forward, pushing the British back into Saratoga. Gates, wily old fox that he is, surrounded the town. In the end, Burgoyne had no choice but to surrender."

Cheers rang out across the hills around the Watauga settlement that night as one and all celebrated a victory captured months before. No one, not one amongst them, dared turn and walk away as none was a Tory, or at least confessed to such leanings.

Building upon the news brought by their traveling storyteller, spirits remained high at the Watauga settlements throughout the coming months.

"You meet people who forget you. You forget people you meet. But sometimes you meet those people you can't forget. Those are your friends." Mark Twain

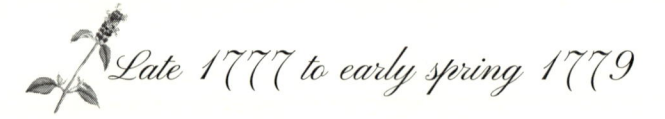

Late 1777 to early spring 1779

Benjamin's next letter and newspapers presented the siblings with details of the outside world that winter of 1777. It also began a whole new chapter in the family's life. Benjamin suffered with so many others at Valley Forge. Lucky, that as an officer and a doctor he shared a log cabin with others of his profession, he unluckily, more often than not, shared it with the ill and the dying. Like the entire army at Valley Forge, Benjamin suffered with them in their hunger, their lack of firewood, warm clothing, and medicine, and their low morale. Men, whose enlistment expired, saw little reason to remain, to fight for a promise of a republic when their own leaders could neither feed nor pay them. General Washington watched as his army dwindled. Men simply walked away, headed home.

After pleading and arguing with the representatives of the Continental Congress, the General's wife, Martha Washington, arrived in late February with food and supplies. Not enough, not sufficient to see them through, but enough to keep some, those most stalwart, from leaving. Some improvements occurred. Benjamin frequently found himself invited for dinner with his commander, as Martha fondly remembered his father and mother.

Benjamin also relayed news of Samuel, who had, true to his word, left the army when his six-month term of enlistment expired in early December. Benjamin had completely supported his younger brother's decision, as Samuel was not cut out for military life. His journey home to Virginia took over a month, as possessing little money, Samuel walked much of the way. Once there, he found the situation worse than they had imagined. Squatters occupied the two remaining cabins that once housed their indentured workers. Their former home and many outbuildings lay in burned ruins. He found their fields fallow and all their livestock gone.

In reply, Joshua and Esther wrote cheerful letters to Benjamin and Samuel. They did not tell of the tornado, losing their cabin, the attack upon Esther, Lovely's silence, or even their move to Watauga. These were not words meant for brothers suffering from far worse problems than their own.

Along the frontier, the coming Christmas season and the recent news of the war brought an encouraging spirit to the Watauga residents. In early December, on a warmer than usual day, Joshua and Michael arrived at the Ballinger cabin near midday. Woody barked their arrival to let all know that company approached.

"Mistress Sarah, sisters, we bring you good tidings and an invite to a weddin'," Joshua called out as he pushed open the door. "Don yer best, whatever it be, for a minister has come to call and David's done proposed to sweet Betsy Ann. They're to be married at dusk! Oh, and there be dancin' and celebratin' tonight and preachin' on the morrow."

"Joshua, stop your fooling! Surely, they are not getting married today, with no warning, no engagement," Esther replied, though not really shocked to hear of the rushed wedding.

"Sure 'nuf they be, Miss Esther. As soon as David heared there be a preacher at the fort, he dashed off to ask Betsy Ann Walker to marry him. David swears they been secretly promised to each other for months now. Next, he done run around to find her Pa and ask his say in the matter. Bein' as there be a passel of those children, Mr. Walker done gave his permission right smart, and they's to be married," Michael informed his friends, barely pausing for breath.

So, Sarah, Esther, and Lovely donned their best attire and searched among their belongings for suitable wedding gifts. Lovely pulled out a beautiful shawl she had woven as a gift for Betsy Ann. Esther wrote a quick note, promising two hens, and butter and milk for the coming year. Someone would have to read the promise to her, as Betsy Ann could neither read nor write. Sarah, who had brought a small trunk from Virginia which contained her more valued possessions, pulled out two pewter spoons to give the new couple.

Walking to the fort, accompanied by Michael and Woody, the party sang and joked along the way. Lovely tried to teach Michael their favorite ballad while Sarah and Esther playfully covered their ears, for the young man could not carry a tune or remember the words. As they neared the fort, greetings rang out from others coming from the outlying cabins, for such festivities occurred rarely. Despite the presence of a minister, the evening's gathering promised to be one of dancing, laughing, talking, and drinking. No doubt there would be at least one squabble.

Within the fort, women had settled long tables, now covered with dishes of all types. Nearby, several men worked to empty and sweep a clearing large enough for dancing. The groom, David, paced back and forth until Joshua and Michael could stand his restlessness no longer.

"David Lusk, come with me," Joshua demanded, grabbing his friend's arm. "Ye as well, Michael." Turning toward the gate, he led them out of the fort with a shouted promise to Mistress Sarah, "we'll be back with time to spare."

Michael placed the pot of stew he had carried from their cabin on the table and ran to join up with his friends. At the gate, Waya turned and accompanied the groom's friends as Joshua explained the excitement of the evening. Esther noticed Waya carried a new rifle. He looked well and fit. The Cherokee man raised his hand, greeting the ladies before hurrying off.

As dusk approached, lanterns were lit. Fires built up around the clearing provided a bit of warmth and an additional glow to the evening's events. From one blockhouse stepped a large-framed, stern-looking young man with a grave countenance. In a wool topcoat, brocade waistcoat, white linen shirt, and black tie, he stood better dressed than any man at the fort, except possibly John Sevier. He looked the part of a preacher in every manner, only younger than the ladies expected. As Esther listened to him speak, she knew him to be educated and later heard how he had recently graduated from Princeton University.

When the crowd finally quieted, Pastor Samuel Doak introduced himself and declared his liking for the countryside about the fort, his liking for the people of Watauga, and his desire to settle in the area. Then he proceeded to marrying.

Before David and Betsy Ann were ushered forward, a couple Esther did not recognize stepped up and asked to be married. The young woman, still in her teens, appeared resolute and embarrassed, as she would obviously soon be giving birth. Her husband-to-be simply smiled at his bride and the preacher.

Recognizing her embarrassment, Doak began, "Now, now, young Elizabeth," for that was her name, "living as you do so far from civilization and churches, I know you and your young man most likely made promises to each other before the justice of the peace before you created that life within you. So, this evening, we will just make all official within the eyes of our good Lord and all our friends."

The couple smiled sheepishly at each other, sharing each other's chagrin and their relief at the preacher's acceptance, before Pastor Doak continued.

In the coming dusk of evening, Elizabeth said her vows and married Greenbury Shook before God and all at Watauga. When the words had been said, the attending crowd clapped and cheered as an embarrassed Greenbury led his new wife to a bench. Moving among them, he smiled at and greeted all the women and shook hands with all the men. Elizabeth sat beaming, hand resting upon her stomach.

Then Pastor Doak called forth for the Walker bride. As a fiddler played a lively tune, Patrick Walker led his daughter from the opposite blockhouse. Esther and Lovely knew and liked the girl, as David had introduced them months before and had even brought her once or twice to the cabin for the evening meal. Betsy Ann was near about Esther's age.

Betsy Ann's dark blonde tresses gleamed in the glow of the candles and fires. As there were no flowers available, it being winter, someone had created for her a wreath of holly leaves intertwined with pink ribbons. She wore a pink homespun dress, a gray wool shawl, and moccasins showed as she stepped forward. The fort had no shoemaker, so most everyone wore moccasins purchased from the nearby trading post. Even Esther and Lovely, who had each outgrown their worn out half boots a year or so earlier, had taken to wearing moccasins.

"Esther, where's David?" Lovely whispered.

"I can't see him, Lovely, but I'm sure Joshua and Michael will make sure the groom attends his own wedding."

Sure enough, as Betsy Ann approached the pastor and glanced around for her intended, David half fell and half stumbled into place nearby the pastor's left hand. Esther noticed his hair appeared dripping wet, yet he beamed at Betsy Ann, and she at him.

Joshua stepped up beside him, while Waya and Michael moved to stand beside Esther and Sarah.

Hours passed as the people of Watauga ate, danced, and celebrated. Sarah slipped off to check on Elizabeth Shook, and then took a seat along the fort's wall to chat with the older women. Lovely met up with Jane, who had attended with her brother William's family. Both girls were asked to dance over and over again.

Although the celebration belonged to Betsy and David and the Shooks, as evening fell into night, Esther attracted much more attention than either bridal party. She danced with the grooms, both of them, with Michael, with others from the militia, and twice with Jesse Bean. Lydia's son stood about five feet-ten inches tall and was solidly built but did not lean to fat. He kept his dark brown hair neat in its queue. Jesse's smile captured any onlooker's attention, for it revealed an outgoing, fun disposition. Still, Esther knew the young man to be an excellent shot, trapper, and always ready to protect those about him.

Joshua watched as Esther glowed, which drew men to her again and again. In an instant, he recognized wanting and lust on the men's faces when they stared at his sister, for she had grown into a strikingly beautiful young woman. At nearly sixteen years of age, an age when many girls of the frontier married, Esther stood out. As she danced, her long hair, earlier tamed by ribbons and braids, hung loose, its long auburn curls bouncing and swirling with her every move. She stood taller than most women and many of the men. With her tiny waist and full breasts, she stepped with a grace and lightness few possessed. Yet Joshua believed it was her face, her smile, her countenance, men noticed.

At the edge of the light stood Waya, watching Esther's every move. His face beamed. His eyes followed Esther's every step. And Joshua recognized the look of love and desire in his friend's expression.

Approaching Waya, Joshua asked, "Wolf, do ye know how to dance?"

"Not such dances, only know dances of warriors. Warriors not dance with women. Women dance with other women and girls, not men."

"Oh, so ye don't want to dance with Esther," Joshua teased.

Suddenly, Waya turned and stared at his friend. "Ah, brother see Waya's heart. Worry not, I go."

"Wait, Waya. I understand. Please, do not leave. Stay. We must see David to his cabin to bed his bride. Ye would be missed."

"No. Go now."

Joshua watched as Waya left through the fort's main gate and walked into the night. He wondered if he would ever see his friend again. Wondered if he should have remained silent. Joshua held no misgivings, no qualms about Waya and Esther. He had months earlier noticed Esther watching the Cherokee man. He saw her smile upon his arrival. He saw how she stood watching each time he left their cabin until he disappeared into the trees. Sometimes, even then, she lingered.

In January, Sarah delivered the Shook's baby girl. Sarah stayed on for two days to help at their cabin, as Elizabeth and Greenbury had no family in the area. Lovely spent more and more time with the Bean family, staying sometimes for a week. Late in the month, the siblings and Sarah celebrated both Benjamin's and Esther's birthdays. Despite Benjamin's absence, the evening was full of fun and laughter. David and Betsy Ann attended, along with Jane and Jesse Bean. Michael arrived with a girl newly come to the fort, Lucy Trimble. A little mite of a thing, Lucy joined in the fun as if she had known them all for years.

Only Waya remained absent. Each time Esther or Sarah asked Joshua if he had seen Waya about the fort, he would only shake his head and move off without answering.

In early April, two events brought joy to the Ballinger siblings. On the second day of the month, a letter arrived from Samuel. As usual, when either brother's letters arrived, they came via Moore's, Captain Gass, and Waya.

First of March, the year of our Lord seventeen seventy-eight,

My dearest Esther, Joshua, and Lovely,

I arrived at our home in late February to find it as described in Benjamin's previous letter. I reside currently with the Elliott family and will most likely remain here for now. I have secured what is left of our father's funds, now safely deposited in a different bank. However, much was spent, illegally it seems, by our uncles. They still reside on their respective properties, though I have been led to understand they both wish to sell out and return to England.

As for our father's land, it is in ruins except for the two small outlying cabins. There is no longer a house, a stable, or a barn. Of course, there is no need for those last two since we own no livestock. I do plan to buy a horse for myself from the Elliotts.

Please, I beg you, DO NOT return here. War is everywhere around. I believe it will intensify once the weather changes for the better.

I am well, as was Benjamin when I left him. I think of you every day as to your circumstances, your health, and your safety. My prayers be with you, one and all. You may write to me in care of the Elliotts.

With love,
God's Blessing upon you,
Samuel

The second proved to be a joyous one for Esther, for toward the middle of the month, Samuel Doak returned with his young wife, also named Esther. Unlike Esther Ballinger, Esther Doak stood only a little over five feet tall and was petite in every way. Her dusty blonde hair, often astray from her cap, looked as frenzied as her actions, for this Esther seemed always in motion. She had instantly accepted her role as a Reverend's wife and seemed to think it her mission to solve all problems and situations. Something she proved adept at doing.

As the Doak couple settled into a cabin built for them during Samuel's absence, Esther Ball found she greatly enjoyed Mistress Doak's company. The two had much in common. As both had received liberal educations, they found they enjoyed books and reading. Esther Doak had much to learn about living in the wilderness, so Esther Ball, Lydia Bean, and others took to helping her establish her household. Additionally, Esther Doak owned her own horse, a gift from her father, so the two young ladies, unburdened by children, could often be found riding across the safer areas of the settlement to visit friends. Mistress Doak often insisted upon accompanying Esther on her visits to tend the sick or wounded.

In late April, Jesse Bean shared the recent news of Daniel Boone and some twenty-eight or so men having been captured by Shawnee warriors while boiling for salt at a place called Blue Licks. The news greatly disturbed William Bean, who considered Daniel a close friend as they had hunted together many times one winter several years back. Across the frontier, settlers worried over the captured men's lives and the possibility of more attacks.

Days and months ran into each other with memories that lasted only days and scarcely remained in their thoughts. The year passed with three more letters from Benjamin and four from Samuel. Samuel, with little to occupy his time, and a restlessness often found in youth, had joined the Virginia militia. Reading between the lines of his letters, Esther and Joshua had determined Samuel also felt guilty about leaving the military. By joining the militia, he could still be in Virginia to monitor their old home. Due to his education and prior experience, he served as a lieutenant.

It seemed, as the year progressed, more and more the world across the mountain moved into their realm. Joshua's role often brought stories to their ears from battles fought far to the east. In mid-summer, Jesse Bean came to relay the story of a militia action near to Watauga, involving his father and others from the fort.

As he sat scratching Woody behind his ears, Jesse told how Isam Yearley, a Tory who lived nearby on the Nolichucky River, had been driven out of his home by a company of Whigs, led by Jesse's brother, Captain William Bean. A few residents with Tory leanings still lived quietly within their community, staying mostly to themselves.

"Now, ye ken, Yearley had been causing trouble and threatening his Patriot neighbors. So, William led the militia out to put a halt to his doings. After rousting Yearley from his home and giving him fair warning to cease his threats, William's company pursued another party of Tories, led by a Captain Arthur Grimes. William believes he be sent here to disrupt our peaceful ways. Now the Tories led by Grimes had killed Mr. Millican and attempted to kill one of the Roddy family. Nice folks, all of them Roddy boys, good Patriots. Then these same Tories took Mr. Grubbs up on a high pinnacle along the Watauga River and threatened to throw him off. Scared for his life, old Mr. Grubbs surrendered all his property to them in exchange for a chance to live out his life in peace. William and his men, now incensed by this unchristian lawlessness, ferreted out the entire party. They put the fear of God in each and wounded the Tory leader, Captain Grimes. Despite our men's actions, all those bastard Tories escaped."

"Jesse, take care with your words. Now, were any of our men wounded and in need of medical care?" Esther asked, turning to gather up her basket of medical supplies.

"Nah, all the men came home safe and sound. Ye ken they be the best trackers and shots in all of Watauga," Jesse bragged. "Just wish I could have been with them."

"Jesse Bean," Lovely shouted, "how dare you wish such a thing. Your mother's been beside herself with worry, and you being along would have made it all the worse for her."

"Sorry, Lovely, I just meant that I want to be part of the action. I'd take care. No need to fret, girl. You know I already be a member of the militia."

During the more peaceful times that summer, Esther, now sixteen years of age, often found local men standing outside their cabin's door facing a barking and growling Woody. Some would bring flowers or small gifts, ask her to walk out with them, and then accept her negative replies with good grace. While Mistress Esther Doak often teased Esther about her numerous suitors, she never asked her younger friend why those suitors held no interest for her.

Lovely continued as Lovely had always been, quiet and often withdrawn. At fourteen, the older boys of the fort and, in particular, Jesse Bean, began paying her compliments, bringing her flowers and small gifts, and trying, always without more than a simple acknowledgment from her, to win over her affection.

These courting gestures spurred many a giggling session between Jane, Lovely, and young Sarah. Lydia Bean, ever the mother of a busy family, advised Lovely, along with her two girls, about how to respond to such advances. Despite little or no encouragement from Joshua, the three girls often spent hours gossiping about the girls who had recently expressed their desires concerning Lovely's brother.

In mid-October, a rider from Boonesborough brought news of a twelve-day siege of the fort by over four hundred Shawnee warriors, led in part by a French captain paid by the British. While not as dramatic in his telling as their sometimes troubadour, the visitor told first of Daniel Boone's escape from his Shawnee captors, and his arduous journey back to the fort to warn of the Shawnee's plans to attack. The rider had few details about the siege, only that it began about the sixth of September and ended on the eighteenth.

All of Watauga rejoiced over the news that only two within the Kentucky fort had died though four were wounded, including Daniel Boone, who the courier assured them had recovered. Still, the news of this event led their leaders to reinforce and repair Fort Caswell, in preparation for such an attack. Several times during the autumn, warnings of Cherokee and Shawnee raiding in their vicinity forced residents into the fort. Their enemy attacked and burned a few outlying cabins.

In mid-January 1779, returning home wet and half frozen after caring for a sick family, Sarah took ill. Esther nursed her for twelve long, bitter days and nights, rarely leaving Sarah's bedside. At first, their dearest friend shook with the cold of the weather, then the fever took hold, and Sarah suffered bone-wracking chills. Joshua and Esther built up the fire and covered her with warmed blankets. Esther gave her sips of spiced tea. Still, Sarah frequently coughed until she could no longer catch her breath. Despite trying all the remedies she had learned — teas, poultices, and such — Esther feared for Sarah's life.

Early on, Joshua had delivered Lovely to the Bean's cabin and requested she stay until Sarah recovered. Lydia Bean welcomed the girl and promised Joshua to care for her like her own. When Esther could no longer deny that Sarah's time lay near, she sent Joshua to escort Lovely back.

In her last day, Sarah lay still, her rasping breath her only sound. Only Esther and Lovely remained in the cabin on the day Sarah breathed her last. Woody, who had lain at her side for days and nights, barely leaving to eat, howled into the stillness, as quietly, in her sleep, finally at peace, Sarah went to join her William. Esther's tears joined Woody's howls, as she now understood the pain of losing a loving mother and friend.

Lovely's tears flowed silently until suddenly she stood and moved about the cabin, tidying up and setting each minor task to rights. For three days, she did not speak.

The siblings buried Mistress Sarah Porter in the fort's small cemetery on a frosty morning, the first day of February 1779. The Reverend Doak spoke at her graveside. His wife stood with Esther and Lovely, holding each close, giving them what peace her arms and warmth could provide. Despite the biting cold and a stiff wind, most all the surrounding community's residents turned out. Each had, in some way, through some illness, or a birth, turned to Sarah Porter, their healer and friend. As the Ballinger siblings rode back toward their cabin, the wind died, and a soft wet snow fell. That evening, Esther wrote to Sarah's sons, still living near Fort Harrod in far off Kentucky. She told of Sarah's last days, her burial, and their deep regrets.

More at Watauga took ill in the coming weeks. Esther moved from isolated cabin to cabin, often escorted by Michael when Joshua was absent. Lovely stayed once again with the Beans. Most of the younger citizens overcame the illness. Still, in early March, Esther stood with two sets of parents as they each buried a small infant. Many, many more of the older residents succumbed. In late March, Esther too became ill—more from exhaustion and grief than the grippe that had spread all winter.

Lovely came home and cared for her. Betsy Ann stayed over for days on end. Esther Doak visited frequently and sat at her side, reading from first one favorite book and then another. Finally, as the trees budded, and the grasses turned to green, Esther, weak still, stepped from their cabin.

All about, forest plants greened in the promise of a beautiful spring when Esther took to walking the forest alone, to gather the herbs and plants she needed to replenish her medicine bag. Armed with the small pistol Benjamin had given her, now loaded, and her knife, she felt secure. She rarely made any noise that might bring attention to herself. She covered her tracks when possible, and was constantly aware of her surroundings, the songs of birds and calls of animals, especially when they suddenly hushed.

Admonishing Woody to stay, some days Esther disappeared from the cabin in the early morning hours, before the others awoke, and returned only in the late afternoon. During her wanderings, her thoughts often turned to Sarah, the woman who had given her love without boundaries and a purpose for her being. After a few weeks, Esther looked healthy again. She no longer seemed deep in grief over Sarah and the ones they had lost during the winter.

"The best thing to hold onto in life is each other."
Audrey Hepburn

Spring 1779

Much had changed in their lives during the previous months. Michael had married Lucy Trimble and settled in a cabin many miles from theirs. Already, they had a baby, a girl, they named Sarah. David and Betsy Ann, as well, had added to their family, a boy, and built a cabin near to her parents.

Now a striking young man, tall and capable, Joshua attracted the attention of all the fort's girls and even a few married women. He attended dances and gatherings at the fort, when possible, but never seemed interested in any one girl. He danced with them all. He joked and hunted with his friends. The older men respected the young man for his abilities and his character, for all knew him to be honest and good to his word. None of the fathers would have balked at his daughter marrying Joshua.

Never one for formal schooling, Joshua had over the years adopted the frontier speech, using "ye" and "nay" and such. Now a sergeant in the local militia, he often traveled from station to station, delivering and gathering news. In every fort, cabin, and settlement, they welcomed Joshua Ball as a treasured friend and a good man in times of trouble.

Of an evening, at their cabin, Esther sometimes found herself alone, for Joshua would be off on a mission, and Lovely with the Bean family. The young men of the fort had at last stopped calling on her, for word around the fort was that Esther, despite being friendly to all, refused all who came courting. Strangely, the men seemed to hold no hard feelings against her, for they revered her healing and caring ways in time of need. Many, during the last year, had come to Esther with minor wounds, rashes, fevers, and even the occasional gunshot or knife wound. Having learned much from Sarah and Benjamin, she'd become the communities' healer, midwife, and nurse. Her compassion, her soft caring ways toward each and all, brought her a well-deserved respect within the Watauga settlement.

The three Ballinger siblings lived modestly. Esther served as her siblings' cook, their wash woman, and their carer. Lydia Bean allowed Lovely use of her loom in exchange for her needlework skills. Lovely kept them in blankets, shawls, and cloth for clothing. Lydia often sold items sewn by, or cloth woven by, Lovely and gave her the profits. Esther and Joshua insisted she save this money or use it for herself alone. In the last year, the girl had woven cloth and made Esther a much-needed new skirt, bodice, and undergarments.

Lovely helped tend their small garden and took care of the livestock when Esther was called away. Joshua made sure his sisters had meat for the table, firewood, and protection. Many a night, a militia man slept outside the isolated cabin at Joshua's request. On some occasions, especially in rough weather, Esther and Lovely would invite the man to sleep before the fire.

If Joshua traveled to see Evan Shelby at his home, he sometimes returned with a new book for his sisters. More often than not, the book was a gift from Evan or Isaac, for each knew the young man had no coin to spare for such luxuries. His and others' loving talk of his sisters swayed them to be generous.

From Evan, Joshua obtained a copy of *Thoughts on Government, Applicable to the Present State of the American Colonies* written by John Adams, Massachusetts's representative to the Continental Congress. The small book, written in the spring of 1776, stood as his response to a resolution of the North Carolina Provincial Congress. That body had requested Adams's opinion on the establishment of their new government and its constitution. Ideas put forth in Adams's writings had been adopted in December 1776 by the framers of North Carolina's first constitution.

Unlike most young women of the time, Esther's liberal education had provided her with the knowledge and logical thinking to make her an ardent supporter of such essays and ways of thinking. Like in fellow Virginian Thomas Paine's *Common Sense*, Adams proposed three branches of government, and more than one single legislative body. Joshua and Esther spent hours debating the arguments for and against these novel approaches toward government, the new North Carolina constitution, and what their federal government might become if freedom from King George was achieved. Such conversations brought into play Joshua's education, despite his willingness to ignore all the various tutors had tried to instill.

The other volume from Evan Shelby, *The History of Lady Barton* by Elizabeth Griffith, foretold, in the preface, the dangers to a young woman's character by reading novels. Esther found this to be quite amusing, as the book's story included such acts as seduction, attempted rape, illicit sex and such, in a novel, written from a woman's perspective, about a woman who had committed the sentimental sin of marrying without love. As this book arrived during one of Lovely's weeklong absences, Esther read it while alone, and then decided it was not for Lovely's pleasure. She, therefore, hid the book until which time she could share the volume with Esther Doak. Though her friend would most likely hide the volume from Samuel.

Infrequently, news sheets and the occasional letter enlightened their everyday lives with stories from the world far removed. Sometimes, a letter would arrive from either Benjamin or Samuel. Twice their brothers sent packages containing newspapers, books—and a coin or two, if from Benjamin. These came by way of military couriers.

Although Samuel continued to serve in the Virginia militia, he wrote of hiring two families to live on their Virginia home place. He had given the families the tasks of clearing overgrown fields and planting crops. They were to be caretakers of the property during his and Benjamin's absence. With Benjamin in complete agreement, they paid the families well for their labors and promised a share of the proceeds, though profit and coin became even harder to come by.

In the little cabin, war news often filled their evening conversation, for Joshua had no fear of sharing the latest with his two Patriot sisters. Often this news centered on attacks by

Chickamauga Cherokee. Two years earlier, British officers had met with and convinced the Chickamauga and some Overhill Cherokee men to fight alongside them. Promises of no further encroachments into their lands by white settlers, and gifts of muskets and other goods, won over many of the Cherokee, especially those of the Chickamauga settlements along the Tennessee River.

All that winter, Watauga's residents shared, from cabin to cabin, stories of Cherokee warriors fighting side by side with British forces and carrying out atrocities against civilian populations. While a few settlers moved back east of the mountains, the more stalwart determined to keep their holdings and to fight.

However, seeing the results of these increasingly frequent attacks, residents and leaders called for action to be taken. Working together, Governors Thomas Jefferson of Virginia and Richard Caswell of North Carolina decided to send a force of men along the Tennessee River to wipe out the Chickamauga settlements, knowing most of the warriors would be absent, the towns populated only with the elderly, women, and children.

Their goal was not to kill these innocents, but simply to destroy the villages seizing goods and supplies. Such destruction would force the Cherokee men to return to help reestablish their settlements and to protect and feed their own families.

Having returned from Evan Shelby's home, Joshua carried the news to Lieutenant Isaac Lane and other militia leaders at the fort. Shelby had been asked to form a unit of men, some one thousand from their region, to accompany a regiment of Continentals under John Montgomery on this raid deep into Chickamauga territory. Joshua had requested to be included.

Upon relaying news of this expedition to his sisters, Joshua paused, and then angrily announced his decision, "Esther, Lovely, I have asked to join the expedition. I be seein' firsthand the death caused by these rovin' bands of Chickamauga Cherokee, sportin' rifles and muskets given them by the British. I feel the need to act. I can stand by no longer and watch as friends be murdered in their homes, their wives and children with them."

Shocked silence followed his words. Esther returned to sorting her plants, roots, and bark, while Lovely looked to her stitches. Several uncomfortable minutes passed.

Finally, turning to face her brother, Esther whispered, "Why now, Joshua? Why?"

Ramrod straight, despite being weary from days of travel and little sleep, Joshua stepped forward. "I can stand by no longer, out of the fight!" he shouted vehemently, slamming his fist against the table. "I have stood by watching as my friends and neighbors take action. My own brothers fight. William Bean and his sons, the Russells, the Lanes, have most all fought for our liberty, for our safety, and I, . . . I carry messages . . . I know 'tis a need, a need to move from place to place and share news and carry militia dispatches, still . . . still," turning, once more shouldering his rifle, Joshua left the cabin without finishing. Esther and Lovely listened as his horse could be heard moving off.

Woody, upset by the turmoil in the cabin, hid under the table, whining, until Esther reached down to stroke his coarse fur, giving him and her both a bit of comfort.

"What if they kill him, Esther? What will become of us? I would rather die than go back to Virginia, even if Samuel is there. I won't go!" Within seconds, the girl moved from her emphatic turmoil of thoughts and fears to withering silence.

Esther paced, tidied the already neat cabin, built up the fire, and moved about, often without purpose, as she waited for her brother's return. Over the previous months, Esther had witnessed Joshua's building anger over his role in the revolution. She, like her brothers, understood the need to contribute to the cause, to fight, to commit.

In the following weeks, recruitment of sufficient men and the needed supplies for the expedition proved easier than the leaders expected. Evan Shelby gathered over a thousand men, including three hundred and fifty from the area around his own home. Captain William Bean and his brother-in-law, Captain George Russell, were among the party from Watauga. They spent several weeks building dugout canoes for the trip down the Tennessee. As all around Watauga, men collected their necessities and marched off to do their duty. Joshua remained at his duties.

Seeing Lovely's silent distress had reinforced in Joshua's mind his role of protector. Additionally, Lieutenant Lane had refused his request and instead sent him east, into North Carolina, with a message for Captain Robert Bean's company of raiders. As it happened, Joshua would have been safer with those along the Tennessee, for many weeks later, as they arrived back in the settlements, all rejoiced over the successful raid. They had lost not one man among their party and only a few wounded—none seriously. The raiders had destroyed eleven towns, killing only four inhabitants. They captured hundreds of pounds of corn and other crops and several hundred rifles belonging to Dragging Canoe, the Chickamauga military leader, who at that time fought in South Carolina, unknowing of what befell his people.

Joshua came home, still limping after several weeks' recovery at Shelby's Fort. Attacked by a small group of Tories, he'd suffered a wound to his upper thigh from a musket ball that had struck the bone but not broken it. After his fortuitous escape, a frontier healer, a Negro man owned by Shelby, had removed the musket ball along with small fragments of bone and stitched the wound.

In late April, as Esther worked, far from their cabin, abruptly, she perceived she was no longer alone. Around her, the forest animals stood quiet. No birds sang or even moved about overhead. Suddenly, fear mingled with Esther's memories of that day long ago at Moore's. Rising from her kneeling position, she reached to secure her pistol when a voice she recognized spoke quietly.

"Miss Esther, Waya means you no harm," he said, stepping out into the small clearing.

"Oh, Waya, I have missed you. Where have you been? You have been gone for such a long time."

"Waya go home to my village. Stay all winter. Hunt with my brothers and friends."

"Is all well with your family?" Esther asked hesitantly, wanting to understand his absence.

"Yea, mother gives us new sister. Strong baby girl, loud voice. Waya come back to trading post and stay with aunt. Much quieter. Waya came to see Lieutenant Lane."

"Our cabin is quiet as well. Mistress Sarah died in the winter."

"Yea, Waya talk with Joshua in morning. He tell me all news. Tell me about Esther's sickness. Be ye well?"

"Yes, Waya, I am well. I was just going to have a bite to eat. Would you share with me?"

So, it began. Esther wandered almost every day into the woods, searching for healing plants. On some such days, Waya would find her and stay for hours. Not every day, as he was often absent, delivering messages between the various stations and forts. When together, they talked, laughed, and shared gossip and food furnished most often by Esther, but occasionally by Waya.

Esther helped Waya improve his English after he requested she do so. She would have never done so before, as her regard for him came to mean so much. They talked of his family and his Cherokee ways. She told him of her extended family, and the reason for the siblings' departure from Virginia. They discussed the revolution, Benjamin, and Samuel.

Back at their cabin, Esther did not share with Lovely or Joshua that she spent time alone with Waya. She didn't know if Joshua would understand and did not want to take the risk of asking him and hearing his negative reply. She understood, all too well, how others at the fort would not approve. While it seemed to be accepted on the frontier that a man might marry or at least live with an Indian woman, the way Waya's aunt Nancy Ward and trader Bryant Ward did, it was not acceptable for a white woman to take an Indian husband or lover.

Infrequently, in the coming weeks, Waya came to their cabin to share the evening meal. Without ever discussing it, Esther and

Waya continued as they always had on these occasions. They met as brother and sister, close friends, nothing more. They tried to exchange no glances, no quiet words.

In May, Esther and Waya found and gathered wild ramps and spring onions. Waya showed her other plants his people gathered for food or medicines. Their days together continued with each learning from the other. Waya taught her his people's names for the various animals and birds. He taught her how to make bird calls, and they picked the call of the wood thrush to announce their coming to each other. Waya's trilling call of the thrush, Esther always answered with the thrush's chirping reply.

Spring moved into full summer, and as the heat of the days climbed, so did their affection for each other. Waya, at first, only took Esther's hand when helping her across a stream or up a slope. Soon, he took her hand and held it just to be near her, to hold her close by. As they explored the surrounding hollows and mountains, they also traversed their own emotions, their growing love, and their respect for each other.

Those silent days, when Waya did not join her, Esther often found herself deep in thought. Within herself, she recognized how much her happiness depended upon Waya's affection, his friendship, his love. On other days, she worried about Waya and, of course, Joshua. For while the two men were held in high regard by the militia officers for their backwoods skills, Esther understood the dangers each faced while delivering messages and orders between the various back country forts, stations, and homesteads.

Waya and Esther's first kiss came on a cool afternoon in late June as they sat under a hickory's low boughs and shared a bit of venison jerky. "May I?" she asked, brazenly. At his confusion, Esther simply leaned across and kissed him. First on his cheek, and then on his lips.

Not to be outdone, Waya laughed before framing her face with his hands to return her kiss. He added one to her nose and then, more lingering ones to her neck. With each kiss, their laughter and playfulness died away and passion arose. Yet before long,

Esther drew away, quietly wondering how she had dared to be so bold. Waya felt only a satisfying happiness that held no regrets.

Remembering those stolen moments of affection, within days, they began each meeting by kissing and touching, often forgetting to hunt for herbs or early berries, and instead spending their first hour together sharing their affection. At other times, they sat side by side and talked. Esther read to Waya from books as he held her head in his lap. She taught him songs, and he taught her more Cherokee words as they climbed hills or sat quietly beside meandering forest streams. She taught him dances in open glades, while singing the songs of her childhood. He showed her, as best he could, the dances of Cherokee women.

Some days they walked, taking in the beauties of the forest and hills that surrounded Boone's Creek. One such day, they discovered a long dead body—a man, his flesh now gone, only his bones lying amidst his clothing. Waya carefully searched the man's torn and rotting buckskin garments for anything that might identify him. Finding nothing except his rifle with the initials F.A. carved into the stock, they left the bones where they lay. Days later, Waya carried the rifle to the fort, yet no one could identify it. Esther carried away the trade tomahawk found in the man's belt, leaving it hidden in the woods where she often met Waya. In later days, upon Waya's absence, she sometimes practiced throwing it against trees.

In early July, Waya and Joshua left to carry messages to Shelby's Fort and to Evan Shelby's farm, and even farther into settlements in the hills of North Carolina. They stayed away for a bit over two weeks. During their absence, Esther thought constantly of the tall, slender Cherokee man whose face she saw in her daydreams and her nightly visions. Never having known the love of a man, or even experienced a true infatuation, Esther, when alone, mused, rationalized, and even scrutinized her feelings. At seventeen, she remembered her father's words to her when barely thirteen, "Esther, my bairn, ignore your mother's words and ideas about the subject of beaus and marriage. Learn to live and to love before you give your heart and hand to any man."

"Have I learned to love? Have I lived?" Esther questioned herself, and then thought back to the previous three years. In so doing, she understood more deeply her father's serious words. Learning and living had little to do with time, with the passing of days or years. Instead, becoming an adult, learning to truly live and to genuinely love came from experience, the experiences of life. In the almost four short years since their nighttime flight, Esther recognized and recalled every event that had made her a woman. Loss, death, and brutality stood in her past as harsh, savage signposts of her life. Yet other events, other emotions, rose swiftly to be foremost in her thoughts—those of strength, brotherhood, family, affection, fortitude, friendship, and love. She knew these stood as pillars of her heart and soul, of living, of life. These factors created in her a woman, a woman ready to love a man.

Upon the men's return late one evening in mid-July, Joshua and Waya stopped by the cabin on their way to the fort, as Joshua'd brought presents for his sisters. Though Waya waited outside for Joshua, allowing their horses to drink, Esther could not abide missing the chance of seeing him, if only for an instant.

So, as Lovely and Joshua spoke, Esther stepped outside and into Waya's arms. At that moment, Esther Ballinger knew she loved Waya, a Cherokee man, above and beyond all others. Waya had known of his love for the young woman for many, many months, even years, as she had haunted his dreams since that day along the trail when he first beheld her.

Joshua stepped from the cabin to find his sister in Waya's embrace, his sister's head on his Cherokee friend's shoulder. "Come, Waya. Esther, we will return soon."

As they rode, Waya waited for some sort of rebuke from Joshua, yet none came. Only after they had finished their business at the fort and turned back toward the cabin did Joshua speak.

"Waya, I see love between my sister and my brother. Many will not understand. Esther will be shamed. She will be an outcast, if all know of your love. While I have no objections, ye must think on that. I will say no more, brother."

"To love is to burn, to be on fire." Jane Austen

Summer into Autumn, 1779

Esther and Waya first lay together in August. The heat of that day rose quickly and by midday, both knew it to be one of the hottest days of the season. Even under the thick canopy of the forest, the humid, unmoving air was unrelenting with its misery. Soon their bodies required, desired, immediate relief from the sultry conditions of the day. Both knew they could always find respite in a deep green pool on Boone's Creek where it meandered through the forest. Esther, the first to disrobe, left on only her shift as a claim of modesty. From the high bank, she dove into the cool water below as Waya watched. As nakedness was not unseemly among his people, he stripped completely and joined Esther in the waiting coolness.

Esther watched as he shed his clothes. Somewhat shyly, she secretly rejoiced at the sight of his body and his desire. Waya's long, glossy black hair spread about his head as he swam over near her. After splashing each other playfully and swimming about, enjoying relief from the afternoon's searing heat, they playfully tried kissing underwater. Floating and laughing with this new shared experience, they held their bodies against each other, finding passion on a summer's afternoon. Soon they left the pool and lay together on a soft bed of moss and their own scattered clothing. Waya explored Esther's womanhood, and likewise, she his manhood. Esther gave no thought to indecency and sin, only to the pleasure and the sensations of their mating. Their release came together, and each rested before moving once more to touch and enjoy the other. As the day grew late, they reluctantly parted for the evening. Each going their own way.

The late summer's temperatures continued to be oppressive, and the pattern of their days became established. Most every day ended with passion underneath the canopy of the forest, far from the fort and the Ballinger cabin. Esther walked out almost every morning with her basket, which often contained lunch for two. She only returned in the late afternoon—always alone. In his innate understanding of their illicit relationship, politely, Waya began to decline Joshua's invitations to join their evening meal. Despite their guarded behavior toward each other when they met in Joshua's company, her brother soon recognized their new closeness. Joshua said nothing to either his sister or his Cherokee friend. Still, his mind puzzled to find a future that might allow the two to find acceptance.

September came and Waya met Esther in their usual spot, carrying a small package. Though curious as to its contents, Esther's mind stood rooted in pleasure. Stripping from her clothes, she approached Waya with no reluctance, no embarrassment. Without words being shared, they made love, both finding gratification in their coupling there amidst a setting of oaks and hickories, the animals of the forest, and the heat of the early morning. Later, they once more swam in the creek, splashing and playing like children.

As the afternoon grew long, Waya opened the buckskin-wrapped bundle and placed a white wool blanket around Esther's shoulders. "Ni hi ga-no-lv-v-s-gv. Ni hi a-tsi-lv. Ni hi a-ma. Ni hi elo-hi. Waya's a-ge-yv."

"Waya, I only know two of those words in your language," Esther whispered as he pulled her close.

"Esther, you be my wind. You be my fire. You be my water. You be my earth. Waya's woman. Understand?"

"I understand. For Waya is my life. Waya is my future. Waya will always be my man, my lover, holder of my heart, my thoughts, and my devotion."

Waya smiled down at her, gathered her into his embrace, and shared the white blanket until the heat of this traditional garment—and their lust—drove them once more to the softness of the forest floor.

Unwilling to part from Waya, Esther arrived home just after dusk to find Lovely pacing the floor, almost in tears with worry. Once again, Esther saw the child in the young woman's body.

Placing the wrapped blanket upon her bed, she took her sister in her arms. "Hush sister, hush. It being so hot, I bathed in the creek before returning. I lost track of time. Be calm, Lovely, be calm. I'll not worry you again with my lateness."

Though Lovely's periods of silence had lessened to almost none, Esther still saw in her sister the timid child she became in times of strife or stress. Little things like a noise in the night, a late knock at the door, or Esther's late homecoming, would cause shaking, tears, and then silence. Esther wondered, time and time again, to where Lovely's mind wandered when these spells overtook her. It did no good to ask, for silence rarely serves as a suitable answer.

Days passed. Esther, herself, noted changes in her wellbeing. She sometimes found herself singing. Her lovely alto voice rang with songs of her childhood as she carried out her chores and prepared her many herbal teas, salves, and poultices. Her appetite grew, and she craved sunshine and the company of women. She often rode her horse, Athena, into the fort to visit with Esther Doak, or to the Bean's cabin to gossip with Mistress Lydia and her daughters—to learn about their small community's happenings.

During Waya's absence on a mission with Joshua, Esther realized she was happy, blissfully happy. Her terrified dreams came no more, and thoughts of that day at Moore's rarely passed through her mind, even in moments of daydreams and ebbing sleep. Only with this realization did she understand how often she had been lonely, scared, and downhearted since leaving their Virginia home. The young woman now grasped how the grief suffered by them all after Mistress Sarah's death had pulled a pall over her for months.

Sometimes, while alone, her thoughts would wander back over the years since they had run from their uncles. In these thoughts, she came to marvel at their survival. She took pride in their accomplishments in a wilderness full of hardships and peril. Esther recognized within herself a strength, a resiliency strong enough to face any hardship or tasks she might encounter.

On a mid-October early dawn, as the leaves showed off their first range of autumn colors, Esther stood beside a kettle over a fire nearby the cabin when her thoughts ran to Waya. As the wash water heated, she thought back on their first meeting. She recalled the circumstances. Suddenly, the memory focused so clearly it was as if she once again stood beside that small Virginia steam. She saw, as if in a mirror, her reaction to Waya's whispered warning, the look of his clothing, his clean smell. A calm befell her, just as it had that day. As Esther recalled each detail, the reflection awakened within her another memory, for she realized her last moon courses had been in late summer. She had missed at least two cycles. Laying her hand upon her stomach, Esther felt no shame, only intense joy.

"The risk of love is loss, and the price of loss is grief - But the pain of grief is only a shadow when compared with the pain of never risking love."
Hilary Stanton Zunin

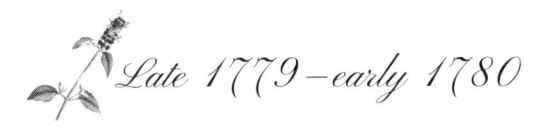

Late 1779 – early 1780

Joshua returned in early November, bringing with him letters from both Samuel and Benjamin.

August 2nd, the year of our Lord, seventeen, seventy-nine

Dear Joshua, Esther, and Lovely,

By now, if you have received any news of the war, you have realized I serve under General Washington. As this letter will be passed from military courier to courier, I feel safe in writing to you of my whereabouts. This year has been a busy one, with the most important battle being that at Stony Point, New York, on July 16th. Led by Brigadier General Mad Anthony Wayne — yes, everyone calls him that — our forces attacked the British outpost there in a daring assault. I must say, the stories of how it was carried out are inspiring. The British took heavy losses.

Elsewhere, skirmishes occur frequently in most of our colonies, even in Georgia, where the British hold almost total control. In South Carolina, Francis Marion and his followers constantly attack British troops and supply shipments. Many now call him the Swamp Fox, for that is where he hides after his wily raids and assaults.

As for myself, my health is good despite our still- poor rations. My days are long, but our men value my skills. I serve under a powerful, intelligent man, whom I come to admire more each week.

I have not heard from Samuel recently. I hope he is well and stays safe. Joshua, you know I expect you to care for our sisters. At some point, this war will most likely come south, and I expect you will want to fight. Consider how desperate our sisters will be without your protection when you are faced with such decisions. If you must fight, do so knowing my prayers are with you and your commitment to our family and our cause.

I hope to be with you all soon, as surely this war will end. Take care of each other,

Your loving brother,
Captain Benjamin Ballinger

After finishing Benjamin's letter, all three siblings, eager to read Samuel's letter, reached for it. Lovely's hand reached it first. With a bit of giggling, she held it over her head and dared the others to grab it. Esther tried but failed before Joshua, much taller than his youngest sister, smirking, took it from her grasp and handed it to Esther.

After the joy of hearing from Benjamin and recognizing his rank for the first time, Esther began reading, expecting more cheerful news.

26 September, the year seventeen seventy-nine

My dearest sisters and brother,

I was wounded in late August. I will not say more at this time. My health is currently suspect. I am now returning to our home to recover, as I am unfit to continue with my unit. I will stay in one of the cabins on our land and strive to regain my strength. Our tenants have proved a wise hire, and I know I will find shelter and safety there. I hope in the coming months to join you.

Until then, with love,
Samuel

After Esther read, she walked back and forth across the small cabin, deep in thought. Lovely stood silently and then reached to reread the letter. Joshua sat, head in hands at their table, quiet and solemn.

"Joshua, I should go. I *must* go to Samuel. Will you take me? Shall we prepare to stay in Virginia? I know Lovely does not want to return. Still, I am needed. Perhaps we might leave as early as tomorrow, or at least by the day after?"

Raising his head from his hands, Joshua sharply retorted, "No, Esther, there be further news. Travel from here to our home would be extremely foolish and difficult. The local militia, as well as British forces, patrol the roads, and many travelers find themselves trapped in skirmishes between the two. All over North Carolina and Virginia, Tories and Whigs fight, neighbor versus neighbor. Chickamauga Cherokee and Shawnee attack almost daily along the backcountry trails and far into North and South Carolina. I be with the militia. I am needed here and must serve out my enlistment. We can't just pack up and go home. Winter be upon us. Besides, ye cannot travel in yer delicate condition. You cannot ride a horse all day and sleep on the cold ground."

"What do you mean? My condition?"

"Sister, I can tell ye carry a child. I have suspected since late September. Lovely suspects as well."

"Lovely knows? But how? She is only a child," Esther replied, ignoring the girl now standing, listening, only a few feet away.

"She is fifteen. She be more observant than ye care to notice. Besides, she be often with the Bean families. They multiply like rabbits. Ask her yourself and stop treating her like a child. She needs to be consulted and treated like she is an adult."

"I am an adult," Lovely whispered.

Ignoring Joshua's harsh words, Esther continued to pace before suddenly turning back to her brother. "Does Waya know? Did you tell him?" Esther whispered.

"No, sister. That be yer news to share. I suspected Waya be the father, as I have known since David's wedding of his feelings for ye."

Noticing the tension between her siblings, Lovely grabbed a heavy shawl and stepped toward the door. "I might just go gather the eggs and feed the hens. Joshua, should I unsaddle your horse and brush him down?"

"Yea, go on if you wish. I be out in a while to help ye."

Pacing back and forth across the small cabin, Esther whispered, somewhat afraid of the answer, "Oh, Joshua, where is Waya? Why did he not return with you? I hoped and prayed he would return soon. He does not know of our child."

"Colonel Russell of the Virginia militia sent him to his Cherokee village with a message. I don't expect we'll see him until late December, if even then."

Esther, sitting upon her bed, silently wept. She wept for Samuel. She wept for wanting of Waya. Yet, she did not weep for herself, for she felt only joy for the baby she carried. Waya's child. Without speaking, Joshua gathered his sister into his long, capable arms. "Sister, I be always with you."

Later, there in that little cabin on Boone's Creek, alone except for each other, the three schemed and talked. Joshua and Esther wrote to Benjamin of Samuel's condition and whereabouts. They did not dare write about Esther being with child. Lovely, readily agreed to spend more time at their cabin and to take over some of Esther's chores. All this, her older brother and younger sister discussed while Esther paced back and forth, worried over Waya's absence and, even more so, of Samuel's injury.

An hour or so later, tired of watching Esther pace the small cabin, Joshua forced her to sit at the table and handed her a cup of warm spiced cider. Sitting, Esther released the tension in her shoulders and, after several minutes, asked, "Joshua, what shall I do? I love Waya. For the sake of this child I carry, will the Reverend Doak marry us? I shall go tomorrow and speak with Esther Doak. She'll be the best to advise me."

"Esther, I consider Waya my brother. For he be closer to me than Benjamin and Samuel. He is a good man, and he loves you. I know in my heart, the good Reverend would be willing to marry ye in a legal ceremony. Still, he cannot, for such a marriage would nay be legal nor recognized by most. Esther, ye would become an outcast. I doubt ye'd be asked to care for anyone once talk begins of yer condition. Let us three think on this and try to keep your secret until Waya returns," advised Joshua, trying to ease his sister's worries. "Esther, one other thought. Waya may be hung for rape if it be known he be the child's father. You must keep this secret."

"I cannot even tell Esther Doak?"

"Best not," Joshua whispered. "Let us ponder on it awhile first."

"I don't care what others see as proper. As I see it, many on the frontier have only common law marriages. Mistress Lydia once told me the Bean family believes in the Scottish practice of handfasting," Esther thought aloud.

Neither Lovely nor Joshua responded to her mutterings.

After a few moments, Esther stated firmly, "I shall have to get along as best I can, brother, for I know my heart. Lovely, let us finish those corn cakes. Perhaps you might cut off a bit of that ham Lydia sent. I find myself quite peckish."

Putting Esther's condition aside, the siblings worried over the news from each brother. Esther worried about Benjamin's lack of food and his being so close to the war. All three harbored a deep concern for Samuel. Was he alone? How bad was his injury? Had he any medical treatment? Could he care for himself?

A deep pall fell over the cabin. Worries on so many concerns, issues they could not affect due to distance, clouded the mind of each. As dusk fell, so did silence. Lovely turned in first, after quietly taking to her knees in prayer.

Joshua tended the fire and nighttime chores. Esther prepared for the morning meal. At last, she whispered a good night and kissed Joshua upon the cheek, before taking the white blanket from its buckskin wrapping and placing it across her bed.

Understanding its significance, Joshua's heart filled with hope while his brain fretted over Esther's love and devotion for his Cherokee friend. Knowing, they had little chance of happiness together.

The Ballinger siblings slipped again into a monotonous routine of daily chores and the harder job of keeping a monumental secret. As autumn turned to winter, a miserably cold winter set in. Esther carried on with her tasks and chores much as she had always done, except she rarely ventured into the woods and never alone. Hiding her growing babe under loose clothing, she struggled to keep her secret throughout infrequent but necessary visits to the fort.

Lovely began, in secret, to sew clothing for the baby. She wove several small blankets on a small loom Jesse Bean had constructed for her and tore old cloth into clouts. Still, Waya did not return.

Unlike previous years of mild autumn weather continuing well into November, that year, in late October, the cold of winter set in early. As the days grew shorter, winter enveloped them all in a shroud of freezing temperatures, sleet, freezing rain, and then snow. Even Woody, who had taken to sleeping on their doorstep some time before, begged to enter the cabin and would often lie upon the hearth until shooed away. When the cold did not relent, Joshua and Jesse shored up their lean-to, giving their horses more protection from the biting wind and severe temperatures.

For weeks on end, Esther and Lovely wore most of their clothing, layer upon layer. By December they had taken to sleeping together. They hung deer skins, the few they had, against the cabin's wall beside Lovely's bed, it being wider than Esther's. Here they could often be found, even in daylight, seeking warmth. Occasionally, Woody joined them and neither girl made him leave the bed.

Joshua worked to store up additional firewood and kindling, filled the few cracks in the cabin's chinking, and, when absent, made sure someone from the Bean settlement or the militia would ride by and check in with his sisters.

Within the Watauga community, more frequently than ever before, families existed without their menfolk. Men like Robert Bean had long ago joined the North Carolina militia and rarely returned home. Most all on the frontier still had extended family — parents, brothers and sisters, aunts and uncles, cousins — who yet lived east of the mountains. With no access to recent news and scarce few letters among those who could read and write, worry over loved ones in the line of battle dampened spirits and inhabited prayers for their safety.

Sometimes, it seemed Samuel Doak's prayers continued for longer than his sermons.

As it had been for several years, the same situation existed within the Ballinger cabin. Their lack of news from Samuel and Benjamin kept them anxious and fretful. Additionally, recent news of a battle in Virginia kept them worried over friends near their old Virginia home. Each one's evening prayers included a plea for blessings and safety for men such as Robert Bean, George Russell, Isaac Shelby, John Sevier, and others from their community who served. Jesse Bean had recently been appointed a lieutenant with a small party of sharpshooters. Now he roamed far and wide in search of Chickamauga raiding parties.

The three siblings kept a quiet Christmas. Pastor Doak held a Christmas eve service at the fort, attended by all three. No one could have possibly noticed Esther's condition, for everyone arrived wrapped in many layers of clothing and stayed that way throughout, for the small church was unheated. Hands clasped within a fur muff, Esther prayed for Waya, for Samuel, and for Benjamin, amongst many others.

Once again bundled up against heavily falling snow, Lovely and Joshua left their cabin to attend the New Year's Day festivities without Esther, telling all who asked that she felt ill. Several days later, David and Betsy Ann stopped by with little Sarah and their new son, David, and the cabin knew a day of happiness with old friends. They ate and laughed at the antics of the couple's two small children. If either noticed Esther's condition, they did not comment. Secretly, Joshua had asked David to keep Esther's secret.

Jesse Bean stopped by less often, sometimes in search of Joshua. Other times, he showed up with sewing for Lovely, or small gifts of grain, game, or salt pork for their pot, lengths of yarn, and once a length of soft cotton cloth he had purchased at the sutler's shop for Lovely. Everyone at the fort knew he was sweet on the girl and suspected he had purchased the gift for her. If any of their friends noticed anything amiss with the Ballinger siblings, they kept it to themselves.

Waya did not return, nor did any news of his whereabouts come their way. Only in quiet, peaceful times of rest did Esther fret over his absence. Most times found her simply expecting and awaiting his imminent arrival. Those periods of worry increased after she felt the baby move, growing ever stronger with his kicks. Within her own thoughts, Esther became convinced she carried a boy.

Throughout January, the unnatural cold continued. Creeks, and then rivers, froze solid. Thick drapes of solid ice hung heavily from trees until branches broke and fell, shattering upon the deeply frozen ground beneath. At times, the sound of falling limbs, and even entire trees, echoed like rifle shots throughout the hills and hollows. At night, the sounds of winter's distress and destruction disturbed their sleep and held them in constant wakefulness and watchfulness.

In early February, another, even heavier, snow covered the surrounding landscape. Trees hung with layer upon layer of white, frozen curtains, icy and opaque. Upon the earth, the upper crusty layer of snow froze into a sharply defined vista. This inclement weather prevented Esther and Lovely from leaving the cabin except to care for their animals and to bring in firewood and water. Many mornings, they had to shovel a path before they could leave the cabin. With Boone's Creek frozen solid, and access to the spring buried, the girls boiled snow for themselves and their animals, when Joshua was not around to break the stream's ice and carry it indoors to melt.

Joshua found their calf frozen to the ground, icebound in death. Their chickens now roosted in a partition off the lean-to. Still, they lost over half their flock. Joshua reported seeing frigid, frost-covered turkeys and other birds lying in the snow, where they had fallen from trees. Large and small game became extremely scarce. Their meals were often corn cakes and salt pork, or a small slice of the ham Lydia had sent at Christmas.

The girls read to each other, caught up on their sewing and household chores. Esther wrote letters for Joshua to carry away on his next journey. For hours at a time, the cabin stood quiet as neither spoke. They turned to reading, once again, the few books they possessed, often while bundled into Lovely's bed.

After his few brief trips outside each day, Woody returned with frozen fur and ice between his paw pads. Trying to help, Lovely sewed four little fur slippers for him, made of rabbit hide. Her first attempt at placing them on his near-to-frozen paws had Esther in stitches as she sat watching the spectacle. For as soon as one was in place and tied securely, Lovely would move on to the next while Woody pulled on the ties of the first and deftly removed the slipper. Soon, at Lovely's insistence, Esther held Woody, coaxing him to lie still while his shoemaker placed all four on his feet and tied them with strong knots.

Upon releasing the large dog, Woody began a torrent of loud obnoxious barking and bounced around the small cabin in a raucous dance while trying to shake loose what he obviously considered odious foot coverings. After Woody had knocked over two stools, the musket, a basket of kindling, and upset the table, he blundered toward the fire. Luckily, Lovely tackled him and coaxed him to lie down while Esther removed the slippers. Hours later, one or the other sister would break out in giggles just thinking of Woody's dance.

Despite the cold, Joshua's travels continued. He often rode alone, but sometimes with another militiaman. Often it was Michael, who had rejoined the militia. Arriving home from one such trip to Shelby's Fort, Joshua carried news sheets and a letter. As the letter was addressed only to him, he'd opened it soon after Shelby's agent placed it in his hand.

Upon their return, he sent Michael home and stopped at their cabin before bringing the messages and letters he carried on to the fort.

Delaying, Joshua removed his frozen clothing and warmed his hands and feet before the fire. Lovely presented him with a hot cup of spiced cider and a warmed corn muffin. Finally, Joshua pulled the opened letter from his pouch and settled his sisters into listening. Then he reluctantly reread the missive.

20 October, the year of our Lord seventeen seventy-nine

Mr. Joshua Ball,

I regret to inform you of your brother Samuel's passing on 15 October. He had returned from the militia with a serious wound to his upper thigh, which became putrid. Samuel had planned to return to your old plantation. Instead, we kept him here after he stopped to rest upon his return journey. He was possessed of a high fever for several days. We sat with him day and night and plied him with food and such medicines as we could obtain. He spoke of you and his sisters. Near the end, he relayed to us your whereabouts and how to direct this letter.

Please know, we buried Samuel in your family's small cemetery next to your father and siblings. It was a quiet, private ceremony with just our immediate family and your tenants in attendance.

I have posted a letter to Benjamin. Alice and I deeply mourn Samuel's passing, as does our daughter, Felicity. Knowing Samuel as we had come to do, he most likely failed to mention the circumstance of their relationship, as they had become sweethearts during his previous stay. Felicity remains broken-hearted, for she loved him dearly. She sat with him continuously during his last days.

Sincerely, in deepest sympathy for your loss,
George Elliott, Esquire

After reading the letter aloud, Joshua swept his sisters into his arms and held each one tight, afraid to let go of even one for fear they too might slip from his grasp. Much to his surprise, Lovely soon quieted her sobs and set about making the evening meal.

On the other hand, Esther paced the small cabin, angrily shouting at her brother for not taking her to their Virginia home after they'd received Samuel's last letter. Having rarely heard Esther raise her voice in anger, Joshua took her, once again, into his arms and held her tight against his chest. Then Joshua recited to her the dates of Samuel's last letter and George Elliott's letter of his passing.

"Esther, Samuel had most likely passed by the time we received his letter about his wound. Ye be not to blame, and neither be I, nor Benjamin, nor Lovely. Some Tory devil killed our brother. Now, we will mourn, and we will remember."

Taking each to himself, he pulled them in close and whispered. "I be home before dark. Here be some news sheets. Esther, sit and read to Lovely as she prepares our meal. We will speak of Samuel when I return."

Among the news Esther read, one small article captured her fancy, taking her thoughts away from Waya and the death of her brother, at least for the time being. So, she read aloud.

Our Continental Navy's Loss of the Bonhomme Richard

Earlier this year, Scottish-born patriot and naval captain John Paul Jones began making a name for himself in support of our cause. Our infamous Captain Jones, commanding the USS *Ranger*, successfully captured the HMS *Drake*. In the North Channel between Ireland and Scotland, this naval battle of wits announced our naval presence and our patriot cause to the world.

A seasoned captain, Jones was afterward placed in command of sailing the converted French merchant ship, *Duc de Duras*, given to our Continental Navy by our French allies. Jones promptly renamed it the USS *Bonhomme Richard* after Benjamin Franklin's pen name, *Poor Richard*. He sailed forth from Lorient in France toward eastern England on the fourteenth of August in the previous year with three members of our own fleet, the *Pallas*, the *Vengeance*, and the *Alliance*.

On the twenty-third of September, off the coast of Yorkshire, England, at Flamborough Head, our small fleet encountered a group of forty British merchant ships under escort of the HMS *Serapis* and the HMS *Countess of Scarborough*. Captain Jones maneuvered his ships behind the convoy.

Immediately, the various crews began preparing to fight. Cannons were loaded with double shot and grapeshot. Captain Jones ordered the *Pallas* to ride in his wake to deceive the British of their numbers.

In the evening's dusk, the HMS *Serapis* hailed the USS *Bonhomme Richard*. Captain Richard Pearson shouted, 'What ship is that?' Captain Jones replied, 'I can't hear you!' Pearson then demanded, 'What ship is that? Answer at once, or I shall be under the necessity of firing into you.'

A battle of wits ensued and as Jones yet refused to reply, tempers flared, and the two ships fired at almost the exact same instance. Direct hits on both ships' facades resulted in holes and splintered wood. The Battle of Flamborough Head had begun."

As Esther read, Lovely finished making the meal and poured cider for them both. Taking seats across from each other, Esther moved their one lantern, a seldom-used luxury, closer and continued to read.

Four hours passed as the two ship's crews fought a bloody and deadly battle. As the sea began to show streaks of red, on-shore spectators watched in horror as the *Bonhomme Richard* ripped the *Serapis* apart with blast after blast. Considered a pirate by many of our English enemies, Jones' attack seemed to prove himself to be a savage and terrifying foe. It is reported, by members of his crew, how Jones took control of a nine-pound cannon on the deck of the *Bonhomme Richard*, while continuing to shout orders and rally his crew to the battle.

Amidst hand-to-hand combat and small arms fire, the Americans proved both deadly and accurate as the

Bonhomme Richard stood taller than the *Serapis*. The battle still raged on until half past the eighth hour of the evening, when suddenly the USS *Alliance* fired shots directly into both the *Bonhomme Richard* and the *Serapis*.

Alas! Fired upon by his own fleet! Captain Jones called for the *Alliance* to cease fire. Only later did he learn the ship's name, and that the *Alliance's* captain had hoped to sink the *Bonhomme Richard* and steal the glory of sinking the *Serapis*.

As both nations' ships began to burn and sink, *Serapis's* master-at-arms, believing Jones was wounded and not seeing their flag, shouted that the Bonhomme Richard had struck their colors. This being the accepted naval sign for surrendering. The British officers shouted toward the *Bonhomme Richard*, asking if they surrendered. According to his own sailors aboard the *Bonhomme Richard*, Captain Jones said in reply, 'I may sink, but I'll be damned if I strike. I have not yet begun to fight!'

Instantly upon hearing those words, American sailors threw a grenade across the now blood-red water and onto the *Serapis*. In a chain reaction, the *Serapis's* gunpowder storage ignited and exploded. Immediately, the *Alliance* fired another barrage at the *Bonhomme Richard*. Captain Jones ordered the release of the brig's prisoners and implored them to help save the ship, and in so doing, their own lives.

At nigh on half past ten, Captain Pearson surrendered the HMS *Serapis*. His crew had suffered some one hundred and seventeen casualties. As Captain Pearson climbed aboard the *Bonhomme Richard*, and holding forth his sword, he reported to our daring Captain Jones, with the words, 'It is with the greatest reluctance that I am now obliged to resign this, for it is painful to me, more particularly at this time, when compelled to deliver up my sword to a man who may be said to fight with a halter around his neck!'

Despite Captain Jones' heroic actions and masterful command, the *Bonhomme Richard* sank. American casualties numbered some one hundred and seventy. Jones captured two enemy ships and sank one. He yet lives to command another ship. *Hurrah! Hurrah!*"

In the following days, the Ballinger siblings grieved, each in their own way. Never one to sit idle, Esther kept busy, as did Joshua, who often spoke of Samuel and how brave he had been. Esther found solace in remembering the caring brother who had sheltered two girls from harm and led them off into the wilderness on a dangerous journey in search of safety. She shared with Joshua more tales of their journey and Samuel's attempts at keeping the girls safe and happy.

Lovely insisted upon speaking of Samuel as if he still lived and was simply absent from their everyday lives, as he had been for the last year or so. Not understanding how to deal with Lovely's version of grief, the older two quietly allowed her to be. Esther wrote to Benjamin about Lovely's talk of Samuel, knowing it could be months before she might receive any reply.

"Death leaves a heartache no one can heal, love leaves a memory no one can steal." From a headstone in Ireland

Spring 1780

After the harshness of the previous winter, March came in mildly, bringing with it a promise of an early spring. Lydia Bean came to call on one of those beautiful early days, one bringing forth gay moods and a promise of good fortune. Riding her small gray mare and carrying gifts, she approached the Ballinger cabin, calling out as she drew near, "Hail, the Ball cabin."

"Mistress Lydia, please do come in," sang out Lovely, having rushed to the door upon hearing Lydia's voice. "We've not had visitors in such a long while."

Across the room, Esther watched all this as she sat reading, her hand resting on her now obviously expectant stomach. Esther reached for a blanket to cover herself, but Lydia's quiet, motherly tone halted her movement.

"No need, Esther. I know, and I bring news," Lydia announced to the young women she now knew so well.

"Lovely, I brought some mulled cider. Ye'll find it in a jug tied to my saddle. Perhaps ye might fetch it and warm some for us?" Lydia requested, unpinning her wool cape and removing her traveling bonnet. Esther saw her flinch with pain during the tasks, for her shoulder had never healed completely after her injuries. Esther reminded herself to offer Mistress Lydia some ointment before her departure that might relieve the pain.

Lydia, a rounded woman of average height, a mother of seven, wore a soft white lace-trimmed cap over her dark brown hair, now lightly streaked with gray, and a plain gray wool dress with a lovely white collar. Esther recognized it as Lovely's hand work. Having the previous year attended Lydia's birthday celebration, Esther knew her to be fifty-six years of age.

"Yes, Mistress Lydia, please be seated," Lovely offered, still smiling at Lydia's coming, as she busied herself with the chore.

"How be ye, Esther?"

"I am well, Mistress Lydia. How is your family faring this winter?"

"Oh, my men be off and about hunting, trapping, and such. As you know, Robert be in the East with the militia, while Jesse roams here about, keeping the Chickamauga at bay. William rarely remains at home most weeks. My youngest, Russell, be learning to hunt with George when he is about. Lovely, you'll be glad to hear that Sarah has taken to the small loom and makes lively patterns. She might never be as skilled as Jane, still, my youngest girl tries so hard."

Lovely handed them each a tin cup of warm cider before Esther finally asked, "Mistress Lydia, this smells lovely. You said you come with news."

"Yes, my dearest Esther. I bring news of Waya," Lydia answered quietly.

Shocked to hear his name from Lydia's lips, Esther gasped, "Oh, hurry, please tell me, I have waited so, so long."

For a moment, Lydia sat sipping her cider and watching Esther's countenance. There, upon the young woman's face, she found hope, anxiousness, and worry. Esther remained seated. Moving her hand to her stomach, she leaned in toward Lydia, urging with her movements for her friend to continue.

"Now, child, pray don't interrupt, for my story be a long one. Let me bare to you all I know, for I know most, if not all, of what befell you and Wolf, as we called him," Lydia answered as she took Esther's hands in hers and began her story.

"We had a visitor. My friend, Nancy Ward, came last week and stayed two nights with us. She and her husband had journeyed through deep snow and across frozen rivers to bring me the news. As in our own settlement, among the Cherokee they hold great respect for family and the needs of such. Nancy taught me to see the Cherokee as people who live, love, and work for their families, much as we do. During those days at her home, we taught each other to trust. Nancy traveled so far in winter to bring us word of Wolf, for she is his family, just as you are. She dared not come to ye as she did not know if ye would welcome her. I assured her ye would open your door to her, and urged her to come herself, yet she asked that I come with her news."

Seeing Esther's bewildered face, Lydia rushed into the message.

"Nancy relayed how, some time ago, as the trees turned colors, Wolf came to her and his people with messages from our militia. Those words between her people and our militia concern us none at all, and not be the purpose of my visit. Nancy told me about how, some weeks after Wolf returned to his village, after winter had begun, he journeyed south into the mountains, despite the deepening snow and cold, with several men of his family. They planned to bring back deer meat, and, if possible, elk, to the village as supplies were running low. Like us hereabouts, the Overhill Cherokee have suffered from the lack of game.

"Now, my dear Esther, comes the hardest part to tell. Only one of their party of five returned, the youngest—a cousin to Wolf—who was made to hide by Wolf, during an attack upon their camp by Chickamauga Cherokee warriors. After pushing the boy into heavy brush, Waya turned back to the battle. The boy watched as Wolf and the others fought. He told how they fought bravely against superior numbers. None was spared. The boy watched as his uncles and cousins' bodies were mutilated. Hours later, when he believed it to be safe, he covered their bodies with rocks and then wandered for weeks trying to return to his village. He traveled alone. He had no rifle, no horse, and no warm covering except what he wore and a buffalo skin. He had only his bow and arrow. Even now, Nancy says he is still not well in mind or body."

Seeing the anguish in Esther's face, as tears pooled, Lydia took the young woman into her arms. "Esther, when Wolf first returned to his people, he told his aunt of his marriage to you and his suspicion you were with child. Nancy said he told of his great happiness, and his pride in his beautiful bride. He openly declared his love among their village. Some of his people showed him anger at his choice of bride, but never once, she relayed, did Wolf back down. She said he expressed his love for you over and over again.

"Wolf had made plans to return to you when he was asked to join the hunting party. As a warrior, he understood his obligation to his family and his people, and so he put off his return. I am so sorry to be the one to bring you this news," Lydia finished, her voice breaking, her tears now flowing from eyes saddened by her friend's loss.

So many thoughts and feelings ran amok in Esther's mind. Unable yet to express in words her grief, nor to question Lydia for additional details, still one particular element of the story worried her more than the others. "But Mistress Lydia, Waya said we married? We were never married."

"'Twas his belief you two be married. Did Wolf wrap you in a white blanket, like that one, laying upon your bed? Did he claim you as his woman?" Lydia questioned.

"Yes, in the forest near Boone's Creek. Waya placed the blanket around my shoulders and said many words in Cherokee, and then repeated them to me in English, as I had understood so few. Waya told me the Cherokee words meant I was his wind, his fire, his water, and his earth. He said I was *his woman*."

"Esther, I learned from Nancy many Cherokee customs during my time recovering at her cabin. As I understand it, when a Cherokee man wishes to take a wife, he wraps his desired bride in a white blanket or a very pale doeskin and says such words. If she wishes to refuse her suitor, she simply hands the blanket back and walks away. If she agrees, she walks into his arms. That white blanket symbolizes their union. In Wolf's eyes, you were married."

Relief flooded Esther's thoughts, followed sharply by grief. Gripped within her heartbreak, she shook with sobs. Tears flowed from all three women, each dealing with despair and mourning in her own way. In her young mind, Lovely, ever the romantic, saw this as a beautiful fable of love and loss.

Older, and experienced in the ways of their society, Lydia Bean saw a difficult future for a young woman she much admired for her education, her skill, her caring nature, and her devotion to her siblings. She also realized while Esther had loved and been loved, she had also married and was now widowed. Like so many frontier women, Wolf's death left Esther with a child to raise alone. So, Lydia waited, holding back for now the words of advice, words to ease Esther's way.

Minutes later, through her tears, Esther haltingly spoke, posing the question Lydia had come to answer. "Mistress Lydia, what will become of me and this child . . . Waya's child?"

"Esther, Lovely, I came now, not only with this heartbreaking news, but with a plan."

As was her usual way of handling difficult situations, Esther took to the puncheon floor and began pacing. All around, back and forth, she walked, one hand massaging her stomach, the other wadding and unwadding a strip of cloth she used as a handkerchief.

"Mistress Lydia, what plan can you have that will make my situation acceptable by the people of Watauga? I cannot claim to be married to Waya. Joshua and I have discussed how our community would not accept such an arrangement."

"I understand. I also know what will happen when your condition or the birth of a bairn becomes known. You cannot claim to have been married to Wolf, as these God-fearing Christian people will not accept a Cherokee marriage or a religious marriage between a white woman and a Cherokee man, or even a relationship between the two.

"No, instead, we must let it be known that you married a man of the Virginia militia that has been secretly visiting you for the last two years. We can tell how you met him during your time at Moore's. We can spread gossip about Watauga, telling how he often arrived with Joshua and kept to your cabin during his visits, for he desired to keep such visits a secret as some might recognize his family name and report his presence to Tories within our community. William and I plan to tell everyone how this man cannot marry you outright in the eyes of the Lord before the Reverend Doak, for he would lose his inheritance. Instead, he must wait until this bloody revolution comes to a close, bringing with it our freedom. Then he may claim the land his Tory parents hold. If word of his marriage, without his father's consent, came to be known, his father has sworn to cut all ties and give the land to a cousin. We will tell how his father only continues to leave the status of the inheritance as is, because he is of the firm belief that the revolution will fail, or his son will recognize this war as foolishness. William and me believe this story 'twill be accepted if we be the ones spreading it."

"Mistress Lydia, constructed you alone this entire tall tale?" Lovely asked, amazed at the thoughtfulness of Lydia's solution.

"No, William and me discussed it with our boys, well just Jesse and William, as we will need their help to spread and verify the story. Jesse is known to visit your cabin often and will tell of meeting the young man and witnessing the ceremony before a Justice of the Peace—in this case, my William."

"So, now, I must pretend to be happily married to some unknown man and that this baby is his. Might I not just instead be married to some unknown man who is now dead, and then I can grieve for Waya? I can keep to myself. Why must I hold forth this charade?" Shaking with both anger and grief, Esther drew the Cherokee wedding blanket about herself and hurried from the cabin.

"Shall I go after her?" Lovely whispered, anxious with her worry.

"No, your sister needs this time alone to deal with her grief. She has much to dwell on. It be a milder day than most this winter. In her own time, she will return."

As Lydia and Lovely sat quietly, sipping their now-cooled cider, Esther walked about. Sometimes, she wailed loudly against all the world. At other times, she sobbed almost silently. Mostly, she tried to understand Waya's absence in the world, and in so doing, she realized he had been absent from her dreams for well over a month. As the day drew to a close, a sharp wind arose. Clutching Waya's blanket for warmth, Esther resolutely returned to their small cabin.

"Mistress Lydia, might you stay the night?" Esther asked upon entrance. "I believe the weather is turning."

"I came prepared to do just so. Seems we will have yet another snow before the morning. May I put my mare in yer lean-to?"

And so, three women prepared the evening meal, speaking little, and when they did, in hushed tones. Esther, quiet, a bit withdrawn, ate little, and then took to her bed. Lovely shared hers with Lydia, just as she shared with Jane while visiting the Bean family. For two days, the snow fell, wet and heavy. At its end, over two feet lay against the cabin walls. As the snow fell, Lydia and Lovely cared for the animals, carried water and firewood, cooked, and played checkers on a homemade board that once belonged to Mistress Sarah. Esther mostly slept. On the third morning, Lydia and Lovely awoke to find Esther carrying in firewood and adding small logs to the already blazing hearth fire.

"Be ye cold?" Lydia asked, worrying over Esther. "Might I find you a warmer shawl?"

"No, I wanted to boil water and use the last of our tea, a gift from Evan Shelby. I have some stinging nettles to add to yours. It will relieve the pain in your shoulder. I'll make up some for you to carry home," Esther replied. "Then I thought we might talk of my babe."

So, over steaming cups of tea sweentened with honey and griddle cakes flavored with pumpkin, Esther, Lovely, and Lydia completed the details of Esther's story. First, they would explain her most recent absences from society as a difficult early pregnancy. This would be whispered to, and then spread among, the wives of the fort, knowing all would repeat the story to their menfolk and their friends. William Bean, senior and junior, along with Jesse, would quietly spread the word of the marriage Jesse had witnessed at the Ball cabin back in the previous year's spring. As all three served as respected officers in the militia, their words would be accepted as truth.

Jesse planned to spread about how the ceremony had been conducted by his father, William, a Justice of the Peace. The only thing missing from their story's details would be the name of the young man who had claimed Esther as his bride. Details such as a promised inheritance, Tory parents, and him being in the Virginia militia would be let slip by first one, and then another, of them. Giving the gossip time to circulate and to be embellished with more fictitious details would be essential for its success. Also, someone had to waylay Joshua upon his return should he go first to the fort instead of stopping by the cabin, as was sometimes his custom.

In Lydia's concept of the story, only those seven of the community were to know the truth. Joshua would be number eight. Jane would not be party to the rumor's creation, as Lovely knew her friend could not keep a secret. William Jr. had agreed not to tell his own wife.

"One other person must know this story is a lie," announced Esther, "for I must tell Esther Doak. If I do not, I fear I will lose my friend for want of keeping such a secret."

"Can you command Mistress Doak's silence so that she'll not share the truth with the good Reverend?" Lydia asked hesitantly.

"Yes." No doubt entered her mind that Esther Doak might reveal the true story of her babe's father.

Before she left the cabin on the fourth morning, Lydia presented Esther with a lovely white linen cap. "Esther, you be a married woman now in the eyes of all. Here, be a marriage cap to cover yer hair. I be no longer *Mistress Lydia* to ye, only Lydia.

Ye be married, so abide by these customs and more will accept this story."

Unfortunately, Lydia and her menfolk did not have time to complete the deception to their satisfaction before Esther was anxiously called upon for a difficult birth at the fort. Lydia had returned to her home and put all into action only three days before the frantic rider called upon Esther and begged her help.

A bit worried about the expectant mother, whom she had met only once previously, and her acceptance at the fort, Esther rode in with the young father-to-be and carried on as Lydia had instructed. Wearing her new cap, she spoke with the neighbors as she approached the cabin's door. She carried herself with pride and took charge of the situation.

After chasing the girl's own mother out the door on an unnecessary errand, Esther took the expectant mother's small hand in hers and reassured the girl that all would be well. Some twelve hours later, Esther delivered a good-sized baby boy, who took to wailing immediately upon birth. Then, sitting and sharing a cup of warm cider with the new mother, she watched as the boy latched on and suckled. All was well with her world.

Finally, letting the husband and the girl's mother return to the cabin, Esther allowed herself to be led away for food and rest.

Much to her surprise, a friend of the family escorted her to the Doak cabin. "Esther, my dear, might we help you with anything? Anything at all? You must be plum tired out," Mistress Esther Doak asked.

"Oh, I am a bit weary. Perhaps I might stay the night if someone could ride out and stay with Lovely?"

"Dear, dear, now don't you fret. The Reverend Tidence Lane was here at the fort, and he sent his daughter and her brother out many hours ago to check on Lovely, with orders to stay until you returned safe and sound," the Reverend Doak replied. "Rest easy, Esther. We take care of those in our community, especially those who care for others."

Before Esther could express her appreciation, Esther Doak steered her toward their table. "You may take our spare bed for the night. First, I have some sassafras tea and a bit of soup and bread. Please sit. We are so happy to see you out and feeling well," Mistress Doak replied. "That is a lovely cap you wear. Do I detect Lovely's stitches about it?"

As Esther Doak helped Esther prepare for bed, loaning her a nghtgown and bringing her a glass of water, Esther quietly apologized for keeping her condition a secret.

"Tis no need for an apology. I have seen so little of you this winter due to the cold. Still, how did you keep from me this man you married? I would have understood and kept his secret."

"My friend, I wanted, many times, to tell you and now all I can say is someday, someday soon, I hope to tell you all my story. Can you wait?"

"Esther, my friend, how dare you even ask such a thing! For the love of Mary, I hold you as dear as my sisters, even more dear than one of them, for we never became close. Never you fear, never you fear."

So, Esther's story became common knowledge, for one accepted by the Doaks was therefore accepted by everyone. There were questions about her unknown husband, all of which Esther evaded. In the days to come, she spent more time around the fort, checking in on the ill, those in a delicate condition, and the children, for all knew late-winter-early-spring fevers could strike without warning.

Lydia Bean frequently visited their cabin, sometimes bringing Jane and her youngest daughter Sarah. Joshua learned of Esther's marriage *story* a week or so after its inception. He readily adopted this lie but took the news of Waya's death hard. In the days to come, he and Esther discussed it quietly in their few moments alone. Sharing his grief with his sister, being able to talk together of Waya, and relief over a solution to Esther's situation seemed to help them both find solace. The anticipation of Waya's child becoming a part of their family gave them each, in one small way, a bit of comfort.

Esther found that keeping busy left her little time to grieve. She walked with Joshua and Lovely when the weather allowed. She sewed, she read, and at times, she sat in her own silence, seemingly in a world apart from all around her. These times proved to be the hardest—those, and the early hours of the morning before others awoke. In these stolen, silent moments, Esther remembered her days with Waya, together in the forest, the feel of Waya's hand in hers, the laughter in his eyes, and their times lying together beneath the forest canopy. She recalled how Waya was ticklish behind his knees and down the sides of his rib cage. She reminisced. She smiled at memories of days filled only with love, and she shed tears over the story of his torturous death.

Sometimes, as her babe's birth grew nearer, she wondered which of them her baby boy might resemble. In her prayers, she begged he look like Waya.

"A baby is God's opinion that the world should go on." Carl Sandburg

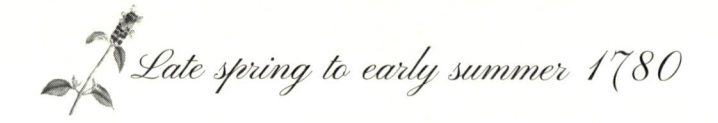

Late spring to early summer 1780

On a visit to the fort, Esther asked the Reverend Doak to remember Waya's family in his prayers. Many at the fort had known and respected the young Cherokee warrior, especially those of the militia. News of his death had passed quickly through the community. Esther explained that Nancy Ward had relayed to Lydia Bean the story of Waya's death. Without asking more, Samuel respectfully asked for prayers for Waya's family the following Sunday.

As the weather warmed, so did talk about Indians in the area. Joshua often found himself pulled here and there to verify rumors of outlying cabins being attacked and families massacred. Too many times, he returned to report the loss of an entire family, a burned-out cabin, and scalps having been taken. In mid-April, Joshua ushered his sisters and Woody to the fort for their protection. Esther and Lovely stayed with the Doaks for three days as Chickamauga Cherokee and Shawnee attacked surrounding cabins and often raided within sight of the fort.

On the first morning after their arrival, Esther called upon Sarah Sevier, John's wife. After having just given birth to their tenth child—a girl they named Nancy—John had loaded Sarah, the new baby, and all his other nine children into a wagon and transported them to Fort Caswell as it was not safe at their home, Plum Grove. Upon entering the small cabin Sarah now shared with six of her younger children, Esther discovered a pale woman, shaking with cold, fear, and exhaustion. She soon discovered the new mother suffered from milk fever.

Sending one of the older children for Mistress Doak, Esther prepared some tea to ease Sarah's misery and help her sleep. Warm compresses on each breast eased her agony. Esther sent another child for additional firewood, and yet another to borrow blankets from other nearby families. Mistress Doak took all the children off to a nearby blockhouse and returned with a woman, unknown to Esther, who had agreed to suckle tiny little Nancy.

Despite Esther's care, Sarah Sevier lasted only one more day before her strength gave out. During that one day, Esther, or Katherine Sherrill, sat at Sarah's side. Bonnie Kate, as all knew her, had been sweet on John Sevier for many a year, and some said he on her. Still, she sat with Sarah, urging her to drink teas and nourishing broths. Esther, being heavy with child herself, deeply felt for Sarah and wondered and worried if she could have done more.

Tears flowed all around for John Sevier's loss, a friend to all, and a greatly respected leader and protector. They wrapped Sarah's body and prepared for burial once it might be safe to journey outside the walls to the burial grounds. Hers proved to be the only death within the fort during the attack.

While Esther sat with Sarah Sevier, Lovely had stayed with the Doaks. The Reverend's wife watched as the girl stopped talking and shook with fear during the raid. The sounds of Chickamauga war cries and rifle shots had sent her scurrying under a bed, where she stayed until all became quiet several days later.

Understanding Joshua's need to be with his sister as the baby's birth approached, Lieutenant Isaac Lane allowed Joshua to take leave from carrying messages and kept him about the Watauga settlement most days. Joshua returned most every evening, relieving Lovely's fears of being unable to care for Esther when the baby arrived. Still stranded within the fort, Lovely helped Mistress Doak carry out many of the chores, leaving for Esther only the easiest tasks.

Often women, and even a few men, stopped by, bringing small gifts such as bread, small articles of clothing for the babe, and once, a small cake filled with pecans and topped with a sweet glaze. Rationed out between them, they savored the cake, as it had been baked with white flour, a rarity at the settlement, and topped with a real sugar glaze.

When called on for a birth or an illness, Esther always found that someone had found her a helpmate before she arrived. That helper stood by, awaiting her commands. Very often, she was told to sit and simply to give instructions to her appointed helper.

In her eighth month, word came by Mistress Lydia telling her the ladies of the community had put their minds together and decided that, unless absolutely necessary, Esther was not to be called to any ailment or injury. Despite the ladies' plan, during April, Esther delivered two baby girls and stitched a hatchet wound in a young boy's leg. For as children will forever be rumbunctious, several young boys playing soldiers and Indians had taken to throwing tomahawks. None too accurately, it seemed. Yet only one had been struck and needed stitches. Esther's quiet soft hands attended to his injury, before the boys, and as it came to be told, one younger girl, received a strong lecture and more than one had a switch applied to their backside.

By late April, the situation had ebbed. Esther and Lovely decided to return to their cabin. Joshua and the Doaks quickly expressed their dismay at such a plan. None could understand Esther's desire to be in her own home when her time was so close, especially as the danger still existed at isolated cabins.

However, Fort Caswell, now filled with many families who had lost their homes to Indian warfare or had recently traveled west to avoid the ongoing conflict in western North Carolina, had become extremely overcrowded. Many a soul slept upon the hard ground of the commons, on firing stations along the fort's wall, or the blockhouse floors. Food and water became scarce. Many could not find shelter, even those with small children and babies. John Sevier, after seeing to Sarah's burial, had packed up his children and ridden for home, escorted by willing friends and militia.

Esther refused to bring her child into this unbearable and aberrant situation. Quietly, she gathered their belongings. After asking David and Jesse to round up their horses, she prepared to return to their cabin.

"And just where do ye think ye might go, Esther Ball?" Joshua snapped.

Continuing to load her horse with the few goods they had carried to the fort, Esther replied, stating firmly, "Home to our clean, quiet cabin. If Lovely wishes to remain with the Doaks, she may do so. However, I'll not give birth to my baby within this overcrowded, stinking cesspool of a fort. It is filled with men who do not bathe, who are unruly, loud, and crass. I dare you to try and stop me. You may be my brother, but you are not my husband, and I shall do as I well please."

"Do you count me as one of those crass, stinking men? Besides, just how do you plan to mount that horse, my dearest sister?" Joshua shouted in anger.

By now, a small crowd had gathered to watch sister and brother argue like cats and dogs. Some even placed bets on who would win the argument.

"I plan to walk and lead Athena home. I have my pistol and my knife. I have Woody. Perhaps you might like to escort me? Though you do smell, I guess I would be willing to have you along."

Some onlookers laughed at her statement and Joshua's stunned look. Others called out, questioning Esther about her plan, as Lovely rushed up and begged her not to leave. It took Samuel Doak to diffuse the situation.

"Now, Esther, perhaps we might speak with Mistress Lydia or my wife to seek a more promising solution?" he ventured.

Resolved to act after being consulted by her husband, Mistress Esther Doak, married some five years now to the good Reverend, took it upon herself to find a solution. However, before Mistress Doak even had time to scheme, disturbing news reached the fort. The militia reported how Chickamauga Cherokee had attacked several of the more distant cabins the previous day.

The fort residents and all those taking refuge now understood how dire the situation had become. Soon more families arrived at the fort, seeking protection. Pulled hither and yon, the Reverend and his wife rushed to help those families get settled. They even took one now-widowed woman, holding a small infant, into their own home. Previously a resident of upland South Carolina, months earlier, the woman had been raped and brutalized by the men under Lt. Colonel Banastre Tarleton. They had slain her husband before her eyes for refusing to take an oath of loyalty to King George. She had journeyed over the mountains with her father and mother, seeking safety. Now, because of raiding Chickamaugas, she was orphaned as well as widowed, for they had slaughtered her parents.

The militia was called out in force and Joshua, along with several others, rode with a small party to warn those in outlying cabins or, if they wished, to escort them to the fort.

Despite the flood of refugees to the fort, Esther Doak found time to send one of the younger Lane boys for Lydia Bean. Between the two women, they found a solution. As Esther, with or without Lovely, could not live alone in a cabin outside the fort's wall and there was no place for them inside, Lydia Bean concluded that their small compound on Boone's Creek was the safest place for the young women. Mistress Doak agreed and arranged for a wagon to go with the sisters to gather their remaining belongings. Several of the fort's men volunteered to ride out and escort them to the Bean settlement.

After several years of occupation, William and Lydia Bean's cabin stood nearby several others of the family. Soon after their arrival to the area, in 1769, William and his sons built the two-story cabin with their protection foremost in mind. As the first settlers in the area, the family understood the need for the additional protection palisade walls might provide. A paling stockade protected the cabin and several outbuildings. It had already withstood several attacks since its construction.

Since 1769, more of the Bean and Russell families had joined William and Lydia on the far frontier. Building close by provided the large family group with help in all manners of life. Along with building the stockade, the family's menfolk all made sure their wives and older daughters were accurate shots. For many times over the years, a shortage of men around the settlement left the women vulnerable to attack.

Lydia arrived at the Ball cabin not long before the wagon. She helped them pack up their belongings and directed the menfolk in loading the wagon and gathering up their livestock. Patiently, their escort helped Esther and Lovely into the wagon. Lovely found it all to be a grand adventure. For a few hours, Esther realized her sister's anxiety had eased.

So, once again, the siblings moved. Esther looked back longingly at the place where she had spent so much time with Sarah, with their friends, and with Waya. Two days later, William Bean reported how, that very night, the Ball cabin fell under attack and was torched. By the following morning, nothing remained but smoldering timbers.

On the first day of May, Esther fussed about their small upper story room in the Bean cabin. The room held three single beds built along the walls under sloping eaves. Jane still occupied one, although Sarah had moved over to the matching room on the other side of the loft. One had always been the girls' room, with the younger boys taking the other.

Moving about while placing preparations for the baby here and there, Esther tried to remember not to bump her head on the ceiling. Worrying once more over every small arrangement she had previously made, Esther wished aloud several times she had the cradle of her childhood in which to place her own babe. In its absence, she had prepared a soft bed in a slatted wood box beside her own bed. Cushioned with a piece of soft doeskin as a base, a folded wool blanket that had been one of Mistress Sarah's lay next. These were topped by a light-yellow blanket, the thread dyed with yarrow and woven by Lovely. Esther felt the bed would suffice. A nearby basket contained folded clouts and small gowns, some lovingly stitched by her sister or herself, while others were gifts from residents of the fort.

Meanwhile, the visiting Mistress Doak helped Lovely wash their few bed linens and blankets from their cabin. During the daylight hours, Esther Doak tended to her charges like a mother despite being herself only four years older than Esther, and not yet a mother.

As the sun dropped that evening, the ladies, now friends all, gathered by the Bean's fire, and Mistress Doak revealed a new side of herself by pulling from her tote a lovely little leather-bound book. She read to the sisters and the Bean womenfolk from *The Life and Adventures of Sir Launcelot Greaves* by Tobias Smollett — a book she much enjoyed, hoping its comic events would enliven the evening.

As the darkness deepened, the gathering of women laughed over and chatted about the stories in the book. Esther Ballinger sat contented, safe, surrounded by friends.

While William prepared to escort Mistress Doak back to the fort the following morning, she whispered to her friend Lydia, "I fear it will be soon. Yesterday, she went about like an old cat preparing for a litter of kittens. I have seen my sisters do the same. Send for me if needed."

Charlotte Bean, Lydia's sister-in-law, visited for the day. After the daily chores, Charlotte, Lydia, and Lovely prepared yarn for weaving. Joshua, who had stopped by the cabin for a bite to eat and to check on his sisters, helped Russell Bean and a cousin unload a large baby cradle from the Bean's pack horse. Lydia had tasked Russell with retrieving the cradle from a nearby relative.

The cradle, the Bean's own, had served the family through the years for most all their little ones. Lydia's father, George Russell, had built the cradle and carved upon it designs of native flowers and vines, many, many years earlier. Designed to hold two children, a toddler and infant, the cradle rocked softly and quietly. After Lydia's last, they passed the cradle around among the Bean and Russell families as needed. As the women exclaimed over its beauty and remembered the many, many babies it had held, Esther felt a great relief at having a true cradle for her babe. Russell and Jesse carried it up the steep narrow steps, carefully maneuvering it around the turn of the landing, and onto the second story. Russell then brought in a smaller cradle to sit before the fire. There the babe would spend each day.

As the brothers departed, each to their own chores and assignments, Lovely, Jane, and Sarah slipped off to talk and giggle as only girls can do. Esther, Charlotte, and Lydia cleaned after the morning repast before Esther took to sweeping the floor. A few swishes of broomcorn rustled across the floor before a quiet rush of water fell amidst her skirts, soaking into the rough wood planks.

"Charlotte," Lydia whispered, "it be Esther's time. Now, there be no need to rush, but might you tend to the morning chores while I help her get changed into dry clothes and then settled? Call Lovely and Jane to help ye. Sarah can bring in firewood while the older girls go for water."

Despite some unease from time to time, hours passed before Esther's labor pains commenced. Lovely and Jane finished the morning chores with Charlotte's help. Sarah chopped the few spring greens the girls had gathered, while Charlotte began a rabbit stew for the evening meal.

As day turned to dusk, then dusk to dark, Esther kept quiet. Sometimes she paced. She sipped honeyed water. At other times, she sat restless and anxious with her Bible in her hands. The lanterns now lit, Lydia and Charlotte sat waiting, as did Lovely.

Outside, Joshua, retrieved from the fort by young Russell, paced, worried, fretted, and prayed. The menfolk had built a bonfire and gathered around, telling stories, keeping watch, and worrying in the way of men, knowing that a woman, dear to their heart, struggled to bring a child into the world.

"Esther, what book be ye reading?" Mistress Bean asked, breaking the quiet.

"The book of Ruth, for it is about women and their trials and troubles. This is my favorite part,

So Boaz took Ruth, and she was his wife: and when he went in unto her, the Lord gave her conception, and she bare a son.

> *And the women said unto Naomi, Blessed be the Lord, which hath not left thee this day without a kinsman, that his name may be famous in Israel.*
>
> *And he shall be unto thee a restorer of thy life, and a nourisher of thine old age: for thy daughter in law, which loveth thee, which is better to thee than seven sons hath born him.*

"Alas, the book of Ruth is also short and keeps my mind from the pain."

"Seems to me the good Reverend Doak should preach more from the books of Ruth and Esther, being as most of us womenfolk cannot read. We deserve to hear comforting words from our Bible rather than hell and damnation," Charlotte responded. "I be of a mind to speak to him about it. Or perhaps just to Mistress Doak, as she be more likely to say the right words to him."

As Charlotte spoke, Esther watched Lovely's face grow pale and saw tears pool in her eyes. Not at Charlotte's words but those last from herself. "Sister, sister, come sit with me. There is nothing to fear, for my pains will bring my babe into this world as all babies arrive amidst pain."

"But, Esther," Lovely sobbed, "Mother and our little Lydia died from such pain. How can I not be afraid to lose you as well?"

"My dearest Sarah," Esther replied, calling Lovely by her given name, a name not uttered between them for many, many years, "because I am strong. I possess a great will to see my babe born, to hold him in my arms, to see him grow, and learn. I want him to be strong and brave like his father. Our own Mother gave up such wishes long before her own tiny Lydia arrived. Mother held no hope, whereas I hold all the hope of the world here, within my heart. Come sister, bring me a cup of water, and we will tell Lydia and Charlotte our story."

After each woman had promised to keep within herself their tale, Lovely and Esther began. Revealing Lovely's real name, the story of their Lydia's birth and death, its aftermath, through their journey west to Moore's, and then onto the Watauga settlement,

Esther and Lovely spoke. Still, both sisters held back their actual family name.

Between pains, Esther walked and talked. Lovely, often by her side, listened as much as she said, never once mentioning her uncles by name. At their story's end, the women passed Esther's time in quiet reflection.

Esther's labor lasted until the wee hours of dawn. As the sun's first rays streaked the dark sky, morning birds chirped their welcome to the day, and Lovely dozed, Esther gave birth to a strong baby girl, with hair as dark as midnight and eyes as green as her own. The babe's healthy cry awoke Lovely. She rushed to her sister's side and proffered a linen towel to wrap the newborn, soon placed in Esther's arms.

"Oh, Esther, look, she has our father's eyes, green like ours. Her hair is darker than yours, but some say a newborn often has dark hair for a few months."

"She? I have a daughter?"

"Ye do, Esther," replied Lydia, "a big healthy girl."

Charlotte slipped out and down the stairs to find Joshua waiting at the foot. "Ye have a niece, a lovely, dark-haired baby girl. Esther be doin' well. Ye sit and relax. We be lettin' ye up to see her soon."

Through both a smile and tears, Joshua nodded, and then grabbed Charlotte in a big hug. "Thank ye, thank ye! Esther and the babe really be well?"

Charlotte nodded. Minutes later, Charlotte returned and asked, "Joshua, can ye carry this pail up to Mistress Lydia while I gather some stew for Esther?"

"Yes, ma'am, I rightly can."

Through tears rolling down her cheeks, Esther smiled at the babe in her arms—Waya's babe. She stroked her face and whispered, "Oh, you surprised us all, for I was sure you would be a boy and look like your father."

"Have you chosen a name?" asked Lydia.

Quietly, anxiously, Esther smiled and answered, "Only for a boy. For now, I shall call her Naomi, for in the Bible, Naomi is a compassionate woman who faces many challenges in her lifetime. If my daughter's life is anything like mine, she will need to be strong, like Naomi."

At that moment, sloshing water from the pail he carried, Joshua rushed into the room, startling the women. "Esther, Esther, be ye well?"

"Come see yer niece. I have named her Naomi."

Charlotte and Lydia stood back and watched as Joshua cradled Naomi in his long arms. Laughing, with tears of joy and relief, the tall, lanky man, dressed in worn buckskin, cooed and smiled at the tiny baby.

"Oh, Esther! Wa... her father would have been so proud!" he exclaimed.

Truly understanding his statement, Lovely and Lydia responded with tears of their own.

In the days following, Esther loved her baby girl in ways she never imagined. She loved holding her, putting her to breast, smelling her baby sweetness, and watching her sleep. She often thought back to her own mother, who never showed any genuine affection for any of her children, and wondered how that could have been.

Her own father, on the other hand, had doted on each and every child. Esther remembered well how she would often find him asleep in the nursery's deeply padded chair, holding one of the little ones against his chest. He'd heaped love upon his children. Perhaps, Esther thought, to make up for that missing from their own mother. He'd praised, he'd taught, and he'd reared his children with a devotion rarely seen in fathers.

Joshua quickly took to the baby girl as if she were his own, instead of his niece. He walked the cabin floor with her when she fussed. He brought her small gifts and asked about her first upon entering the Bean cabin, especially if gone for more than a day. Esther realized Joshua had learned much from their own father. She wondered why he had never found a girl to marry and make his own children, knowing he would be an excellent father.

Lovely took her role of aunt seriously. She provided clothing and blankets, fussing over every little whimper. Still, she drew the line at changing heavily soiled, smelly clouts, something Joshua learned and carried out with military efficiency. Jesse Bean often visited and felt right at home holding the baby. Of course, he'd been raised with several younger siblings, along with a slew of nieces and nephews.

Lydia and William seemed happy to have the additions to their family. Jane and Sarah adored Naomi and argued over who loved her most. Esther recovered quietly and quickly. As they had no cabin to return to, the Beans invited them to stay until a cabin opened at the fort.

While William was often called away on various duties, the womenfolk never found themselves without male protection. Several of the older male cousins, of both the Bean and Russell families, took to staying at the Bean cabin night and day, for the threat of attack remained.

"Rely not on the likelihood of the enemy's not coming, but on our own readiness to receive him." Sun Tzu

Summer into Autumn 1780

In early June, militia couriers delivered dire news concerning Charleston, South Carolina. Dispatches told of the city's capture by the British on the twelfth of May. They now held the city at siege, making it difficult for the residents to purchase food and necessary supplies. British General Clinton, wishing to control all the immediate area around Charleston, had dispatched Banastre Tarleton and Major Patrick Ferguson, to capture nearby Monck's Corner in early April. The brutality ordered by Tarleton upon the civilian population shocked the colonies.

Soon more British forces flooded into Charleston, as over two thousand five hundred soldiers under Lieutenant Colonel Lord Rawdon arrived. Scottish Highlanders, Hessians, the Queen's Rangers, volunteers from Ireland, and even Tory Americans, serving in the Prince of Wales American Volunteers, occupied and surrounded the city. News of this disastrous loss was felt throughout the southern frontier. The situation in the southern colonies had now become critical to the success of the revolution.

Following swiftly upon this devastating news came word of Buford's massacre at Waxhaw's Creek, South Carolina, on the twenty-ninth of May. As settler after settler retold the story, the residents of Watauga reacted with disbelief. With confirmation of the facts, talk of vengeance spread. According to informed sources, in South Carolina, Continental Army forces under Lt. Colonel Abraham Buford, hoping to relieve the siege of Charleston, had approached Lancaster, South Carolina, in late May. Without warning and accurate reconnaissance, they stumbled upon British forces under Tarleton near Waxhaw's Creek.

As Tarleton's cavalry attacked, many of the colonial troops threw down their weapons and ran. Others attempted to surrender by waving white flags, for stories of Tarleton's brutality were well known. According to the story spread about Fort Watauga, a truce was called by Buford. During this truce, a colonial soldier fired at Tarleton, causing his horse to fall and trap him. Incensed at this breach of truce, Loyalists and British troops attacked and slaughtered many unarmed and unresisting Patriots. Buford lost one hundred thirteen men killed with sabers, and over one-hundred fifty so badly wounded they could not be moved and were left to die on the battlefield. Only fifty-three prisoners were taken. Many of these were also wounded.

As Joshua had heard the news of the Waxhaw's Creek massacre directly from Lieutenant Isaac Lane at Fort Watauga, he knew all the gruesome details. The story spread like wildfire among the residents, and throughout the surrounding area. Joshua, himself, sat at Lydia's large table and relayed the gruesome story. His sisters watched and listened as his tears flowed across the anger shown on his face. They observed his ire, his dismay growing stronger as he related the massacre of their men. Soon, his face red and his voice rough with grief and despair, he raged against the British, as many others did upon hearing the news. Never had Esther seen Joshua so angry, so impassioned.

In the days to come, Waxhaw's became the only topic of conversation amongst the men of the fort. Those few Loyalists who remained in the community kept silent for fear of reprisal. Some, dismayed at the British slaughter of helpless men who had already surrendered, turned their support to the fight for freedom. Word came in the weeks to come, from military couriers and news sheets, telling how the phrase *Tarleton's quarter* had come to mean "refusing to take prisoners." Leaders on both sides of the conflict now brutally practiced Tarleton's quarter.

Throughout the colonies, newspapers used the story of Waxhaw's to mount an aggressive propaganda campaign to bolster recruitment for the Continental forces and the Patriot militias. On an evening's stroll beside Boone's Creek, Esther listened as Joshua talked of leaving the frontier and joining the Continentals. Saying little, Esther let her dearest brother vent.

Days later, fearing the loss of a reliable man, an excellent tracker, and a speedy courier, Colonel Sevier promoted Joshua to lieutenant and placed him in charge of all military dispatches and intelligence, in hopes this would persuade him to remain at Watauga.

Even before the news of Waxhaw's had spread to one and all, they'd heard of the battle at Ramsour's Mill in Lincoln County, North Carolina. Joshua himself had carried the story to Fort Watauga in a dispatch from Isaac Shelby. Upon his return to the cabin, he told Esther and Lovely, along with the Bean and Russell families, about how Loyalist forces, under two colonial leaders, had attempted to bring all of North Carolina under British control.

Joshua told how, upon hearing news of British recruiting Loyalists near Ramsour's Mill outside Lincolnton, Patriot officers General Rutherford, Colonel Locke, and Major Wilson, from three surrounding counties, gathered their forces. Nearby, some thirteen hundred Loyalists had encamped near Ramsour's Mill, in Lincoln County. It seemed many of that force did not even have weapons. Colonel Locke, after obtaining recent reconnaissance of the Loyalist forces, decided to attack at first light on the twentieth of June.

In thick fog, for two hours, the battle raged, neighbor against neighbor, brother against brother. As neither side had uniforms to identify their allegiance, the Tories wore green twigs in their hats while the Patriots pinned a white paper on theirs. During the battle, vicious hand-to-hand combat ensued.

Though outnumbered three to one, the Patriot forces soon took the upper hand, causing the Tories to flee. As the morning's fog lifted across the battlefield, they saw some seventy dead and over two hundred wounded, equally divided between the two sides. Shelby reported *we gave no quarter to the wounded Tories*. They buried the Loyalist dead in a mass grave.

The war now totally eclipsed the lives of those across the mountains. Additionally, Indian raids, especially by the Chickamauga Cherokee and Shawnee, became more frequent. Joshua worried about his sisters and his niece. He rejoiced that they no longer lived alone in their solitary cabin. Over the previous years, there had been a few serious scares, and even a few times when the sisters had fled to the fort. Never had he feared for their safety as he did now. Consoled by their presence at the Bean compound and knowing they would flee to the fort if danger warranted, Joshua took on his new role, swearing to use the intelligence they gathered to protect the citizens of Watauga.

In July, Esther wrote once again to Benjamin. She shared with her brother her love for a Cherokee man, his death, her grief, and the birth of Naomi. She poured out her heart, and then told of their deception, made to protect her reputation. She wrote of Samuel's passing. She shared news of their current residence with the Bean family and told of Joshua's promotion. She relayed how Lovely had progressed during the previous months. Esther ended her letter by expressing her deep pride in Benjamin's service and her desire to do more to help their cause. Joshua promised to include the letter in the next communication to Evan Shelby, who regularly sent correspondence north through military channels.

After Joshua returned time and time again from various forts and commanders, Esther always expected another letter from Benjamin. Never had such a long time passed between letters.

Across the southern colonies, especially Georgia and South Carolina, the situation daily turned even more desperate for those fighting for freedom, and especially for the citizens trapped within a revolution. British commanders now considered themselves fully in control of the two southernmost colonies. British ships blockaded the harbors, hindering the movement of colonists and trade. Britain's forces won skirmish after skirmish. Lord Cornwallis set into motion a plan to move north into North Carolina, and then on to Virginia, in a push to reestablish sovereignty and meet up with British forces in the north.

The British expected an easy invasion, as many of the eastern counties of North Carolina now found themselves filled with Loyalists fleeing the western settlements. Most of the western counties of North Carolina, South Carolina, and Virginia, along with settlements across the Appalachians, remained staunchly

Patriot. Filled with men and women who already knew freedom and desired even more so to protect their hard-won existence, who continued to fight with a vengeance, these westernmost colonists remembered Monck's Corner, Waxhaw's Creek, Ramsour's Mill, and Hanging Rock—battles fought by militia, not Continental Regulars. These men fought for their freedom most every day. They were rough men, men experienced with rifles, knives, and even the tomahawk. Men who cried out yells patterned after their ancestors from the Scottish Highlands, or the Indians they now fought regularly.

At Watauga, a brief respite from warfare, worry, and summer tasks took place on the fourteenth of August, when the Reverend Samuel Doak conducted a wedding ceremony for the recently widowed John Sevier to *Bonnie* Kate Sherrill. After the quiet ceremony, John kissed his bride goodbye and rode east toward South Carolina.

Two days later, in that state, the Battle of Camden proved a disaster for the Patriot cause. There Patriot regulars and militia under General Griffith Rutherford, General Baron DeKalb, and General Horatio Gates, fought against General Cornwallis's regulars. Cornwallis maneuvered a stunning victory, driving the defeated Patriot armies from the field and chasing them north. British forces captured all the Patriot's ammunition, seven brass cannons, one-hundred and thirty wagons, and one thousand one hundred rifles. Colonel Banastre Tarleton pursued the fleeing Patriot armies and destroyed all in his army's path—civilian homes, crops, outbuildings, and livestock. Tarleton's severe measures further incensed the Patriots.

Serving in South Carolina's uplands, British Major Patrick Ferguson, himself a Scot, had earlier announced his great loathing for *those damned yelling boys* from over the mountains. Ferguson, who had lost the use of his right arm at the Battle of Brandywine, suffered another serious injury at Camden when a bayonet wound robbed him of strength in his left arm. Still, Ferguson had a knack for recruiting and training men, making them loyal to him and the British cause. Arrogant and tactically brilliant, he led his men into the northwestern regions of South Carolina, and occasionally into North Carolina, where he forced the population to succumb using brutal tactics. Some residents took the pledge of loyalty to King George, some fled into the mountains where they hid, and others fled west over the mountains.

On August eighteenth, in the upper northwest corner of South Carolina, a battle took place between Patriot militia and volunteers against British forces at Musgrove's Mill. Among the Patriots, Isaac Shelby and John Sevier led a sudden, striking attack against Ferguson's Corps. The Patriots inflicted about two hundred casualties before they just as suddenly withdrew back into the dense woods and disappeared. Rightly believing Ferguson's Corps was in pursuit, Shelby and Sevier led their forces deep into the mountains before deciding to return home to recruit more men. They invited the men from North Carolina to join them, knowing Ferguson would punish any who had fought against him. Many of these Patriots agreed, bringing their families with them, thereby assuring their safety from Ferguson's ire.

Returning home for a brief visit, Robert Bean brought news of the South Carolina battles and their aftermath to the Bean settlement. He told of Sevier and Shelby's kind invitation to those brave men and their families. The Beans, the Russells, and the Balls, along with several others, talked openly about all that had occurred and welcomed each bit of news. Esther often listened to their tales of wounded men suffering from horrible wounds that putrefied, leading to death or amputation of limbs. Along the frontier, trained doctors did not exist. Residents treated their own wounds and illnesses or called upon a local healer if one lived nearby.

Before long, led by North Carolina Colonels Charles McDowell and Andrew Hampton, one hundred sixty men arrived at the Watauga settlement where they built crude huts and lean-tos. Some brought their entire family—wives, children, parents and even grandparents—their livestock, their household goods. After traveling for days, even weeks, each man, woman, and child sought peace and a place to rest their head each evening.

Soon, rustic, temporary camps held over two hundred refugees. With little sanitation, the camps smelled of rotting meat, garbage, human waste, and unwashed bodies.

The people of Watauga willingly supplied them with food and other necessities. Esther visited the camp, day after day, to provide medical care, often carrying little Naomi in a pack. She treated wounds, illnesses, and spread hope. Lovely and Jane sometimes came along, carrying fresh vegetables or eggs and cheese. They played with the children, helped the women with chores, and found friends amongst the girls near to their own age.

The Reverends, Samuel Doak and Tidence Lane, worked diligently to ease the suffering of these men and their families, forced to flee their homes by a war now closer than ever to Watauga. Esther met women heavy with child and children marred by the violence of war. Each night at her home with the Beans, Esther, often in tears, prayed for the refugees, seeking relief for their suffering.

Not long after the first group arrived from near Gilbert's Creek, North Carolina, someone hailed the Bean cabin long after dark and all had settled for the night.

"Hail! Bean cabin! Hail!" a voice called in the darkness. Jesse, at home after gathering supplies at the fort, rushed to the outer gate and opened it to find Isaac Lane ready to shout again.

"Please, Jesse, Esther be needed at the camp. I brought an extra horse, 'twould be good to have ye with us."

Esther, who had just reached the bottom of the steps, followed by Lovely and Jane, answered, "I can come. I must dress first and grab my bag. What be the need, Isaac?"

"'Tis not a pleasant story. So, I not be wishing to say more." Isaac answered, glancing toward the girls. "Please hurry."

Seeing the concern on Isaac's face and tears in his eyes, Esther and Jesse rushed to dress.

They rode into the darkness under a waning moon, keeping their horses at a sharp trot for darkness prevented them from riding faster. Along the way, Isaac told some of the story. "Two of my men scouting the trails in the east met up with the family some ways out of the camp. They heard their story and saw how sick the girl be so one rode ahead to the fort to send for ye."

As they neared the quiet camp, where most families seemed to sleep, they noticed a large fire where a small crowd gathered.

As Isaac helped Esther from the horse, he whispered, "'Twill be hard to see."

Esther spent the rest of the night treating and comforting a young refugee girl. Rachel, only five, had threatened Ferguson and his officers with a wooden sword just after the man killed her father for refusing to take the oath of allegiance to King George. Her mother told how Rachel's father had died instantly, before their eyes, after being struck twice across the torso with Ferguson's sword. As her mother, expectant with another child, screamed and cursed the British, Rachel had screeched her threat *to kill all the damned whoresons* while running amongst the British horses and striking them with her play sword, a handmade gift from her father.

One of the militia officers accompanying Ferguson had pulled his sword and struck the child just below the elbow, severing her lower arm. Ferguson's doctor, Dr. Uzal Johnson, had treated and bandaged the wound and given the child a mild sedative to help with the pain. In the meantime, despite her obviously expectant stomach, Rachel's mother had been raped at least twice and their cabin burned. According to neighbors who had rescued the woman and her child and accompanied the family west, their trip had taken four days. By the third day, little Rachel lay feverish and listless in her mother's arms as they rode west.

Rachel's mother, Martha, spoke little and refused to leave her child's side. Toward morning, as Rachel became quiet, and no longer awoke begging for water or her mother, Martha asked, "will she live? Do ye believe she might live?"

"Perhaps," replied Esther, taking Martha's hands in her own, "if the good Lord wishes."

The first streaks of sunlight came just as Rachel gasped and breathed her last.

"Oh, God, no! No! Don't take my Rachel, please Lord!" Martha screamed into the coming morn.

Within two hours of Rachel's death, Esther helped as Martha gave birth to a stillborn son. Then she too breathed her last.

No one nearby at the camp now slept. Martha's wails at Rachel's death, followed by her cries during childbirth, brought many to tears. Even grown, battle-tested men quietly cried and hugged their own children and wives. Others raised a hue of hatred heard everywhere about the camp against a British sovereign who could send such men to enforce his rule.

"Come, my child. Esther, come and rest. You can do no more. They are in God's hands now and once again together," Samuel Doak pleaded.

"No, Reverend, Naomi will be awake soon, if not now, and crying for me. I must ride home. There I may rest. I can tend to my grief over these losses when time allows."

Isaac and Jesse escorted Esther home, where she took to her little room, just her and Naomi. Not once did she speak except a soft *thanks* to Lydia, who carried up food and drink. Mostly she slept, Naomi tucked in beside her.

Life went on, across the Watauga settlement, men and women dedicated themselves to the gathering of late summer crops, planting for winter, storing up hay and firewood, as those chores made ready for the coming cold. Men built cabins, paddocks for horses and other livestock, for the refugees, and shored up the palisade at Fort Caswell. Others took to the woods in search of game. Women dried fruit and gathered nuts and berries.

Esther once again took to scouring the woods, this time around the Bean cabin, for medicinal plants. Lydia had retrieved an old baby pack given to her by Nancy Ward. On nice days,

Esther loaded Naomi into the pack which hung across her chest and carried her daughter into the forest with her. Joshua once found her sitting on a log, nursing the small babe while eating late summer berries.

"Sister, ye look so content."

"Yes, Naomi is happy and well. I have all I need, except Waya. Joshua, I wish to announce that my imaginary husband has been killed. To make it more believable, perhaps you can bring me a message about such when you return from Sapling Grove," Esther replied as she offered Joshua the remaining berries.

"If ye wish. Why now?"

"I have been in mourning since the news of Waya's death. Those around me will see little difference in my manner, and those closest to me will understand. Besides, soon others will wonder about a man who does not come to see his daughter. Charlotte and others have already asked about him. I am tired of lying. Sometimes I think this entire story was a mistake."

"I have sensed your sadness, your longing for Waya every day. I most often see it when you hold Naomi. Perhaps this be for the best. But ye must remember, your lies have kept your honor intact in the eyes of all hereabouts. They all think highly of ye, and therefore of Lovely. This story protected her, as well as ye and little Naomi."

"And you, brother?" she teased solemnly.

"Hardly. As ye well know, the lasses here about think me arrogant and disreputable as I pay them no courtesy. May I share a secret with ye?"

"A secret? You mean the young woman who lives nearby to Evan Shelby that you visit each time you venture that direction?"

"How do ye know about Elizabeth?"

"Ah, now I know her name. You call her Beth in your sleep. Wish to tell me her surname?"

"Nay."

As Esther teased, Joshua reluctantly revealed a few more details about his sweetheart—blonde, not very tall, and could read and write. Esther, however, did not learn the girl's surname.

Soon, word arrived from the Carolinas, where Ferguson continued to recruit and force loyalty from the residents, but upon hearing of the Patriots' migration west across the mountains, he sent a warning. He chose young Samuel Phillips, a rebel captive who he knew to be a cousin to Isaac Shelby, to deliver his ultimatum. Ferguson's warning read, "If you do not desist your opposition of the British Arms, I will march this army over the mountains, hang your leaders, and lay your country waste with fire and sword."

Shelby shared the message with Sevier, McDowell, and Hampton. Soon, all the men of Watauga heard the ultimatum. If ever there had been words doomed to start a fight, those words served their purpose.

About the area of the Catawba and Broad rivers in South and North Carolina, using force and threats, Ferguson continued to lead his army—recruiting some—punishing those who refused. Reports estimated his tactics had enlisted another five hundred Tory militiamen.

After a call to arms, in the west, men from far and wide flocked to Watauga and other western settlements such as Shelby's Sapling Grove. Many of these men were Indian fighters, some had fought in the French and Indian War and Lord Dunmore's War. Most all had withstood not only individual attacks but had held out during siege warfare against overwhelming odds. They each knew the backcountry, they possessed remarkable skill with a long rifle, most able to hit a target at three hundred yards, and each could hold his own in hand-to-hand combat. They fought well with a knife and tomahawk. These lean, well-muscled men often traveled long distances on horseback or on foot in wet, cold weather or searing heat. They slept rough, lived rough, and believed in their own dignity, and their role as protectors of their women, children, and the weak. Each believed in the righteousness of their cause. Most important of all, they held forth courage and believed strongly in freedom.

Word came that in the Carolinas, other militia leaders now heeded the call and formed companies to join in the fight against Ferguson. Joshua and the other couriers found themselves sent hither and yon to announce meeting places and urge men to unite.

Even before the ultimatum from Ferguson, Shelby and Sevier had recruited men for a force to march across into South Carolina for an assault on Ferguson's army. Both leaders, along with the McDowell brothers, knew their success depended upon the support of Colonel William Campbell. Another backwoodsman. A Scot by birth, Campbell had received a liberal education and held many responsibilities, including serving as a Washington County judge. All on the frontier remembered how early on, in 1775, Campbell and his fellow North Carolina backwoodsmen had declared themselves for freedom. They had gone so far as sending a message to the newly formed Continental Congress expressing their view, that as freemen, their rights would not be trampled:

> *We declare that we are deliberately and resolutely determined never to surrender them to any power upon earth but at the expense of our lives. These are our real, though unpolished, sentiments of liberty and loyalty, and in them we are resolved to live and die.*

Now, despite some early reservations about such a venture, Colonels Shelby and Sevier persuaded Campbell to join the fight. He contributed more men to the mission than any other region. Joshua reported how Campbell was gathering his men at Dunn's Meadows in Abingdon, Virginia. From there, Campbell would lead his men south to join up with Isaac Shelby's men at Shelby's Fort. Next, the mounted horsemen, and a few afoot, moved toward another meeting place at Sycamore Shoals on the Watauga River. There they would join with the men recruited by John Sevier and the McDowell men who had fled to Watauga. Among them, would now ride Lieutenant Joshua Ball, a well-known shot and courier, who knew the trails of these mountains better than many. He served directly under Lieutenant Colonel John Sevier and with Lieutenant Lane as a scout.

Nearby to Watauga, along Powder Creek, Mary McKeehan Patton, their local gunpowder miller, began making her fast-burning gunpowder, the kind she had learned from her father to manufacture. As she worked, Mary also tended to her three daughters as her husband David was off fighting in the North Carolina militia. With some help, Mary manufactured over five hundred pounds of gunpowder and presented it to Colonel Shelby. All around the area, women silently took pride in their small contributions as they prepared their menfolk to follow the call to battle.

Just past dawn on the morning of the twenty-fifth of September, Esther and Lovely stood among the Bean women to watch the family's men take their leave. Lydia watched as both Captain William, senior, and William junior mounted up beside George Bean. Captain Jesse kissed his mother on the cheek and doffed his hat to Lovely before taking to his horse. Soon, Captains George and John Russell rode up to join the Beans. William Russell, Jr., a lieutenant, galloped into sight, blew a kiss to the womenfolk, and rode off. Captain Russell's daughter called out to her father to give her love to Lieutenant Isaac Lane.

Each man and woman, in their own way, understood the seriousness of these leave-takings. They knew some men may not return. Some women might, from this day forward, count themselves as widows and their children as orphans. Others might never see the faces of their loved ones after this morning's goodbye. Those left behind stayed watchful until the last of the dust settled and their men were truly gone.

As the menfolk, at last, rode from sight, Lydia turned and entered her cabin, left with only her daughters Jane and Sarah and son Russell.

Esther and Lovely talked quietly on a bench outside the door. Esther had suspected that Lovely might become silent once again. Instead, Lovely spoke of how brave the men looked, especially

Jesse. Esther wondered if her sister understood that some and maybe many of these men and boys would never return.

The day brightened and proved to be one of spectacular beauty as the trees had progressed from green to yellow and orange, with only hints of red just now dotting the hillsides. Although the last few days had come and gone with the nippiness of autumn, this day proved gently warm. In the surrounding settlement, women and children went swiftly about their chores. Some women moved essentials into other's cabins for protection and company. Older boys, still too young for war, now carried rifles and watched as they went about their chores.

Esther knew she could no longer roam the surrounding forest on her own, for with the men of the community absent, the threat of Indian attacks would grow stronger with each passing day. Still, Esther's thoughts rarely dwelt upon that once joyful aspect of her life. Other matters kept her mind occupied until late in the day.

> "Some souls just understand each other upon meeting."
> N.R. Hart

September 25 to October 4, 1780

The following afternoon, Esther Doak arrived, escorted by Samuel. As Esther settled at the table, with a cup of cider, the good Reverend rode on to an outlying cabin to check on an elderly resident.

"Did ye attend the muster at Sycamore Springs with the Reverend?" Lydia asked.

"Nay, I stayed at the fort. Samuel rode out with the rest of the officers, and I stayed with Mistress Robinson. She became quite fretful as John departed. I didn't think she should be alone on such a day, especially in her delicate condition."

"Esther, do you believe her baby might come early? Should I go to the fort?"

"Oh! Heavens above, the woman is just such a worrying soul. That baby won't fall until after John has returned. Now, let me hold Naomi. I haven't seen her for nigh on a full week?" Esther Doak replied.

After an hour or so of talk, cooing over the baby, and gossip, Esther Doak pulled from her pocket a piece of parchment. "I thought you might like to hear Samuel's sermon and prayer for our menfolk. I was not there to hear it, of course, but Samuel said he received many thanks and much praise for his words."

"Please," pleaded Lydia, "read it to us."

> *My countrymen, you are about to set out on an expedition which is full of hardships and dangers, but one in which the Almighty will attend you.*

The Mother Country has her hands upon you, these American Colonies, and takes that for which our fathers planted their homes in the wilderness — OUR LIBERTY.

Taxation without representation and the quartering of soldiers in the home of our people without their consent are evidence that the Crown of England would take from its American Subjects the last vestige of Freedom.

Your brethren across the mountains are crying like Macedonia unto your help. God forbid that you shall refuse to hear and answer their call — but the call of your brethren is not all. The enemy is marching hither to destroy your homes.

Brave men, you are not unacquainted with battle. Your hands have already been taught to war and your fingers to fight. You have wrested these beautiful valleys of the Holston and Watauga from the savage hand. Will you tarry now until the other enemy carries fire and sword to your very doors? No, it shall not be. Go forth then in the strength of your manhood to the aid of your brethren, the defense of your liberty and the protection of your homes. And may the God of Justice be with you and give you victory.

Let us pray.

Almighty and gracious God! Thou has been the refuge and strength of Thy people in all ages. In time of sorest need we have learned to come to Thee — our Rock and our Fortress. Thou knowest the dangers and snares that surround us on march and in battle.

Thou knowest the dangers that constantly threaten the humble, but well beloved homes, which Thy servants have left behind them.

O, in Thine infinite mercy, save us from the cruel hand of the savage, and of tyrant. Save the unprotected homes while fathers and husbands and sons are far away fighting for freedom and helping the oppressed.

Thou, who promised to protect the sparrow in its flight, keep ceaseless watch, by day and by night, over our loved ones. The helpless woman and little children, we commit to Thy care. Thou wilt not leave them or forsake them in times of loneliness and anxiety and terror.

O, God of Battle, arise in Thy might. Avenge the slaughter of Thy people. Confound those who plot for our destruction. Crown this mighty effort with victory, and smite those who exalt themselves against liberty and justice and truth.

Help us as good soldiers to wield the SWORD OF THE LORD AND GIDEON.

AMEN.

Silence followed upon Esther Doak's reading. Esther Ballinger glanced toward Lovely and Lydia. Both's eyes shone with tears. However, young Sarah quietly quoted, "And all this assembly shall know that the Lord saveth not with sword and spear: for the battle is the Lord's. I believe that be from first Samuel."

"Indeed, it is First Samuel, chapter 17 verse 47, my dear child. You have an impressive memory," stated Samuel Doak from the doorway. "Good afternoon, ladies, might I join you?"

Discussions followed of safety, the war, the Reverend's sermon and prayer, and the fall harvest. The Doaks stayed for an early evening meal and then rode back toward the fort just at dusk. As day turned once more to night, Esther's thoughts stayed where they had been most of the day.

Quietly and secretively, the following morning found Esther gathering up her herbs, potions, and bandages. She packed each carefully in one of two saddlebags and a lidded basket that could hang over her saddle horn. She quietly raided Lydia's store for apples, parched corn, maple sugar, pears, nuts, and strips of dried deer jerky. While Lovely remained absent from their room, Esther completed her tasks and then rolled two blankets into a waterproof hide before hiding all in the stable near Athena. One last item remained of her preparations. Taking quill to hand, she penned a letter to Lovely and Lydia.

"I find myself called to duty as a healer. I cannot - no shall not - refuse this call, for my brothers and friends serve and even now ride into battle. Worry not for my safety, I will not be alone for the Lord, our Saviour, rides beside me. Please do not come for me. Instead, honor my service by caring for Naomi.

Lydia, two of your family have new babes and will, I believe, take Naomi to breast. My love for her is so strong I know I shall return. However, if I should not, then Esther Doak should be asked to raise her. I would have her know of her father, for he will always be with me and shall always watch over our Naomi.

Lydia, I know you will care for Lovely as you do your own daughters. She knows how to contact Benjamin. Lovely, please understand that Joshua and I love you and will strive to return to you.

Keep me in your prayers, as you will all be forever in mine,
Esther Ball

That evening, Esther helped with the chores before retiring with Naomi. Taking her daughter to breast, she smiled as her babe latched on, enjoying that pleasurable moment of motherhood. Whispering, she explained all to her Naomi, a babe much, much too young to understand, promising over and over to return.

After she and Lovely retired for the evening, Esther lay awake, waiting for Lovely's soft snores before gathering some of Samuel's old clothing, her heavy cape and a man's cap.

Early the next morning, upon hearing Lydia rise and begin her day, Esther once more placed her babe to her breast. As Naomi, satisfied, drifted off to sleep, Esther placed her lovingly back into her cradle. Then, dressed in her riding clothes, Esther went down and explained Samuel Doak had asked her to check in on the elderly woman he had visited a day earlier. Grabbing a couple of hot hoe cakes, Esther slipped out, added the boy's clothing to her satchel, then quickly saddled and loaded Athena. All before riding off with a wave to Russell, who sat nearby milking a cow.

Riding first southwest, after a quarter of a mile, she turned north toward Sycamore Shoals, for she knew there she could easily determine the path of their departing army. Arriving at Sycamore Shoals, Esther hurriedly turned once again south. Knowing the men had traveled south, she laughed at her folly when she saw she had wasted valuable time going all the way to the shoals, as she should have known the men would follow Gap Creek into the mountains.

All day Esther rode, stopping only to water and rest her horse. South, then southeast, along the Yellow Mountain road — the road Joshua had traveled so many times, she rode. Marked by signs of many men traveling on horseback, and followed by a herd of cattle, their path remained clearly evident, even two days after their passing.

Late in the afternoon, well off the path in a small glade, Esther rested Athena and slept awhile herself. Later, she changed into men's clothing, just as a waxing gibbous moon rose in the east. Once more, she took to her saddle and rode on. Several hours later, the moon, now often obscured behind the forest trees, left her in darkness, so leaving the path, she unpacked and hobbled Athena, and settled into a deep sleep.

The next day, Esther followed the trail by daylight, stopping only for short periods of rest. She often took small meals of the pilfered foodstuffs while in the saddle, munching on nuts, dried apples, or jerky. Many times, she found herself forced to take to the woods and stay quiet as men and a few families passed going, more often than not, toward Watauga. Late in the day, she watched as a few of Watauga's younger boys drove some cattle, that had earlier accompanied their army, back toward the settlement.

Recognizing one of the young men, as she had treated him for a wound earlier in the year, Esther rode out to question him. She remembered him being called Young Samuel by his family, as both his father and grandfather, all living in the same cabin, had the same name.

"Young Samuel, why are these cattle being returned? Has something happened to our army?"

"Mistress Esther, why be ye ridin' out here so far from the fort? Ye be alone?"

"Never mind that now. Please, why are you driving these cattle back to Fort Caswell?"

"Colonels Sevier and Shelby decided the cattle and men on foot be slowing the army down. They done slaughtered some for meat, put some men on our horses, and send some back with the cattle. So, I be walkin'. Sure don't like the thought of ye bein' out here alone, Mistress Esther."

"Oh, I am not alone. My companions are back off the trail, resting. Thank you, Young Samuel. Now you take care." Esther had some regrets about lying to the young man. However, she knew he would raise the alarm at the fort if she did not make him believe she traveled with others.

Esther turned back into the woods and then circled around to the road over Roan Mountain. Later that day, she came across the large meadow where their army had camped and slaughtered the cattle. The terrible, lingering smell of rotting carcasses forced her to cover her mouth and nose with a scarf Lovely had woven for her and to push Athena faster.

On the twenty-ninth, as she crossed Roan Mountain, an early light snow fell, coating her and her horse. The biting icy wind almost drove her to stop and build a fire before she remembered the buffalo robe she had found hanging on a hook in the Bean's small stable. Pulling it from under her packs, Esther covered herself and then wrapped a scarf about Athena's head, leaving her eyes and nose mostly uncovered.

About an hour later, while descending the mountain, the young woman discovered the temperature in the surrounding valleys remained milder and almost pleasant. For several hours, she made good time. Passing a young couple, Esther asked for directions into South Carolina and learned she was traveling south on what they called Bright's Trace. Named for Samuel Bright, an earlier settler to the area, the trace had existed for centuries as an animal trail, one also used by Indians to cross the mountains from the coastal plains to the lands west beyond the mountains.

Esther saw and heard only one other rider, a man she easily avoided simply by moving off the path into the dense forest. He rode by so quickly that he didn't even notice when Athena snorted at his horse. Given his rapid pace, Esther wondered if he was on a mission for the militia.

On the fourth day, as she rested beside a small brook just off the trail, Esther heard yet another horse approaching. She watched from the surrounding trees as a tall and slender, older Negro man rode into sight. She could not make out his face, for he rode while constantly looking downward along the trail, as if he tracked someone or something.

Suddenly he halted and called out, "Mistress Ball, I knows ye be hereby. Come on out her'and talks with me awhile. Mistress Doak done sent me. I mean ye no harm."

Recognizing the voice of the blacksmith's helper from Watauga, Esther grudgingly left the cover of the trees. "Walter, I will not return. They may need me after the battle. Our men may be wounded and require healing. They have no surgeon, no healer," Esther stated with quiet determination.

"Mistress Doak done said ye mightn' 'fuse to come back home. That be why I done come. I know some 'bout traveling, also 'bout healin' from my time with the Shawnee. More important like, I 'spect ye could use a friend 'bout now. Awful lonely out her' 'lone, 'specially for a woman. I done carried 'long a rabbit, I done shot aways back thinkin' we might share this evenin'."

After a few more minutes of Walter's slow, deliberate persuasion, Esther agreed to allow Walter to ride along with her. They trotted side by side until near dark before they settled in for the evening. After deciding on a campsite, Walter built a fire, roasted his rabbit, and produced from a bag a bit of cornbread wrapped in cloth. "Sorry, Mistress Esther. Couldn't find no way to tote butter nor no buttermilk."

Almost two more days of riding had passed when suddenly Walter pulled up and suggested they rest a bit. "Now, Mistress Esther, seems to me there be a campfire up ahead. I be goin' to ride up to 'vestigate. Ye just rest here."

"Walter, will you try to find out about our army?"

"Will do, Mistress Esther. Promise."

Sometime later Walter returned to announce, "I think best we'uns ride a bit more and then rest up till morn. Travelers sayed our boys done left out yesterdee morn, but we still close on behind."

As Walter and Esther prepared to settle that night, she realized her desperate need for rest. The strain of riding so far each day, her fear of being discovered and returned to the fort, and her lack of sleep fell upon her as she dismounted. Also, her breasts yet ached each day, as even though she had bound them on her first day out, her milk still flowed. She excused herself and took to the woods to see to her private needs.

Being a kind, considerate man, Walter built a brush arbor for Esther to sleep under after having declared that rain would start during the night. Esther bathed in a nearby stream and gathered a few late berries. Walter provided them with some fish for the evening meal and insisted upon preparing everything while Esther rested. She awoke at dawn to a pouring rain, hungry, having slept through the evening meal, and thirsty. Beside her sat a bundle of cold fish, berries, more cornbread, and a full clay bottle of water. Walter slept nearby under his own shelter.

For that long, wet day, Esther and Walter stayed put. Walter tended to the chores, shot a couple of squirrels, and gathered nuts, firewood, and water. Esther mostly slept. When awake, she worried she would not arrive in time to be of assistance. She worried about Naomi and Lovely. She feared for Joshua and all the men from Watauga. Several times, Esther turned to prayer.

That evening, as the weather cleared, Esther, having wondered since his arrival, asked her companion, "Walter, how did you know which way I had gone?"

"Well, Mistress Doak say'd ye done left a letter. She say'd your sister, Miss Lovely, done found it early the next morn. Mistress Bean said the girl screamed and screamed your name. Would have done come for ye herself, had Mistress Bean not stopped the child."

Now warmed to his answer, waving his hands about and smiling, Walter continued, "So Mistress Bean rode in with Russell and told the Reverend and Mistress Doak while I be standin' near on. I done volunteered right off to come fer ye. I be a free man and knows my way about a trail, 'specially this here trail. All around the fort folks knows that. I also knowed ye be a smart woman and ye would follow our men's path.

"Mistress Doak done pulled me aside and give me the vittles and telled me not to bring ye back — to leave ye be and be ye protection. I 'member how ye done cared fer those folks around the fort, so I knows ye gonna do right by our men. 'Sides, this way, I might be there to help put a ball into that Ferguson fella."

For two days, Esther and Walter followed the overmountain men at a distance. The Patriot army grew larger and larger as more men arrived from parts of North Carolina and Virginia to join up. Stopping and asking about in small villages and hamlets, they learned the overmountain men were searching for Ferguson and his militia army, as they had little information as to his whereabouts.

Riding along, Esther and Walter often chatted, and she learned his life story. Born a slave in Virginia and owned by a wealthy planter, Walter had been trained as a blacksmith. Early in life, he'd saved the planter's daughter from drowning and, when the planter died, had been freed in the man's will. Walter still carried his papers, declaring him a free Negro. Moving westward over the years, he'd been captured by a roving band of Shawnee warriors, up near the Ohio River, and stayed with them for some seven years. He had taken a Shawnee wife and fathered three children, all girls. After the death of his wife and daughters during a raid by the Iroquois, Walter determined God wanted him to leave the Shawnee.

Weeks later, traveling south along a trace, Walter encountered several long hunters and joined up. They loaned him an extra rifle, taught him how to hunt, and took him along, further south to Fort Caswell. There, he found work with the blacksmith.

"Walter, do you have a surname?"

"Yeah, Mistress Esther, I do's. While traveling west, I once met a man I greatly, greatly 'mired. He be a doctor, owns a large plantation, and has himself a passel of chillens. Guess they's mostly grown now. Name be Benjamin Ballinger. So, I done named myself Walter Ballinger. What ye think on that? Fine name for sure. I believes."

When no answer came forth from Esther, Walter turned to find the young woman had stopped her horse and sat stone still smiling while tears streamed down her face. "Oh! My! Mistress Esther, be no need for those tears, even if you don't take to my name."

"No, Walter Ballinger, I love your name, for it is the same name as my own. I am Esther Ballinger, the oldest daughter of Dr. Benjamin Ballinger. I am quite proud you chose your name to match mine."

"Now, Mistress Esther, I done heared ye and Joshua and Miss Lovely called by the name Ball. No need, no need at all to tell ol' Walter such a tale."

"Tis no lie, Walter. My true name is Ballinger. My older brother Samuel, Lovely, and I took a different name after fleeing from our home. Someday, I might just tell you that story."

"Funny thing, Mistress Esther, first time I sees yer brother, Joshua, he reminded me of one of Dr. Ballinger's young ones.

See, that boy found me near to the doctor's house, injured. He done took me home to his Pa for doctoring. That's how I come to meet your Pa. But then, there at the fort, Joshua done stated his name be Ball, so I reckon it not be the boy I 'membered. My, oh my, how connected we all be."

After riding in silence for several miles, Walter asked quietly, "Mistress Esther, I needs to know, be yer father amongst the livin'?"

"No, Walter, he passed five years ago. I have only my brothers Benjamin and Joshua and, of course, Lovely."

While no more secrets passed between the two riders, a friendship built first upon a name and then a sincere liking for each other grew. Esther, who knew Walter's reputation as an honest, hardworking man, never feared for her safety while in his presence. Walter now claimed a brotherly attachment to the young woman who shared his name. Weeks later, thinking back on their journey, Esther realized she had trusted Walter completely.

Over the campfire that evening, Esther stated, "Walter, I believe it is the third of October. I know we are close behind our army, but I have, we have, no idea where they are headed and when a battle might occur. Perhaps I could stay here until morning, and you could ride out now and join up with our army to gain some information."

"Done been thinkin' on that myself. I be so doin' iff'in ye promise to remain here and take care to stay hidden. I be back by dawn iff'in be possible. You keep that fire aburnin' and don't get no chilblains."

"I promise I'll remain right here and stay warm until morning."

Walter returned just after dawn on the fourth of October. He looked exhausted. Esther pushed the remaining bit of rabbit she had roasted the previous evening toward him. The small fire had burned down, and she reached to put more wood on the fire when Walter spoke quietly, "Shouldn't Mistress Esther, some

Tories might be about. I be warm enough. Found this here tacked to a tree. Might be important. Don't know fer sure, can't read."

In the light of early morning, Esther first quickly read the notice to herself. As she reached the end, she gasped and glanced up to see Walter awaiting her words. Without pausing, Esther read it aloud.

>Denard's Ford, Broad River,
>Tyron County, October 1, 1780.
>
>Gentlemen: Unless you wish to be eat up by an inundation of barbarians, who have begun by murdering an unarmed son before his aged father, and afterwards lopped off his arms, and who by their shocking cruelties and irregularities, give the best proof of their cowardice and want of discipline; I say, if you want to be pinioned, robbed, and murdered, and see your wives and daughters, in four days, abused by the dregs of mankind-in short, if you wish to deserve to live, and bear the name of men, grasp your arms in a moment and run to camp.
>
>The Back Water men have crossed the mountains; McDowell, Hampton, Shelby, and Cleveland are at their head, so that you know what you have to depend upon. If you choose to be degraded forever and ever by a set of mongrels, say so at once, and let your women turn their backs upon you, and look out for real men to protect them.
>
>Pat Ferguson,
>Major 71st Regiment

"Well, I be rightly damned, Mistress Esther, that Major Ferguson be a fool, a right stupid ol' fool. Everyone knows you don't kick a wildcat for that screamin' cat most likely turn and tear you to pieces, limb from limb."

"I could have not put it better myself, Walter. Now, what else did you find out? Where is our army headed?"

"Well, I done spoke with Black Mike, you know Sevier's man, and he says they now believe that Major Ferguson done camped his army on top a ridge called King's Mountain. That be right on the border between the two Carolina colonies. Don't know much more 'exceptin' we be about two days hard ridin' from her' to that there place. As for when those colonels be figurin' to attack, well, I reckon they done planned to surprise that there Ferguson. That be what I'd do and our leaders be somewhat smarter than me."

> "On wounded soldiers, in their anguish lying,
>   Her gentle spirit shall descend like rain.
> Where the white flag with the red cross is flying,
>   There shall she dwell, the vanquisher of pain." Joyce Kilmer

October 4 to October 7, 1780

Clear cool, autumn weather allowed them to ride easy for the rest of that day and into the fifth. While they rode toward where they believed King's Mountain to be, Esther and Walter found it necessary to stop and asked for directions in several small villages. Esther thought it best to ask at isolated cabins they saw along the road, but more accurate information came from an older couple on the outskirts of Gilbert's Town.

"You be right near two days behind that Patriot army headed south, young woman. Be you Tory or Whig, I shall say no more."

"Sir, perhaps we can convince you we are Patriots?"

"Don't rightly know how you'd do so. You got papers?"

"Papers? Well, no, sir."

"No mind, can't read."

"Perhaps I might pay you for the information?"

"Pay me! Pay me! To be a traitor!" he shouted.

"George Lawson, stop harassin' that girl right this instant," another voice, this one female, shouted in return.

"Now Molly, you just be goin' on about your business while I be tendin' to mine," he answered, turning about to face the tall, slim older woman who'd appeared in the doorway of their large two-story cabin.

Marching forth, arms swinging, she spoke quietly into George's ear before turning back to their visitors. "Now miss, just where might ye be headed? Perhaps I be of more help than this ol' fool of mine."

Flustered, Esther carefully chose her words as she decided on a partial truth instead of a deception. "Mistress, my brother be with the Patriot army that came by here two days ago. I need to find him. Will you please give me their direction?"

"Why, yes, I can. That army 'twas headed south toward Cowpens. You might come near to reaching there tonight if you just follow this path down to the river. At Alexander's Ford you go across the Broad, from there you turn southeast. Trail's well marked. I wish you a safe journey. Now hurry along."

Turning back to her husband, she demanded, "George, get you back to the spring and fetch my water. Oh, you got plenty of water for yourselves?" she asked, turning back to Esther and Walter.

"Yes, mistress, we do. We thank you kindly. Come along Walter."

Much later in the afternoon, after fording the Broad River, Esther and Walter turned southeast. As evening approached, Esther urged Walter to ride further on. However, as their horses were worn and hungry, Walter insisted they stop. In a small, sheltered meadow beside a mountain stream, they settled their horses and built a small fire. With little food left, they roasted and shared the remains of a hunk of beef Black Mike had given Walter.

Soon the weather turned, and a cold driving rain quickly enveloped their camp. Walter, always thoughtful of Esther's wellbeing, had already constructed a small shelter. Soon, they both huddled underneath. Throughout a cold, dark, wet night, Esther slept beside Walter, who kept watch between catnaps.

Just before dawn, Walter shook Esther awake. "Mistress, I done got the horses ready. Here be a bit of barely warm tea. Get yourself ready. I be tidying up the camp."

Within minutes, Esther had finished her tea, took care of her needs, and prepared to mount up.

"Mistress, ye be going on back to the trail while I be pissin' on this here fire. Be right behind ye."

Smiling at Walter's words and courtesy, Esther mounted Athena and rode through the trees back to the road.

Side by side, they journeyed on into the morning toward Cowpens. There, around the pens that usually held cattle for auction, they found evidence of the army's encampment of the previous evening. Yet, the fires lay cold, not warm, as if the army had left earlier that morning.

"Seems to me our army done lit out yesterday night for somewheres different. Must be hurryin' to do battle," Walter surmised.

Upon leaving Cowpens, the army's trail became harder to follow. Nigh on impossible, according to Walter. Yet, being a reasonably good tracker, he soon found the trail of a large body of mounted men headed somewhat east. Still, other trails they ran across seemed to track south or even due north. Esther and Walter discussed the possibility that their army had split into smaller units.

"'magine they could ah done so, Mistress Esther, but seems that might make it harder to strategize one to another."

"Yes, but like us, they might not know exactly where Ferguson is. They might split up to hunt for him."

"Could be as ye say. Guess Joshua and his couriers be busy as bees ridin' back and fro between our men."

For Esther and Walter, the rest of the sixth of October proved difficult. They constantly found and lost trails. Only once did they believe they might actually be on the trail of their army. In the late afternoon, Esther, tired and cross, insisted they stop and ask directions. As they approached a rather large white frame home surrounded by open fields, they spotted a ruckus between mounted men and a youngster. Turning back into the tree line, Esther watched as several men held the youth while others seemed to question him.

Unsure of whom or what they observed, they instead turned back toward a deserted cabin they had passed earlier in the day. There they took shelter during a rain shower. Disheartened over their lack of information, Esther welcomed the chance to get dry, warm, and to rest a bit. Walter hid their horses in an isolated paddock and was securing firewood when the door flew open and two men pushed inside, long rifles ready.

Calmly, Esther reached into her pocket for her small pistol before realizing she recognized one of the two men. "Be ye Aquilla Lane?"

"Mistress Esther? How come ye be here? Are ye alone? Mind my manners, yea, I be Aquilla," one answered as they entered the small cabin.

"I thought so. You are Lieutenant Isaac's brother. Is he here about? Have you seen Joshua?"

"Not since early morning. Joshua be with Isaac. I mean the lieutenants, my brother and yours, that is. Is ye sister and the babe well? Be there trouble in Watauga?"

"How 'bouts ye two stands right still like stone statues," Walter instructed, moving through the now empty doorway long rifle first. "I be likely to shoot, . . . well I be damned, Aquilla Lane!"

"Walter, Mistress Esther, might ye two just tell us how ye came to be here afore someone gets killed?"

"Aquilla, Walter is my escort, of sorts. I am here to give aid to your wounded after the battle. Seems we have become lost, and we took shelter from the rain. Has the battle happened? Did they find Ferguson's army?"

"Well, I be! Joshua and Isaac sure not goin' ah be happy to hear you done come all this way."

"They might if someone becomes injured, or shot, or ill and in need of my help, Aquilla Lane. You can just go right back there and tell Lieutenant Lane, or Captain Bean, or Colonel Sevier, or whomever is in charge, that I am here to do my part. I have not left my child and ridden all this way to be disregarded simply because I am a woman. Now, answer me, has the battle taken place?"

"Oh, no ma'am. We still have a ways to go. My brother Tidence here and me been sent to root out any Tories hidin' in the area, 'specially them that might give away our location. We be on connisance."

"I think you mean reconnaissance. Glad to meet you Tidence. Aquilla, is there somewhere nearer to the battlefield where we might find shelter and set up an aide station of sorts?"

"Don't rightly know, ma'am, 'ceptin, perhaps, maybe? How about Tidence and me just stay here abouts tonight and then, in the morning, take ye to a small church we saw earlier today? I reckon ye shouldn't be goin' no closer, as some of our men still be roaming about and might mistake ye for the enemy. Our Pa, Lieutenant Joshua or Captain Bean likely wring our necks for such as puttin' ye in danger."

Worried and tired, almost to exhaustion, Esther took to one of the deserted beds in the cabin. All three men contributed to a store of firewood and the evening's meal.

Early on the seventh of October, Esther arose to find Aquilla Lane missing and Tidence quietly standing beside Walter.

"Now, Mistress Esther, I done promised Mistress Doak to see to yer safety. So Tidence here and me be planning to take ye to that church nearby and stay there with ye. Aquilla, he done volunteered to go straight to Colonel Sevier and tell him yer whereabouts and yer comin' all this way to tend any wounded."

"So, you decided this on your own, did you?" Esther answered, a bit peeved at not being consulted.

"No, ma'am. Talked it over with Aquilla before he left out. Tidence here done put in his words as well, though they not be many. Still, seems like the best for all. 'Specially since none of us wanted to be shot by Joshua or Isaac, both bein' right smart with a rifle."

Several hours later, they reached the small church the Lane boys had come across during their reconnaissance. Unlike many rural churches, this one had a small wood-burning stove. Numerous benches and two large rough tables stood against the back wall of the sanctuary. Outside, Walter found a hitching post and a privy of sorts. Esther instructed Walter and Tidence to find water and firewood.

Shortly after their arrival, near to three in the afternoon, they heard rifle shots ring in the distance. The sound echoed forlornly around the little valley where the church stood.

At the suddenness of battle sounds, Esther rushed outside and stood looking into the wooded hillsides to the southeast. Soon Walter and Tidence stood nearby, rifles aimed at an enemy too far away to be seen, yet too close to ignore.

"Tidence, how many men are with our army?"

"Right near nine hundred, I done heard Captain Bean tellin'."

"Do you know the strength of Ferguson's corps?"

"Not rightly, ma'am. I hear'd tell somewhat over a thousand. No need to be worryin'. Our boys be riled something fierce. That Major Ferguson insulted us and called upon our honor. Least ways, that what my brother said."

"Tidence, can you not read?"

"Oh, yes ma'am. Pa insisted we all learn to read an' write an' do our numbers. I be the best of all us boys. I would've read the words myself, but someone else done grabbed the paper we found stuck on a tree and made off with it."

Taking it from her apron pocket, Esther handed Tidence the folded broadsheet with Ferguson's ultimatum. She watched as the young man quickly read the warning directed toward the local inhabitants.

"Been wondering jist what had riled up our boys so much the last few days. Guess they done read Ferguson's words, or had his words read to them," Tidence replied, turning back toward the echoing sounds of many rifles and muskets. Solemn and quiet, he watched, as did Esther and Walter, a battle they could not see but only hear unfold amongst the trees on a nearby mountain, named for an early settler, not the king they now despised.

"Does Ferguson have cannons?"

"Oh, no, ma'am. Ferguson's boys be militia, not one British soldier among them. They walk near 'bout everywhere. Most don't even have horses. Course, our men be on foot now. I heard Isaac telling the boys that mountain be covered in trees and brush, and they'd go in on foot. Least ways, they can hide and shoot from the trees. I wouldn't worry myself much, if'in I be ye. Any our boys need tendin' Aquilla ken where we be."

Slowly, time crept forward as Tidence, Walter, and Esther stood listening to a battle fought between men who had been raised together as family or neighbors or friends. Men who had many times fought, hunted, worshiped, and celebrated side by side. There on that wooded hillside, all thoughts of fellowship and family seemed now forgotten. There on King's Mountain, men fought beside and even against their sons, their brothers, their cousins, their friends, their neighbors. It was militia against militia, except for one lone British officer.

Esther thought on Joshua, on the Bean men, and all those she knew at Watauga. Men she had danced with. Men whose wounds she had tended. Friends such as Michael and David and Jesse.

An hour after hearing the first shots, the sound of rifles rang out across the hills and valleys louder than ever before. A crescendo of battle. As they listened with hearts and minds full of fear and dread, within minutes, silence. Signaling an end? A silence of death? The silence of surrender? Sometimes still, a lone shot rang across the hills, little more. Somehow, the fear of knowing how the battle fared became more intense. More real. Esther believed she could hear screams and moans of agony, of fear, of death.

As the stillness continued, Esther turned back toward the small church, opened the door, and fell to her knees. Walter, who had followed, let her be.

Turning back, he said, "Tidence, ride out toward the battlefield. If our men be the losers, some might be headed back home. Ye can direct them here."

"No need, Walter, no need. Aquilla knows where to bring the wounded. Told me to wait here."

So, Walter and Tidence waited in silence. Their prayers and thoughts their own. Inside, Esther prayed on in soft whispers. Alone with her thoughts — her fears.

Near on to dusk, two men carrying a wounded man on a sling between their horses rode into sight. Another horseman carried what appeared to be a small boy across his chest.

Mistress Esther, ye be needed!" Tidence shouted through the open door. "Hurry, our men bring wounded!"

Arising at once, Esther stumbled toward the door on legs, now numb from hours of kneeling. Leaving the church, she spied the first two riders and their wounded comrade. Walter had already moved to help.

As the three carried the wounded man into the church, Esther turned at Tidence's shout, "Mistress Esther, there be more a comin'."

"Go," Esther ordered Walter, "the other man carried a child."

The first of the wounded to arrive, carried in by his own cousins with Walter's help, lay seriously wounded.

"This be our cousin, ma'am. He be a hero, took down several Tories after being stabbed," one man whispered.

192

Esther began, and upon finding a bayonet wound to the lower abdomen, knew even as she examined the wound that he had little chance of surviving.

"Can you tell me your name?" she asked quietly, as more battle-weary friends carried their wounded comrades into the church. Walter and Tidence guided their efforts, asking that they place the wounded on pews or on the floor.

"Lieutenant William Blackburn, ma'am. Be I badly wounded?"

"Yes, Lieutenant, but I'll see to you. You rest now and let me get your wound cleaned and bandaged. Have you much pain?"

"Some, less now that I am here and not moving, ma'am."

"I'll see to your pain in a minute. Now, just rest, William."

"My family calls me Will."

"Then so shall I, now rest, stop talking, and let me work."

As evening's darkness settled in, Esther and Walter diligently worked, side by side, to tend each and every one of the men relegated to their care. Walter assigned Tidence to carry and distribute water to the wounded and to keep the stove burning hot as they needed warm water. Not long after dark, Aquilla arrived with yet another brother, Dutton. They took on the task of carrying out the dead and seeing to the newly arrived.

The brothers located lanterns and candles in a small storeroom and gathered more firewood as the evening turned cold. Esther worked on. Turning to each man repeatedly, she kept calm, reassuring each one. The most agitated, she supplied with a tea made from peach tree bark, knowing its sedative powers would supply comfort to mind and body.

One young boy, only fifteen in age, arrived with slight powder burns to his eyes. His tears flowed silently, as he sat embarrassed on the floor in a dark corner.

"Someone fire their rifle too close to yer eyes, young man?" Walter asked, squatting in front of the boy.

"Yes, sir, I mean Walter."

"I answer to either. Now let me consult with Mistress Esther."

"I heard. Bring my bag, and I'll find the pouch of eye bright. Mix the powder, just a spoon full or a bit more with cold water and have him apply it to his eyes with a clean rag. You can use part of a bandage. Does he have other injuries?"

"No, ma'am, just powder burns on his face, bright red he be, flecks of powder in his skin, too."

"Eye bright should help. Have him change the compress frequently. I will check on him later. Aquilla, might I have your help?" Esther called over the moans and groans of over twenty wounded men as she turned to recheck Lieutenant Blackburn.

"Yes'um."

"Help me turn the Lieutenant here. I need to see to his back. I believe he still bleeds," she directed, as Aquilla arrived at her side. Then, glancing down, Esther sighed as tears clouded her sight. "No need, Aquilla. Lieutenant William here has passed."

All around, men felt the quiet, the silence, the finality of Esther's words, and as she stood praying over the young man lying before her, all around the room, heads bowed. From one corner of the church, sitting, leaning against the wall, an older soldier began singing "Rock of Ages" in his powerful baritone.

While I draw this fleeting breath,
When mine eyes shall close in death,
When I soar to worlds unknown,
See Thee on Thy judgment throne,
Rock of Ages, cleft for me,
Let me hide myself in Thee.

Others joined in. They sang all the verses, and with the last, heads still bowed, many a man wiped away tears. William, while the first to be lost, was not the last.

"Esther, I needs ye to see to one more."

"Another soldier, Walter? When did he arrive?"

"Not a soldier, a child. He arrived with Lieutenant Blackburn. He done broke his arm. Set it best I could and found him a place to rest and some vittles. Come see, ma'am."

Quietly lying on Walter's blanket in the corner of the church up behind the altar, Esther saw a small Negro boy of about eight years of age. Skinny, dirty, the rags he wore for clothes hanging off in tattered strips, lay a child.

"He don't talk much. Said his father be made to fight and he followed him to the battlefield to bring him home as his mother was about to give birth. He fell from a tree where he hid when the fighting commenced. His name be Levi."

"Levi, my name is Esther. May I examine your arm? Walter, did Levi have some food?"

"For sure, I brung him most of mine as he done gobbled down his own portion."

Examining Walter's handiwork of thin wood shakes and a tight bandage wrapping, Esther answered, "well, it seems I could have done no better, Walter. You did an excellent job. Levi, did you find your father?"

"Told me he saw his father die."

"Well, young Levi, I guess you can stay with us for now. Rest and call out for Walter if you need help."

Esther noticed the boy never took his eyes off Walter.

Esther and Walter moved from man to man all night. Some needed only a clean bandage and a bit of encouragement. Others with more serious wounds lay quiet as they cleaned and dressed their wounds. Several murmured in confused words, making no sense, and, at times, cried out. Esther made sure each of these had a less wounded watcher nearby, to call out for her if needed.

At dawn's first light, Tidence Lane placed a blanket around her shoulders and led Esther to a pallet placed behind the altar. There, upon that cold floor, Esther prayed once more for Joshua, for none here had word of him since the battle's end. Only then did she sleep. Quiet overcame the room, as Tidence, Walter, Aquilla, and Dutton continued to tend the wounded.

Only an hour or so passed before a ruckus outside awakened almost all within the small church, including Esther.

"Esther, Esther Ball!"

Exhausted, but suddenly alert, Esther recognized Joshua's voice. As she rushed to the door to silence him, Joshua stepped into the church, followed by a very tall, slender man, carrying what appeared to be a doctor's case.

"Joshua, stop your shouting. You'll awaken one and all."

"Stop my shouting? How dare ye sister! I should shout at ye, shake ye, and demand ye return home immediately. Where is Naomi? Where is Lovely? Are ye well?" Joshua shouted, shaking with what Esther realized was anger mixed with a large dose of fear.

"Just which question do you wish me to answer first?" Esther replied, hands on hips and temper flaring. For despite her weariness, and with the relief of knowing Joshua was unharmed, Esther found the strength to stand strong and defend her position.

As Joshua tried to find calm, Walter walked up and took his arm. "Friend, let me answer for her, for I know all. Mistress Esther, I believe the young man they just put up on the table done need your help."

With a firm hand, Walter led Joshua away. Esther heard him ask, "Young Joshua, did you know'd I done ken ye as a young boy? Why, we even have the same name..."

As she turned back to tend her newest patients, Joshua's companion spoke. "Ma'am, I understand from Lieutenant Isaac Lane, you have been tending these men. I am Doctor Seth McIntosh. Might I be of assistance?"

From his Scottish burr, Esther immediately recognized Dr. McIntosh's homeland. He stood some over six feet tall, even taller than Joshua. He had obviously pulled his dark auburn hair into a queue earlier in the day, but now most fell loose and in curls upon his shoulders. Blue eyes shown above a shadow of freckles and a day's growth of stubble which covered his handsome face.

"Dr. McIntosh, oh, yes, please, there are several wounds that could use your training. Over here is Private Cox. He has a musket ball in his shoulder. Perhaps you might remove it? Several others have serious wounds. Might we examine them as well?"

"Only if you call me Seth. I know it is improper, but I find as we work it will reduce time addressing each other. May I call you Esther?"

"Yes . . .," seemed to be all Esther could utter, in response to Joshua's arrival, the presence of a doctor standing beside her, and her exhaustion.

Esther and Seth worked side by side for the rest of the day. Seth made quick work of William Cox's shoulder and soon the young man lay bandaged and resting after a dosing of feverfew. As they worked around the room, side by side, checking on each man, Esther noticed Seth's efficient, caring manner. He seemed knowledgeable, and she enjoyed hearing his Scottish burr and his casual way with all, both the injured and those assisting.

Very late in the afternoon, Joshua approached with a tin plate of roasted venison and a cup of cider. "Sister, I be happy to see ye well. I be sorry for my manner earlier, but the news of yer presence so close to the battlefield left me worried and angry beyond all reason."

"Oh, Joshua, I wanted to tell you, but I knew you, most of all, would ensure I did not make this journey. Putting that aside, Joshua, where is Walter? I haven't seen him in hours."

"He and some of the Blackburn boys took Levi home. Seems the boy lived close by. I expect they be returning soon. Now, sit sister, eat. Walter has told me much. I know ye be safe. Still, ye look tired. Have ye slept recently?"

"Only an hour, just at dawn. Joshua, are there more wounded men?" she asked, while attacking the plate of food.

"Only a few, Robert Sevier be badly wounded, still he refuses to come to seek aid. Dr. Seth bandaged him and gave him some bit of medicine back at our camp. Don't rightly know what. Robert just wants to head on home. Most of our men be headed on home, as we fear Tarleton might be comin' this way. Oh, and Moses Shelby be ridin' here now for aid. Robert Edmonson, too, the younger one. They killed his pa and two uncles."

"Joshua, what about the wounded Tories?"

"No need to worry over them. One of their surgeons survived the battle, and he be seeing to their care. We be only bringing our wounded here. Not many over fifty, course we have some twenty-nine killed. Some of our men just needed bandaging. Not near as many as those damned Tories."

"So, our men were victorious. It is true what these men have said? Ferguson was killed, and our men won the battle?"

"Did no one tell ye? We snuck up on those damned Tory bastards and killed or wounded near on four hundred, including Ferguson himself."

"Joshua Ballinger, how dare you curse like a heathen?" Esther whispered. "We can take pride in our victory without vicious talk and defamation. Except maybe for Ferguson. Walter found one of his broadsheets. I must say, I believe the man to be a fool, saying those things he did."

Joshua's countenance changed, and he grasped Esther's hands in his. "I saw him die, sister. Our men shot him as he charged into our position with a drawn sword. Anger and fire in his eyes, he took down several of our men before the first rifle shot hit him. He died instantly from over five shots, hitting him all at once. Then his horse dragged his body as his foot was caught in his stirrup when he fell dead. Once his horse was held, our men mutilated his body. They stripped him of his clothing. Just when I thought the worst be over, later as their forces surrendered, our men continued firing, giving no quarter, until Shelby and Sevier forced them to stop . . ."

Joshua suddenly spoke again. "As the battle began, our forces quietly snuck up on the lower reaches of the mountain. Some ground was swampy and slowed us immensely. Then the British began firing. Our men fought from behind trees, moving ever upward toward the enemy. As the fighting became more intense, the noise of rifles and muskets and men yelling became almost more than a man could endure. Jesse Bean stood nearby, and we fired as soon as we could reload, repeatedly, then their militia charged with bayonets. That's when the fighting became personal."

Esther waited as she could see Joshua struggling with these fresh memories, some almost too intense to be recalled. She felt his fear, his sorrow, his remorse.

"As the Tories waved their white flag and lay aside their muskets, seems some of our men could not stop fighting, could not accept surrender, could not accept we had been victorious until all the enemy lay dead."

"Oh, brother, the horrors you have witnessed," Esther whispered.

"Not only witnessed, sister. I shot my share and killed one with my knife and another with my tomahawk. I have killed before to protect myself and my companions, but never another in a battle such as this. May God protect my soul," he whispered, and releasing Esther's hands turned and walked toward the darkness outside the church door.

From across the room, Seth called out, "Esther, perhaps I might have your help. You as well, Joshua."

With those words, Joshua drew into himself what little strength that remained and turned to help. As they rushed across the small room, others carried inside the last of the Patriot wounded. Moses Shelby's wound required immediate attention. As they labored to ease his pain and tend his wounds, Esther requested Joshua brew up a tea using her pouch of black cohosh.

After encouraging both Moses and young Robert to drink, they shared the sedative tea around the room with those who most needed relief from their pain. Others drank heartily from a shared jug of rum, Tidence had procured from somewhere thereabout.

Heroes are people who rise to the occasion and slip quietly away.
Tom Brokaw

October to Early December 1780

Much later, Walter returned, holding tight to a sleeping Levi.

"Did you find his family?"

"Rightly did, Mistress Esther. Mother and baby be dead, murdered in their bed as was a sister, about five, she be. Thank the good Lord I done left Levi outside when I went in the shack to check. Something about the place made ol' Walter know evil had been done. Not much to do but bring the boy back, as he has no more family. Guess he be my son now." Tears rolled down the old Negro's cheeks and into his sparse stubble, as his body shook with grief over what he had discovered.

"Come, friend, have you had food? Settle Levi down here beside my pallet. Use my blanket, so he does not feel the night's chill."

"Did I do's right, Mistress Esther? Did I do's right, taking him away from that place? Reckon the child done belongs to someone, seems like. . ."

Taking Walter's hand in hers and squeezing it, Esther replied, "You did exactly as I would have done. We'll make it so that Levi can stay with you if you wish. Let me worry about that."

A while later, Esther took to her pallet at Walter's insistence. He bedded down nearby to make sure no one disturbed her. Levi slept peacefully at his side. Esther, lying awake, wept silently for Joshua and Naomi, for the wounded, for the dying, and prayed for the dead. She drifted into small snatches of weary sleep only to awake to mourn for their losses.

Still three times, she arose, lit a candle, and checked on each of the wounded. Checking if they slept peacefully. Asking those yet awake if they were cold or in pain? From one to another, she moved. Some who woke saw her as an angel in the darkness. Others conversed with her in whispers, so as not to wake those sleeping nearby. A few slept through her ministrations, her care, without waking.

Finding the young man with the powder burned eyes and face, she removed his compress, wrung it out in a basin of cold water, and checked he was sleeping peacefully before placing it back on the lad's face.

Sitting quietly against the back wall near the door, Dr. Seth had dozed a bit before waking immediately upon hearing movement within the room. Seth watched as the beautiful young woman, still dressed mostly in men's clothing, moved from man to man. She seemed an angel of mercy, yet very much a woman. As she returned to her pallet, he quietly rose and left the church. Outside, a chill wind blew, although the skies held clear. There, Seth found Tidence and Aquilla standing guard, both alert and instantly aware of his presence.

"Tidence?"

"Yes sir, Dr. Seth, somethin' amiss?

"No, all is quiet. Just needed a bit of fresh air. Also, I wanted to ask, do ye ken Esther well"?

"All about Watauga know Mistress Esther. She be a healer, and, of course, ye know she be Joshua's sister. Joshua be a lieutenant now, the militia's best courier hereabouts. Mistress Esther be one determined young woman. Capable in all things for the ill. Soft hands, so Isaac says. She done treated him for a wound several years back. Everyone at Watauga respects Mistress Esther."

Hesitantly, Seth probed a bit more, asking, "Mistress Esther, is she married? I thought I heard her brother ask about a baby."

"Oh, no sir, not now anyways. Her husband done died not long after the baby was born. Most of us never met the man. Just be her and Joshua and a younger sister, Miss Lovely, now. They be staying with the Bean family as their own cabin got torched by the Chickamauga. I believe you met Captain Bean and his sons?"

"Yes, William is a brave and dedicated leader. I understand he had several sons and relatives in the recent battle. How old be Esther's child?" Seth asked, turning the conversation back to Esther.

"Oh, let me think on it, well . . . seems she be right on half a year. A girl, think her name be Naomi. Mistress Esther be our carer and midwife about Watauga. I think I done said that. She learned from Mistress Sarah. Mistress Sarah died a year or so back. Some say her brother be a doctor with General Washington. That be Esther's brother, not Sarah's. Sarah was old when she passed."

Having now determined that Tidence would answer any question he posed and a lot more he never thought to ask, Seth probed a bit more, "Do you know how she came to be near the battlefield? I understood us to be several days' journey from the Watauga settlement."

"Ol' Walter done told us all 'bout her headin' out here on her own just a day or so after our men done left out. Left a note with her sister, Miss Lovely, tellin' where she be goin'. Mistress Doak, she be the preacher's wife, and Mistress Bean was debatin' who to send after her, to bring her home, when Walter done volunteered. He caught up with her and brung her the rest of the way. Walter swears Mistress Doak told him to do so. Walter never lies, so I guess it be truthful what he told."

"She left Watauga and traveled over the mountains on her own?"

"That be Walter's tale. I believe it be true. My mama once said Mistress Esther done be a powerful, headstrong, smart young woman. I always believe what my Mama says. I once said she be pretty to look at and almost got slapped down for talking such. I's just statin' my opinion!"

Early the following morning, Lieutenant Isaac Lane and several men rode up to the little church, followed by two wagons and extra horses. "Dr. McIntosh, Private Aquilla!" he shouted.

Stumbling to his feet, Tidence answered, "Brother, ye be waking the wounded! Quiet down."

"That be Lieutenant Brother to you!" Isaac teased. "No time, Tidence. We need to load everyone up and move out. A larger escort will be along to assist. Find Aquilla and get a move on. Be Dutton here about?"

Within minutes, Seth and Esther began evaluating each of the wounded men's condition and needs. Meanwhile, Isaac Lane organized loading the seriously injured into the wagons and saw that those who could ride were mounted and assigned a member of the escort as their helpmate and protection. Being as many were family, this chore resolved itself as the men rushed in to assist their wounded relatives and friends. All the wounded were to be carried off toward Watauga, even those from further east or north into North Carolina.

Walter gathered Esther's belongings, saddled the horses, and helped pack up all the items needed to care for the wounded. With his every step, Levi followed like a puppy behind his mother. Once everything was in place, Walter lifted Levi up onto his saddle and gave him strict instructions to stay put.

"Seth, will you be going along to Watauga?" Esther questioned as Aquilla arrived with the doctor's horse.

"Only partway, then I must ride back to join our forces, as they will need me after yet another battle."

Within the hour, twenty more men approached the little church. As the party loaded up, Esther approached Isaac Lane and asked about Joshua. "Isaac, is Joshua about?"

"No, ma'am. Captain Bean done sent him out to do some reconnaissance. Don't reckon we shall see him for several days, if not longer. Now, Mistress Esther, ye ready? We need to bemovin' along. There be word Colonel Tarleton be hot on our trail. All know that man has no respect for the wounded."

That first day, Isaac Lane led the men back toward Cowpens and then north along the same route they had taken to the battle.

To ease the suffering of the wounded, the wagons moved slowly. Their journey progressed at a snail's pace, though they stopped only as absolutely necessary. Between stops, Esther and Seth checked on the wounded, carried water to each, and changed bandages when needed.

Having slept so little in the previous days, Esther often felt herself dozing in her saddle. At such times, Walter or Aquilla would speak to her, asking her if she needed to rest. Walter wanted her to ride in a wagon with the wounded, where perhaps she might sleep. Esther declined all such offers.

Just before they reached the Broad River at Alexander's Ford, Tidence, who had ridden ahead to survey the crossing, returned with the news that the water ran too high to risk crossing with the wagons.

After much discussion among the militia leaders, Seth, Esther, and even Walter, they helped each invalid mount up with another rider to be ferried across the Broad. As this maneuver began, Seth and Esther tended to each of the seven seriously wounded. Soon mounted, each one, brave to the man, crossed the icy stream without complaint.

They abandoned the wagons as the trail onward over the mountain would not accommodate that mode of travel. While this would make travel faster, Esther and Seth worried about the strain of hours of riding horseback for each of the more seriously wounded.

On the far shore of the Broad, Isaac begged at a large cabin for shelter for the night. The residents quickly agreed to his request and helped the wounded to be settled and fed. Many in the small hamlet brought food for the soldiers and their wounded.

Soon, those under their care lay bedded down within the home, while outside, their escort built fires and shelters for the night as rain threatened.

Late in the evening, Dr. Seth asked politely, "Mistress Esther, please allow me to escort you upstairs, where I have been told a bed awaits you."

"No, if there is a bed, our wounded need it. I'll sleep on the floor. I have a blanket and a buffalo robe, though it is a mite damp."

"Lieutenant Lane insisted, Esther," Seth replied, smiling.

"Sleep there if you wish. I will be here in this room on a pallet. You sleep. I'll tend our wounded. You need rest as much as I."

"Please, Esther, rest upon the bed. You have done enough."

"Enough! How dare you decide *when I have done enough!*" Esther replied in a harsh whisper so as not to wake those sleeping nearby. "Have I stood up to our enemy's rifle and sword and fired upon him in defense of our freedom? Have I marched across mountains or forded streams with an army? Have I faced down British bayonets or stood against Hessians? Did I starve and freeze at Valley Forge, as did my brother Benjamin? Did I give my life as did my brother Samuel? Have I ridden hither and yon delivering military correspondence? No, Dr. McIntosh, I will never have done enough until I have saved the life of each and every one of these men and all those that will need my care in days to come. How can *you* not understand? I have made only a simple sacrifice, whereas you serve on battlefield after battlefield. I no more deserve to sleep in a bed than I do to be treated with deference. I am simply a woman, yet a Patriot, who came to serve our cause, in the best way I can. Still, I fall far short in my service to our freedom and find myself lacking."

Despite her anger and rage, exhaustion pushed Esther to tears. Seth moved to pull the young woman into his arms to comfort her.

Walter reached her first and spoke. "Mistress Esther, Doctor Seth only asked ye to sleep in a bed. Ye wish to sleep here near the men, then so be it. Come with Walter, sister, into this here kitchen. There be warm bread and butter and a cup of hot tea with a bit of honey. I be seeing to your pallet here before the fire. I done hung your buffalo hide before the fire, so it be near on to dry. Even warm. You be able to hear the men from here, if you be needed. Come, sister, come with ol' Walter."

Seth stood silently as Walter led Esther quietly down the short hall into the home's attached kitchen, her words echoing in his mind. How could this young woman believe she had not done enough? She had toiled day and night, caring, softly, prayerfully, attentively for their wounded. All while mourning for her lost brother and husband, and most likely seeing his suffering in each of these wounded. Then Seth remembered Esther had not listed her own husband among her losses.

Later, Seth thought on how, after previous battles, he had watched as untrained wives and young women faced the same tasks as Esther. Not one had worked as diligently as had Esther, and none with as much training and skill. Then, Seth remembered her face at Joshua's asking the young woman about her child. First her dismay over her desertion, then her love for the young babe she had left behind. How hard it must have been to ride away from her baby so soon after losing her own husband.

He had once read a word that had captured his attention — *enigma*. Esther's character was such — puzzling, contradictory. He wanted to know more, to learn more about her. As he turned back toward the cabin's entrance, Seth felt the first pangs of longing. Longing to know more about this woman, longing to shelter her from the harshness of life, and if that was not possible, to stand beside her as she struggled to find herself worthy.

The next morning, near to Gilbert's Town, Dr. Seth McIntosh turned back south toward South Carolina, after saying a quiet goodbye to Esther, Walter, and young Levi.

"Dr. Seth, where might you be headed?" Esther asked, as they said their quiet goodbyes.

"South, back to join our militia and our armies. I go where I am needed. Seems like some in command believe there will be another battle in South Carolina soon."

Answering Lieutenant Lane's sharp, urgent call, Esther smiled once more, and moved toward one of the wounded.

"God be with ye, Dr. Seth," Walter answered with a handshake and a smile, "and if ye find yerself near Watauga, I be the blacksmith's helper. Mistress Esther, she be about as well."

"Walter, what is Mistress Esther's surname?"

"Oh, Mistress Esther be called Ball. She never revealed her husband's surname, nor does she use it now. I believe it be only hers to tell."

"Thank you, Walter. Take care of her and young Levi."

"Ohs, I rightly do."

After the battle of King's Mountain, some of the overmountain men had traveled quickly home through the mountains to Watauga. Back to their families, their homes. Each held a deep desire to return, knowing even now their kinfolk and friends might be in desperate peril.

While some overmountain men would have continued to fight, knowing their wives, daughters, and sons could, in most circumstances, defend themselves quite well, others recognized the dangers of the wilderness. Also, the harshness of winter approached, when each member of a family would be needed to fight the elements as well as the Chickamauga.

While Lieutenant Lane escorted their wounded home, a large body of overmountain men, some from North Carolina and some from Watauga, escorted their British and Tory militia prisoners north.

Others who fought there on that mountain moved quietly toward their own homes in North Carolina, Virginia, and South Carolina. Some, those who no longer had a home to return to since Ferguson's forces and the Tory militia had laid waste to the region in the previous months, rushed to reunite with their family and find shelter for the coming winter.

Upon nearing the crest of Roan Mountain, Esther pulled Walter aside while Levi slept nearby. "Walter, does Levi talk to you? I haven't heard him say a single word."

"No, young Levi done gone mute. He spoke that first day at the church, but after we went and found his home, not one word. Sometimes I see him crying when he thinks I not be noticin' but no, not one sound."

"Walter, we must keep Levi with you. He trusts you."

"I's intend to do just that. That boy be mine now. Always wanted a son."

"We'll speak with Reverend Doak. He might know how we can keep Levi safely with you."

Because of the need to move slowly and carefully with the wounded, Esther, the three Lane boys, Walter, and their escort did not arrive home until the sixteenth of October. All along the way, one or two scouts lingered in their wake, keeping watch for Tory militia or British regulars under Lieutenant Colonel Banastre Tarleton. Neither came.

At midday, as they approached Fort Caswell, anxious residents and those proud militiamen who had returned earlier flooded forth through the fort's gates to welcome them home. Cowbells rang! Men, women, and children shouted! Some fired off rifles to let others thereabout know their wounded had returned home. The good pastors of their community, Tidence Lane and Samuel Doak, rushed about blessing and praying over the wounded and their families. They asked about the needs of each man. Esther Doak took notes.

Finally, Esther gave each wounded man over into his family's care. She reassured each family and offered guidance for the care of the most seriously wounded. Only after she had finished with the last one did she turn to Walter.

"Oh, Walter, I am going to miss having you at my side. You have been my rock, my protector, and my friend. How can I ever repay you for your kindness?"

"Mistress Esther, there be no need for payment. Far as ol' Walter sees it, I jest been helpin' and protectin' my sister. 'Sides my reward be right there in young Levi."

Taking him in a hug, "Walter, brother, please call me Esther and come to visit me soon. Bring Levi. I want to introduce you both to my Naomi, your niece."

"Oh, sister Esther, I be calling you so, only when we be alone, so no one mistakes my meanin'. Today, I be seein' to ridin' out with ye to the Beans. Can't let ye wander into the wilderness alone, no, not ev'r again."

"Fine. You can meet my daughter today. Though I am eager to go, first, I must speak with the Reverend and Mistress Doak. There are several families that will surely need help in the weeks to come."

Several hours later, an exhausted Esther, escorted by Walter and two of the Lane brothers, set out for the Bean cabin. Along the way, Esther thought back on the heroes' welcome they had received at the fort. Not one had rebuked her for leaving and going to their soldiers' aid. Esther and Samuel Doak, among many others, had called her a hero. Quietly, Esther denied the term, for in her mind, a hero protected all under their care, while she had lost three young men. She had done so much less than any man in the militia.

Now, as she and her escort rode along, Esther urged them to hurry, for she wanted nothing more than to hold Naomi and to see Lovely.

When they approached the Bean settlement, Woody gave the alarm that riders were coming and then let out a howl of welcome when Esther dismounted, knocking her to the ground.

Levi laughed! Smiling, Walter chuckled at the sound, while the Lane brothers quickly helped her to her feet.

Many a watching eye filled with tears at Esther and Naomi's reunion, for as the baby woke to find herself once again in her mother's arms, she smiled, chuckled, and then burrowed her face into Esther's chest. Later, in the Bean cabin, safe and content, Esther sat holding her daughter for nothing and no one could make her turn loose.

Lydia Bean immediately noticed the small boy wrapped in a blanket as he had no jacket or shoes. "Walter, perhaps we might find some things among Russell's old clothing for the boy. If not, I can ask around amongst the family."

"Would be mighty appreciative, Mistress Bean. I got coin to buy him some moccasins."

So, within the hour, young Levi had been bathed and owned two pairs of trousers, both with patched knees, three cotton shirts, socks, undergarments, and a jacket a few sizes too big. Lydia had rolled up the sleeves to fit his short arms before Lovely and Sarah tacked them in place.

One of the Bean cousins, a girl about Levi's age, appeared with a wooden spinning top and showed Levi how to make it spin. While they played in a corner, Lydia pulled Walter aside.

"Walter, I don't ken how ye went off to protect our Esther and came back with a child, a Negro child at that. Still, he be here now."

"Someday mightn' tell you the story. Not one for tender ears. Mistress Lydia, I's all Levi has now for family. So, he be my son."

Lydia and Charlotte passed around food and drink to all who gathered. They shared news and the joy of having lost not one member of the large Bean and Russell clan.

Soon, a deep weariness overcame Esther. Only after she fell asleep, did Lydia take Naomi away and pass her along to Susan, her niece, who had served as wet nurse for the baby. Still sitting in the Bean's only stuffed chair, now covered in her white blanket, Esther slept through the night.

In the days following Esther's return, her heart filled with a deep desire never to part from Naomi ever again. She wondered how mothers could ever watch their child wander out to play alone, especially knowing the dangers. Esther constantly held, played with, and cared for Naomi, except for those hours she spent continuing to care for the wounded soldiers and others needing her skills. Each time, rushing back to be with Naomi.

While her milk had dried up and Esther could no longer nurse her own child, she had little choice but to continue living with the Bean family. Not to mention, she and Lovely had no home to return to.

Esther felt she owed them so much for taking care of Lovely and Naomi during her absence. The Bean clan, on the other hand, felt that Esther owed them nothing at all, for they recognized the sacrifice she had made by going to King's Mountain.

Every day, Walter, with Levi, rode out from the fort and escorted Esther to three of the wounded men's homes to see to their care. After a week, two were well enough to no longer need more than an occasional visit. Walter also escorted her to an outlying cabin to deliver a new baby and to the nearby home of an elderly widow who had fallen ill.

As the days passed into weeks, most all the Bean and Russell men had returned relatively unharmed from King's Mountain. Still, each espoused their opinion that the threat from British forces was not over. During the autumn and into early winter, Cherokee warriors continued to harass outlying cabins, hunters, and travelers. A few of the younger men from Watauga traveled back east to join the North Carolina militia.

Joshua did not return until several weeks had passed after Esther's have arrived back at Watauga. Having caused much worry between the sisters, he explained his absence, then kissing each in turn, he turned once again to Esther.

"Esther, let me hold my niece. No matter if I stink, she won't care. Look, she be reachin' for me," Joshua demanded, laughing all the while as the babe's tiny arms waved about reaching for the tall young man.

"Where have you been for so long? We expected you days ago," Lovely asked.

"Oh, here and there."

"Did you spend time with Beth?"

"How do ye know about Beth? And yes, I did, nosy child."

"I will have you know, I am not a child, being as I am sixteen years old."

"Oh, so you spent your time with Beth? Exactly where was that?" Esther asked.

"Near to Isaac Shelby's and that is all you need to know."

"Is there news of the war?" Lydia asked, hoping the answer would bring news of William, her sons, and nephews.

"Some, some," Joshua took a couple of minutes to smile and play with the babe before continuing. "Colonel Campbell and Colonel Shelby put some prisoners on trial for their actions against local citizens. William and your sons mostly be with that party, Campbell and Shelby's that is. They hung nine prisoners, and the rest were being escorted to General Gates. Mistress Lydia, William and Jesse be on their way home soon. Robert stays to fight with a few of our other men. Couriers have gone north to General Washington and to the Continental Congress about the victory. All across North Carolina, men and families have turned to our cause."

"Oh, Joshua, what good news!" Lovely exclaimed, while Russel hooped and hollered until his mother insisted, he take himself outside.

"I'll go round and tell every family, shall I Ma?"

"Go on with ye," Lydia answered, smiling.

The following morning, both Joshua and Walter, again with a now mostly silent Levi, escorted Esther to check in on the widow Bassingham. As Emily Bassingham had been suffering from grief over the loss of her husband and inflammation of the lungs for several months, Esther was not surprised to find Emily had passed during the previous few days. Several times, Esther had begged Emily to allow someone to stay with her. Emily had insisted no one was needed.

Walter and Levi rode off to find the Reverend Doak. Joshua stayed to help Esther wrap Emily's body in a quilt. Then the siblings built up the fire and set the cabin to rights. They milked and turned the cow loose and fed Emily's two hens.

The chores completed, Esther and Joshua sat down to chat while waiting. Esther tried to pry from her brother more details about this mysterious Beth, while Joshua learned more about her ride to King's Mountain. Soon, Samuel and Esther Doak arrived with the small cart, often used to carry bodies to the fort's small cemetery.

"Thank you, Esther, for sending for me. Emily's been right poorly for a long time. Ever since Albert died, now that I think about it."

"Yes, I believe she simply gave up on living. Do they have family hereabouts?" Esther asked, while Joshua helped Walter place the body in the cart.

"No more, no more. They arrived long before me, but Reverend Lane told me how their daughter died soon after they arrived here. She had consumption. Their son joined up with the Continental forces and died at Valley Forge. Someone once told they had a son in Kentucky, but Tidence says if so, he never heard them speak of him."

"So, what's to become of their cabin and their belongings?" Joshua asked.

"Well, custom her' bout' be that whoever finds it first it be theirs if'n they so wish. Guess it be yours," Walter answered.

"Could be yours using that logic," Joshua retorted.

"Personally, I think it should be Esther's. She and Lovely and Naomi and Joshua need a home," Samuel Doak replied.

"Family is not an important thing. It's everything." Michael J. Fox.

December 1780 through January 1781

So, it came to be that Esther, Lovely, and Joshua accepted the Bassingham cabin and prepared to make it their own. Emily and Alfred Bassingham had not been wealthy, still by frontier standards, they had accumulated a right good stock of belongings.

Over the coming weeks, Esther, Lovely, Lydia, and Charlotte cleaned the small cabin from top to bottom. The Ballinger sisters donated all the excess belongings and clothing to those families in need. To prepare for the fast-approaching winter, Joshua and Russell gathered and chopped firewood. The surrounding community gifted the family with dried fruits, nuts, grain, beans, meal, and bits of their late autumn harvest, for all knew the small family had no produce from their own garden, as it had been destroyed the night their cabin burned. Many donated in acknowledgement of Esther's care of their men at King's Mountain.

The Lane brothers, Aquilla and Tidence, arrived on a clear day toward the end of November and helped to enlarge a lean-to at the back of the cabin for the Ball's dairy cow and their horses. They also constructed a small, covered pen for the three chickens Lovely had purchased with coin from her earnings. During their work that day, Esther quickly realized both young men worked hard to impress *her* more so than Lovely. Courting on the frontier was often more labor intensive than just bringing flowers or gifts. Young men used their skills to impress young women. Their own not-so-subtle way of proving their worth.

Walter and Levi took to checking on their livestock every day as Esther and Lovely did not feel comfortable going off to the cabin without an escort. Esther learned the two often spent the night in the cabin, for within the fort, Walter had only one small half cabin behind the blacksmith shop for himself. Esther happily acknowledged to all that Walter and Levi were now a part of their family.

Unusual for the frontier, the Bassingham cabin had four rooms—two lower and two upper—though the last had steeply pitched ceilings. A rough stone chimney and fireplace dominated the lower, large room and ran all the way across the cabin's width. A small room, barely housing a bed, had been framed in along the back next to a small, covered porch.

Only a mile or so from the Bean settlement, along a small tributary of Boone's Creek, the cabin sat in a deep hollow surrounded by tall hardwoods and a few cedars. A short walk, out the back of the cabin, along the creek, lay a large, secluded meadow with a paddock for their horses and cow. Now overgrown and dormant, an enormous garden plot, laid out by Albert and Emily several years earlier, lay further along the creek.

Silently, for weeks, Esther stressed over her worries concerning a move to the cabin. She contemplated the difficulties a move would bring. Unlike their first small cabin at Watauga, it would not be just her and Lovely. Now she had Naomi to think of. Her first concern was Naomi's need to be put to breast at least thrice a day, for though the babe now enjoyed cramming soft foods into her mouth, she needed a mother's milk. While Esther often attempted to teach her daughter how to drink from a cup, she felt her Naomi needed the breast.

The second worry centered on the isolated position of the cabin. The British defeat at King's Mountain had stirred the British commanders into a rage, and in retaliation, they had increased their pressure on the Chickamauga Cherokee to wipe out the overmountain settlers. Attacks on isolated cabins and settlements intensified. Fighting those threats kept Captain Jesse Bean and his sharpshooters constantly on the move.

In early December, following several days of intense thought and concern, Esther approached Lydia with her doubts as the two prepared the evening meal. Rushing ahead, she stated, "Lydia, I don't feel right moving to the cabin. I might place Naomi and

Lovely in danger with us living in such an isolated place. Besides, Naomi needs Susan. Perhaps we should offer the cabin to one of the newly arrived families and move back to the fort. I could find another wet nurse."

"Might you just postpone your move until Naomi be weaned? William told just yesterday how the fort be overcrowded with burned out families and those fleeing from the British. So I don't believe ye can find a cabin."

"Lydia, I dwell constantly on the danger. With Joshua continually away, it would just be myself and Lovely. Did Emily and Albert ever have trouble from the Indians?"

"None I be knowing about. Course, they kept to themselves after their daughter died and their son marched off to war. We rarely saw them. They were not the visiting kind. Albert spent all his time workin' on that cabin and tending their crops. I only remember seeing Emily at the fort once, and that was for Albert's burial. Seems to me they just kept to themselves."

"Still. . .," Esther hesitated.

"Esther, I think on ye and Lovely as daughters. My home, while not large nor empty, with our menfolk off to war . . . well, it has room enough for ye three. Yer presence here provides me with friends and a house full enough to keep my mind busy. Ye know the worry of womenfolk as we sit at home alone, with our children, wondering. . .. Am I yet a widow? Are my children fatherless? Is my brother dead? Is my son wounded? Ye and Lovely and little Naomi keep my mind off the worries. I have needed ye here as much as ye have needed a home. I'll be truly sorry to see ye go, if ye decide to do so. Now let us think no more about that today."

Several weeks passed with Esther's worry for their safety, increasing, for all about the settlements, the Chickamauga continued their deadly raids. Esther never left the Bean settlement without at least two of the militia and Walter as escort. Still, many an evening's talk often focused on the latest atrocities.

A quiet Christmas came and went across the frontier. The weather stayed relatively mild, especially compared to the previous winter. Within the Bean cabin, they exchanged a few small gifts and attended a Christmas service at the fort. With so many of the menfolk off at war, the holiday passed quietly.

Prayers often began and ended with pleas for their menfolk's safety and health. Lydia seemed preoccupied and worried. Jesse had not been home in weeks, as his small unit worked to protect outlying cabins from the Chickamauga. Her son, Robert, had never returned to his wife and children after King's Mountain, having remained with the militia unit he commanded. The Williams, senior and junior, came and went frequently on militia business, rarely able to stay to home for more than a day.

The true cold of winter came in with the new year. Joshua returned on the second day of January with urgent messages for Colonel Sevier and others. After a quick visit with his sisters and niece and a night's sleep before Lydia's hearth, he took to a different horse and rode away once again. Early in the month, they heard talk about several more men from among those who had fought at King's Mountain who had traveled east toward the conflict.

War news was scarce as few travelers came their way. Constantly, Esther worried about the absence of letters from Benjamin. The last had been written in August 1779. More than a year had passed. Even knowing the fallibility of the colonial mail and military couriers, Esther's worries over Benjamin grew with each passing day.

Lovely stayed as Lovely most always had. She seemed to live from day to day by ignoring the turmoil of war. Esther accepted this manner, believing it was Lovely's way of dealing with death, sadness, and things she could not change or bear to contemplate. Her sister simply lived as though such things did not exist. Some days Esther wished she herself could adopt Lovely's attitude.

On the last day of January, just at dusk, Joshua rode into the Bean settlement, leading a pack horse and accompanied by a young woman on horseback. As Esther had done many times, the woman had worn men's canvas trousers for what must have been a long journey, for each looked travel worn. Snow had begun to fall hours earlier along with quickly dropping temperatures. So, Russell and Joshua quickly moved toward the small barn to unpack their horses while Esther, grabbing her cloak, approached the visitor.

"Mistress Lydia Bean is nearby visiting her elderly cousin, but may I welcome you inside? You must be chilled and tired. I am Esther, Joshua's sister."

"I have been wanting to meet you for so long. Joshua shared with me much of you and Lovely and little Naomi. I am Beth."

"Finally, we meet. Please come in and warm yourself. There is a meal awaiting. Joshua and Russell will care for the horses. No need for you to help."

"Joshua was not sure if you had moved to your own cabin but thought it best we stop here first with the weather being so harsh."

"You must be frozen through. Come, come, get warm and meet Lovely. She and Jane and Sarah, those are Lydia's daughters, are preparing the evening meal. I hope you like rabbit stew and corn cakes. I believe they have an apple cobbler for afterward."

Just as introductions were being made, Joshua entered carrying a small satchel.

"Here be yer clothing, Beth. Esther, where might Beth go change?"

"Oh, show her up to our chamber. She can share with us. Do you need anything more, Beth?"

With a quiet shake of the head, Beth followed Joshua up the steep stairs, leaving all below completely befuddled.

"Sister, is that the girl Joshua whispered about in his sleep?" Lovely asked.

"I expect she is."

"Why is she here? Did she come alone, just her and Joshua?" asked Jane.

"Well, did ye see anyone else?" teased young Sarah.

"No. But, 'tis strange, a young woman should not be travelin' alone with a man unless they be married. At least that's what Mama says," replied Jane.

"And if they are married, then may a young woman ride about the wilderness with a man?" queried Joshua, taking the steps two at a time on his way back down.

"Yes, but you are not married," Lovely stated. "How could you be? You would not dare get married without us in attendance? Isn't that so, Esther?"

"Why ask her? I be your newly married brother who did just so without your permission or attendance. Being the oldest of us three at twenty years of age, I not be needin' either."

While the younger girls stood stunned at the announcement, Esther gave Joshua a hug and congratulations just as Lydia and Russell returned to the cabin.

"Mama, we need to hold a party. Joshua done married some strange girl named Beth, without tellin' Esther and Lovely, and brought her here wearing trousers! Have you ever heared of such a thing? Getting married without telling yer own family?" exclaimed Sarah.

"As a matter of fact, I have. I married yer father without telling one soul besides my mother. Seems to be it worked out quite well. Also, I should hope Joshua be wearing trousers as it be cold and snowin'. Now where be this young woman, Joshua? Ye didn't leave her with the horses, did ye?

"No, Mama, Beth be wearing trousers, the girl he brung," corrected Sarah, interrupting Joshua's attempt at a reply.

"Yea, my child, I ken. Now see to the corn cakes, please."

"Mistress Lydia, Beth be changing into her women's clothing. I have messages for ye and news for others. First, as far as I ken all yer sons be safe and well. William senior said he be home soon. Robert be also well, and I have a message for his wife. I be going in the morning to see her, as 'tis not urgent."

"This sweet babe, Naomi, I believe, woke as I changed. I fixed her with a clean clout and brought her down. Figured she might be peckish, as most babes are when they awake."

As Naomi reached for her mother, the younger girls began pestering Beth with a dozen questions.

"Beth, do yer parents know ye got married or did ye jist run off?" asked Sarah, despite her mother's rush to tell her to hush.

"Perhaps I be the one to answer," interrupted Joshua.

"Nay, 'tis my question to answer, and I believe I can speak for myself, Joshua Ball. So, I'll answer Sarah's question. You are Sarah, are you not?"

"Yea, I be Sarah Bean. Do we only get to ask one question?"

"Let me consider?" posed Beth, keeping each in suspense before continuing. "One question each for me, and then you may ask Joshua one question each."

"What if I be not wanting to answer?"

"As your bride, I say you must, or there are consequences."

"What be a consequence?" ask Sarah.

"Is that your question?" replied Beth.

"Oh, no, no, I still be wantin' to know about you runnin' off and marryin' Joshua."

So, the newly enlarged family settled in around the Bean's large table, crowded but happy, as first Beth and then Joshua answered questions.

"Two members of my family were present the day I married Joshua. They welcomed him into our family. My mother is also Elizabeth, and my father is Matthew. Our surname is

Shelby. I have eight sisters, all younger than me and all but one still be home. Jane next."

"Was it a big weddin'?"

"No, just two of my family and the justice of the peace. Now, before you waste a question, we married on the tenth day of January 1781. Now Lovely."

"Beth, do you love Joshua?"

"Yes, more than life itself," Beth replied, blushing. "Esther's turn."

After the girls finished giggling while watching Joshua blush at Beth's answer, Esther simply replied, "no questions from me."

"Mistress Lydia?"

"Just Lydia, please. I will not be askin' ye questions. Like these four, ye now be a considered a member of our family. I hope to get to know ye better in the comin' weeks. Ye and Joshua be welcome here as long as ye wish to stay, however, we be tight for beds."

"No need for a bed. We be plannin' to bed down on the floor in front of the hearth, as be my custom. We be warm there. Was not a long ride today, Lydia. We spent yesterday evening with the Seviers as I rode there first to deliver correspondence. John be home for a few days, and Kate insisted we stay the night."

"Are you sure, Joshua?" Esther questioned. "You and Beth must be tired from your trip. Perhaps you can take my bed and well . . . oh, how can we arrange this?

"They will take my bed, and I shall take the small bed in the boys' room. I insist, young Joshua, so no need to even begin arguin' with me. I be lost and cold in that bed each night without William," insisted Lydia.

Laughter and talk and more questions filled the early evening. Later, just as all turned to their beds, Joshua asked, "Esther, come walk out with me?"

Passing a sleeping Naomi to Lydia, Esther grabbed a cloak from the peg near the door and followed Joshua out into the night.

"Esther, I did not mean to tell ye of my marriage in this manner. Beth and I planned to wait until spring. When I last saw Colonel Shelby, he relayed to me news of Beth's family. They recently fled north into Virginia as all the Shelby family be hunted down by the British as traitors. Beth refused to go. Instead, she fled, alone, to Shelby's Fort and awaited me there. I could not leave her alone and stranded, so we married with Evan as witness."

"Oh, Joshua, has she had word her family is safe?"

"No word of their arrival to be with family near Moore's had yet come when we departed. Evan promised to send word once he hears. Esther, I love her. I have for nigh on two years. I have told her all. She knows all about our family. Just her, Evan and Isaac Shelby and the justice of the peace know our true name. Not her parents. I married her with my true name to make it legal. Evan and Isaac understood, for I be not the only man on the frontier using another man's name."

"Will you be here for a while? Must you ride out again soon?"

"Nay, I have a fortnight's leave, at Isaac Lane's insistence."

As the siblings turned to walk into the cabin, the harsh, screeching scream of a wildcat stopped them both. Russell, who had just walked out to check on the livestock and that all was well inside the palisade, stopped in his tracks. "Joshua, I heard a wildcat just before you rode in."

"So did me and Beth, young Russell. Now, how many times have ye heard a wildcat twice in one day?"

"Never. I'll fire off the alarm to those nearby," he replied. "Esther, can ye go tell Ma? She kens what to do."

Within the hour, two nearby Russell families and another Bean family arrived and were ushered into the compound. Russell and Joshua watched over their movements as they came from cabins within hailing distance. Struggling through the cold and snow, each sought the security of the palisade's walls. The menfolk and womenfolk all came loaded with extra rifles and muskets and plenty of ammunition. Each hoped it would not be needed. Yet, each knew the threat, as they had faced this peril from the day of their arrival across the Appalachians.

Lydia and the girls checked all the rifles and muskets and placed them where needed. Beside each was a powder horn and shot bag. Esther, Lovely, and Beth prepared beds and pallets for the younger children and helped an aging Russell aunt into Lydia's bed.

"Joshua, will they attack soon?" Lovely whispered, pulling her brother aside.

"Unlikely to. Chickamauga tend to attack at dawn. Now, go off to bed, ye and Jane and Sarah. Esther already put Naomi down. Susan and her babe be there with you."

"Where be Beth?"

"Oh, she be changing back into her trousers."

"Why would she not take to her gown?"

"Because, my darling sister, she be an excellent shot and says she be able to fight better and will be warmer in trousers than in skirts! Besides, she has no nightgown. Now off ye go. No more questions."

"Blood makes you related; love makes you family." Unknown

January into February 1781

Once inside the Bean homestead, everybody took to their stations. The palisade itself was constructed of upright split logs. Inside the sturdy surround stood the Bean family's large two-story cabin, a small shelter for horses and dairy cows, a paddock, a spring house over a free-flowing limestone spring, and two solid-log, two-story blockhouses, one on the north corner, and the other on the east. The cabin, along the south-west of the enclosure, created that wall of the palisade.

Each blockhouse, diminutive in interior space, allowed only two men to stand on each level to defend the homestead. Like the back of the cabin, the blockhouse walls had numerous firing slits. In summers, the structures were like ovens, while in the winter, nothing kept out the cold. The Bean men had also built firing stations along the palisade wall, especially on the northeast wall near the gate, where men might fire in two directions at potential enemies. The Bean compound had stood against Indian assaults on two previous occasions.

George Russell, and his two older boys, took to the north blockhouse, leaving the other to Joshua and Beth. As the night grew colder, the wind arose, making the heavily falling snow swirl all around within the quiet darkness. Within the blockhouses, wrapped in buffalo robes, each stomped their feet and clapped their hands to keep the cold from becoming totally unbearable. Soon, those few souls standing sentry took turns coming inside the cabin to warm hands, feet, and backsides before the roaring fire. Lydia kept hot cider and warm blankets ready.

Neither Joshua nor George came in for many hours. Finally, Russell Bean relieved Joshua, while Lydia stood with her nephews. Handing each man a cup of cider, Esther asked, "Should someone sneak out and go for help?"

"No need, Mistress Esther," replied George. "Done sent my young William as soon as Russell fired off the warning."

"You sent your son riding off for help alone in this snowstorm!"

"Ridin'! Young William, no ma'am, he be runnin'. William be the fastest runner I ever see'd. 'Sides, that boy can hide where no man can find him and see in the darkest night better than an ol' hooty owl. Why, several years back William, that is Lydia's William, and me done challenged the boy. Told him to take off running for the fort on a dark night with no moon to speak of. We followed or tried. Lost him within the first bit of trees and never saw him again. When we got to the fort, there was my young William, sittin' havin' hisself a cider. The gate sentry said he had come runnin' in about half an hour before us."

Shaking her head in amusement, Esther then turned more serious when she asked, "Have you seen any movement outside the walls?"

"Large fire off to the right, seen some movement about it sometime back. Not recent though," George answered.

"There be five or so smaller fires scattered off to the left. All built up several hours previous. I saw no movement at all," Joshua answered. "Still, would be hard, as the snow is falling thick and heavy. Besides, the trees stand thick thereabout."

Hours later, just as the first streaks of light pierced through the still-falling snow, now over knee deep to a grown man, a single, chilling war cry rang out. Then another, followed by another, then yet another, from all around the compound. The Chickamauga cries persisted, circling around and around, for several minutes. Esther, knowing it was not possible, believed she could hear echoes. Perhaps the cries simply reverberated within her own fear.

As the shrieks woke almost all who had managed to sleep, Susan quietly brought both babes down and placed them, still sleeping, in the hearth-side cradle before picking up her own musket. Jane, Sarah, and Lovely followed. Each stepped up beside a rifle man, or woman, to reload as necessary.

After the cries fell silent, a quiet more fearful than the previous echoing howls encased them within their own fear. Silence overwhelmed their senses, and each one within the cabin answered the others with almost silent whispers.

Esther and Lydia stood sentry at two of the firing slits in the back wall of the cabin. One of the Russell boys, barely eleven, if that, stepped up to a nearby corner. Watching through the falling snow, Esther saw movement from her slit near the opposite corner of the cabin. As she raised her rifle to fire, the wind swirled the heavy snow into a blinding curtain of white. Now she could see nothing.

Quiet, as only a heavy, blinding snowstorm can bring, sent foreboding into her soul, for their enemy stood well hidden within feet of their positions.

The terrifying quiet of knowing your enemy stood within the stillness of dawn captured, and began crushing, Esther's heart. Not so much for herself, but for all those she loved who stood poised around her.

Paralyzing silence. Deep apprehension felt within her bones. Silence thundered in her soul, telling her the end was near.

Not one within the compound dared move nor speak.

Then Lovely screamed. One scream after another, seemingly louder with each utterance. Horrible, eerie, hideous, never-ending screams, one, then another and another, until there was no end.

Laying down their arms, and rushing to the girl, Esther and Lydia pulled Lovely into them, holding her upright, tight within the circle of their arms. Still, her screams continued, ever increasing in their shrillness. Esther reacted in the only way she thought to do. She reached back, and with all her force, slapped her sister hard across the girl's distorted face. Lovely's ghastly shrieks fell silent. She fainted.

Esther and Lydia lowered the girl to the floor. As Lydia covered Lovely with a nearby blanket, Woody moved beside her and lay tight against her body, his head upon her shoulder. He had not barked once, only omitting a low growl while Lydia and Esther tried to calm Lovely.

Stunned and shaken, Esther walked back to her station, resumed her position, and, aiming her rifle, almost instantly took down a buckskin-clad warrior, his face painted with red streaks. He had been so close, the spray of blood shot through the firing slot, splattering her clothing and her face. His burning torch dropped into the snow, placing all about in a soft reflective light until it burned out.

At once, rifles and muskets roared, both within and outside the palisade walls. Carrying their rifles, Russell, Susan, and Charlotte rushed up the stairs to the upper rooms, seeking a better vantage point through those rooms's slots. Esther heard Russell's quiet footfalls above her seconds before his rifle rang out. She watched as a warrior grabbed his shoulder, turned, and left the fight. Blood ran from the exit wound into the snow as he stumbled away.

As the noise increased, so did Naomi's and little Sue's frantic cries. Some of the older children rushed to comfort them. Yet, neither mother moved toward their child. Instead, each intensified her will and turned back toward their enemy. Both had heard stories of babes killed by Chickamauga warriors.

Taking care with their shots, both Lydia and Esther struck another Chickamauga each. Lydia's shot propelled their attacker backward into the snow. He fell silently. Esther's prey howled with pain and anger as he rushed on toward the cabin. Nearby, Sarah and Jane worked quickly, reloading and handing them another firearm after each fired. Not taking time to aim as the warrior was so close, Esther fired yet again. This time, he fell.

Then, as suddenly as it had begun, all the firing stopped. Silence. Esther watched cautiously as two warriors sneaked in and removed their fallen comrades. One of the fallen still lived, for Esther could hear his quiet moans. She felt a moment of remorse, nothing more.

Several minutes later, George Russell slipped in the cabin door. "Everyone safe? We heared screams."

Hearing his question, Esther turned and answered, "'Twas Lovely. She panicked. Anyone hurt out there?"

"Nah. We took down several, and then suddenly they quit advancing and began gathering up their dead and wounded. Joshua believes they be leaving."

As George turned to return to his post, horrible, blood-curdling yells rang through the surrounding forest. Yet, these cries sounded different from the earlier Chickamauga battle cries, for they seemed to be words, not just yells. Then rifle fire crackled, adding to the melee of sounds.

"God be good! That be Jesse's men! I ken that call, heard it enough over the years to know my boy's yell. It be the militia. George, our young William done got through safely and brung us salvation!" Lydia rejoiced, hugging her brother.

Within minutes, only the silence of heavily falling snow reigned thereabout. George helped Esther place Lovely on Lydia's bed, beside his sister-in-law, who still slept, her being almost totally deaf. Meanwhile, Susan comforted and nursed two hungry, scared babies. Jane, Russell, and Sarah tidied up, made sure all the rifles were loaded and placed nearby. The older girls began preparing food, for despite the heavy snow, morning's light shone upon a new day. Beth arrived, and after warming her hands, pitched in to help.

Figuring the Chickamauga had had enough and were fleeing to their own village with their dead and wounded, Jesse recalled his men and sent several off to warn and check on nearby cabins. Esther stepped outside into a beautiful landscape of now softly falling snow to assure herself that none were wounded and needing attention,

"Sister, where be ye headed?" Joshua asked, taking her in his arms. "All be well? Lovely?"

Shaking with the built-up tension, Esther replied, "Not one was harmed. Our Sarah, our Lovely, oh Joshua. She screamed, and screamed, and screamed. I needed her to stop."

"I know, George told me. Be she still asleep?"

"Yes, we laid her on Lydia's bed. She did not awake. What if she does not? Oh, Joshua, I should not have struck her." Now filled with remorse, Esther continued, "She needed love and understanding, not. . . "

"Dwell no more on it, Esther. Lovely will awake. She must learn to face her fears. Now, let's go find your Naomi and my Beth."

The blizzard drifted over two feet of heavy, wet snow across the Watauga settlements. Days of quiet reigned, as few felt the need to leave their warm cabins and to venture out into the frozen wilderness. At the Bean settlement, Esther and Joshua watched as Lovely moved about as though nothing untoward had happened. She never asked about the Chickamauga attack. She never apologized for her outburst. She never spoke. Not once.

The deep snow kept most everyone inside. When they ventured out, they quickly finished their chores and ducked back in to stand before roaring hearths, warming their feet and hands, before hanging wet, cold garments up to thaw and dry. Despite the snow, Walter appeared three days later, with Levi, to bring news from the fort. Seems not one settler died, or was even severely wounded, during the raid. Isaac Lane and Jesse Bean had sent one tracker after the Chickamauga. He had reported back that the Indians had fled toward their own village along the Tennessee River, carrying with them their dead and wounded. Most everyone believed they would stay put until the spring thaw.

"What would life be if we had no courage to attempt anything?"
Vincent Van Gogh

1781 Winter into Spring

The Williams Bean rode in on the fifth and declared themselves to be home for a month or more, at least. William senior had a slight wound that Esther treated. With so many occupying such a small space within the crowded cabin, tempers flared much too often. Knowing their presence had finally become a burden instead of a blessing, Joshua and Esther decided the time had come to leave. So, on a slightly warmer day than those previous, they packed their meager belongings and moved to the Bassingham cabin.

Having heard of their plans from Jesse, Walter showed up with two rabbits and the butchered hindquarters of a deer, his horse weighed down by two large baskets mounted on either side of his saddle. Levi sat astride his own horse, a gift from Joshua, who had found the small piebald wandering the woods after the Indian raid. Tidence Lane, had shown up at the fort one day with a small saddle once used by the Lane boys in their youth. Bundled up in heavy clothing, Levi beamed with pride.

On the day of their move, Lydia cried as they packed up. Jane begged to be allowed to go along, a request Lydia quickly denied. Sarah sulked. William Bean joined in the venture as he and Russell transported the smaller of the two cradles to the Ball's new home.

"Have ye sufficient blankets and coverings?" Lydia asked.

"I am more worried that *you* do not have enough. My dear Lydia, you have given us too much," Esther teased. "Lydia, we are only going a mile away, not much farther than our old cabin. May I tell you a secret that might calm your worries?"

"So, it be a good secret?"

"Yes," Esther whispered. "Walter and Levi will be staying. They shall take the back room on the porch as theirs. It is larger than Walter's half cabin at the fort. Now, we shall not be alone when Joshua returns to duty."

"Oh, Esther, that do be a good secret. 'Course, people shall talk, but most shall grumble about his not being at the blacksmith shop and ready to hand. Can I tell William?"

"He will soon hear it from Lieutenant Lane, so yes. Please come often to visit. I know it be hard to find the time, but we will miss you all so much."

So, following hugs and promises, the Ball siblings, Beth, Walter, and Levi rode off into the mostly melted landscape, leading their packhorses once again to a different home. At the cabin, while the men and Beth unpacked, Esther lit the already laid fire to take off the chill.

After much discussion during the previous week, they had decided as to the allocation of rooms. Joshua and Beth soon occupied the larger of the two upper rooms. It was above the hearth and would stay warm most nights. Lovely and Esther would share the other, and there she placed most of her belongings. As another bed, built against the wall, already stood in the larger ground floor room, Esther expected that, more often than not, she would sleep downstairs, for there the cradle would stay, as the upper rooms could be reached only by a steep ladder.

Lovely, who still had not spoken, quietly moved her things into the upper room that held only one bed. Once settled, she took up the chores that had earlier been her responsibility, and seemed content, though withdrawn.

In the days and weeks following their move, Joshua and Walter hunted when meat was needed. When necessary, one or the other would escort Esther to do her *doctorin'*, as Walter named it.

Levi took it upon himself to make sure the cabin always had fresh water and plenty of firewood. He talked more and more as the days passed, but never about his past or his own family. He spoke only of Walter and the people at the fort. Levi developed an exceptional ability to mimic the voices of the fort's residents. His favorite being that of Samuel Doak. This talent proved useful for calming an upset and crying Naomi, for she would instantly hush, and then giggle, as Levi pretended to preach quite interesting sermons full of admonitions against sin, fornication, drinking, and, of course, King George. Apparently, King George was a sin against mankind. Levi's arms would raise and lower with his voice. His sermons often contained bits of hymns, some of which Esther had never heard. She assumed they had been taught him by his mother.

"Walter," Esther whispered one evening after listening to such a sermon, "does Levi know what fornication means?"

"Oh, no, Esther, I done asked him 'bout that, and he jest said that it be really bad. I believe, if I 'member right, he said it were bad enough to send a man or woman to hell and damnation, forever and ever. I done figured that was enough for a child to know."

"Well, he seems to have Naomi impressed with his words. I've never been able to make her giggle that much."

A week after their move, Beth pulled Esther aside. "Sister, be there anything we can do to bring Lovely from her silence?"

"No, we have found it best to just wait it out. Once she stayed silent for almost a month. My brother Benjamin believes some great harm done her in the past has injured her brain or her being. He said, while in Edinburgh studying to be a doctor, they read and studied such cases. They called it *lunacy*. Benjamin says it can come on and go away for no recognizable reason. Lovely's silence seems to come with times of great fear."

Several days later, Esther found Lovely huddled in a corner of their small room, covered in several blankets, shaking and moaning. With Beth and Joshua's help, they placed her upon her bed, and forced her to drink a calming tea Esther concocted. On that occasion, they could not determine any real reason for Lovely's fear.

While February remained somewhat cold, the snow melted away and, with proper clothing, the days proved nice enough to make improvements around the cabin. As a family, they spent several days clearing old growth and debris from the sizeable garden. Lovely helped repair the wicker rabbit fencing. Some days she spent hours with her small loom, making cloth for a growing Naomi's clothing. Still, she did not speak. After several visits by her friends, Jane and Sarah, the girls simply stopped coming by, for Lovely did not speak or share secrets, as girls are known to do.

Like most of the previous winters, Esther found herself frequently requested by those suffering with the ague or winter fevers. Escorted by Walter, she roamed far and wide, sometimes staying overnight. Beth, having helped raise her many younger sisters, took on Naomi's care during Esther's absences.

Recently, Naomi had grasped the idea of drinking from a cup and was now quick to grab any cup within reach. Each adult, and even Levi, learned to place their own cup in the middle of the table, out of her reach. Otherwise, they often found themselves doing without and cleaning up Naomi's latest spill. Beth quickly gave up trying to keep the child's gown clean, and simply tied a cloth around her neck to catch the almost constant spills after her drinking attempts. While the babe seemed to love the milk from their cow, her other favorite drink became the locally made cider. This Esther and Beth refused to give her, while Osh would occasionally give her small sips, just to see her pucker up her face and then smile up at him, begging for more.

At nine months, Naomi learned to pull herself up and climb. She climbed on benches, which often overturned, and beds. She even tried climbing the log walls. She climbed on and over Woody, who, overnight, learned to move outside, away from the busy baby. Not a quiet child, Naomi gabbled almost constantly. Her only proper words were *Mama* and *Osh*. Osh, better known as Joshua, would grab up the baby upon entering the cabin, throw her into the air, swing her to and fro, and tickle her until she giggled in his arms. Naomi loved Osh and called for him frequently, especially upon hearing a horse arrive at their cabin.

While Joshua played with her and made her giggle with delight, Walter became her calming influence. Tired, hurt, hungry, or simply mad, Naomi's cries would stop in minutes if placed in Walter's capable, muscular arms. He whispered to her, crooning old words to even older songs, until she calmed down and often fell asleep.

"Walter, what are those words you sing to Naomi?"

"Don't rightly know, Mistress Beth, my mother sang them to me. I 'member her voice. 'Twas soft, yet strong and steady. Mama came here from Africa on a ship afore I be born. Said my daddy still be in Africa. She learned some English. 'Nuf to survive. I jest 'member the songs."

"Does she still live?"

"She died givin' birth to my sister when I be about Levi's age."

"Walter, does you sister yet live?"

"Don't rightly ken," he answered quietly, returning to the song.

In those early months of 1781, Beth, Walter, and Levi created a family with Joshua, Esther, and Lovely. Each had a role to play within the unusual gathering, and love blossomed.

"There is only one kind of shock worse than the totally unexpected: the expected for which one has refused to prepare."
Mary Renault, *The Charioteer*

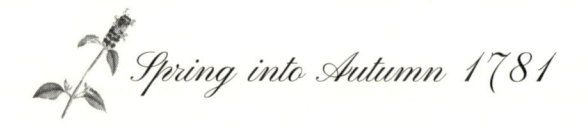

Spring into Autumn 1781

At the beginning of March, on a clear day under bright blue skies with a light breeze, Esther heard horses just before Jesse Bean hailed the cabin. Naomi, having heard the horses, yelled out for Osh.

"Ball cabin, it be Jesse," a voice hollered.

As Esther grabbed a shawl and stepped outside, she realized Jesse was not alone. Beside him rode a tall man, dressed in mud-splattered and worn clothing, leading a pack horse.

"Esther, I brung Dr. Seth," he announced sharply. "Hope ye don't mind a visitor."

"Seth, oh my, please do come in. You are always welcome here. You, as well, Jesse. It is so nice to have you visit us. Seth, what brings you to Watauga?" Esther soon realized she was asking too many questions and talking too much for either man to answer.

She hushed. Embarrassed.

Smiling down, Seth answered, "I rode all this way to see you and your siblings, Esther. I wanted to see you, and I have news. Perhaps we might talk inside, but first I need to unload and turn my horses out, for I have traveled far."

After Jesse took his leave, Esther helped Seth unload his horses, placing his packs and bags inside their cabin for safekeeping. They turned his horses out into the nearby paddock. Esther had already sent Levi for Walter and Joshua, who worked nearby gathering firewood.

After introductions all around, they took seats at the cabin's table. Lovely brought cider and milk in cooled jugs and placed warm hoe cakes on the table. Meanwhile, Esther gathered up Naomi, worried, as Seth's demeanor seemed anxious.

With all settled, Seth explained, "Esther, Joshua, Lovely, I rode to Watauga to bring you news of your brother, of Benjamin. But first, I find I must tell you how I came to learn of your connection to my friend, for your brother and I first met in Edinburgh."

As Esther gasped and started to speak, Seth took her hand and asked, "Please, let me tell this in my way. 'Twill be easier for me to do so, and for you to hear."

Joshua started to speak and then sat back, closing his mouth. Beth took his hand and placed it in hers, for she sensed the tension in her husband's being.

"Esther, Joshua, when we met at King's Mountain, Walter told me your name was Ball and that you had a brother, who was a surgeon, serving with the Continental army. Still, I never associated you with the Benjamin Ballinger I knew. Then, last month, not long after the battle of Cowpens..."

"What battle at Cowpens? The place near the Broad River? We have not heard of such!" Joshua interrupted. "Were we victorious?"

"Oh, yes, that is the place. I assumed you had news of the battle. It took place on the 17th of January. I guess you have heard our General Washington sent General Nathanael Greene to take command of the Southern army. Soon after his arrival, Greene split his army into two parts. On Greene's orders, General Daniel Morgan went southwest, toward the Catawba River, to cut supply lines and organize Patriots in the western settlements. Being as I had served in that area before with many in the militia, I volunteered to go along. Soon it became known by Morgan that Cornwallis had sent Tarleton to block any such activity. 'Twas about the second week of the past month, when Tarleton's scouts located Morgan's army on the Pacolet River in South Carolina. Upon hearing the report, Tarleton took up pursuit. Morgan moved his army northwest on the Green River road, but when he reached Cowpens, knowing the Broad was in flood, he decided to make his stand."

"Against Tarleton? Was he mad? I had always thought Morgan to be presumptuous. Still, he had no place for retreat with the Broad in flood!" Joshua exclaimed angrily.

"Many believed him to be so. Seems Morgan wanted a place to force his army to take a decisive stand. Morgan then sent word into surrounding areas for the militia to rendezvous at Cowpens. As more and more men gathered, Morgan settled on his eventual plan of battle, and asked the militia to stand and take two, or perhaps three, volleys, before fleeing to the rear. I heard his speeches to the men. He spoke of past battles and called the British every name for evil men you can imagine. He called for a victory like we saw at King's Mountain and revenge for every defeat our cause has suffered. Before long, the men commenced to cheering his talk, then reluctantly agreed to stand through two volleys.

"It was bitterly cold the morning Morgan's scouts told him Tarleton's army approached. Some men later told how Morgan had slept not one wink the previous night. Still, he strutted about, giving orders like a young man ready to take on the world. He placed his troops into three lines. Out front, the sharpshooters hid in the surrounding trees. Many of those had been there at King's Mountain. They silently waited, as they had orders to accomplish one thing, to take down as many officers as possible, especially those among the Dragoons. And that they did. Soon Tarleton's Dragoons fled the battlefield. Then the sharpshooters moved back to the second line while the front line, the militia, took two volleys. Some fell, but they stood before fleeing. All happened as Morgan expected. Those of us watching from the trees saw, once again, our militia flee the battle.

"As Morgan anticipated he would, Tarleton believed the Patriot army to be in full retreat, so he pushed forward. He sent his remaining Dragoons against the fleeing militia. As planned, William Washington's cavalry rode into the field of battle and took on Tarleton's Dragoons, unfortunately losing some eighteen of his own men in the clash.

"Joining the fray, Morgan's Continental line stepped up and fired volley after volley. Morgan cheered on his men while the sharpshooters and militia rejoined the battle. Old Morgan cried out, some said, *form, form my brave fellows! Old Morgan never was beaten!*

Seth's small audience sat stunned, waiting for more. Was this to be another horrible massacre of their army or another stunning victory?

Seth continued his tale. "Tarleton sent in his reserve, the 71st Highlanders, with bagpipe and drum. Almost immediately, our line broke again, but Morgan rode up and down, ordering our retreating men to face about and fire. Soon they did so, carrying our flag back into the fight to great success. Then they charged with bayonets. I watched, stunned, as the British line broke! Our cavalry and remaining militia reentered the battlefield and surrounded their forces. Soon the British line began to surrender in mass.

"Some told afterward that William Washington rode in pursuit of the fleeing Tarleton and dueled with him and two of his officers, sword to sword. They say he survived only because his bugler, who had followed the pursuit, fired his pistol at one of the Englishmen just as he raised his sword to strike Washington down.

"What we did not capture of the British forces fled in disarray. I watched most all the battle from our aid station before the wounded began to arrive. Then I listened as our men cheered yet another victory, another liken to King's Mountain."

"Who is this William Washington?" asked Beth.

"Some say he is General Washington's kinsman. I know he is from Virginia and is considered a brilliant and brave commander. I have met and immensely liked the man."

Talk of the victory and its aftermath continued for several minutes before Esther interrupted the talk, turning it back to their brother.

"Ah, yes, Benjamin. I met Benjamin Ballinger in Edinburgh, not long before I left for the colonies. I didn't know him well. Still, he told me of his large family in Virginia, and that his father had also studied in Scotland. I saw Benjamin again, briefly, after my arrival to volunteer at Washington's headquarters in New York. So, when General Greene arrived at our southern headquarters, understanding he had recently been with Washington's Continentals, I took the opportunity to ask about my friend. It was Greene who gave me the news.

"Benjamin volunteered to accompany Major Benjamin Tallmadge and his dismounted dragoons on a raid on Lloyd's Neck on the fifth of September 1779. Tallmadge took him along, as he had no surgeon or physician, and expected casualties. After Tallmadge's successful attack, which captured some three hundred and fifty Tories, a prisoner stabbed Benjamin while he attempted to treat the man's wounds. They said Benjamin died instantly. General Green told me of his death and how, later, among Benjamin's belongings, Washington's staff found reference to his siblings being at Moore's Fort in Virginia and living under the name Ball. Washington knew of Benjamin's fight to regain his inheritance, and of his siblings fleeing from their Tory uncles. General Washington was devastated, and he, himself, wrote a letter to be sent by courier. General Greene said Martha Washington wept upon hearing the news of Benjamin's death."

After glancing at a stricken Joshua, and more firmly clutching Esther's hands, Seth continued, "I had not made the connection until Green told me this. I did not ken you are my friend's siblings. Once I knew, I had to come. I had to be the one to tell you, for I knew from what you said that day at King's Mountain that you did not know. Esther, Joshua, Lovely, I am so sorry for your loss." With tears in his eyes, Seth stood and walked toward the door, leaving them to their own grief. No one moved to stop him.

Walter quietly took a sleeping Naomi from Esther's arms and placed her in the cradle, covering her gently. Passing by Joshua, he squeezed the young man's shoulder, and then took Levi by the hand. They stepped out the back door of the cabin.

Esther began to shake with the misery of learning, acknowledging a truth she had suspected for months. Benjamin lived no longer. He had been gone for two years. There were only three where once there had been nine. As her own tears flowed, Esther turned to see the tears in Lovely's eyes reflecting the late afternoon light. Then her sister stood, cleared the table, and began the evening meal. Lovely's tears ran in streams down her cheeks. Still, she worked, occasionally wiping her face with the sleeve of her bodice.

Beth and Joshua left the cabin together, hand in hand.

Seth stayed. During the weeks that followed, he became a friend. He worked with Walter and Joshua, never shirking from any chore they took on. Levi followed him wherever he went. Soon, the child had perfected Seth's burr. Several weeks after his arrival, Esther overheard Beth tell Seth he was becoming the brother she never had and always wanted. Lovely stayed silent but smiled more, and occasionally laughed aloud at one of Seth's stories, or at Levi's repeating one.

Esther struggled. Beth and Joshua tried to take from her part of the grief, the guilt she seemed to carry. Each understood how Esther had taken upon herself the role of protector for her family from the day their father passed.

Once Joshua's leave ended, he once more took to his courier duties. Having Seth and Walter at the isolated cabin lessened some of his worries over leaving his new wife and his sisters alone. On his second return trip, he carried news about Beth's family in a letter from Evan Shelby, telling of their safe arrival in Virginia's wilderness.

War news filtered in, and the outlook for the first time in three years looked favorable. Cornwallis moved his army northward, leaving the two southern-most colonies to the feuding militias, although the British still occupied both Charleston and Savannah.

Along most of the frontier, days passed quietly, with only occasional disruptions. At the Ball cabin, the womenfolk, with Walter's help, planted a large garden. Esther once again roamed the hills in search of medicinal plants, and Lovely returned to her small loom, and some days rode to the Bean's to work their larger loom.

In early April, Naomi took her first steps and by mid-month, attempted to run everywhere possible. It took all their combined efforts to keep the tiny girl from the stream, and away from the horses and cows, as she held no fear of man or beast. Esther and Beth hoped Woody would be her companion, yet the dog most often stayed very near Lovely, even following her to the Bean cabin.

In late May, Joshua requested and received, from Colonel Shelby, permission to carry correspondence into Virginia's Tidewater. After taking and almost destroying Richmond, British forces had withdrawn, leaving the city and nearby Goochland county, their old home, almost free of strife. After telling only Beth of his mission and its reason, Joshua left for the long journey. He planned to stop at Evan Shelby's to get directions, for first, he wished to travel north to visit Beth's family. From there, he would proceed east, toward their former home.

As the months progressed, Seth came and went. Sometimes he stayed away for weeks. His travels took him as far as Lincoln and Mecklenburg counties in North Carolina, and once into South Carolina to meet with General Greene. Not long after he had arrived at their cabin with the news of Benjamin's death, Joshua had questioned the young man as to his position with the Continental army.

"I am simply a volunteer, Joshua. I signed no papers. I receive no pay. I wanted to see America, the colonies, to determine if I wanted to emigrate. Unfortunately for me, I arrived during a war. As I am a Highland Scot, I saw no reason to fight for an English king. I decided to serve, in some capacity, your own revolution as all our attempts have failed to throw off the English yoke."

"Ah, and your family? What do they think about your exploration?"

"I no longer have close relatives. I lost my father and brothers in the struggles, and after being left an orphan when my mother passed, a widowed aunt took me in. We resided in a small village, Pitlochry, where I attended a boys' school run by the local Presbyterian minister. My aunt passed just after I finished my medical training. I sold her house and set sail only three weeks later."

"So, you arrived in?"

"Early summer of 1776. After four years, I find I no longer wish to go back to Scotland. There are too many memories there to haunt me. Besides, I have found so much here in America to love. I find the mountains remind me of Scotland's Highlands. I suspect that's why there are so many of my fellow Scots here about. I wish to see more of this land. I have thought about going on westward, into Kentucky, perhaps even later this year. I have money for land and have heard I can get it at a good price."

"Ah, that is why Beth married me, at least part of the reason, she says. I have dreamed of Kentucky since I first heard of Boone's trips across the mountains. My father had a friend who lived in the western regions, and often wrote of his journeys into the mountains and beyond. Our father would read aloud the letters and point out places on a poorly drawn map. Not long after I first met Beth, she asked, *be ye willing to go west to Caintuck?* From there, things seem to move along quickly between us."

Esther wondered, day after day, why Beth seemed not to worry over Joshua's absence. Perhaps she had adopted Lovely's attitude. Esther, on the other hand, became quite concerned after the first month with no news, and on a quiet day rode in to near Fort Caswell, to where Samuel and Esther Doak were building a home for themselves.

As she rode near the fort, she passed near Lieutenant Lane and several of the militia, and called out, "Isaac, Isaac, a word, please."

"Good day to ye, Esther. What brings ye out today?"

"Off to visit the Doaks, but I had hoped to see you. Has there been word of Joshua?"

"No, Evan has sent no word since your brother left there. I expect 'twill take him several weeks to go into Virginia and back.

"Joshua went to our old home? Why did he not tell me?"

"I assumed he had. I should not have said, Esther. Did he not tell you he wished to do so? He said he needed to deal with matters after the death of his brothers."

"He did not say where he was going. I never asked. Still, no need to worry, Isaac. I asked, and you answered. I appreciate knowing. Good day to you."

Throughout the afternoon, Esther Ball discussed her fears and worries for Joshua with the Doaks. Samuel said, as always, *it is in the hands of the Lord*. Out of her husband's hearing, Esther Doak whispered, "I'd like to give your brother a swift kick in the backside for keeping such a secret. Do you think Beth knows?"

"I think she must. Yet, she has said nothing."

Changing the subject, the Reverend's wife asked, "And Dr. Seth? Is he back in our community?"

"Yes, he arrived yesterday. Worn and tired from a long journey, as he had recently been with General Greene. However, he says he is here until Joshua returns. I believe he may know more about Joshua's journey than even Isaac."

"And you, my friend. How fare you?"

Before answering, Esther thought back on the previous weeks and decided to be honest with her friend. "I still often find myself almost lost to my grief. I know so many have lost more than me. Even little Levi. Yet, in some six years, I have lost all my siblings, except two. I think I may have also lost Lovely, for still she does not speak, and sometimes slips into uncontrollable sobbing and shaking. I have only Joshua and Beth, who becomes more every day my *sister*."

"And Dr. McIntosh?"

"What about him?"

"Is he yet a brother, or something more, something different?"

"Neither. I still mourn for Waya. Now I must go, 'tis late and I have no escort to go after darkness falls."

"Esther, stay. Talk with me, please. I didn't mean to pry. It's . . . well, I see your loneliness. I also see Seth's eyes on you. He is at least smitten, and probably loves you. Even my Samuel has noticed, and you know he barely notices such things."

"Nay, you are wrong, my friend. It is nothing more than friendship. Now, I am going. Come visit me when you can get away from watching your home being built," Esther teased.

Weeks later, Joshua arrived just before dark, wet from a heavy thunderstorm that had passed an hour earlier, and dead tired. While he unloaded two heavily loaded pack horses and his own mount, Walter and Beth helped carry and settle the goods.

Once dry and fed, the young man told of his latest travels. "Ol' Evan gave me good directions to your family, Beth. All be well. Yer sister Martha carries a babe and says ye shall be an aunt by Christmas. Oh, and little Anna has found a beau, but as he be in the militia, she simply pines away for his return. Or at least so she says, constantly. They are all quite well, settled, and expect to stay in Virginia until at least next spring, before returning home."

"And our home?" Esther abruptly interrupted.

"Isaac Lane told me when I stopped by the fort with messages that he had told you of my destination. I had my reasons for keeping my destination secret, for I knew ye would want to go along. Esther, Lovely, our home, as ye know, was burned. I stayed with the Elliott family for two nights. I cleaned our cemetery and ordered a stone for Samuel, as the previous one ordered by George Elliott has not arrived. I saw a solicitor and placed all our holdings in trust with George for a time."

"I am not going back!" Lovely screamed out. Her first words since the Chickamauga attack. As they turned and stared, Lovely began to shake, and then once again, to scream. This time, Walter stepped in. He took her bodily into his arms and held her tight as she broke down in sobs. The minutes passed.

Once Lovely became quiet, though still held tightly by Walter, Joshua spoke. "Lovely, we will not go back to Virginia. Mr. Elliott's wife's brother wishes to buy the land, and I have agreed. George will see to the sale and place the money in his bank for us to use. I plan to split it three ways—Esther, Lovely, and myself."

Before he could continue, Esther broke in, "No, Joshua, as the oldest male, the money is yours. Lovely and I should not receive a third. Perhaps only a dowry for Lovely, should she decide to marry."

"Then you will each receive a dowry of one third of Father's estate. I shall listen to no argument. As for my portion, Beth and I plan to go on to Kentucky as soon as possible. We hope ye and Lovely shall go along."

While Lovely did not answer, Esther hesitated before stating, "I need time to think on it." Then, changing the subject back to Virginia, she asked, "Joshua, what did you learn of our uncles?"

"Oh, some, perhaps not all there is to learn. Michael Hollowell managed to sell his plantation to a neighbor in 1779 and sailed for England. George Elliott had asked among friends but could not learn more. As for Gabriel, a Tory militia hung him not long before Michael absconded. As the story was told to George, Gabriel raped a thirteen-year-old planter's daughter, near to his own plantation. He left her with child. When the militia surrounded and took his home, they found two Negro girls and one white child being held captive, one severely beaten. They found Gabriel several hours later and, after whipping him near to death with his own crop, hung him and left the body hanging."

Turning to Lovely, Esther saw no change in her sister's expression or demeanor. Instead, Lovely picked up her cup and poured more milk for herself as if they had only been discussing the weather.

All this time, while Joshua spoke, telling of his journey and his plans, Seth had remained quiet. Now, hoping to ease the tension, he said, "Esther, I had a few belongings shipped over when I journeyed to New York. I recently was able to retrieve some few items. I thought you might like this book. 'Tis *Clarissa* by Samuel Richardson, 'twas my aunt's favorite."

"Seth, you have been silent about your travels and your ideas about Joshua and Beth's plans. What say you?" Esther asked, completely ignoring the gift.

Nodding to each, Seth said, "Esther, Lovely, as Joshua well knows, I have wished to travel to Kentucky since not long after my arrival on this continent. Now, it is my intent to do so, to travel with Joshua and Beth. I believe there to be great opportunity for me there, both as a surgeon and a landowner."

"Well, it seems you three have decided to travel into a dangerous wilderness, leaving Lovely, Naomi, and myself here to fend for ourselves. I assume you expect me to marry, so that we have protection and someone to depend on. Well, I shall not. I will not marry. I married Waya, and not one man I have met since he... he...." Then pushing aside the proffered book, Esther rose and walked out of the cabin.

"Joshua, go after her," Beth pleaded. "Please explain we wish for them to go along."

"No, Beth. Esther needs this time alone. I have told her much tonight and made decisions without her regard. Let her be. Esther will come to her own mind in her own time."

"When one door of happiness closes, another opens; but often we look so long at the closed door that we do not see the one which has been opened for us." Helen Keller

Autumn into Winter 1781

As the day grew long and darkness overcame the surrounding forest, Esther slipped back inside and lovingly carried Naomi upstairs to their bed. Lovely had gone up not long after Esther left the cabin. Knowing Esther was now safe within their cabin, Joshua and Beth moved toward the ladder soon afterward, leaving Seth sitting before the fire.

"Joshua, who is this man, *Waya*?" Seth asked quietly, halting Joshua just at the ladder.

"Waya was my friend, a Cherokee man. He is Naomi's father. He and Esther married in a Cherokee ceremony. Few about know this, so I ask you to keep Esther's secret."

"Where is he now?" Seth whispered, almost afraid to know if the man yet lived.

"Dead, killed by his own tribal brothers. Esther's marriage, the marriage others told you of, be simply a fable, nothing more, told to protect her and Lovely. There be much to keep Esther here at Watauga. Memories. There be little to make her go. If ye truly love my sister, as I suspect ye do, then ye must become the reason for her to go. Good night, Seth."

Despite her outburst of the previous evening, Lovely remained silent. In the days to follow, Esther, the sister who almost always let her feelings and opinions be known, strangely, also seemed to brood silently over Joshua's pending move.

In the following two weeks, much occurred. Joshua ended his service with the militia. As his commitment had expired some weeks earlier, this was simply a formality. Seth and Joshua traveled to Fort Caswell frequently to ask recent travelers about the Wilderness road, the Cumberland Gap, and the hazards of their proposed journey.

After one such visit, they discussed recent information about how and why Daniel Boone had removed his family from Boonesborough to Boone's Station. They often asked travelers about other stations and settlements in the new Virginia counties, as Kentucky was now recognized. The two men, with Beth's input, endlessly discussed where they might decide to settle. On his return journey from Virginia, Joshua had come upon *the traveling church*, a large party of westward travelers. According to Captain William Ellis, the military leader of the expedition, it seemed a group of Baptist, most from a small church near Fredericksburg, Virginia, had emigrated, in mass, to Kentucky in search of religious freedom—to preach as they saw fit without being taxed to do so. Their religious leader, Lewis Craig, and some five hundred or so souls had packed up their belongings and moved westward toward the Cumberland Gap, when Joshua had chanced upon them.

Joshua, after having provided some information on their route of travel, had discovered the party planned to settle near Logan's Station, in an area somewhat south of Boonesborough, near Dick's River. Having told Seth all he had learned, the two decided the area might be a good place to settle, or at least to winter, before deciding on a final destination. On his return journey, Joshua had also discussed his planned move with Evan Shelby, who had informed him that his son, Isaac Shelby, looked to purchase land just west of Logan's Station.

Esther sometimes kept quiet throughout these discussions, often held at the cabin's table. At other times, she just stood and left the room, going either outside or to her upstairs room. Each time, Seth's eyes followed the woman. He wondered how he might bring up the subject of Waya, for he wanted to know more. To understand.

In mid-September, called to the Bean's cabin to treat a wound, for Esther was carrying out her midwife duties, Seth found time to talk alone with Lydia Bean. Finished treating and bandaging a wound on Russell's leg, Seth found time to speak with Lydia. "Mistress Bean, perhaps, I might ask you a question about Esther?"

"You might. I might answer," Lydia replied hesitantly.

"Joshua told me briefly of Waya. Of this Cherokee man who married Esther in a Cherokee ceremony. Joshua says you know their story."

"And why might ye, Seth McIntosh, be askin' me now?"

Without hesitation, Seth answered, "Because I love Esther. I think I have since King's Mountain. In that small rural church, lit by candles and lanterns, she stood as a lovely vision among the wounded. I watched her elegant ways and heard her refined, soft manner of speaking. Despite being dressed in men's trousers under her apron, she seemed the most beautiful woman I had ever seen. We worked side by side. We shared the horrors of those wounded men. . . of death. I thought we had made a deep connection, an understanding of at least friendship. Now, she seems angry. . . lost . . . and will not let me get close. I have tried, but she will not let me show her my love or convince her to love me."

Quietly, but vehemently, Lydia asked, "Why should any woman let a man love her, let alone a woman who loved a man so different from herself that others would refuse to let them marry? A woman who had to live a lie to protect her own, her child's, and her sister's dignity. A woman who has, in the last few years lost two brothers to war, worried over another, and seen her own sister suffer with overwhelming fear. Esther be many things, but most of all, she believes herself to be the salvation of her family, and all those she knows and loves. Sometimes I think the woman believes she can save the world. Then her heart almost breaks when one soul is lost."

Lydia paused and held up her hand to halt Seth's reply. Sitting quietly, sipping her cider, Lydia waited, forming the words she wanted to say.

"Seth, that woman be a daughter to me, both her and Lovely. 'Tis my belief that Esther needs to find love again. She needs to let go of her grief, her fear of losing more among those she loves, and she needs to let someone else help her carry her burdens. If ye be willing to be all she needs, then I hope it might be ye, Seth."

"So, you believe it might be possible? You believe she might come to love me?"

"Young man, if there be anything at all I *believe* in as much as our Lord, it be love. I know love can heal all evils. I believe love is possible for all. If they let it be."

Sitting quietly for another minute, Lydia finally broke her silence, "So I will tell you all I know of Waya. Then 'twill be up to ye. Remember, this is Esther's secret, her story, her life, and only hers to reveal to those she trusts. I am taking you into my confidence and know you will respect all I say."

Taking on the most challenging task of his life, Seth made to woo Esther. He carried her loads. From daybreak to bedtime, he did everything he could imagine to make Esther's life easier and more pleasant. He played with her daughter and helped with her care and protection. He consoled her sister when needed. He sometimes tried to reach inside her silence with stories from his homeland. To draw her out of herself.

He brought Esther woodland flowers and plants, some for their beauty and some for her medical bag. He read at night from *Clarissa*, or the family's favorite, *Dr. Samuel Johnson's A Journey to the Western Islands of Scotland*, followed by stories of his own journeys. He taught them songs from his homeland, some bawdy and some love-lorn.

Seth's favorite, *Of A' The Airts*, soon became a favorite of Beth's. Seth had explained how the song spoke of love and how *airts* meant directions, such as north and south. Beth had a lively, clear alto voice, and she quickly learned the tune and timing of the song.

Of a' the airts the wind can blaw
I dearly like the west,
For there the bonnie lassie lives,
The lassie I lo'e best.
There wild woods grow, and rivers row,
And monie a hill between,
But day and night my fancy's flight
Is ever wi' my Jean.
I see her in the dewy flowers -
I see her sweet and fair,
I hear her in the tunefu' birds -
I hear her charm the air.
There's not a bonnie flower that springs
By fountain, shaw or green.
There's not a bonnie bird that sings
But minds me o' my Jean.

For Samuel and Esther Doak's autumn housewarming, to be followed by a dance, Seth dressed in his finest and escorted the sisters to the afternoon's events. His dark blue waistcoat, decorated with silver threads in a Fleur-de-lis pattern, brought out the color of his eyes. His coat and breeches, black and elegant, were worn with his knee-high black boots. The clothing made him look ever taller and more dashing. Most of their guests came planning to camp on the grounds for the night, so Seth carefully prepared all that would ensure Esther and Naomi's comfort.

"Perhaps I might have the first dance of the evening, Esther?" he asked, handing her a cup of punch not long after their arrival.

"I had not thought to dance," she replied, hesitantly.

"You must. I insist." And with no other words, he took little Naomi from her mother's hand and swung her about just to hear her giggle. He tried to anticipate Esther's every need that afternoon.

Later in the evening, Esther relented. As she had many years passed at David's wedding, she danced almost every dance that evening, twirling her dark green gown and white petticoats with every step. While Seth partnered her more than others, she also stepped out with Isaac, and later, with Aquilla and Tidence Lane and Jesse Bean. The men of Watauga honored her with dances, songs, and tributes, for each remembered how Esther had served them at King's Mountain. Seth watched when Esther danced with another, jealous of each having her attention, even if only for the length of a dance. Yet, he watched extremely proud of the woman he now loved.

Lovely danced once each with Isaac and Tidence Lane, but refused Jesse, and instead sat out for all the other dances. Beth watched her carefully, as something in Lovely's manner made her fear for the girl. Approaching Lydia Bean, she whispered, "Mistress Lydia, something seems amiss with Lovely. Perhaps ye might come and see to her? I want to find Walter. He has a way with her when she is upset."

So, while most all enjoyed the cool evening under the stars, celebrating their friends' new home and Samuel's school building, already being constructed nearby, Lydia and Walter led Lovely into a quiet room in the Doaks' new house and let her sob until her shaking stopped. Soon exhausted, Lovely fell asleep. Walter agreed to stay nearby and promised to send Levi for help if needed.

"Beth, did something amiss occur before Lovely took ill?" Lydia whispered as they left the room.

"Not so's I noticed. Lovely sat with David's wife and others. Nearby, some of the older lads played with a bullwhip. I saw her jump each time they snapped it. They hit no one or did anything untoward. 'Twas nothing to be afeared of."

It was late into the evening as they prepared to bed down, havng planned to stay the night, when Esther realized Lovely was nowhere to be found. Seeing her distress, Beth spoke quickly, "Sister, Lovely became upset several hours ago. Walter, Lydia, and I took it upon ourselves to see to her. She sleeps within the house in the Doak's spare room."

"Why did you not come for me?"

"Sister, ye needed yer evening of fun. Sometimes Esther, ye do not need to do everything yerself," Joshua answered, holding a sleeping Naomi in his arms.

"Esther, I have settled you a place here on the porch. Mistress Doak suggested you spend the night inside, but I understand Lovely has taken your bed. Will this be good? I thought you might like to sleep beneath the stars, yet near to Lovely." Seth answered, showing Esther to a quiet spot.

"Sister, I changed her clout before she fell asleep, and she had a cup of milk. Joshua and I will be nearby if needed. Sleep well," Beth informed her, moving away to their own bedrolls.

"Thank you, 'twill do quite well. Joshua, place Naomi here beside me, that I might feel her when she wakes." As she felt her body relax against the soft pallet Seth had created for her, Esther realized she had much to think about, and that she looked forward to being alone with just her daughter.

Though tired, Esther lay for a long, long time into the evening, thinking back on dancing and being carefree. Others had cared for Lovely. Even for Naomi. She thought on now she had reached only her nineteenth year. Yet, most days, she felt as though she was as old as her friend Mistress Sarah had been when they met those years ago at Moore's. Was she her community's old woman who cared for the sick, the dying, those being born, and those injured in battle? Tears filled her sleepy eyes as her thoughts turned to those carefree days spent with Waya. With those daydreams of love and affection foremost in her thoughts, Esther finally slept.

The fall harvest completed, Esther worried to herself about the planting of winter crops such as cabbage, collards, and leeks in their garden. She stressed more about their safety with Joshua and Seth determined to begin their journey on the first day of October. Still, they would have Walter and Levi. Then one day, upon walking out toward the paddock, Esther overheard Walter and Seth discussing the upcoming journey.

"Dr. Seth, ye knowed I done been through that Cumberland Gap with hunters several years back. Think I can rightly remember the trail thereabouts. Ye think Joshua might be willin' to have me and Levi tag along. I be right good with a rifle, shootin' game, and catchin' fish."

"Walter, you are welcome to join us, but what about Esther and Lovely? Would you leave them alone if they refuse to go?"

"Oh, not to worry. Sister Esther done decided to go along with Joshua and Beth and ye. Jest can't find the words to say so. I 'spect any day now, she be packing up little Naomi and tellin' her friends goodbye."

"Oh, so you think you know my mind, do you, Walter?" Esther interrupted.

"Well, yea, sister, ol' Walter does."

"Why might I go on such a dangerous journey simply because my brother wants to go?"

"Perhaps because I am also going, Esther," Seth replied quietly, as Walter turned and walked toward where Levi could be heard calling.

Without further consideration, Seth decided then and there to speak his mind. Stepping closer to her and taking her hands in his, Seth quietly and carefully laid his heart open before the woman he loved more than life itself.

"Esther Ballinger Wolf," Seth whispered, then he paused at her startled expression, "yea, I ken all. I love you, woman, I love you, you Esther," Seth stated, his voice breaking. "I have since those days at King's Mountain as I watched you and saw a woman I could no more let go of than life itself. I thought of no one and nothing else in my days before I journeyed to Watauga. Knowing my words would break your heart, as the tidings I carried were so grave, still, I had to be the one to come, because I needed so badly to see you. To see you were safe. To hold you in your grief, if I be needed. To comfort you. Esther, I love you. Must I tell you again. May I tell you again, I love you. I'll shout my love to the skies! I love you! You, Esther, because of who you are, of how you care, of how you live. I need you. I always will.

If you decide to stay here. Stay, I will. If you decide to go back to Virginia, then I shall follow in your footsteps, or walk beside you if you will allow me. *Never will I believe all is lost until you die without telling me of your love for me."*

"Seth, I lay with a Cherokee man, Waya. We married within his people's custom, outside of the church, for there was no choice. I bore his child. Now you say you knew all this, and yet you love me?"

"I loved you before I knew of Waya. I love you now, knowing all. It makes no difference to my love, Esther. I love your courage to live your life loving . . . loving a man with no regrets, no regard for what others might think. Now. . ., now, I ask. Can you find such love as you had for him with me? Can you? You must, I beg you. I will give you everything I possess. I will cherish you. I already love your daughter and will raise her as my own and with my name, if you wish. I will care for Lovely as I would my own sister, had I one."

"You ask too much, Seth McIntosh. Too much, too much!"

"Esther, love can never be too much, *for it is all that makes life worth living."*

Pulling her hands from his, Esther turned and walked away, leaving Seth wondering if he had gone too far . . ., been too forthcoming. Still, he held no regrets.

Esther spent several days in silence, speaking only about necessary tasks and concerns. Beth worried much over the reason, while Joshua only suggested they let her be. Seth became absent more often. Joshua knew his friend spent time checking on the injured or ill within the settlement, or simply wandering the hills alone. October first passed, and no one departed. Between themselves, Joshua, Beth, and Seth had agreed to wait until early spring. Each wanted to be settled in Kentucky by the first of May, even if it meant traveling in harsh weather. They recognized Esther's need to ponder, to examine her own thoughts and needs, to find her own heart.

Throughout the autumn months, news of the war slowly trickled into the community through military correspondence, and with newcomers to the fort. Word spread about how General Nathanael Greene's forces had pushed General Cornwallis's army north into Virginia, to near Yorktown. Meanwhile, General Washington, with the support of General Jean Baptiste de Rochambeau, moved south toward Yorktown with over fourteen thousand soldiers. Off the Chesapeake Bay, a French fleet, comprising some thirty-six warships, now prevented Cornwallis from obtaining reinforcements and supplies, or being evacuated. Many believed the conflict might soon end.

On a mild day in mid-November, Isaac Shelby rode south with news for John Sevier. Within an hour after speaking together, the two rode to the fort, where they sent runners to outlying cabins. Lydia sent Russell to the Ballinger cabin, for all who were able were asked to gather at the fort. Saddling horses and riding quickly toward Caswell, they wondered at the news, for Russell had said the call had come from Shelby and Sevier. Was this another call for the militia to gather and ride off to some faraway battle? Yet, why were the womenfolk asked to come to the fort?

Upon their arrival, John Sevier, Isaac Shelby, Isaac Lane, and William Bean pulled Joshua aside and quietly told him the news. It seemed the militia was to be the first to know. At Joshua's whoop of joy, followed by his dancing around and shouting *Freedom! Freedom!* Esther and Beth hugged and cried. Walter grabbed up Levi, and they danced around shouting *Hurrah! Hurrah!*

Soon John Sevier stood upon a wagon and announced, "General Washington and some fourteen thousand troops surrounded Cornwallis at Yorktown on the 28th of September. The siege lasted until the 19th of October, when Cornwallis surrendered to General Washington. Cornwallis is being allowed to return to England with his soldiers after his promise to fight no more upon this continent."

"What of the south? Georgia and South Carolina? Is the war over?" someone called out.

"Charleston and Savannah are still being held. For now, there seems to be some sort of minor peace agreement. Still, we must hold strong, as there may be more battles to fight," Isaac Shelby answered. "General Washington believes the war may well be over."

After more questions, and shouts of joy and victory, including the firing off of many a long rifle, the afternoon and evening built into a celebration which had not been seen for some six years. Women and girls carried out tables and set up food. John Shelby had brought a yearling cow to be barbecued, and someone else brought forth a side of venison. Musicians pulled out fiddles, and soon music filled the air. Children laughed and played joyfully about, many too young to understand. As the day turned to evening, and dark captured the exuberant jubilee, Esther stayed near Lovely, watching, ever aware of her sister's mood.

At dusk, the Reverend Samuel Doak took to the wagon, standing where all could see, to offer the blessing. Lanterns and an enormous bonfire lit the evening. Everyone, women, men, and children, suddenly lent their attention. Mother hushed babies as Samuel began to speak.

"Our loving Lord, Let us not forget those who fought, those who suffered, and those who died for our victory. Most all hereabout have lost family members to this fight for liberty. In our newly found freedom, let us never forget to be humbled by their sacrifice. Lord, bless us all tonight. Bless this food. Bless our United States of America."

"Nothing in this world can torment you as much as your own thoughts."
Unknown

Winter of 1781 to 1782

Perhaps the heavy snow of late December brought about the change. Maybe Seth's persistence cut through her defenses. Possibly, seeing love, expressed openly, between Joshua and Beth revived her heart. According to the Reverend Samuel Doak, it was within the realm of possibility that God's will came to be. Lydia Bean and Esther Doak laid her change of heart upon fate and the persistence of true love. Despite the reason—the cause—the events of the winter—by mid-season, Esther Ballinger Wolf knew she had once again found, within herself, love for a man. This time for Seth McIntosh.

On the sixteenth of February, leaving Naomi with Walter and Levi, Seth escorted Esther to the Doak home to ask the Reverend to marry them on the following Saturday. Seth had declared he would wait no longer minutes after proposing to the woman he desired to very soon call his wife.

Esther Doak insisted the wedding take place in the new school, which also served as the community's Presbyterian church. With smiles, laughter, and true unrelenting joy, for they had both believed the couple would soon make this request, Samuel agreed. Mistress Doak started planning.

After first smiling and laughing over the news like young girls, Lydia Bean and Esther Doak schemed, decorated, and strategized throughout that week. Soon, green boughs decorated with ribbons and garlands, instead of flowers—absent from the landscape in the dead of winter—lay ready to decorate the church. Lydia presented Esther with a length of wool she had dyed pale blue using elderberries. Lovely, Jane, and Sarah worked day and night to sew the new bodice and full skirt. Lovely embroidered it with small flowers. The ladies created a dress of pale pink for

Naomi. Esther Doak pulled from her chest, recently arrived from her father's home, a lovely bonnet of white velvet, and insisted Esther wear it for her wedding.

So, so soon, the day arrived. On Saturday the 23rd of February, everything, everyone, stood ready. Lovely donned a dress of darkest purple, with a matching bonnet, for the occasion, the same she had worn to the Doak's housewarming. Seth, dressed again in his elegant suit, seemed not the least nervous. Instead, Joshua insisted to Beth, Seth seemed *the happiest man on earth.* While Joshua tried to better his usual attire, he could in no way match Seth's elegance. So, he donned a new linen shirt beneath his fringed jacket and announced himself ready. Beth, to his surprise, appeared in a deep red gown and matching bonnet, decorated with feathery plumes.

"Elizabeth Shelby Ballinger, ye look lovely. Where did ye find that gown? I know it did not arrive with ye in that small pack ye carried."

"Esther Doak gave it to me. Her father sent her a trunk full of clothing when he sent their furniture and other belongings. She laughed when she unpacked this one, as it was one of her youngest sister's gowns, not her own. As they are not alike in size or stature, Esther cannot wear it. She said she immediately thought of me. Look, there is even a matching bonnet."

So, dressed in the best the frontier offered, they set off for the wedding. Wearing a borrowed coat and breeches, Walter rode beside Levi, who dressed for the event in new breeches and shirt under his wool coat. The boy beamed with pride at being invited to attend.

Esther and Naomi had spent the previous evening with the Doaks. The following morning, the females in the house dressed, laughed, and acted like anxious children. Samuel, a man of good humor, joined in the fun by swinging Naomi about in her new dress. Esther watched with joy as her best friend's husband giggled along with Naomi, for she knew Samuel desperately wanted children of his own.

By mid-morning, Esther stood ready to take Seth as her husband. Several in the community attended, despite the poor weather. Joshua and Beth stood as witnesses. Seated nearby, holding Naomi, Lovely watched as Walter walked Esther down the short aisle. As the small church held only twenty or so seated, and not many more standing, only the William Bean family and Isaac Lane, escorting his bride-to-be, Sarah Russell, attended. Woody interrupted the quiet ceremony by howling and scratching at the door until Levi jumped up and allowed the dog to lie beside Lovely's feet.

As Seth slipped a large ruby anchored on a wide gold band on Esther's hand, he whispered, "'Twas my mother's." The ring fit perfectly. A dinner, a celebration, gifts, and even some tears, followed as they made merry for the rest of the day, and into the evening. From across Watauga, friends and former patients came by with good wishes and gifts. Only when Joshua, Beth, Lovely, Naomi, Walter, and Levi prepared to ride home with the Bean family, did Esther realize they had planned that she and Seth would spend their wedding night at the Doaks. Beth quietly handed her a small bag packed with a few necessities, including a new nightgown trimmed in lace.

As the bride prepared for her wedding night, she thought back to her first love, Waya. At their own wedding, so different and so extraordinary in its own way. Esther knew Waya's memory would always be with her, a reminder every time she looked at Naomi. Tears came, unwelcome, flooding her eyes and spilling down her cheeks just as Seth stepped into the room.

"My Esther, my dearest, why tears? Is something amiss?"

"No . . . yes. I thought of Waya. Of our wedding."

"Do you now regret our marriage?"

"Seth, I hold no regrets," Esther replied, firmly and quickly. "No regrets for marrying Waya, though he never really asked me to marry him. Someday, I'll tell you about our ceremony. Please, please, don't misunderstand my tears. Many years ago, not long before his death, my father told me to grasp love and hold it tight whenever love came my way. I did so first with Waya. Now, I plan to hold to you forevermore. I love you, Seth. If you'd like, I'll shout it to tonight's star-strung skies!"

"We could go outside and do so, if you so wish. However, it is cold and raining somewhat steadily. Also, I believe it might wake Esther and Samuel. So perhaps we can think of a better, and quieter, way to end our wedding day," Seth joked, taking Esther in his arms.

Now called by their birth name, the Ballinger siblings, and the new McIntosh family, prepared for a journey to begin in early March. Once more, their journey's beginning stalled due to weather and Naomi being ill with a cold, or, as Seth called it, a *fhuachd chumanta*. Esther insisted they wait until Naomi's fever, cough, and runny nose had cleared before they left for Kentucky.

Finally, on the first day of April, a Monday, the party left for the land many still called Caintuck. They passed by the Bean compound to say their last goodbyes. Lydia and Jane cried. Sarah sulked. Jesse, Russell, and William wished them well, and escorted them as far as the fort. Then their party turned toward Shelby's Fort, planning to travel much the same path as they had in 1777. From Shelby's, they would ride back into Virginia and turn northwest toward the Cumberland Gap. All who had traveled this route said they had some two hundred miles to traverse.

As many a pioneer had journeyed before them, they each led a packhorse, loaded with household necessities, and luxuries such as a mother hen and her dozen chicks in a basket, and three almost grown kittens that Naomi refused to leave behind. Their cow, followed by her calf, walked behind the first riders with Levi, on his little horse, pushing her along. Walter often rode in the party's rear, keeping watch. Woody walked each day beside Lovely's horse.

For their first week, the weather remained mild, and then a quick snowstorm left them stranded in a bitterly cold log station for two days. Finally, on the road again, they joined, for a few days, with a party of hunters also headed into the wilderness. As

263

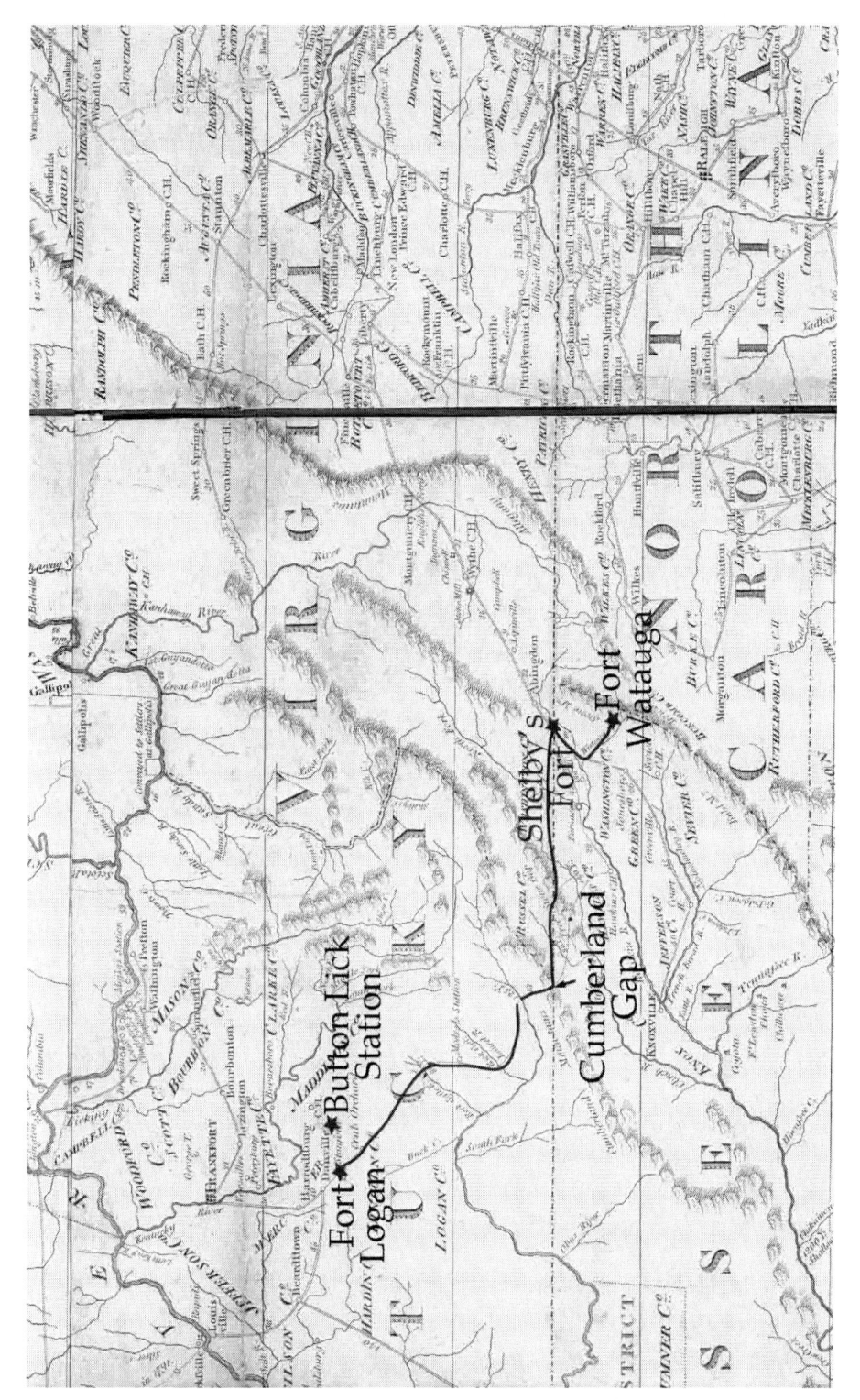

they approached the Gap, the hunters moved on ahead, leaving them to cross the divide alone. Having received a hand-drawn map from Isaac Shelby, with notes as to various streams, rivers, stations, campsites, and dangers, they traveled each day, sure of their route and their destination. Nighttime camps, sleeping on the ground, eating sometimes cold meals, and keeping almost two-year-old Naomi safe occupied their resting hours.

Earlier in the year, Joshua and Seth had settled on buying land near Gilbert's Creek, just east of Logan's Station, near the newly built Craig's Station. Isaac Shelby's choice of land a few miles farther to the west, had greatly influenced their choice. Seth felt the two settlements and stations would provide protection and business for his medical practice, as there were few surgeons along the far western frontier.

On the fifteenth of April, planning to ride through the Gap, they awoke to find a light snow falling. Knowing their trip through the mountains might turn treacherous, they waited one more day, hoping the next might arrive with clear skies. Taking shelter under a nearby rock ledge, they anxiously waited out the day. Only at nightfall, did Esther, tired from chasing a bored Naomi all day, notice Lovely's ashen face.

In the previous months, Lovely never spoke. Yet, she often replied with a nod or shake of her head, and sometimes even wrote small notes. That night, when asked if she felt ill, she simply turned away from Esther and pulled her blankets more tightly against her body.

"Seth, I believe Lovely might be ill," Esther whispered.

Overhearing her, Beth answered before Seth could muster any words, "She has eaten little, if anything, for several days. I didn't mention it, as I thought her courses might be upon her. I know I am rarely hungry at such times."

"I'll check on Lovely," Seth answered. "I had also noticed she has lost weight since our journey began."

After a night of worry for those around her, Lovely seemed herself the following morning. However, Seth and Joshua watched as the young woman poured her tea onto the ground and threw her cornmeal porridge into a nearby bush.

Determined to make his sister understand she must eat and drink sufficient food each day, Joshua pulled Lovely aside and scolded her severely. Lovely stood and listened. She nodded. Then she mounted her horse and rode into line after Beth.

For two days, Lovely ate while her family watched to make sure she did.

Each day, they descended farther from the Gap and followed the Wilderness Trail, cut by Daniel Boone and his woodsmen back in 1775. While the trail had seen many travelers and had, in sections, been improved, their party had to ford streams and rivers, for few ferries and no bridges existed in this wilderness. Spring rains and melting snows had created near-flood conditions in many waterways along their journey.

At the Cumberland River, they met with a group of woodsmen floating over on a recently constructed ferry of sorts, with loads of bundled goods and their horses. The men readily agreed to help them cross safely, for such was the custom of the frontier. Seth insisted Beth, Esther, and Naomi go over first, leaving their horses to cross later. They would take across almost all their belongings. Several young men, already on the other side of the broad river, helped them disembark, ushering them toward a blazing fire to warm themselves and wait for the others to cross.

Lovely, having refused to go on the first crossing, agreed to cross instead with Walter and Levi and the rest of their baggage. Their horses would come over last with Joshua and Seth. Joshua watched and helped as the men struggled to pull the ferry across. His mind wandered to his youngest sister. Having noticed the flatness in Lovely's eyes that morning, he wondered if it was just from her ever-constant fear, or the weariness of travel, or even something more.

Suddenly, just as the ferry reached mid-stream, Joshua watched as Lovely walked to the platform's edge, slipped under the rope barrier, and dropped into the stream. Joshua heard Levi's scream and watched as Walter threw himself into the river after the girl. Levi, who had been holding tight to a rope tied around Woody's neck, pulled the dog close and sat on him to keep him from jumping in. Woody's howls echoed across the river. The man helping guide the raft rushed to Levi's side to protect the boy from being pulled to his own death.

Without pause, Joshua pulled off his hunting jacket and dove in, swimming swiftly toward the ferry. Several of the woodsmen watched in horror as Walter and Joshua swam in circles, diving frequently, searching and calling for Lovely.

Others ran downstream, hoping to glimpse the girl bobbing in the stream. Seth, noticing Esther's rush to the river's opposite bank, yelled across, "Hold her back. No Esther! Stay there! Joshua and Walter will find her." Unable to do more, he watched as Beth, holding Naomi, and two of the young hunters, held Esther away from the river's bank. Over and over, she screamed, "Sarah! Sarah!" Then she fell to her knees and began to shake and wail.

At dark, unable to see into the murky water, they gave up the search. Joshua and Walter, exhausted from their attempts at a rescue, huddled near the fire. All the woodsmen, who had pitched in to help search downstream along the banks, had returned to the camp when it grew much too dark to see properly.

While many searched, the other men had transported their horses across the river. Seth and Beth laid out their camp near the men's fire. Well into the evening's darkness, Esther sat holding a sleeping Naomi. She ate nothing and spoke only when questioned.

Near dawn, Seth awoke to see Esther standing beside the river, talking with Joshua and Walter. He walked closer and listened. Feeling like an outsider, he did not wish to interrupt.

"Joshua, did she really jump into the river? Why would she? Sarah was never a strong swimmer."

"I watched helplessly as she simply walked to the edge, slipped under the rope, and stepped into the water. She did not jump, it was like she walked off the edge," he answered, so quietly they had to lean in to hear him as his voice broke with grief. "It was not an accident."

"We should have stayed in Watauga. She was happier there, not as afraid," Esther declared angrily.

"Was she, Esther? Truly, was she happier?" Walter asked. "Seems to ol' Walter, Lovely just gave up living a while back. Yes, she ate and slept and did her chores. Now, as I's see it, that not be living. I done watched as she sent away her friends. Ignored Jesse Bean and all those other young men that came courtin'. That girl never smiled. She never laughed. I think something inside our girl broke the night of the Chickamauga raid. I's believe she's been wounded sometime long, long before and that night her spirit died of fear. That be how ol' Walter sees it."

Three days of searching followed. They walked for miles along the riverbanks, searching through thick stands of trees, brush, and tall grasses. On the fourth day, Esther and Joshua finally accepted that Lovely was gone, and her body would never be found. They gathered up their belongings, loaded their horses, and moved along.

A different mood fell over the journey. Esther and Beth cried often. Joshua lost his temper at the slightest brief delay or obstacle. Seth tried, within himself, to puzzle out how Lovely's mind had failed, and what he might have done differently. It was Walter who kept the group moving. He took on extra responsibilities and tried to lift spirits as best he could. Levi became Woody's new companion. He made sure the large dog ate and slept beside him in Lovely's absence. He had to keep Woody tied to his saddle each day to prevent the dog from turning back toward the Cumberland.

Not far from their destination, Seth pulled Esther aside one evening. "Esther, I remember you once telling me about something happening to Lovely before you left your home in Virginia. You told me that even then, she lapsed into silence. Thinking back on all this, and the atrocious actions of your uncle upon that girl in Virginia, perhaps we now know what befell your sister."

"Could I not have done more to help her?" Esther pleaded.

"No . . . perhaps . . . for in her mind, her thoughts, I believe Lovely saw herself as damaged. She most likely relived that horrible event over and over within her mind. She feared it happening again and could not stand the thought of it. Had she spoken of it, asked for help to deal with the shame, the horror, then perhaps, perhaps. . .," Seth finished.

"Now, I cannot even bury her. Like with Benjamin, I cannot place a marker somewhere to mark her being. I find it hard to say her name, to say Lovely. We shall call her Sarah. It might be easier for me to hear."

"We will, my dear. It might not mark her body's last resting place, but we will place a marker on our new land to remind us, each day, of her. Then she might live on in memory and be known to those that come after us," Seth promised.

Days later, they arrived at Logan's Station. Taking shelter in a small empty cabin, they grieved and planned. On the following morning, Joshua and Seth rode out with a local man, one familiar with the area, to look for a place to homestead. Later that afternoon, they returned, pleased with themselves, and hopeful that their lives might once more find peace.

"Esther, Beth, we have found our new home. Seth and I plan to hire a surveyor tomorrow and lay out a large tract near a range of hills almost due east of here. Remember that small village called Crab Orchard? The land we want lies directly north, just southeast of Craig's Station."

"Is there already a cabin?" Beth asked.

"No, we hope to build within the next month. The land agent knows of men we can hire. We found a proper place," Seth answered, "just below the ridge, on a terrace with three limestone springs and two nearby creeks. There are plenty of hardwoods about, and some cedar. We saw deer and turkeys. Dick's River holds plenty of fish and lies nearby. I plan for a rock chimney, not log and chinking."

"And ye can pay for all this?" Beth asked.

"I can and will. 'Twill be our home for a year or so, together as one big family. Then if ye and Joshua wish, we can build you a home nearby," Seth answered.

By mid-summer, the mixed family lived quietly in their own home, surrounded by the hills and knobs of Kentucky's wilderness. Nearby, the small towns of Crab Orchard, Stanford, and Lancaster attracted more and more new settlers and even some businesses. One of which was Walter's blacksmithing shop, for Seth had loaned him the funds to purchase equipment. While Indian raids continued sporadically, fewer and fewer worries over such events kept the settlers near to forts and stations.

In August, miles north of their homestead, on the Licking River, one last battle occurred in the Revolutionary War. Led by three British officers, some fifty or so Loyalists and over three hundred Shawnee warriors, attacked Bryan Station. The siege began on the fifteenth of August. Hearing of a large militia force approaching, the Loyalist forces departed on the eighteenth and fled north toward the Licking River. Not waiting for reinforcements, the militia followed, rushing toward the Licking at a place called Blue Licks. On the nineteenth, ignoring pleas by such as Daniel Boone and other leaders to wait for reinforcements, the militia pushed across the river at Blue Licks, directly into an ambush. Seventy-two militia men soon lay dead, including Daniel's son, Israel. Eleven were captured. Although the British-led force retreated immediately, losing so many men in one battle shocked the frontier.

In retribution, General George Rogers Clark launched a raid across the Ohio River in November. Over one thousand men, including Benjamin Logan and Daniel Boone, rode with him. They destroyed five unoccupied Shawnee villages and all their crops and stored supplies.

As those brave men crossed the river into the Ohio territory, two babies were born in a two-story log cabin at the bottom of a knob, a hill the residents had named Button Lick for the funny little button-like fossils and the salt lick found upon its slope. Esther gave birth first and easily, to a boy who she and Seth named Benjamin. Joshua's Beth struggled more with her first. Seth and Esther aided her labors and brought forth a strong, large boy the parents named for Isaac Shelby.

Many more children joined the Ballinger and McIntosh families in the years to follow. Seth practiced medicine in Lancaster, and Esther served often as their community's healer and midwife.

Joshua and Beth added three more children, all girls, to their family before the west pulled at them once again. In 1800, they left, headed toward the area of Kentucky between where the Cumberland and Tennessee Rivers flowed north into the Ohio.

Epilogue:

14 August 1805

My dearest Uncle Osh and Aunt Beth,

I write today with sad news. Mama passed on the twelfth of August. Levi found her sitting on that old bench across the porch. Her rifle had fallen to the floor, yet she sat slumped as if in slumber. Jeb's howls had drawn Levi to the porch as he carried water toward the cabin. Earlier in the summer, Mama had discovered a growth protruding from within her stomach. She refused to go see the new surgeon at Stanford, or the ones in Lexington. Instead, Mama insisted on remaining in the cabin with only Levi nearby.

Matthew and I asked her time and time again to move back to this house, her own home for so many years. We had room for her. She could have had her and Papa's old room. It about broke my heart, yet she refused. All this time, I never understood why she moved back to your cabin after Papa's death.

We buried her early this morning, between Papa and Sarah, in our little family cemetery. Levi helped dig the grave, and I ordered a marker. Governor Isaac Shelby attended along with several others of our area who remembered her service at King's Mountain. Levi says he'll stay on at the cabin for a while, then he plans to travel west to see your family.

I must write to Benjamin, for he is still in Scotland studying medicine, and plans to travel on to Berlin later in the year. I'll encourage him to do so, as there is nothing for him here. The twins, Ruth and Lydia, had just left for Virginia last week, where they will stay with the Jeffersons until Christmas. Seth always wanted them to do so and made sure there were funds set aside, and for their dowry in his will. Perhaps each will find a suitable husband! I shall write them later today.

Mary married a local boy in June. Always the stubborn one, she looked and acted so much like Mama. They live in town and help out at his father's mercantile.

One final bit of news, after three years of marriage, I am finally with child. Matthew is overjoyed. His lawyer work provides well for us, and would do so, even if we did not have father's inheritance to support my siblings.

Osh, one last note, unlike custom, I will have Mama's full name on her stone, Esther Ballinger Wolf McIntosh, instead of "Esther - wife of Dr. Sean Thomas McIntosh." She lived a full life, and it should all be memorialized. I buried her with her flag, the one the people of Watauga presented her not long after her return from King's Mountain. A few years back, Mama told me how Sarah had sewn the flag at Colonel Sevier's request and insistence. It was the one they carried to the battle at King's Mountain.

With so much love and sorrow,
Naomi Wolf McIntosh Russell

Author's Notes

In my efforts to make this story's setting and narrative as timely and historically accurate as possible, I relied on both primary and published sources. For the Battle of King's Mountain, I turned to two major sources, J. David Dameron's *King's Mountain: The Defeat of the Loyalist, October 7, 1780* and the ultimate source Lyman C. Draper's *King's Mountain and its heroes*. Now, while I'll readily admit to reading only sections of this 612-page volume, its excellent index made it easy to find the information I needed to tell accurately Esther's story. Draper, a collector of stories, first-hand accounts, documents, and such, is often the ultimate source on early Kentucky and colonial history. Other books consulted included two by Robert M. Dunkerly: The *Battle of Kings Mountain: Eyewitness Accounts* and *Bravery and Women of the Revolution: Sacrifice on the Southern Battlefields*. While Esther Ballinger may be a figment of my imagination, many women served as nurses on various battlefields during the war. They also served as messengers, supplies of food and other necessities, and even served in combat.

For the chapters set in the Watauga settlement, I discovered several sources at the Kentucky Historical Society that revealed minor information about the residents. Two readily available books filled in the gaps. *The Overmountain Men* by Pat Alderman supplied much of the history of that area as did *The Wilderness Road, The First Family of Tennessee, and Other Stories That Need to be Told* by Ken Coffey. However, neither book had footnotes or indeed much information as to their sources.

Very late in my writing, I discovered a thesis by Brian P. Compton entitled "Revised History of Fort Watauga." Compton's thesis confirmed many of my previously written statements about the fort. However, this scholarly work also provided a great deal of doubt about the inaccuracy of the written sources previously mentioned. Oh, well, this is my story to tell, and I can only hope I have not made too many historical inaccuracies.

Tidbits from other sources filled in gaps. One interesting note was that the word Watauga is perhaps Cherokee or Creek for broken waters, as in Sycamore Shoals.

Often readers of historical fiction wonder who was a real person and who was manufactured within the author's imagination. The Bean and Russell families are indeed historical. William (born 1721) and Lydia (Russell, born about 1726) Bean are considered the first white family to settle in what we know as Tennessee. It is very possible that John Bean, William's brother, and George Russell, Lydia's brother, came into the area at the same time. Otherwise, they arrived soon after William Bean and his family.

In a side note: William Bean is my husband's fifth great grandfather. My husband descends from Jane Bean Shipley, who was killed by Cherokee Indians while sitting at her loom outside Bean Station, Tennessee, in either 1789 or 1790. Jane and Andrew Shipley had one child, Solomon Shipley. William Bean descended from the McBean/McBain/Bean clan of Scotland, a clan who once lived on the eastern shore of Lock Ness. Most family trees place the first McBean in this family line as having emigrated to the colonies in the late 1600s.

Real men at Moore's Fort include Thomas and David Gass. Real families and individuals at Watauga include the Reverend Tidence Lane and his family. Tidence established the Buffalo Ridge Baptist Church at Watauga in 1776. Reverend Samuel Doak and his wife Esther arrived in Watauga about 1778. Samuel established a church and a school. Many of his descendants still live in east Tennessee. Leaders named in various battle descriptions are all real. I worked very hard to make this book a true accounting of the American Revolution.

The story of Mary McKeehan Patton making the gunpowder for the Battle of Kings's Mountain is documented in various sources. Of course, John Sevier, and his two wives, are well known, as John later served as Tennessee's governor. Isaac and Evan Shelby are recognized as esteemed Patriots. Like his friend

John Sevier, Isaac later served as governor, but in Kentucky, for he did indeed settle in Lincoln County, near Danville, Kentucky. For more information, S. Roger Keller's *Isaac Shelby: A Driving Force in America's Struggle for Independence* is an excellent read.

Establishing who fought at Kings Mountain was both easy and hard. For example, were both William Bean senior and junior there? Which one served as a captain? Personally, I believe both served in some manner, for it seems one was with the North Carolina militia for a long period during the war while the other served nearby to the Watauga settlement during the same time. William senior would have been 60 years old in 1780 while William junior was 36. Many other members of the family served at King's Mountain including Captain Jesse Bean, age 25. From the Russell family, George, Andrew, and William served as lieutenants, while Robert and Moses as enlisted. There are most likely many more from the Bean/Russell family that served.

Lieutenant Isaac Lane was at King's Mountain and served at Watauga. Yes, he did marry Sarah Russell, niece to William Bean. Most references list him as Tidence's son while others list him as a nephew. Tidence Jr., Aquilla, and Dutton were also real and served at King's Mountain along with seven or eight others of the family. The same problem of lineage can be said for Jesse Bean for he may have been John Bean's son, not William's. However, Jesse did serve in the militia and commanded a group dedicated to dealing with the defense of the Watauga population from the Chickamauga Cherokee.

The story of Samuel Moore and Lydia Bean's capture and Lydia's rescue by Nanyehi, or Nancy Ward, is true and was reported in various documents of the period.

Being a retired archaeologist and historian, I have always loved learning about our Native American cultures. I own several books on Native Indian legends and beliefs. Waya's Cherokee origin story (Chapter 7) was paraphrased from *American Indian Myths and Legends, Selected and Edited by Richard Erdoes and Alfonso Ortiz*.

I saw a bronze roadside marker near my home while writing this book, that told of the Gilbert Creek Baptist Church and its origin with the Traveling Church. However, it was not until I found George Washington Ranck's *The Traveling Church* that I understood the significance of this group of religious pioneers to Garrard County, Kentucky. I have discovered we often live near a historical site we never knew about until some small tidbit compels us to learn more. Ranck's book and its wonderful story enlightened me about my adopted home.

About the Maps!

While the three maps may not have been essential to this novel, my editor advised they would be greatly appreciated, especially by those not knowledgeable about United States geography. She is British. She also suggested that since she knew little about the American Revolutionary War (I guess they do not teach British children about wars their country lost.) a timeline of the War would also be helpful.

Now making the timeline was easy, being as I am a historian by experience and training. Making a map, well, not so easy. As I cannot draw even a decent stick figure, I decided to use an early American map as the background. Oh, my! What trouble that caused! For without satellites and all the global positioning gadgets we have now, early American map makers made lots of mistakes. I truly mean thousands of mistakes. I found one late 1700s map showing South Carolina with a northern section, above North Carolina, and a southern section below North Carolina that encompassed a lot of Georgia. Then there is the "upside down map of Kentucky" but that is a discussion for another day. One major problem I discovered was most maps made prior to the American Revolution did not place many details west of the Alleghenies as that was "Indian Territory."

Finally, a series of daily searches of online map sites revealed "A map of the United States exhibiting post roads & distances" produced by Abraham Bradley and printed in 1796. This map contained all the areas the novel is concerned with, had almost every place in its true location, and was easily available from the Library of Congress at http://hdl.loc.gov/loc.gmd/g3700.ct001192.

Now some might ask why I did not include a map of Esther's journey to King's Mountain? The answer is easy: because I could never make one as nice as the National Park Service maps for the trail. They can be found and downloaded at: https://www.nps.gov/ovvi/planyourvisit/maps.htm (scroll down to find the links to each map)

Sarah Lovely Ballinger

Sometimes I find myself creating a character and telling his or her story without any idea where their life will take them. Lovely was such a creation. It was only as I wrote of her death that I knew why my subconscious had placed Lovely within this story, for I could have left her out. It would have been easy to erase her. If I had, much would have been lost, for mental illness within historical fiction is rarely touched upon. It is a story too hard to tell . . . too horrid to imagine . . . too personal.

Today, we have a much better name than lunacy. We treat mental illness with more compassion. Still, the hurt, the grief of losing a family member to suicide is much the same no matter what we name the disease. I know for I lost my son to mental illness—to suicide. It has been over ten years now, almost twenty. Still, I think about him daily and find that my tears still come easily. My heart breaks all over again, and again, and again. . .

The National Suicide Lifeline number is 988. Learn this number. Tell those you know and love about this lifeline. Don't be afraid to ask for help. Believe me, there are so many willing to help you live. So many who will love you—beg for you to be with them instead of gone. I promise this is true.

About the Author

C.M. Huddleston lives in a log cabin near Button Lick Knob in Kentucky. Now retired from several careers, she writes most days—sometimes fiction, sometimes history, sometimes just nonsense that no one will ever read. She believes everyone needs to do this as it empties the mind of all that stuff you don't really need to know.

She is lousy at sending out emails to those few who have signed up for such things. So, if you sign up on her website at cmhuddleston.com don't expect a lot of contact. She does make the ones she sends worthwhile.

Connie is even worse at updating her other website at Caintuck.com which is about the Boone family and early Kentucky history. But when she does, she has fun telling snippets about her beloved home state.

Books by C.M. Huddleston
Middle Grade Fiction
Greg's First Adventure in Time
Greg's Second Adventure in Time
Greg's Third Adventure in Time
Greg's Fourth Adventure in Time
Greg's Fifth Adventure in Time
Winter Wonder (with several other authors)

Adult Fiction
Leah's Story
Caintuck Lies Within My Soul: The Jemima Boone Story

Pictorial History
Marshall County (KY)
Georgia's Civilian Conservation Corps
Kentucky's Civilian Conservation Corps

History
Seldom Told Stories: Daddy Luke, Maum Charlotte, Maum Grace, and Daddy William of Bulloch Hall
James Stephens Bulloch: Aristocratic Southern Gentleman

The Bulloch Letters Series:
Mittie & Thee: An 1853 Roosevelt Romance
by Connie M. Huddleston and Gwendolyn I. Koehler

Between the Wedding & the War: The Bulloch/Roosevelt Letters 1854-1860
by Gwendolyn I. Koehler and Connie M. Huddleston

Divided Only by Distance & Allegiance: The Bulloch/Roosevelt Letters 1861-1865
by Connie M. Huddleston and Gwendolyn I. Koehler

Made in United States
North Haven, CT
19 December 2023